DEATH
OF A
NIGHTINGALE

Also by Lene Kaaberbøl and Agnete Friis

The Boy in the Suitcase
Invisible Murder

DEATH
OF A
NIGHTINGALE

LENE KAABERBØL

AND

AGNETE FRIIS

Translated from the Danish by Elisabeth Dyssegaard

Published by
Soho Press, Inc.
853 Broadway
New York, NY 10003

Library of Congress Cataloging-in-Publication Data

Kaaberbøl, Lene.
[Nattergalens Doed. English]
Death of a nightingale / Lene Kaaberbøl & Agnete Friis ;
Translated from
the Danish by Elisabeth Dyssegaard.

Originally published as Nattergalens Doed, in Danish.
ISBN 978-1-61695-451-2
eISBN 978-1-61695-305-8
I. Friis, Agnete, author. II. Dyssegaard, Elisabeth Kallick, translator.
III. Title.
PT8177.21.A24N3713 2013
2013016761

Printed in the United States of America

10 9 8 7 6 5 4 3 2 1

AUDIO FILE #83: Nightingale

"Go on," says a man's voice.

"I'm tired," an older woman answers, clearly uncomfortable and dismissive.

"But it's so exciting."

"Exciting?" There's a lash of bitterness in her reaction. "A bit of Saturday entertainment? Is that what this is for you?"

"No, I didn't mean it like that."

They are both speaking Ukrainian, he quickly and informally, she more hesitantly. In the background, occasional beeps from an electronic game can be heard.

"It's important for posterity."

The old woman laughs now, a hard and unhappy laughter. "Posterity," she says. "Do you mean the child? Isn't she better off not knowing?"

"If that's how you see it. We should be getting home anyway."

"No." The word is abrupt. "Not yet. Surely you can stay a little longer."

"You said you were tired," says the man.

"No. Not . . . that tired."

"I don't mean to press you."

"No, I know that. You just thought it was exciting."

"Forget I said that. It was stupid."

"No, no. Children like exciting stories. Fairy tales."

"I was thinking more along the lines of something real. Something you experienced yourself."

Another short pause. Then, "No, let me tell you a story," the old woman says suddenly. "A fairy tale. A little fairy tale from Stalin Land. A suitable bedtime story for the little one. Are you listening, my sweet?"

Beep, beep, beep-beep. Unclear mumbling from the child. Obviously, her attention is mostly on the game, but that doesn't stop the old woman.

"Once upon a time, there were two sisters," she begins clearly, as if reciting. "Two sisters who both sang so beautifully that the nightingale had to stop singing when it heard them. First one sister sang for the emperor himself, and thus was the undoing of a great many people. Then the other sister, in her resentment, began to sing too."

"Who are you talking about?" the man asks. "Is it you? Is it someone we know?"

The old woman ignores him. There's a harshness to her voice, as if she's using the story to punish him.

"When the emperor heard the other sister, his heart grew inflamed, and he had to own her," she continued. "'Come to me,' he begged. Oh, you can be sure he begged. 'Come to me, and be my nightingale. I'll give you gold and beautiful clothes and servants at your beck and call.'"

Here the old woman stops. It's as if she doesn't really feel like going on, and the man no longer pressures her. But the story has its own relentless logic, and she has to finish it.

"At first she refused. She rejected the emperor. But he persisted. 'What should I give you, then?' he asked, because he had learned that everything has a price. 'I will not come to you,' said the other sister, 'before you give me my evil sister's head on a platter.'"

In the background, the beeping sounds from the child's game have ceased. Now there is only an attentive silence.

"When the emperor saw that a heart as black as sin hid behind the beautiful song," the old woman continues, still using her fairy-tale voice, "he not only killed the first sister, but also the nightingale's father and mother and grandfather and grandmother and whole family. 'That's what you get for your jealousy,' he said and threw the other sister out."

The child utters a sound, a frightened squeak. The old woman doesn't seem to notice.

"Tell me," she whispers. "Which of them is me?"

"You're both alive," says the man. "So something in the story must be a lie."

"In Stalin Land, Stalin decides what is true and what is a lie," says the old woman. "And I said that it was a Stalin fairy tale."

"Daddy," says the child, "I want to go home now."

"GUM?"

Natasha started; she had been sitting silently, looking out the window of the patrol car as Copenhagen glided by in frozen shades of winter grey. Dirty house fronts, dirty snow and a low and dirty sky in which the sun had barely managed to rise above the rooftops in the course of the day. The car's tires hissed in the soap-like mixture of snow, ice and salt that covered the asphalt. None of it had anything to do with her, and she noted it all without really seeing it.

"You do speak Danish, don't you?"

The policeman in the passenger seat had turned toward her and offered her a little blue-white pack. She nodded and took a piece. Said thank you. He smiled at her and turned back into his seat.

This wasn't the "bus," as they called it—the usual transport from Vestre Prison to the court—that Natasha had been on before. It was an ordinary black-and-white; the police were ordinary Danish policemen. The youngest one, the one who had given her the gum, was thirty at the most. The other was old and fat and seemed nice enough too. Danish policemen had kind eyes. Even that time with Michael and the knife, they had spoken calmly and kindly to her as if she hadn't been a criminal they were arresting but rather a patient going to the hospital.

One day, before too long, two of these kind men would put

Katerina and her on a flight back to Ukraine, but that was not what was happening today. Not yet. It couldn't be. Her asylum case had not yet been decided, and Katerina was not with her. Besides, you didn't need to go through Copenhagen to get to the airport, that much she knew. This was the way to Central Police Headquarters.

Natasha placed her hands on her light blue jeans, rubbed them hard back and forth across the rough fabric, opened and closed them quickly. Finally, she made an effort to let her fists rest on her knees while she looked out at Copenhagen and tried to figure out if the trip into the city brought her closer to or farther from Katerina. During the last months, the walls and the physical distance that separated them had become an obsession. She was closer to her daughter when she ate in the cafeteria than when she was in her cell. The trip to the yard was also several meters in the wrong direction, but it still felt soothing because it was as if she were breathing the same air as Katerina. On the library computer Natasha had found Google Street View and dragged the flat little man to the parking lot in front of the prison, farther along Copenhagen's streets and up the entrance ramp to the highway leading through the woods that sprawled north of the city's outer reaches. It was as if she could walk next to him the whole way and see houses and storefronts and trees and cars, but when he reached the Coal-House Camp, he couldn't go any farther. Here she had to make do with the grubby satellite image of the camp's flat barrack roofs. She had stared at the pictures until she went nearly insane. She had imagined that one of the tiny dots was Katerina. Had dreamed of getting closer. From the prison, it was twenty-three kilometers to the Coal-House Camp. From the center of Copenhagen it was probably a few kilometers more, but on the other hand, there were neither walls nor barbed wire between the camp and her right now. There was only the thin steel shell of the police car, air and wind, kilometers of asphalt. And later, the fields and the wet forest floor.

She knew it wouldn't do any good, but she reached out to touch the young policeman's shoulder all the same. "You still don't know anything?" she asked in English.

His eyes met hers in the rearview mirror. His gaze was apologetic but basically indifferent. He shook his head. "We're just the chauffeurs," he said. "We aren't usually told stuff like that."

She leaned back in her seat and again began to rub her palms against her jeans. Opened and closed her hands. Neither of the two policemen knew why she was going to police headquarters. They had nothing for her except chewing gum.

The court case over the thing with Michael was long finished, so that probably wasn't what it was about, and her plea for asylum had never required interviews or interrogations anywhere but the Coal-House Camp.

Fear made her stomach contract, and she felt the urge to shit and pee at the same time. If only she could have had Katerina with her. If only they could have been together. At night in the prison, she had the most terrible nightmares about Katerina alone in the children's barrack, surrounded by flames.

Or Katerina making her way alone into the swamp behind the camp.

It was unnatural for a mother not to be able to reach out and touch her child. Natasha knew she was behaving exactly like cows after their calves were taken from them in the fall, when they stood, their shrill bellowing lasting for hours, without knowing which way to direct their sorrow. She had tried to relieve her restlessness with cold logic. They were not separated forever, she told herself. Katerina came to visit once in a while with Nina, the lady from the Coal-House Camp, who reassured Natasha every time that she would personally take care of Katerina. Rina, the Danes called her. They thought that was her name because that was what the papers said. But Rina wasn't even a name. It was what was left when an overpaid little forger in Lublin had done what he could to disguise the original text.

Maybe that was why she was here? Had they discovered what the man in Lublin had done?

Her dread of the future rose like the tide. Her jaw muscles tightened painfully, and when she crushed the compact piece of gum between her teeth, everything in her mouth felt sticky and metallic.

The policeman at the wheel slowed down, gave a low, triumphant whistle and slid the car in between two other cars in a perfect parking maneuver. Through the front window, Natasha could see the grey, fortress-like headquarters of the Danish police. Why were there thick bars in front of some of the windows? As far as she knew, it wasn't here by the entrance that they locked up thieves and murderers. It seemed as if the bars were just there as a signal—a warning about what awaited when the interrogations with the nice Danish policemen were over.

The fat cop opened the door for her. "This is as far as we go, young lady."

She climbed out of the car and buried her hands in the pockets of her down jacket. The cold hit her, biting at her nose and cheeks, and she realized that she had brought neither hat nor gloves. When you were in prison, the weather wasn't something that really mattered. She had barely registered the snow the day before.

The older policeman pulled a smoke out of his uniform jacket and lit it, gave an expectant cough. The young cop, who already had a hand on Natasha's arm, sighed impatiently.

"Just two minutes," said the heavyset one and leaned against the car. "We've got plenty of time."

The young one shrugged. "You really should stop that, pal. It's going to kill both you and me. I'm freezing my ass off here."

The old one laughed good-naturedly and drew smoke deep into his lungs. Natasha wasn't freezing, but her legs felt weak, and she noticed again that she needed to pee. Soon. But she didn't want to say anything, didn't want the policemen to rush. She looked up at the massive, squat building as if it could tell her why she was here. Relaxed uniformed and non-uniformed employees wandered in and out among the pillars in the wide entrance area. If they were planning to seal the fate of a young Ukrainian woman today, you couldn't tell, and for a moment, Natasha felt calmer.

This was Copenhagen, not Kiev.

Both she and Katerina were safe. She was still in Copenhagen. Still Copenhagen. Across the rooftops a bit farther away, she could see the frozen and silent amusement rides in Tivoli, closed for the season. The tower ride from which she and Michael and Katerina had let themselves fall, secure in their little seats, on a warm summer night almost two years ago.

The big guy stubbed out his cigarette against a stone island in the parking lot and nodded at Natasha. "Well, shall we?"

She began to move but then remained standing as if frozen in place. The sounds of the city reached her with a sudden violence. The rising and falling song of car motors and tires on the road, the weak vibration in the asphalt under her when a truck rumbled by, the voices and slamming car doors. She was searching for something definite in the babble. She focused her consciousness to its utmost and found it. Again.

"Ni. Sohodni. Rozumiyete?"

Natasha locked her gaze on two men who had parked their car some distance away—one of them wearing an impeccable black suit and overcoat, the other more casual in dark jeans and a light brown suede jacket.

"Did someone nail your feet to the pavement?" the young cop said, in a friendly enough fashion. “Let’s keep moving.” His hand pressed harder around her elbow, pushing her forward a little.

“I’m sorry,” she said. She took one more step and another. Looked down at the slushy black asphalt and felt the fear rise in her in its purest and darkest form.

They worked their way sideways around a small row of dug-up parking spaces cordoned off with red-and-white construction tape. Long orange plastic tubes snaked their way up from the bottom of the deserted pit. Next to it was a small, neat pile of cobbles half covered by snow.

Natasha slowed down. Gently. Avoided any sudden movements.

The old guy looked back just as she bent down to pick up the top cobble. She smiled at him. Or tried to, at least.

“I’m just . . .”

He was two steps away, but the younger one was closer, and she hit *him*, hard and fast and without thinking. She felt the impact shoot up through the stone and into her hand and closed her eyes for an instant. She knew that the young cop fell in front of the old one, blocking his way, because she could hear them both curse and scrabble in the soap-like slush. But she didn’t see it.

She just ran.

NINA WOKE SLOWLY, with some kind of murky nightmare rumbling at the bottom of her consciousness. There had been a refugee camp that looked like Dadaab, the flies and the heat and that smell you never completely escape from, the stench of atomized human misery. But the children lying before her on the ground with starved faces and protruding bellies were Anton and Ida.

She rolled over onto her side and tried to escape the dream. 9:02, announced the large digital wall clock that had been the first thing she hung on the wall when she moved in. An anemic February sun was streaming unimpeded through the window; the shades she had bought at IKEA on a rushed afternoon in August were still lying in their packaging on the radiator almost six months later. Luckily, there were no neighbors. Outside lay Grøndals Parkvej, and on the other side of it the park and the railroad embankment, the reason she had bought the apartment. Centrally located yet still a quiet neighborhood, the realtor had said, a really good parental buy—did she have a son or daughter starting college, perhaps? When he had realized that she was going to be living there herself, he had adjusted expectations noticeably. Divorced mothers were difficult clients, it seemed, confused and unrealistic and with no perspective on their own budget.

The cell phone rang. It must be what had woken her, even though she hadn't really registered it, since it wasn't her ringtone. She poked Magnus in the ribs.

"It's yours," she said.

A groggy sound emanated from the fallen Swedish giant. He lay on his stomach, his head buried so deep in the pillow, it was amazing that he could breathe. His broad, naked shoulders were covered with short golden hair, and he smelled of semidigested beer. She nudged him again.

Finally, he lifted his head.

"Oh, my God," he said in his distinct Swedish accent. "What time is it?"

"It's Saturday," she said, since that was more to the point.

He reached for the cell phone, which was lying on the floor next to the bed along with his wallet and keys. Neat little bedside tables, his and hers, were not part of the apartment's inventory. The only place where she had made an effort was in Anton's and Ida's rooms, and they still hadn't turned out right. Everything was too tidy. It lacked the clutter of toys and discarded clothing, the scratches on the wall from hockey sticks and lightsabers, the remnants of stickers that wouldn't quite come off, odd splotches from overturned soda cans and soap bubble experiments. Quite simply, it lacked *children*. She hadn't managed to make it more than a temporary refuge. Home was still the apartment in Fejøgade, and that was where they had their life.

She got up and headed for the bathroom. A small bathtub that permitted only sit-up baths, yellowing white tiles from the '50s, and if you insisted on having a washing machine in there, you had to accept that you were going to bang your knees against it every time you sat on the toilet. But to sit in a Laundromat at an ungodly hour to have clean clothes for the next day . . . No, thank you. "Been there, done that," as Ida would have said.

After peeing, Nina gargled with chlorhexidine. She was susceptible to thrush and other mouth infections after her attack of radiation illness the year before. All in all, her resistance was not what it had been, she noted dryly. Otherwise Magnus probably wouldn't be lying in her bed now. The doctor and the nurse. Damn. How much more clichéd could you get?

He had just been through a divorce. So had she. They were both consenting adults and all that. But she knew perfectly well that it wasn't because they were adults. It was because they were both so unbearably lonely that any kind of intimacy was better than nothing.

Through the bathroom door she could hear his voice change from Saturday grogginess to professional clarity, and a rush of alarm raced through her. She spat out the petroleum-blue mouthwash into the sink, plucked yesterday's T-shirt from the dirty laundry basket and pulled it on, then opened the door.

He was getting dressed, the cell phone still pressed to his ear.

"Okay," he said. "No, don't give her any more. I'm on my way."

"Is it Rina?" she asked with an odd kind of pseudomaternal instinct. There were around 200 females at the Coal-House Camp, yet Rina was the first one she thought of.

"They've given her several doses of Bricanyl," he said. "But they can still hear crackling on auscultation, and she's hyperventilating."

Sweet Jesus, it *was* Rina.

"What happened?"

"Everything," he said. "Come on."

NATASHA HAD ENDED up on the wrong side of the lake, and there was only one way to deal with that. She had to get hold of a car.

The realization had been gnawing at her since the previous evening, or rather the previous night, because at that point it had been almost 2 A.M., and even if she had dared take a train or bus, they weren't running any longer, at least not to where she was going.

She had been so tired that her bones hurt. In particular her knees and the small of her back ached from the many freezing kilometers, and she knew that she couldn't walk much farther without resting.

Most of the houses on the quiet street lay dark and closed behind the snowy hedges. But she could hear music and party noises and beery shouts, and when she got to the next street corner, she saw three young men peeing into a hedge outside a whitewashed house that was alight with boozy festivities. She stopped, half sheltered by the fence of the corner lot, leaning for a moment against the cold tar-black planks.

"Laa, la-laa, la-laa . . ." roared one of the peeing men, loudly and in no key known to man. "Laa, la-aa, la-laaa . . . Come on!"

The two others joined in, which didn't make it any more tuneful.

"*We are the champions, my friend . . .*"

She realized that they were celebrating some kind of sports victory.

Presumably basketball—she suddenly saw how alike they were physically: broad shouldered, yes, but primarily tall, and younger than she had thought at first; she had been fooled by their height.

Yet another young boy emerged from the house. He seemed more low-key than his peeing buddies, just as tall but a little skinnier, a little more awkward. His dark hair looked damp and spiky, and he wore glasses. A girl tottered after him in high heels she could barely manage, the strap of her pink blouse falling halfway off one shoulder.

"Robbie, don't go yet!" she shouted shrilly.

"I need to get home," he said.

"Why? Dammit, Robbie . . . You can't just . . . Robbie, come onnnn!"

One of the three at the hedge quickly zipped up and tried with similarly incoherent arguments to convince Robbie to stay, but he shook them off.

"I'll see you guys," he said and started walking with long, fairly controlled steps down the street in the direction of Natasha. The girl stood looking after him, her arms folded across her chest.

"Robbie," she wailed, but one of the guys by the hedge put an arm around her and pulled her along with him back into the house. Robbie continued down the sidewalk as if he hadn't heard her.

Natasha was about to back up so that he wouldn't notice her, but he didn't go all the way to her corner. Instead, he stopped at a dark blue car not far from her.

"Whoo-hoo," one of the remaining party boys commented. "Does Daddy know you're driving his Audi?"

"They're skiing," said Robbie. "They won't be home until Thursday."

He remained standing with the keys in his hand as if he didn't feel like getting in while they were looking on. Not until they had followed their friend and the girl into the house did he unlock the car.

He was so tall. There was no way she'd be able to hit him and get away with it, and she no longer had a cobble or any other weapon. But he had a car key. And a car.

Without a car, she couldn't reach Katerina. Without a car, they couldn't get away, and they had to. In her mind, she once again heard the voices from the parking lot outside police headquarters. There was nothing recognizable about them, and what they had said wasn't alarming in itself. "It has to be today. Understand?" Ordinary words, not threatening—but spoken in Ukrainian. She felt a fresh rush of panic just thinking about it.

She glided up behind the rangy young man and placed her hand on his, the hand in which he held the keys.

"Not good," she said in English. "Not good to drive after drink."

A good guess—the short delay in his reaction revealed that he had been drinking. Not as much as the others but probably still quite a bit. He stared at her as if he was trying to remember how they knew each other. She took the keys out of his hand, opened the door quickly and got in.

"Hey, wait . . ." He stuck his leg in so she couldn't close the door and quickly grabbed the wheel. "What are you doing?"

Driving, she told herself silently. Driving to Katerina. But clearly he wasn't planning to just let her do so.

"Robbie," she said again in English. "Bad for you to drive. Let me. I take you home."

He looked at her through slightly foggy glasses. Using his name had had an effect. He thought they knew each other even though he wasn't sure how. And he was drunk. More than it had appeared at first.

"Okay," he said slowly. "You drive, er . . ."

"Katerina," she said with her most dazzling smile. "Don't you remember? It's Katerina."

HE DIDN'T FALL asleep in the car as she had hoped. Instead he directed her through the suburban streets, closer to the lake that separated her from Katerina, and finally got her to turn into a drive and park in front of a garage and a yellow brick house with old ivy growing all the way to the roof. The branches from the large silver birch at the entrance were weighted so heavily with snow that they brushed across the car's roof. She turned off the engine and tried to leave the key in the ignition, but he was still too much on guard and pulled it out himself.

"Thank you," he said. And then apparently was struck by a thought beyond getting to his own front door. "What about you?" he asked. "How will you get home?"

She forced herself to look away from the car keys in his hand and into his eyes.

"Maybe you ask me to stay?" she said.

She felt anything but attractive. Her hair had been wet with snow several times, and the shirt under the down jacket was stiff and sticky with old sweat. She only had a little bit of mascara on, if it wasn't smeared under her eyes by now, and she knew she was very, very far from the beautiful Natasha that Pavel had once shown off to selective friends as "my lovely wife."

He sucked in air, making a sharp, startled sound. But somewhere a surprising degree of sophistication appeared from beneath the boyish awkwardness.

"You are very welcome," he said. "This way, madame."

"Katerina," she corrected him gently. "Or you make me feel like an old woman."

SHE WOKE UP abruptly many hours later with a feeling of panic racing through her veins. Her head hurt, and she was once again sticky with sweat. The clean comforter that lay so lightly across her naked body had never been anywhere near a prison laundry, but it wasn't Michael lying next to her; it couldn't be, not anymore. The panic subsided.

It had grown light outside. Grubby grey winter light fell on piles of clothing, basketball shoes, a desk that had almost disappeared under heaps of books and paper, a green carpet marked with white lines like a basketball court. She hadn't intended to fall asleep, but the velvety blackness of her own unexpected orgasm had swept her into unconsciousness.

She felt a sudden tenderness for the overgrown boy who lay snoring with his face deep in the pillow—even more lost to the world than she herself had been. To be touched by another person. A person who hadn't pulled on clear plastic gloves to examine her body. A person who wanted to bring her desire, not pain. When was the last time she had experienced that? Not since Pavel.

She hadn't needed to sleep with him. He had left the car keys on a little table in the foyer. There had been several chances, but she hadn't seized them. Instead she had drunk shots and beer with him, and they had kissed on the sofa with way too much tongue, as if she were a teenager again. As if she were seventeen and had just met Pavel. And now she lay here in his bed, staring up at a huge poster of a towering black American basketball player who apparently was called Magic. Recalled the pressure of his hip against her stomach, the slippery feeling of sweaty skin against sweaty skin, his eager, choppy rhythm, a little too sharp, a little too hard and fast, yet still enough to give her that surprising dark release that had carried her into sleep.

He didn't move when she wriggled free of him and slid out of the bed. She stood for a moment, naked and dizzy on the green carpet, and felt so exhausted that she wanted just to crawl back into the nothingness with a heavy, warm body at her side.

"That won't do, my girl," she whispered, and it wasn't her own voice she heard, but Anna's. Neighbor Anna, Katerina called her, even though they hadn't always been neighbors. "Sometimes you just have to go on. One foot in front of the other. Without thinking too much about it."

She listened, but Anna-in-her-head didn't have anything else to say this time. And the real Anna was probably sleeping safe at home in the yellow farmhouse next door to Michael's.

Natasha pulled on her jeans even though they were stiff with dried road salt all the way up to the knees. The shirt she couldn't bear. She bunched it up and stuffed it into the pocket of her jacket and instead stole a T-shirt and a grey hoodie from Robbie's closet. The sweatshirt sleeves were about a foot too long, but she rolled them up and put on her down jacket before they could unroll again.

There was a saucy drumroll from somewhere on the other side of the bed, and Natasha gave a start as Freddy Mercury's voice suddenly erupted into the same triumphant refrain she had heard the victory-drunk players bawl out at the party the night before. It was Robbie's cell phone. It was lying with his pants on the floor by the desk.

She picked it up and pressed the OFF button frantically. Robbie hadn't moved. Luckily, it would take more than that to wake the sleeping warrior. She stuffed the cell phone in her own pants pocket, wrote a message on a pad that was lying on the desk and placed it next to his pillow. Then she went downstairs.

The car keys were still lying on the foyer table. She took them. In the kitchen she opened the refrigerator and drank a pint of milk without taking the carton from her mouth. She quickly examined the shelves, nabbed a package of rye bread and a big box of chocolate wafers for sandwiches, stuffing four or five pieces in her mouth right away. The sweet explosion of melted milk chocolate went directly to her empty energy deposits. The rest she carefully wrapped in foil again for Katerina.

She glanced at the clock over the sink. It was after ten, and it was high time she got going. Katerina was waiting right on the other side of the lake. And now Natasha had a car.

She took a knife from the kitchen drawer before she left.

UKRAINE, 1934

"DON'T TAKE THAT one. It isn't ripe."

Olga glowered at Oxana, who had followed her into the garden and now drew herself up in a wide-legged stance, with an annoyingly grown-up frown on her face. It was so typical of Oxana to interfere just when Olga had gotten permission to go pick a melon for tea, if she could find one that was ready. Olga was the one who had helped Mother dig and turn the earth and place the small brown seeds in the ground one by one. Shouldn't she also be the one who decided when the first melon was ripe? Oxana might be two years older, but that didn't make her any wiser. No way was this going to be her decision!

To prove that she was right, Olga quickly bent down and rapped hard with her knuckles on the biggest melon, just like Mother usually did. The sound was muffled and hollow, and Olga felt as if she could almost see the red fruit through the rind, heavy and sweet and juicy. Her mouth began to water.

"What about the other side?"

Oxana pushed Olga lightly and hit the melon on its yellow, dirt-covered bottom, making a flat, wooden crack.

"See for yourself," said Oxana seriously. "It won't be completely ripe for a few more days."

"I don't give a fart," Olga said sourly. "We can eat it today, and it'll be perfectly fine—and anyway, I'm the one who gets to decide."

Oxana frowned again. "Speak properly," she said. "You're starting to sound just like the boys. It's better to wait until that melon tastes right. It's only dogs and boys—little boys—who can't help eating whatever is in front of their noses. Anyone with half a brain waits to dig up the potatoes until they are big and leaves the apples on the tree while they are small and green and sour."

Olga shook her head and suddenly couldn't help thinking about Mashka, who had had a litter of puppies last year and had scrounged around the compost heap for food until October. Mother had once slapped Olga because she had snuck a piece of rye bread out to the dog, and after that Mashka had had to manage on her own with whatever mice and rats she could catch. Mashka hadn't had time to wait for the potatoes to get big, or for the mice to get fatter, for that matter. Right after Christmas both she and the puppies had disappeared from the back shed, and it wasn't hard to figure out who had taken her, because at that same time, a group of Former Human Beings had drifted down the village's main street, reaching out with their skeletal fingers for anything edible on their way. The bark had been peeled from the trees, sparrows shot out of the sky; they had even eaten dirt.

Olga shuddered.

Poor Mashka. She herself had looked like a dead dog in the end, so perhaps it had been for the best that she had been freed from her suffering. But still. It wasn't nice of Oxana to speak badly of dogs in that way. They just did what they had to do to survive. Just like everyone else.

Olga grabbed hold of the watermelon and twisted it defiantly so that it let go of the vine with a small, crunchy snap. "It's ripe."

Oxana sighed in the way that meant that Olga was so childish, and Oxana herself so much more grown-up. But she nonetheless quickly followed Olga around to the covered veranda, where Mother had already heated water in the samovar. Mother took the melon, split it in half on the cutting board with the largest knife they had and didn't say a word about it not being ripe.

Olga looked triumphantly at Oxana. But Oxana just laughed and gave Olga's braid a friendly tug. It was odd. Sometimes Oxana pretended to be grown-up even though she wasn't. Other times she was just Oxana, like now, when she lifted little Kolja up from the rough planks on the veranda and danced around with him in her arms, as if there were a balalajka orchestra in her head. Kolja twisted his skinny little four-year-old body to get loose. He was a serious boy; even when he laughed, he somehow looked serious, as if he didn't believe that anything could be all that funny. Oxana's smile, on the other hand, shone like a sun, and she was beautiful, Olga thought, even now when she had just lost a tooth in both sides of her lower jaw and the new ones were growing in a little bit crooked. She was ten years old and a hand's breadth taller than Olga, but her teeth still looked too big for her narrow face. Her eyes were as blue as cornflowers.

Mother pulled off Kolja's shirt and vest so he could eat the first piece of watermelon without smearing the juice all over his clothes. Olga got the next piece and was just about to take a bite when she realized something was wrong.

"Shouldn't we wait for Father?"

"If he's not home in time for tea, there's not much we can do about it," said Mother. Her mouth had gotten small even though she was still smiling. "He'll be here soon enough."

"But . . ." Oxana had also stopped now, one hand hovering about the platter. "I can run down to the office and get him."

"No, never mind," said Mother. She pulled her blouse out and fanned it back and forth to get a little air against her skin. "He'll probably be here soon."

This was wrong.

As long as Olga could remember, they had eaten the first

watermelon together—all of them. When they lived in town, it had been a day of celebration, when Father cut the pieces and said funny things when he handed them out. "To my most highborn princess" or "to the most beautiful flower in the field."

Olga shifted uneasily in her seat, but she didn't say anything. It was one of the hottest summer days so far. Clothes felt sticky and itchy on the body, rubbing at the lice bites that had kept Olga and little Kolja awake all night. Mother had changed the straw in the mattresses, boiled the sheets and rubbed petroleum on the sleeping shelf, but the lice still bit in the heat and darkness until Olga was about to go mad. For some reason they weren't as interested in Oxana.

Olga scratched her neck and looked uncertainly at her big sister. It would have been best if Father was there too, but the large, sweet watermelon pieces lay in front of her, and it was unbearable. Oxana was right about that. She was no good at waiting.

She reached across the platter and took a thick slice. It was so juicy that the water dripped from her fingers, and when she took the first bite, it was wonderfully sweet and immediately pushed away her bad conscience. Mother could keep her rye bread, pickles and thyme tea today, and Oxana could stare at her as sourly as she liked. Olga took another piece.

"You're such a baby," Oxana said, outraged. "I'm waiting for Father."

Olga stuck out her tongue and kicked at Oxana under the table, but for once Mother didn't say anything. She had taken a piece of melon herself, bending her head over the table and carefully spitting out the black, mature seeds onto a piece of newspaper to be dried and saved for next year's crop. Then she pushed the plate of pickles toward Oxana. "Eat."

Oxana shook her head and glanced up the road.

Something was wrong. Olga could feel it all the way in the pit of her stomach. A kind of dark energy shone out of Mother now. It was like the wind that suddenly arrived and stirred up the dust in the road before a thundershower. From the Pretrenkos' house on the other side of the cabbage patch, Olga could hear laughter and Vladimir shouting something or other at Jana. Other than that, everything was quiet in the oppressive afternoon heat.

"Do you want to spoil the food?" Mother asked. She was pale with anger now. "Eat, or I guarantee that you will go to bed without food. Your father is drinking his tea someplace else today."

Oxana looked frightened. Mother rarely got angry, but when she did, she sometimes struck them. Mother's hands were hard and dry as wood. Now she got up abruptly and began shoving the food off the table with angry gestures. Kolja reached out fast, grabbed two more pieces of melon and raced down to the bottom of the garden with his prize. Olga remained petrified, looking at her mother. A kind of hidden knowledge began to bubble up to the surface.

The arguments had woken her in the night several times in the first months of spring. When Mother and Father argued, they whispered instead of shouting, so that it sounded like an excited hissing in the dark. Mother had never hidden the fact that she would have preferred to stay in Kharkiv, where Father had been a factory manager and a highly respected member of the Party. Even in the great hunger year, they had had bread and also a little sugar, salt and vegetables. To return to the village was suicide, she had said, but even though she cried, Father insisted.

It was the Party that had asked him to take over the management of the collective because he was known in the village and had a bit of experience with farming from his boyhood. And the Party was greater than Mother's tears, that much Olga knew. Father loved his Party and his country and would do everything possible to ensure that everyone would be better off. He would build a better future with his own hands. Olga had been on Mother's side, but of course Oxana had been on Father's, as she always was. And he was the one who got what he wanted in the end. Mother had dried her eyes, packed their things in silence and had followed him to the village where they had both grown up.

They had arrived in Mykolayevka in the fall right after the harvest, and Olga had hated the place instantly. Half the village's houses stood empty, with rattling shutters and broken planks and beams. Most of the trees along the main street had been chopped down, and the few that were left had been stripped of their bark and were as dead as the houses around them. Just two poplars remained by the house of the village soviet, their silver leaves rustling in the wind. The few people in the street were thin and starved and dressed in layer upon layer of rags and coats full of holes. Even Father had looked frightened, Olga thought, but then he said that this year, the harvest was already safe. The horror stories of the great hunger year would soon be only that: stories. They would see; it would soon get better. Oxana believed him, but Olga's stomach hurt, and she tried to hide her face against Mother's chest.

The first winter had been just as terrible as Mother had feared. Even though Father was the foreman for the kolkhoz, and the harvest was better than the previous year, the bread rations were meager. Father would not take more for his family than the ordinary workers received, Oxana reported proudly. Just once, he had brought home a load of potatoes and a barrel of rancid salt pork that he had bought on the open market, and that had lasted a whole month.

It had not been enough. Not even the salt pork had staved off the hunger altogether and silenced the hollow ache under the ribs. And spring had been the worst. While everything bloomed around them, hunger had gnawed at their stomachs worse than ever.

It wasn't Father's fault, that much Olga understood. And it had gotten better in the course of the first warm summer months. But

Mother still cried and scolded all the time and was thin and tired and grey even though the sun was shining and they had been able to collect the first potatoes in the garden over a month ago. She had lost two teeth in her lower jaw, which now gaped as emptily as Oxana's.

But it occurred to Olga now that the whispered arguments in the night throughout the spring had not been just about Mother's longing for Kharkiv and her fear of cold and starvation.

Father drank his tea someplace else.

A picture of Father down by the sawmill in the company of a smiling, full-figured woman whirled through Olga's head, followed by the laughing mug of Sergej from school. Sergej had lice and stank, like the little pig he was.

"What do you think of the widow Svetlova?" he had asked.

"What do you mean?"

"Do you like her?"

Olga shrugged. She had no interest in talking with Sergej, who was seven and disgusting to look at, with large pox scars on his forehead.

"You father does," he said and pulled his index finger quickly back and forth through a circle he made of the index finger and thumb on his other hand. It was deeply disquieting even though Olga didn't understand what it meant.

The realization hit her now like a spurt of blood, burning her cheeks and her stomach.

The widow Svetlova had made it through the winter in a better state than Mother. She had no children and was younger. Much younger, with round cheeks and broad white teeth without a single gap.

Oxana sat with her head lowered and picked at the splinters in the table. She was probably pouting because she hadn't gotten any melon, but she didn't deserve any better.

"Now look what you've done," hissed Olga. "You've made Mother sad."

Oxana shrugged. She scowled, eyes full of tears.

"You're such a baby," was all she said. "You wouldn't be able to wait for anything if your life depended on it."

"MAGNUS, DAMN IT," snapped Nina, but Magnus was driving twenty-five meters in front of her and couldn't hear her clenched exclamation. The winding forest road to the Coal-House Camp was not at the top of the municipality's list of priorities as far as plowing went, and with every snowfall the road got narrower and the snowbanks on both sides got higher. Magnus was driving close to the speed limit, with Volvo steadiness on authorized winter tires, while her middle-aged Nissan Micra skated around the turns as if it had never heard the word "traction."

The Micra was an emergency solution. It was almost fifteen years old, the door handle on the passenger side had broken off and the gearshift suffered from a reluctance to return to the middle position unless you gave it a sharp whack. Someone had painted green racing stripes on its curry-green door, most likely in a desperate attempt to give it a bit of personality. It was not the dream car; it was the "what I can afford?" car. She couldn't do without it. The public transportation's tenuous connection to the Coal-House Camp, more officially known as Red Cross Center Fureso, ceased completely at 9 P.M., and night shifts were an unavoidable part of the job of nurse.

The Micra's front wheels spun without effect on the black ice, and Nina had to fight a deep-seated urge to step on the brakes. The car sailed sideways into the curve and only fell into the track again seconds before it would have collided with the snow. She shifted down and waited for it to slow. Ahead of her, the back of Magnus's Volvo disappeared around the next turn. Perhaps she should have come in the Volvo with him. But then there was the problem of getting home again, and they hadn't exactly announced their . . . affair sounded completely wrong, relationship even worse—their mutual loneliness relief to the world. Maybe not arriving at the same time was a good move. But the adrenaline made her stomach burn, and the slow driving necessary on the slippery roads felt completely counterintuitive.

Natasha had escaped custody. As unbelievable as it sounded, it was true. The authorities had concluded that she might try to get hold of Rina and had therefore sent police out to the Coal-House Camp, which was, Nina thought, not something she could really object to, except that they had apparently managed to provoke one of the worst anxiety and asthma attacks Rina had experienced in all the time she'd been in the camp. Nina understood why Magnus was rushing and cursed the Micra's insufficiencies both mentally and out loud. "Damn it, damn it, damn it."

When she finally rolled into the parking lot in front of the camp's main entrance, she instantly spotted two almost identical dark blue Mondeo station cars. Two cars. Presumably at least four people. Apparently there was no lack of resources when the object was to catch single mothers with a foreign background found guilty of attempted murder, Nina thought dryly. It didn't say POLICE on the side, but it might as well have. Did they really think Natasha was stupid enough to wander into the camp as long as they were parked there? The police had errands at the camp fairly regularly, and Natasha knew just as well as the rest of the camp's current and former residents which car makes she should be on the lookout for.

On the other hand, it wasn't particularly intelligent to attack two policemen with a cobble. Nina had a hard time recognizing Natasha in the hurried description of events that Magnus had given her on their way to the cars. Of course, Natasha could be pushed to act violently; probably almost everyone could. But when she stabbed her fiancé with a hunting knife, it hadn't been because he had physically abused her for months; it wasn't until she caught him with his fingers in Rina's panties that she had counterattacked. During all the time she had spent in Vestre Prison, she had been almost alarmingly silent and passive.

Until now.

"What the hell were you thinking?" Nina muttered to herself as she made her way up the barely shoveled walkway in the direction of the camp's little clinic. Something or other had clearly brought this on, but what?

She stomped the snow off her boots on the grate by the clinic's main entrance. Weeks' worth of frosty slush was packed in the metal grid so that it had had become like trying to dry your feet on an enormous ice cube tray. As she opened the door, though, the heat hit her like a hammer. Magnus consistently ignored all energy-saving suggestions on that point. "The people who come here are sick, depressed and hurt," he had said when the chair of the camp's conservation committee had protested. "I'll be damned if I'm going to let them freeze as well!"

Rina was half sitting, half lying on a cot in one of the two examination rooms. In the corner between the closet and the wall sat an aggressively clean-shaven young man in a hoodie that on him looked more like workout clothes than weekend wear. He had placed himself in such a way that he couldn't be seen from the window, and Nina concluded that he had to be a member of the Mondeo brigade. There had been a moment of heightened alertness as she came in, but now he relaxed back into a waiting position, apparently convinced solely by her age and appearance that she posed no danger.

"Hello, sweetie," Nina said, squeezed Rina's hand, which was limp and a little too cool. "What are we going to do with you?"

There was something about the slight, eight-year-old body and the narrow face that reminded Nina of the eastern European little girl gymnasts of the 1970s—Olga Korbut, Nadia Comaneci and whatever they were called. Not the smiling medal photos, but the serious, too-old-for-their-age concentration before the routine, the shadows under their eyes, the contrast between the cheerful ponytails and the hollow-cheeked, pain-etched faces. Rina's hair was blond like her mother's, thick, straight dark blonde hair without even the suggestion of curl or wave. Right now that hair was pulled back with a light blue Alice band, but even though you could occasionally sense that Rina felt she had fallen through a rabbit hole to an alternate universe, there clearly wasn't much Wonderland about it. Her breathing was still terribly labored. Tiny pinpoint blood effusions around her half-closed eyes revealed how hard she had had to fight to get enough oxygen into her tormented bronchial tubes. Yet it wasn't Rina's physical condition that made Nina's own heart contract as if it were something more than a pumping muscle.

"Sweetie," she said, sitting down next to the child and pulling her close. Even on good days, anxiety lay like permafrost just beneath Rina's thin crust of childish trust. Now the trust was gone. There was no wish for contact in the slight body; she just let herself be moved with an arbitrary shift in her weight that had nothing to do with intimacy.

Having changed quickly, Magnus entered, stethoscope in hand. Pernille, who had had the night shift, followed on his heels.

"I had to give her oxygen a few times," said Pernille. "And her peak flow is still nothing to shout about. But . . . well, you can see for yourself."

Magnus nodded briefly. "Hello, Rina," he said. "I just need to listen to your lungs a little bit."

Rina didn't react except with a quick sideways glance. Nina had to turn her partway so that Magnus could examine her.

"Come on, Rina. You know the drill. Deeeep breath."

Rina continued to breathe in exactly the same tormented rhythm, but Magnus didn't try to correct her. He just praised her as if she had done what he had asked. "Very good. And now the other side."

There was still no reaction, no sign that Rina was participating in the examination with anything but limp passivity. Nina gently pulled her close so that Magnus could place the stethoscope against Rina's chest. Over Rina's blonde hair she caught Magnus's gaze.

"Well, I can hear that it's getting better," he said, just as much to Nina as to the child. "Do you want Pernille to get you some ice cream?"

Rina loved ice cream and could eat it year-round, and it had gradually become the ritual reward for various examinations, especially those that involved blood tests or other needle pricks. Rina lifted her head and considered the offer. But then she collapsed again with a single shake of her head.

"Did you eat breakfast, Rina?"

Again a tiny shake.

"She didn't want anything," said Pernille. "Not even ice cream."

Magnus sat down on a stool so he was more or less at eye level with Rina. "Listen, Rina. It's super hard for the body when you have trouble breathing. It's as hard as playing ten soccer games in row. Do you see? And then you have to be a little kind to your body and feed it properly, even if you might not feel like eating."

That didn't make any visible impression.

"Rina, if you don't eat anything, we'll have to keep you here in the clinic," said Nina. "Wouldn't you rather go back to your room?"

The policeman by the closet cleared his throat. "It's best for her to be where she usually is," he said.

Nina stared at him with anger smoldering in the pit of her stomach. "Best?" she said. "For whom?"

"So that the mother can find her more easily."

The anger burst into flame. Only concern for Rina made her control herself. Couldn't he see that this was a child, a sick and tormented child, not just convenient bait for their trap?

"That's a medical decision," said Magnus very, very sharply. "And I'm the doctor."

But Rina had lifted her head again and suddenly looked more present and alive than she had at any point since Nina got there. "I'd like an ice cream," she said.

Oh, Lord, thought Nina. So that the mother can find her more easily. That was the only thing Rina had heard and understood. What if Natasha really did show up? And the police arrested her in front of the child? Nina didn't want to think about what that would mean for Rina's delicate balance and her grasp of reality here in non-Wonderland. She could see that Magnus was thinking more or less the same thing. But they couldn't do anything—couldn't even discuss it here and now while Rina was listening.

"Strawberry or chocolate?" asked Nina.

TEN MINUTES LATER, as she escorted Rina across the icy asphalt lot that had once been the barracks' drill grounds, it was with two of the Mondeo brigade on her heels, though they maintained a certain discreet distance that presumably was supposed to make them look like civilian passersby. Rina held Nina's hand, something she had otherwise stopped doing, and in her other hand she clutched the strawberry ice cream, which she dutifully sucked on every fourth or fifth step. At least it didn't look as if her breathing was significantly more labored now that she was moving and even though the air was cold enough to sting Nina's more resistant lungs. Pernille had done all the right things, had administered Bricanyl and later prednisone, had measured the oxygen and attempted to calm the panic. Physically, the girl was improving. But right now Nina was much more concerned with what was happening in Rina's mind.

In the middle of the grounds, Rina suddenly stopped. She gave a little tug on Nina's hand.

"What is it, sweetie?"

"He's dead," said Rina.

It took Nina a moment before she managed to reply, quietly and calmly. "Who?"

"Poppa Mike."

Poppa Mike? Did she mean Michael Vestergaard?

"Why do you think that?"

"That's what they said. The police."

The wind raced across the open square. Pin-sharp flakes that were more ice than snow bit Nina's cheeks and forehead, and she suddenly felt as if she were standing in an arctic desert, icy and isolated, infinitely far from warmth, shelter and human contact. Rina stood next to her and stared with great concentration at the strawberry ice cream, as if conquering it were a task she had set herself. She wasn't crying—in fact, her face was devoid of expression—but Nina was not fooled. She quickly checked the time—12:31—and looked up at the slate-grey sky with the apparently irrelevant thought that the weather would make it difficult to fly. Only a few seconds later did she understand why flying conditions suddenly seemed to matter. Whenever the situation had escalated from desperate to hopeless in one of the hellholes and disaster areas of her misspent youth, the skies had been her only hope. It was from above that help might arrive.

Unless Rina had misunderstood something, Natasha's former fiancé was dead—the man Natasha had once tried to murder with a hunting knife. And it had happened while she was on the loose after having brained a policeman with a cobble.

"Rina . . ."

"They are both dead," said Rina and took a determined bite of the strawberry ice cream. "Poppa Mike and Daddy."

Jesus. Poppa Mike *and* Daddy?

Nina realized that she knew absolutely nothing about Rina's biological father. She had placed a single-mother-from-Ukraine label on Natasha without giving it a lot of thought. "Are you sure, sweetie?" she asked carefully.

"That's what they said." Rina's voice shrank, got smaller and thinner, not because of Nina's doubt, it turned out, but because the next thing was what had made her world shake. "They said Mama did it."

"Mama?"

"Yes, that Mama killed them. Both of them."

Suddenly the Mondeo brigade's size made more sense. They weren't hunting a woman found guilty of a single—relatively ineffective—homicide attempt. They thought that Natasha was a double murderer.

Nina was all at once extremely conscious of Rina's hand resting in her own. The girl's delicate fingers were trembling, not just from cold and fear, but because the asthma medicine was affecting her. Anton's hand was different, more solid and square and usually more dirty.

Anton was with Morten now, in the apartment in Fejøgade. Maybe they had made pancakes; Morten sometimes did that when he had the time and energy and was in a good mood. Maybe they were all three still sitting at the kitchen table while Morten lingered over an extra cup of coffee and talked about music with Ida, and the checkered oilcloth got more and more spotted by Anton's marmalade fingers. Only Nina was missing.

I'm not sure I can do this, she thought, without completely knowing what "this" was, just sensing that the war had started again, and she was too tired, too old and not suited to fight it. I wouldn't mind if someone came to rescue us right now.

Rina gave her hand a little tug, this time because she wanted to continue. "I'm cold," she said.

"No wonder," said Nina. "It's freezing out here. Let's get you inside."

Somewhere behind them, the two Mondeo men had halted. Now they started moving again. Was it one of them who had said that "Poppa Mike" was dead? And that Natasha had killed him? How could they say such things while Rina was listening? No hope of rescue from that quarter, that much was certain. But who else was there to turn to?

SØREN RECOGNIZED THE number right away even though he hadn't called it in over six months.

He stopped in his tracks, and another runner on the path had to swerve around him. His pulse was at 182 and his breathing so labored that he had to let the telephone ring several times before he took the call, but he didn't for a second consider not answering.

"Yes," he said.

"It's Nina. I don't know if you remember me. I was the one who—"

"Yes. I know who you are."

He saw her with crystal clarity in his mind's eye. The first time he had met her, she had been sick as a dog with radiation poisoning, frightened and furious. The hospital's patient uniform didn't fit her any better than it did anyone else; she was stick thin and smelled faintly of vomit, and her short, dark hair covered her scalp like a matt of shaggy and untended fur. Only her eyes had revealed that there was still life in the ruins—the intensity burned through clearly in spite of the fact that the rest of her had to be categorized as "more dead than alive."

She had been difficult, uncooperative and suspicious, and he had to threaten her with prison, a moment during the interrogation that he wasn't very proud of. She probably had no idea that he had later done his best to shield her—her and her pretty illegitimate network. In his eyes, people like Nina were perhaps a bit too trusting toward some of the illegal immigrants and other borderline cases they supported with medical aid, shelter and other emergency essentials. But damn it, people should not be prosecuted for basically doing a good deed.

Another runner trotted by him in the tense staccato style people tended to adopt when the going couldn't be trusted. Even on this disgustingly cold winter afternoon, there were lots of joggers on the path around Damhus Lake. The route was too short; he had circled the lake four times, which made him feel a bit like a hamster in an oversized wheel, and even though the council did clear the paths of snow, they were still slippery and greasy with a grey-brown mixture of gravel, slush, goose shit and salt. He would have preferred the woods of Hareskoven or some other, less crowded place, but the snow made the forest paths more or less impassable, and when he had tried to exchange his running shoes for cross-country skis a few weeks ago, his old knee injuries had protested so violently that he'd had to toss the skis back up on the carport rafters again.

The phone had gone quiet, long enough for his pulse to drop to around 140.

"What can I do for you?" he asked at last.

"Forget it," she said suddenly. "I shouldn't have called."

The background noise and the faint whistling disappeared. She had hung up.

He stood looking at the phone for a few seconds. There was a limit to how long he could stand still. He was already getting cold, and a harsh wind blew over the lake's frozen surface. An open hole in the ice was teeming with screaming, quacking, cackling waterfowl—mostly ducks and graylag geese, but there were also five or six swans and a raucously aggressive gang of black-headed gulls.

He pressed the DIAL button. She answered at once. "You must have had a reason for calling," he said.

She still hesitated. "It was mostly because . . . you're not an idiot."

An ironic "thank you" was about to slip out, but he stopped himself. Irony wasn't what was needed here. "What's happened?" he asked instead.

"You are the twenty-six-year-old mother of a little girl," she suddenly said, in a peculiarly rushed staccato tone. "You've escaped from Ukraine; you get engaged to a Danish man; he's a sadistic bastard, but you tolerate it because you are more afraid of being sent back than of what he does to you. Not until you catch him with his fingers in your little daughter's underwear do you snap. You buy a knife and stab him in the throat. He survives, but you are found guilty of attempted murder and sent to jail."

She stopped, but he just waited, his muscles getting stiffer, the cold creeping across his skin along with the sweat. He stood perfectly still. He sensed that if he as much as shifted his weight, she would fly away again.

"You spend sixteen months in Vestre Prison doing nothing but what they tell you to do. Passive. Easy to handle. And then you suddenly attack a policeman and escape. And this is where it gets really weird. You don't go to get your daughter. Instead you head directly for your ex-fiancé, and then you kill him."

He could hear her breathing now that his own was calmer. Hers was stressed and shallow. Forced.

"Does that make sense?" she said. "Is it logical?"

"I don't know," he said. "Too much of the picture is missing."

"But your first impression?"

"I can't say," he insisted. "It would be pure speculation."

"Okay. Forget I called."

"No, wait. I just said that I didn't know enough."

She sighed. "That's something. The police here think that they know everything. They are apparently convinced that Natasha murdered both the sadistic bastard and Rina's father."

Rina's father? Who the hell was that? Nina wasn't making it easy to follow her.

"Where are you?" Søren asked.

"The Coal-House Camp. Rina—that's Natasha's daughter—she . . . Damn it, she can't take this!" The anger rose in her voice. "They're using her as bait in their Natasha trap, and they don't give a shit if she's up to it or not."

He would probably have done the same thing—kept an eye on the girl with the assumption that the mother would contact her sooner or later. He didn't tell Nina that.

"What's Natasha's last name?" he asked.

There was a pause.

"I don't remember," she admitted. "Something . . . something Ukrainian. Wait. Dimitrenko or something like that. I don't remember how you spell it."

The computer was not particularly forgiving of alternative spellings, but on the other hand, how many Ukrainian women could there be who had just escaped from Vestre?

"I'll see what I can do," Søren promised recklessly. "I'll call you later."

"When?"

"It'll take awhile. At least a few hours."

"But you'll call?"

"Yes."

"Thank you."

The tension in Nina's breathing was gone. The relief made her voice younger and lighter, and he felt a prick of conscience. There probably wasn't anything he *could* do, and his only reason for trying was deeply unprofessional.

He wanted to see her again.

POLICE. OF COURSE, there would be police.

Natasha felt Katerina's proximity tug at her core. There she was, right on the other side of the fence, not in the family barrack where they had lived together before Michael, but in the rooms reserved for unaccompanied minors. She was there; she had to be there, even though Natasha couldn't see her.

But the police lurked like big, fat barn cats, just waiting for the stupid mice to scurry out of the hay.

"As long as it's light, you have no chance." She once again heard Anna's voice, a voice that calmly and sensibly forced her to listen even though Natasha wanted to run over and throw herself against the wire fence. She wasn't sure when she had stopped thinking of Anna as a real-world source of solace and good advice, and instead turned her into this odd inner fairy godmother who kept an eye on Natasha and made sure she didn't behave too stupidly. Perhaps it was since that night a year and a half ago when she had attempted to stab Michael in the throat with a knife. Was it then?

Natasha was glad Anna was there. It made her feel less alone.

She walked back through the deep snow, well over half a kilometer, to the little clearing where she had parked the dark blue Audi. She might as well try to sleep a little.

She brushed extra snow onto the car's license plate to be safe. She didn't think Robbie would report it stolen for the time being. He was probably still asleep, and when he woke up, he would find the note she had placed next to his pillow: *I'll be back. ❤, Katerina.*

Right now she wished she had called herself something else.

In the Audi's trunk she found a blanket and a thick tarp. She took them both into the backseat and cocooned herself inside. A sleeping bag would have been better, but she didn't have a sleeping bag.

THE BED IN the apartment in Kiev had been a revelation in several ways. Clean and white and delicious smelling, full of pillows, comforters and smooth, light sheets—Egyptian cotton, Pavel had said, and she just nodded. She had never before lain on a mattress that received the body in this way, firm and soft at the same time. At home in the room in Kurakhovo, you could feel the bed slats through the worn foam rubber.

And Pavel, Pavel, Pavel, Pavel.

He had driven into her life in a shiny red Alfa Romeo one day as she was trudging along the road between Dachne and Kurakhovo. She had missed the bus and would rather walk to the next stop than stand waiting in the cold. When he slowed down and asked if she wanted a lift, she had ignored him at first. She didn't want him to think she was one of those girls. But he had kept rolling along next to her, apparently indifferent to the trucks that roared by him honking and all the vulgar gestures and shouts from the passing drivers. He had spoken to her just as if they were walking along next to each other on the sidewalk, although they did, of course, have to shout more loudly. He was a journalist, he said, and was writing an article about safety in the coal mines. Did she know anyone who worked there? Or anyone who once had? "Everyone does," she said. There were practically no other places you *could* work in Kurakhovo; it was the mines or the power plant or unemployment. Her father had lost his job two years ago; her mother still worked in the plant cafeteria. "And what about you?" he had asked. It had gone on like that all the way to Kurakhovo, and finally when they had reached the outskirts of town, she had gotten into his car. Because by now her feet hurt and because she was getting hoarse from shouting, and because . . . because Pavel was Pavel.

She had insisted on a church wedding so that everyone could see that she had married well, to a husband who had both money and culture. An intellectual, as her father said, at once contemptuous and satisfied. Pavel didn't drink vodka. Not even at the wedding party, where he wore a dark Armani suit. Few of the guests could appreciate such details, but that wasn't important. Pavel looked like what he was. A success. At the same time, he had shown everyone else up for what *they* were and would always be. A bunch of drunken, shabby bumpkins with foolish grins and yawning gaps in their teeth. Uncles and aunts and cousins, and girlfriends from school who arrived on the back of their boyfriends' scooters.

None of them drove an Alfa Romeo. And none of them had an apartment in Kiev with a view of the National Museum.

The first night in Kiev, she had felt like the princess in a fairy tale.

"Come on. There's something I want to show you!"

Pavel smiled at Natasha, and she couldn't help smiling back. Genuine smiles that could be felt all the way to the heart, and she thought that it felt precisely like love in the movies and that she adored every detail of his face. The nose, which curved slightly, and the blond hair she knew he had inherited from his Galizien mother, who had been ethnic German. Pavel himself spoke fluent German and also English, and earlier in the evening, he had ordered in a restaurant with the same confidence as the men in the American movies.

"What is it?" she asked.

On purpose she let herself stumble clumsily into his arms. Her breasts under the new bra and the soft silk blouse grazed his chest, and she wanted to get closer, feel his weight and the strength of his arms. In fact, she thought, and felt shameful and happy at the same time, she would undress him all the way tonight and look at him before they did it. In the big white bed, on the sheets of crackling Egyptian cotton. She didn't know if it was normal to think like this, but she didn't care. The night sky turned above them, and she laughed lightly and giddily.

"Take it easy." Pavel gently pushed her away and dexterously placed his arm between them, so that their bodies were no longer touching. "Act like a lady, my sweet. We're in a public place."

The rejection smarted, but only for a moment. Then she let herself be led farther up the steep path toward the lookout in Maryinsky Park.

Pavel took her hand and drew her to an opening in the trees. They were at the park's highest point now, and above them stretched a gigantic shining arch, all the way across the square. The evening air was pleasantly warm against her skin.

"Arka Druzhbi Narodiv. The People's Friendship Arch," said Pavel and pointed at two stiff statues under the arch. "Those are the two brothers. A symbol of Russia and Ukraine. The statues are cast in bronze, and the bow is pure titanium. As strong as steel, but much lighter."

Natasha nodded but didn't know what to say. Or what he expected her to say. She was much more interested in a little enclosure with bumper cars and pounding techno music on the other side of the titanium rainbow.

"Can we?"

"You go ahead," he said. "I'll wait here."

Natasha pouted and deliberately put on a disappointed face. But he didn't budge. He just dug into his pockets and found a few bills that he placed in her hand.

"I'm too old for bumper cars, but you go ahead, sweetheart. Then I'll show you the view afterward."

Natasha had already changed her mind. It wasn't going to be fun. Not when Pavel stood there next to the ring like an adult waiting for a child. The little lecture about the statues had already made her feel like a schoolgirl on a class trip. But it was too late now. In her newly purchased high heels, Natasha tottered over to a neon-yellow car and got in, knees folded almost all the way to her chin. Pavel stood a few meters from the railing and lit a cigarette, a brand with a sweetish tobacco that left a wonderful taste on his soft lips. He'd buried his hands in the pockets of his long black pants. So much for the creases, but that was okay. She'd take care of that for him.

There were only three other cars in the ring. One was being shared by a young couple, and the other two were driven by two teenage boys, absolutely hammered, who were clearly intent on doing maximum damage to each other. Even before the power had come on, the two drunk boys were hanging out of their cars, laughing and cursing and insulting each other. Why on earth had she thought this would be a good idea?

The car in front of her whined and picked up speed, and she reluctantly stepped on the flat little pedal in the bottom of her car. It smelled of burnt rubber, and the heavy, monotonous bass from the techno music made her chest vibrate. A faint nausea came over her, totally different from the feelings of sexual excitement and expectation that had coursed through her only minutes ago. She turned the steering wheel and lost focus for a moment while the car rotated around on its own axis. Then she was hit hard from behind, and her knees slammed against the steering wheel. It hurt, but she still forced herself to laugh giddily and let her gaze seek Pavel's tall figure outside the enclosure. She wanted him to see that she was having a good time.

He wasn't standing there anymore. She caught sight of him farther away, in the shadows under the trees, together with another man. Natasha lifted her foot from the pedal and observed Pavel and the man, who at first looked as if he was having a laugh about something. He spread his arms, and you could see his teeth bared in an odd grin. A friend, Natasha thought. Pavel's friends were influential and important men, she knew—journalists and politicians and businessmen, some of them filthy rich. None of them had come to the wedding, though, because Kurakhovo wasn't the kind of place you invited people like that, Pavel explained.

Now Pavel was the one laughing and gesticulating, but there was something strangely stiff about the scene. As if the two men were performing a play in an open-air theater, with exaggeratedly caricatured gestures in honor of the people in the back rows.

Pavel stepped back and suddenly didn't look like the man who had called the waiter earlier in the evening and confidently left twenty percent on top of the already large bill. There was a touch of uncertainty in his body, as if he'd rather be somewhere else.

Then the other man hit him.

The blow came so fast and with such precision that Natasha only saw it because she was keeping a sharp eye on them both. Pavel's head snapped back and to the side, and his hands rushed to his face, but otherwise nothing happened. The man turned around and walked away, passing under the titanium arch that was as strong as steel but lighter. His steps were angry and smooth and almost synchronized with the noisy music from the bumper cars.

Natasha tumbled out of the car, though she was still in the middle of the black arena. She barely escaped being torpedoed by one of the teenage boys on her way to the exit.

Pavel stood leaning against a tree when she reached him, with two fingers pinching the bridge of his nose to stop a trickle of blood.

She wanted to ask him what had happened, but something in his gaze stopped her, and she just handed him a napkin from the new Dolce&Gabbana purse he had given her.

"It's nothing. You don't need to worry," Pavel said and smiled behind his hand. "The things I write are not popular everywhere in Kiev. Journalism is a risky business, you know."

She didn't know.

Yes, of course she had heard about journalists who were threatened and shot. Idealists. But for some reason she had never connected that with Pavel.

He must have seen the confusion in her face, because now he was laughing for real and lifted her chin so that her face was turned up toward his.

"No, of course you don't know anything about that, my beauty," he said. "But come on. I still haven't showed you what we came up here for."

"Let's go home," Natasha said, glancing in the direction where the man had disappeared. It was almost completely dark now, and the square was emptying out. Only a few small groups of young people still sat there, laughing and smoking in the warm evening.

Pavel shook his head and took her hand again. Pulled her with him. "A jerk like that is not going to ruin our evening," he said. "He's not worth it. Have a look . . ."

She turned obediently.

Beneath them Kiev's millions of lights glittered, reflected in the great black mirror of the Dnieper River.

"Our city, Natasha. Isn't it beautiful?"

He pulled her close, but the night's intoxication had receded, and the world had become more real again. She had a bad taste in her mouth, and a pile of garbage next to them gave off a sweet-and-sour smell.

"I love you," she said, hoping the magic words would banish the unpleasant grittiness of the reality around them.

"And I love you. Like mad. Like a total lunatic," said Pavel. And now it must've suddenly been all right even though they were in a public place, because he pulled her close, and she could feel his short, excited breath against her neck.

His kiss tasted sharply of beer and sweet tobacco, and a little bit of blood.

SHE WOKE UP in a forest far from Kiev, in an ice-cold car, and still with a bloody taste in her mouth. She had bitten her cheek while she slept.

Pavel was dead and had been so for a long time. And the thing that had killed him was now stretching its tentacles toward her and Katerina.

UKRAINE, 1935

"WHAT KIND OF person are you if you believe in God?"

Comrade Semienova rose from her desk and looked at the class with a mild, questioning gaze.

Olga squirmed on the bench. The question wasn't difficult, and she knew what she was supposed to answer if she was asked. People who believed in God were anti-Soviet and not quite right in the head, and like the kulaks, they wouldn't work and especially not on Sundays. The kulaks wanted to be fed by the proletariat, and the religious by their God, and their faith was so strong that they would rather starve and freeze to death in the street than acknowledge that they were wrong.

That was the truth.

But in a way there were more truths than that, and they rubbed strangely against one other in her head and made her uncomfortable as she sat on the hard school bench. Because Olga remembered that her grandmother had had a little gold crucifix hanging under her blouse that she sometimes pulled out and kissed with her big, wet lips, and that must mean that she believed in God, even if she worked with her hoe out in the turnip field until the midday heat forced her inside.

Her grandmother died three summers ago. She had been found out in the field lying next to her hoe. Father and Mother and Oxana and

Olga had taken the train from Kharkiv to be part of singing her out, and even though Olga was smaller then, she could still remember the stench in the tiny living room where Grandmother lay waiting for the burial party. It was because she had been lying there too long, Father said then. Much too long, out there in the field. Even now Olga hated to think about it—Grandmother in the field in the roasting afternoon sun. Even if Grandmother *had* believed in God.

Olga would have liked to ask Comrade Semienova if work in the turnip field didn't count as work for the Soviet state for some reason, because perhaps that was the explanation. But she didn't dare. If there were something wrong with Grandmother, it would be embarrassing for both Oxana and her. Comrade Semienova would definitely frown and might even get angry.

And that must not happen.

Comrade Semienova was the most beautiful thing Olga had ever seen, and she knew that Oxana felt the same way. Small and straight and with hair as fair and shiny as stalks of wheat. When someone answered correctly or when there was particularly good news from Uncle Stalin in Moscow, her glowing smile brought out two lovely dimples in her soft cheeks. She smoked cigarettes like a man, which somehow seemed incredible and wonderful.

She had come from Leningrad, arriving in the early spring to replace old Volodymyr Pavlenko, who had died of hunger-typhoid sometime during the winter.

The school had been closed until April because there wasn't wood or petroleum, and therefore no one knew how long old Pavlenko had lain dead and frozen solid in the house at the back of the school. Because he was frozen, he didn't smell like Grandmother had, but Olga couldn't help shuddering when she thought about it. Still, that was long ago, and now it was autumn.

"Fedir? How does the religious person think?"

Comrade Semienova let her gaze rest on Fedir, who sat all the way at the back of the class. He was thirteen and strong as an ox but also similarly slow.

"They are stupid." Fedir grasped for more words. "They want to steal from the people."

Jana, who sat next to Olga, groaned quietly and imitated Fedir's slightly out-of-focus gaze and open mouth. But Comrade Semienova was satisfied.

"Correct, Fedir," she said and lit up with her wonderful smile. "But you can also express it in a different way. Oxana?"

"They are counterrevolutionary parasites who do not wish to have a strong state."

Now it was Olga's turn to groan. Oxana was good at remembering all the long words. The best in the entire class, and that was probably why she also sometimes dared to stand next to Comrade Semienova's desk after class to speak with her at length. Oxana was neither shy nor afraid she might blush and stammer. It was annoying and disgusting to watch, Olga thought, because Oxana wasn't that much better than Olga and Jana. She just had no shame. But the worst thing was that Comrade Semienova couldn't see that Oxana was sucking up to her. On the contrary, it seemed as if she liked speaking with Oxana and in fact listened to what she said, even though Oxana was only ten and Comrade Semienova at least twenty. As if they were friends.

Now she nodded to Oxana with a confidentiality she didn't share with any of the other children. Then she raised her voice.

"Comrade Oxana is the best student in this school," she said, offering a slender hand in Oxana's direction. "Therefore, I have decided that she is to accompany me next week to a group meeting with Komsomol and the pioneer division in Kharkiv. I would like Oxana to sing the Internationale."

The class was completely silent. Even that little worm Sergej, who sat next to Jana, had for once stopped rolling boogers on the table and was keeping his arms and legs still at the same time.

Now Oxana was blushing. It was from pride, not shame, thought Olga.

"Oxana is talented," Semienova continued. "But you should know that we all, regardless of abilities, must strive to be better comrades, to work harder for Uncle Stalin's ideas about the dictatorship of the proletariat. Next time it could be one of you going along to Kharkiv if you work hard and improve yourselves."

Jana bent her head toward Olga and stuck her index and middle fingers into her mouth with a telling gagging gesture. Olga giggled deliberately. But inside something had begin to gnaw and rub, like the many truths she saw. Were you allowed to hate your own sister? She had a feeling that both Uncle Stalin and Semienova would disapprove of her thoughts if they knew of them, but it was hard enough to control her words and behavior. To control her thoughts was completely impossible. No matter how hard she tried, they often drifted into black areas and made her think that she might be a kulak, or on her way to becoming one. There were things she wished to have, even though no one was supposed to own anything. Bread and silk dresses and shiny headbands. And Semienova.

That was why she had begged and made a spectacle of herself—as Jana put it—until she had been included in one of the photographs taken when Oxana had been chosen as the school's model student in September. Semienova got the *Pioneer* magazine to come all the way to Mykolayevka. Of course, only the picture of Oxana made it into the newspaper, but Semienova had also asked to have the other developed and had placed it next to her bed in the room behind the schoolroom. Olga knew that she was included because Semienova had felt sorry for her, but the picture was a nice one all the same, with Olga and Oxana in the beautiful and almost identical traditional dresses Mother had sewn for them when they still lived in Kharkiv.

Olga wished that she was the one Semienova had chosen to sing at the pioneer meeting, and she wished that Oxana wasn't so beautiful, didn't have such blue eyes and didn't sing like the stupid, goddamn nightingale in the poplar tree down by the stream.

OXANA'S CHEEKS WERE still blushing when they passed the last house in the village and continued on the dirt road between the hills.

The trip to school was terribly long now, ever since they had moved out to Grandfather's farm, and every day when they passed by the old house, Olga cursed the widow Svetlova and her bloated cow tits. All Jana had to do was run along to the Petrenkos' house right next door, while Olga and Oxana had to trudge along the stream and over the rise. It was all right while it was summer and the road was dry and warm so that you could take off your socks and shoes and walk barefoot. But now it was September, and the rain had already transformed the road into two black muddy wheel tracks. Neither their bark shoes nor the extra socks could prevent the cold mud from getting all the way in between their toes as they walked. Disgusting.

In addition, on the road to Grandfather's, there were Former Human Beings who had dug themselves dirt hole shelters among the birch trees and sat staring at them with starving eyes as they passed by. Sometimes they whispered and hissed up there among the trunks, begging for bread—"*khleb, khleb*"—but mostly they just stared. The worst was the children wandering around with bloated bellies and sores on their arms and legs. Most of those children had disappeared during the winter. The ones who remained were more dead than alive, and Olga had more than once thought about giving them a piece of her bread.

But hunger gnawed at her too—every day, all the time. Through gruel and porridge and nettle soup. When she closed her eyes, she thought about all the things she had eaten when she was younger. Whole plates filled with potatoes roasted in oil. Salt pork and sausage and cheese and pierogi. It would all come back, Oxana said, and she also said that Olga had to be strong and save her bread for herself, because the children among the birches were already marked for death by scurvy and typhoid. No matter how much bread they ate now, they would die, crushed between the great millstones *golod* and *kholod*—hunger and cold. Olga could not ease their suffering with a single piece of bread. And Olga knew that Oxana was right. In the spring she had seen boys by the pond behind the house catching tadpoles and swallowing them live. That kind of hunger consumed everything and could not be satisfied by Olga's two half-eaten crusts, and every time she had the thought, she let her bread slip back into her pocket and felt how her stomach, which at first had protested in panic, grew calm again.

Once she had decided to keep the bread, she discovered that she actually hated the Former Human Beings. They had stolen from the peasants and now sat there begging bread from her, so terribly hungry herself, who had never stolen as much as a stalk of wheat. That truth warmed her all the way down into the pit of her stomach. But she was still angry at Father too, because it was his fault that they had to walk the long way through the birch grove every day.

It was Father's fault that they had had to move. Father and Svetlova's cow tits.

Jana had told her that Svetlova had moved into their old house with Father just two days after Grandfather had come with the horse and wagon to collect Mother, Oxana, Kolja and her, and that Svetlova on that very same day had used Mother's laundry bucket to rinse her dirty underwear and hang it up on the veranda so everyone could see it. Mother had cried when she heard, and after that no one spoke of Father any longer. It was forbidden.

"Just think," said Oxana dreamily. "A whole day in Kharkiv, and I'm going by train with Comrade Semienova."

"Hmmmm."

Only once in her life had Olga traveled by train, and that was when they had to attend Grandmother's funeral. Otherwise, she had only seen them at a distance in the railroad town of Sorokivka. You needed permission from the GPU for that kind of travel. And money. Something occurred to her.

"But who will pay for your ticket?" asked Olga. "It costs at least five rubles."

"It will be taken care of," said Oxana importantly. "I've already discussed it with Comrade Semienova. Oh, Olga, I wish that you could come too."

Olga shrugged and smiled faintly. It was hard to resist Oxana when she was happy. And Olga wished that she would be happy all the time because then she herself might escape from the gnawing and disconcerting worms inside.

"Maybe you could ask Comrade Semienova if I could come along. We can sing together. 'Zelene Zhyto'—'The green, green wheat.' We know it. We can do it in harmony."

Olga hummed the first soft notes of the song that Mother had taught them. A harvest song that everyone who had grown up in a village had heard in the fields when the wheat and oat were harvested. But Oxana just shook her head.

"I don't think so." There was genuine sympathy in her voice. "Only one student can be selected from each school in Kharkivka Oblast, and besides, you are still much too young to understand what a political meeting like that is about. That's not at all the kind of song you sing there."

She looked around and quickly handed Olga a piece of bread. They never ate in school. Oxana especially didn't like the hungry eyes of the others, and Mother had carefully instructed them never to show that they had bread. Instead, they crumbled the bread into little pieces and ate them quickly and discreetly on the way home. Preferably before they reached the birch trees.

Comrade Semienova said it was the dirt-hole people's own fault that they were starving, and that was another truth. Olga knew that it was true. Still, it was nasty that they were there, and she was happy when Oxana described how everyone would be fine as soon as the next five-year plan was put into action. Uncle Stalin would make the country so rich that even the Former Human Beings would acknowledge their mistakes and receive salt pork and butter on their bread every day. Oxana was certain because she knew it from Comrade Semienova, who told her things that were not said in class. Great things were on the way, she said and winked teasingly.

"Soon, little Olga, you'll be able to stuff yourself. You'll become so fat that Sergej will need longer arms if he is to reach all the way around you when you kiss."

Olga couldn't help laughing and swatted at Oxana, who broke into a clumsy gallop toward the house. Oxana's bark shoes sank into the mud with small, soft squelches, and she lifted her dress so you could see her thin, stockinged legs and large, bony knees.

For a brief moment, she turned her head and looked back at Olga. Her blue eyes glittered savagely and exuberantly above narrow rose-colored cheeks. Behind her, the chestnut's wine-red leaves and the yellowing birch trees shone vividly, and all at once Olga felt a choking fear shoot up, paralyzing her as she stood in the muddy wheel track. A sort of premonition.

"Oxana," she said, "don't go."

But Oxana didn't hear her.

SØREN FOUND HIS boss in the well-equipped exercise rooms under PET's headquarters in Søborg. The Danish Security and Intelligence Service believed in keeping its employees fit. Søren knew Torben didn't like to be disturbed in the middle of training, but they usually came to an understanding more easily in person than over the phone. Torben did put down his weights and listened with at least some patience while Søren sketched the circumstances surrounding Natasha's escape and the killing of her ex-fiancé. Then he leaned back on the bench and grabbed the weights again to complete another set before answering.

"Spot me?" he asked. "I'll try for twelve."

"Okay."

Søren positioned himself so he could help with the last repetitions if necessary. Lips pursed, Torben breathed in through his nose and out through his mouth, in time with the motion. The weights shot up in an explosive press. Then he lowered them slowly, very slowly, to the outer position. Then up again with something that sounded like a snort. The Adidas shirt was dark with sweat and could probably be wrung out. At the ninth repetition, his extended arms began to shake, but Torben didn't give in, and when Søren moved to put a hand under his elbows at twelve, he hissed an angry "no" and took it by himself.

He lay on the bench, hyperventilating for a few seconds, before he sat up and gave Søren a triumphant look. "Not bad, huh?"

Søren handed him the water bottle without commenting. He knew he should offer a friendly "Well done" or something like that, but he couldn't quite do it. It felt increasingly false, like a scratchy old record that should have been thrown out long ago. He no longer felt at home in that sweaty, towel-swiping changing room community but didn't know what to replace it with. Perhaps it was just that he didn't have much in the way of relationships outside of work. Maybe he had made a mistake all those years ago when he hadn't just agreed to have children with Susse. Maybe they would still have been together. Now she lived with her jazz musician husband in a bungalow with a white fence and cocker spaniels and pear trees in the yard, and her youngest had started high school. They were still friends—that much he had salvaged from the fire. And he wasn't exactly envious of the family idyll, just . . . a bit pseudonostalgic. That could have been me. But it couldn't have been, of course, because with him it would have been a different story.

He wrested his concentration back to the case, if it could be called that. Right now, there wasn't much PET meat on it, he knew.

"I've called police headquarters," he said. "They have a Ukrainian policeman sitting there who doesn't speak English. From GUBOZ, apparently." GUBOZ was the special division that dealt with organized crime in Ukraine. That was pretty much the only alibi Søren had for looking into the case. Fighting organized crime was, after all, a PET concern.

Torben considered him over the top of the water bottle with his cool steel-grey gaze. "That's right. You used to be a language officer," he said.

"Russian and Polish. Nineteen eighty-one and nineteen eighty-three." Possibly the most intensive schooling Søren had ever been subjected to—a bombardment of words that approached brainwashing, constant tests, an eternal rhythm of classes, homework, physical training, sleep—classes, homework, physical training, sleep . . .

"Yes, today they're learning Arabic and Afghani," said Torben and screwed the lid onto the bottle again.

"Pashto. Or Farsi, depending."

"Yes. Is your Russian still usable?"

"Pretty much."

Torben nodded and dried his face, neck and shaved head with an often-washed greyish-white towel.

"Okay. Go ahead and give them a hand, since you're so curious. And why is that, by the way?"

It was stupid to try to lie to Torben. As Søren's boss, he took that kind of thing very badly, and besides, they considered each other old friends. That Søren had begun to doubt whether constant physical competition really could be called a friendship didn't change the fact that they had known each other for over twenty-five years. "Natasha Dmytrenko's daughter apparently lives in the Coal-House Camp. And Nina Borg, you know, the nurse from . . ."

"Yes, I remember her."

". . . Nina called because she was worried about the girl. And about the mother too."

"What did she imagine you could do? Save mother and child from the cruel Danish police?"

Søren shrugged. "Something like that, I guess."

Torben shook his head. "Aren't you a little too old to be playing Don Quixote?"

"Don Quixote *is* old. Or at least middle-aged. That's the point."

Torben got up and returned the weights to the rack. "Thank you," he said. "If there are other literary niceties I need to have explained, I'll be sure to tell you. The point here, my friend, is that you are getting involved in something that most likely doesn't concern either you or us."

"I know. But the man is from GUBOZ, and that must mean—"

"That there is some suspicion of organized crime, yes, thanks, you don't need to spell it out. Okay. Talk to the Ukrainian if you absolutely have to get involved. And if there's something in it, it goes directly to our own OC boys. I want my group leader back on his counterterrorism perch by Monday at the latest. Understood?"

With PET's usual fondness for English terms, OC was the accepted abbreviation for the Center for Organized Crime.

Søren mentally clicked his heels and saluted. "Yes, sir."

Torben gave him a look but otherwise ignored the sarcasm. "Want to grab a brew later?"

That was Torben's way of dealing with the boss/friend issue. The beer invitations usually came when he had been most boss-like.

"Maybe. Or . . . There probably won't be time."

"Up to you. You can join us for dinner if you feel like it. Annelise is doing a roast."

"Thank you. But . . . maybe another time."

"Mmm. Okay." Torben had already turned around and was making his way over to the pull-down machine. Søren suddenly realized that Torben hadn't for one moment expected him to say yes.

"I NEED A WORD with you."

It sounded more like an order than a request, Nina realized, but she didn't care. The policeman was so young, he automatically started to obey. He was on his feet before it occurred to him that a nurse was not actually above him in the chain of command. But by then it was too late for him to sit down again without looking like an idiot. He was also young enough that not looking like an idiot was pretty high on his list of priorities.

"What about?" he asked.

"Let's go outside," she said.

Rina looked at them with the alertness of a wounded animal, and the policeman apparently realized—much, much too late in Nina's opinion—that there were certain things you didn't discuss while an eight-year-old was listening. He followed her into the hall. Rina's eyes trailed them the whole way. She sat on her bed with the Moomintroll-patterned comforter pulled all the way up to her chest. Nina had found her a Donald Duck comic, which she dutifully had looked at, but judging by the random page turning, she wasn't getting a lot out of the story.

"We'll be right outside, sweetie," said Nina, and she didn't know if that sounded like a comfort or a threat to the child. Her anger swelled another notch, and she closed the door carefully before letting loose on the policeman.

"I understand that Rina's stepfather is dead." She didn't like to give the bastard the legitimacy of having any kind of place in Rina's life even now, but Rina had called him "Poppa Mike." Whether Nina liked it or not, he was, in fact, a part of what Rina had lost after Natasha's ill-considered attempt at homicide.

"May I ask where you received that information?" asked the young policeman, possibly in an attempt to regain his authority.

"From Rina, who got it from you."

He actually blushed. The color rose along his neck and washed over his well-defined cheekbones. He couldn't maintain eye contact.

"Fuck," was all he said.

"Yes," Nina said and felt her attitude soften. He didn't try to explain it away or apologize, and that was something. "How could that happen?" she asked.

He shook his head. "We didn't think she spoke Danish," he said. "She didn't answer when we asked and didn't say anything at all to anyone. We were told that she was mute."

"Mute?" Nina's voice rose again.

"No, that probably wasn't the word. 'Speech issues' is what I think they said."

"That just means she has a hard time talking to strangers," said Nina. "And that she often can't speak in stressful situations. And no matter how little she says, she hasn't lost her hearing."

"No. I'm sorry."

"When was he killed? And how?"

He shook his head. "I'm not at liberty to discuss the case with . . . anyone."

"A little late for that, isn't it?"

He didn't answer.

"Did it happen after Natasha escaped?" asked Nina. "Is she a suspect?"

"I can't comment on that."

"And what about Rina's father? Is it true that he was murdered too?"

But if there had been an opening, it had closed again. He was once more annoyingly police-like and looked as if the word "fuck" had never crossed his lips.

"I'm sorry," he said. "I can't comment on that."

"Well, then comment on this," she said, irritated. "I don't want you in Rina's room. I don't want any of you in there. She's traumatized enough already, and as long as you are there, I don't have a snowball's chance in hell of talking with her about it or getting her to relax. We can easily make it an official medical order if that's necessary and outline precisely why your presence has already had a powerfully negative effect." The last part was pure coercion.

He squirmed. "I have to consult," he said.

"Consult all you want," she said. "As long as you do it out here and not in there."

She turned her back on him and went back into Rina's room.

The Donald Duck comic lay on the floor like a discarded prop. Rina sat with an old, broken cell phone, the only toy she had brought with her to the camp when she had arrived at the age of not-quite-six.

The psychologist had found it interesting, Nina remembered. "Does she ever speak into it?" he'd asked.

"She whispers," Nina had said. "Mostly she just presses the buttons and listens. But sometimes she whispers as well."

"Is there any pattern to when she does it?"

"I think it's mostly when she's feeling sad," said Nina. "Perhaps it distracts her."

"I think it's encouraging that she attempts to communicate her feelings," the psychologist had said. "Even if it's not with us. You should definitely let her keep it."

Now, more than two years later, Rina still had her phone and clearly needed it more than ever. Her bitten nails pressed the buttons with almost manic intent.

Nina picked up the Donald Duck comic and placed it on the little dresser next to the bed. "Would you like another ice cream?" she asked.

Rina looked up. She shook her head silently and finished dialing. She held the telephone up to her ear and listened.

It occurred to Nina that that was precisely what she was doing—listening. She wasn't pretending; this wasn't an act-like-the-grown-ups game. She was listening in earnest. For the first time, Nina wondered what it was Rina expected to hear.

She sat down on the desk chair and pretended to look out the window, but she was really keeping an eye on Rina's expression, and that was why she saw it.

Suddenly the girl's face opened, and she smiled. A completely open smile that, for some reason, gave Nina the chills. She felt like grabbing the phone out of the child's hands but held herself back. As the psychologist said, it was good for Rina to attempt to communicate with someone.

But what did you do if this "someone" began to answer?

There was no doubt in Nina's mind that Rina had indeed heard a reply, and it was highly unlikely to be because the defective phone had suddenly started working.

There was a quiet knock on the door. The young policeman stood outside.

"I've spoken with the chief," he said. "She says that it's okay for us to be in the room next door on the condition that you and your colleagues have someone with the girl at all times. Press this if you notice anything alarming."

He handed Nina a little black box with a red button. A personal attack alarm. Nina remembered that not long ago, they had discussed whether the night shift at the center should be equipped with them.

"Okay," she said. Not an insignificant victory. "Thank you."

Rina looked at the policeman with her animal gaze until Nina closed the door again. The cell phone had disappeared into her pink backpack. The psychologist would probably consider that a step backward, but Nina couldn't help feeling relieved.

THE WALLS WERE a calming dove blue; the chairs and tables of light wood and lacquered steel all looked like something you might find at a high school from the '70s. But the fact that the tall patrician windows were covered with bulletproof glass cooled the atmosphere a bit, Søren noticed, and made it impossible to characterize the police headquarters's combined coffee-and-lineup room as cozy.

"He speaks almost no English," said the detective inspector, discreetly flipping his thumb in the direction of a young man who sat drumming his fingers impatiently on his jean-clad thigh. "And the other one, the one we could at least speak to, seems to have vanished into thin air."

"The other one?" asked Søren. Until now he had heard only about one man.

"Yes, there were two of them. They came to speak with the fugitive—well, at that point she wasn't a fugitive yet, but . . ."

"So you've lost both an inmate and a foreign police officer?" Søren spoke with a certain coolness. He knew that the safety involving the transport of inmates wasn't ironclad, at least not unless the so-called "negatively strong" inmates were involved. If one of the more peaceful ones got away, it was usually pretty anticlimactic. They often turned up on their own when they had taken care of whatever it was that was so important to them, or if not, you could collect them undramatically a little later in the day at the home of a much-missed girlfriend or at the birthday celebration of some family member. The system responded with an extra thirty days and the revoking of a few privileges, and that was that.

But this was different. Natasha Dmytrenko didn't miss her fiancé—she had done her best to kill him once before, and now he was dead. It also worried Søren considerably that a member of the not ill-reputed Ukrainian militia appeared to have given his hosts the slip.

The DI grew defensive. "We can't just lock our foreign colleagues in a cage," he said. "He got pretty upset when he heard that she had escaped, and suddenly he was gone as well."

Søren regarded the one Ukrainian policeman they still had under control. The man had short brown hair and a face broader than the average Scandinavian ones Søren was used to seeing. There was a restless, coiled energy in the drumming fingers and the tapping heel. A dark tie and a white shirt lent a bit of formality to the jeans getup and the '70s hippie suede jacket that hung over the chair back behind him. He must be around thirty, Søren estimated, young but no kid.

"What's his name?"

"Symon Babko, police lieutenant in some subdivision of the criminal police."

Søren just nodded and elected not to tell the young assistant criminal policeman that this "subdivision" could swallow the entire Danish police force more than once without even noticing.

Even though it wasn't said very loudly, the Ukrainian policeman must nonetheless have picked out his name through the ambient noise of chair scraping and cafeteria talk. He raised his head—what a chin, Søren thought; there was a warrior-like determination to that chin—and looked directly at Søren.

"*Dobry den,*" said Søren, holding out his hand and presenting himself. "Søren Kirkegard, PET."

"Hello," said Babko.

He had unusually large hands, Søren noticed. They looked out of proportion to his thin, knobby wrists. As if someone had attached an inadequately thin handle to a spade.

"I'm sorry. I speak only Russian, not Ukrainian," said Søren.

Babko laughed. It was an amazing volcano eruption of a laugh that started far down in his skinny middle, moved up through his entire body and made his shoulders shake before finally rolling out across the cafeteria landscape with such power that conversations around them ceased.

"My friend," he said, with laughter still in his voice, "when you have sat in a chair for almost twenty-four hours without being able to say anything but 'Hello,' 'Thank you,' and 'Where is the toilet?' there suddenly is not as much difference between Ukrainian and Russian as there usually is. We will no doubt understand each other."

THEY BORROWED AN office on the second floor with a view of the parking lot.

"It was down there," Symon Babko said, pointing. "Down there she got away."

"Natasha Dmytrenko?"

"Who is really called Natasha Doroshenko," said Babko. He pushed a worn file folder toward Søren. "She was questioned in two thousand and seven in connection with the killing of her husband, Pavel Doroshenko. Immediately afterward, she disappeared. There is, therefore, a request for detention."

Søren opened the folder. Natasha Doroshenko looked like a frightened teenager in the photo that was glued to the first page of the detention order, but that was the way she looked, he remembered, in most of the photos that accompanied the Danish case files he had had the chance to skim. He attempted to speed-read to get an overview but had to accept that his linguistic proficiency wasn't quite sufficient. The Ukrainian differences from the Russian he was used to teased his eyes, similar to the way Norwegian or Swedish forced him to read more slowly. It would take a while to digest the material, and right now it was more important to engage with the man who sat across from him.

"Tell me," he said instead.

"In Ukraine, she is still wanted in that connection. She hasn't been found guilty. Not yet. But she's wanted. So when we learned that she had been recognized in Denmark, we were naturally interested."

Søren nodded. "Are murder cases normally handled by GUBOZ?" he asked neutrally.

"At first it was a simple murder case under the jurisdiction of the criminal police. I wasn't attached until a week ago when the extradition case started." Babko looked closely at Søren. There was a subtext here, Søren sensed, but he wasn't sure that he could read it.

"So you have formally requested her extradition?" he asked.

"Yes. But even before the extradition got properly underway, Colonel Savchuk had successfully requested an interview. The Danish officials were apparently very forthcoming."

That searching gaze again. Søren was annoyed that he was clearly missing something, but he sensed that a direct question would be a mistake.

"I assume Savchuk is your English-speaking colleague?"

"That is correct. *Colonel* Jurij Savchuk."

Finally Søren understood. With his slight emphasis, Babko was making it clear that Savchuk had a higher rank than he did and that he therefore was in a pinch right now. He couldn't officially criticize a superior, though Savchuk had apparently left without being polite enough to tell his hosts where he was going or why.

"Where is Colonel Savchuk?" asked Søren.

"He is presumably investigating Natasha Doroshenko's disappearance," said Babko carefully.

"On Danish soil?"

"I assume he is doing so by agreement with the proper authorities." It was clear that if this was not the case, Babko wasn't at fault.

As far as Søren knew, there was no such agreement, and he strongly doubted that the "proper authorities" would take kindly to an unauthorized freelance effort from the Ukrainian police. But he let it pass. "The killing of Pavel Doroshenko," he said instead.

"Yes. On September twenty-third, two thousand and seven, Doroshenko was found in his car near Lake Didorovka. At that point he had been dead for a few days. It was at first assumed that he had been murdered, since he had some obvious lesions, mostly on the hands, but it later turned out that the cause of death was heart failure, presumably caused by pain and shock."

"He was beaten to death?"

"Yes and no. Four of the fingers on his left hand had been crushed—extremely painful, but under normal circumstances not lethal."

"Crushed how?"

"In the car door."

"And I assume it couldn't have been an accident?"

"Unlikely. The door was slammed shut across his fingers several times. Normally you put a cable or thin rope around the victim's wrist, and the hand is pulled toward the door while the victim sits bound in the car and already trapped by the seat belt. It's said that the best tactic is to stick your hand as far out of the car as possible, so that the door slams closed on the wrist instead of the fingers, but it is very difficult not to attempt to pull your hand toward you. That's the most natural reaction."

Søren listened to the cool and almost routine description of the torture. "In other words, that happens regularly? This type of violence?"

"Yes. It's a fairly common way of punishing people who, in one way or another, have had their fingers in the wrong pies."

Søren's eyes fell on the teenage-slim Natasha Doroshenko. "It doesn't seem likely that this is a . . . punishment . . . that his wife could administer."

"Not on her own, no. A petty criminal called Bohdan Pahlaniuk later took credit for providing the muscle. But he claimed to have been paid by the wife because she was upset that Doroshenko couldn't keep his hands off other ladies. Pahlaniuk said that the intention wasn't to kill him." Babko tapped the case file with a square index finger. "Page two."

Søren turned the page. Yes—page two was a confession signed by Bohdan Pahlaniuk and dated November 16, 2007.

"How was he caught?" he asked.

"Pahlaniuk was arrested and held for another assault a month or so after Pavel Doroshenko's death. The Doroshenko confession surfaced in connection with that. But a warrant was out for her just a few days after the killing."

"Why?"

"The most obvious reason, of course, was that she took off and left the country with her daughter a few hours after she had been questioned. But there were some other suspicious circumstances as well. Even though her husband had disappeared four days before he was found, she hadn't reported him missing."

"How long had they been married? How was their relationship?"

"They were married in two thousand. She was only seventeen. He was quite a bit older, in his mid-thirties."

"Twice her age?"

"Yes, it's not that uncommon. She's from a small town near Kurakhovo in Donetsk Oblast. It's not the greatest place in the world to live when you are a young girl wanting a bit of fun in life. Since the coal mine began shutting down production, everything has ground to a halt. There are whole neighborhoods that are practically ghost towns. He was a journalist, lived in Kiev in a fancy apartment—her ticket to the city and a completely different lifestyle."

"Do you know whether there were, in fact, 'other ladies'?"

"He had the reputation at least for being a bit of a *babolyub* before he married. Maybe the leopard hadn't changed his spots just because he signed a wedding license."

Søren considered the possibilities. There was apparently a certain amount of substance to the case against Nina's young widow, and yet . . . certain peculiarities jumped out.

"Am I correct in assuming that Colonel Savchuk is a man of a certain position?" he asked.

For the first time in the course of the conversation, Babko sat totally still. The bouncing heel stopped bouncing; the fingers ceased drumming against the coffee mug.

"That's correct," he said. "In SBU."

SBU was the Ukrainian secret police. Not exactly an organization with a spotless reputation.

"Not GUBOZ, then."

"No."

"What is his interest in this case?" asked Søren. "Wouldn't it normally be handled by someone at a lower level?"

Babko looked at him for a few seconds with a poker face. "Correct again," he said finally.

His replies became more and more minimal, Søren observed, the closer you got to Savchuk.

"Is he carrying his cell phone?"

"Presumably."

Now we're down to one word, thought Søren dryly. What would be next? Syllables?

"Do you have a number?" He deliberately shifted from the formal to the informal address to reduce the distance between them. *We are colleagues*, he tried to say. *Help me out here.*

Babko shook his head—a single abrupt gesture.

Silence filled the office. You could hear the traffic outside in Hambrosgade accompanied by the hissing of radial tires through slush.

"So you have no way of contacting him?"

"No."

Not only was Babko a man playing away from home, but his only teammate was apparently more of an opponent than a fellow player. Søren could almost pity him, but only almost. Because one thing was clear: Babko was by no means telling Søren everything that he knew.

The Ukrainian militia was no knitting circle. Every year Amnesty International registered countless instances of torture, misuse of power and corruption, and the country's own ombudsman in this area had had to note that up to three-quarters of those arrested were subjected to some form of abuse. In many instances the interrogation methods appeared not to have changed significantly since Soviet times when quick confessions were necessary if you were to solve the required 80 percent of your cases. Whether you had the correct guilty party was less important. It was all about closing the case in a hurry.

Was Babko one of the bully boys who routinely beat detainees with water-filled plastic bottles or kept them handcuffed for days? He didn't look like the type, but then, not many torturers did.

UKRAINE, 1934

"YOU'RE TO KEEP your mouth shut. Understand? What I do in my own house is none of your business or anyone else's."

Grandfather pounded the table so hard that the warm tea in his mug sloshed over the rim and soaked into the rough grain of the wood. Oxana started, but she didn't lower her eyes. On the contrary, she raised her chin in defiance, giving him a small, stubborn smile of the kind she normally offered Olga when she thought Olga had done something particularly childish.

But Grandfather wasn't a child. How did she dare? True, he was little and bent and moved with difficulty, but when he hit, he hit hard, fists to the face. He had gotten up, swaying and threatening, planting both his broad, lumpy hands on the table for support while he glared at Oxana. The smells of rank body and goatskin and vodka billowed in the air around him.

"But Russian vodka is the people's enemy," said Oxana. "We have to fight drunkenness, crime and religious sloth."

"Shut up."

Oxana collected herself. "But Grandfather," she said. She wasn't completely unaffected, because her voice had gotten a little bit shrill now. "You yourself have seen what vodka does to people. When men drink, they can't work. They fight and kill each other. It's the capitalists' weapon to anesthetize the masses."

Grandfather's eyes were half closed and swimming now. "*Kapitalistki, sotsialitski, kommunitski*," he growled. He shoved the table so hard that all the mugs teetered, and one fell down and shattered on the floor. "That crazy teacher of yours means trouble. Stay away from her. You're smart, they say. It shouldn't be so hard to understand."

He stumbled around the table and fell toward Oxana, who had positioned herself by the brick oven, Grandfather's vodka bottle in one hand. She was furious. A bottle of vodka was not only hard to come by, it was also expensive, and the money could have served a more useful purpose. The standard bread rations from the kolkhoz were only enough for bare survival, and bread and butter were expensive in the open market. Kolja needed the extra nourishment, as did Mother.

Grandfather raised his fist, and Olga instinctively ducked in her seat by the chimney. She expected any moment to hear the sound of Oxana's skull being split open by Grandfather's fists, but instead it was Mother's icy voice that broke the silence.

"Leave her alone."

Olga opened her eyes again and saw Mother standing in the doorway. The draft made her heavy skirt flutter faintly. It was cold outside now, with frost at night, and Mother's face and hands were red from the chill. Grandfather backed away from Oxana. He had wrenched the dirty vodka bottle out of her hand and was staring meanly from Mother to Oxana before he finally ambled out of the living room. He slammed the door hard behind him. Olga caught a glimpse of him through the dirty window. He looked like an angry wounded bear, thought Olga, crossing the little courtyard with short, lurching steps before he disappeared down the road toward the village.

Mother signed deeply and sat down with little Kolja on her lap. The clay bowl that she had brought in from the barn was almost empty again today. Zorya's milk barely covered the bottom. The calf from the spring was long gone, and the cow was not a miracle machine that could produce milk from potato peels and straw. No matter how much you boxed her sunken udders, it was usually only possible to extract a few drops at a time. Now Mother brought the bowl up to Kolja's mouth.

"Drink, my boy," she hummed. "Milk from Zorya for you."

Kolja squirmed, wrinkled his little face and turned his head away.

"Drink, Kolja." Mother's voice was sharp now, and she pressed the bowl against Kolja's lips until he reluctantly emptied it in one swallow. Then he placed his face against Mother's throat and closed his eyes.

"Why doesn't he help us?" Oxana's voice flicked like a whip through the living room. "I've heard the widow doesn't lack for anything, and we are his children. You are his wife."

Mother didn't answer, just sat with half-closed eyes and stared straight into space. Olga didn't like it. Mother's neck, which used to be smooth and brown and smelled of herbs from the garden, had gotten wrinkled and stringy. Dirt caked her chest and breastbone darkly, and in a few places it had cracked and fallen off, the skin beneath showing a transparent pink. Olga knew that it had something to do with Father, even though she didn't completely understand why Mother had stopped washing from one day to the next. Just as it was clearly also Father's fault that they were living here instead of in the house in the village next to Jana.

It was Oxana who took care of bathing Kolja now, and Oxana who woke up Mother so that she made it to work in the morning, but the caked dirt on Mother's neck they couldn't do anything about, just as they couldn't get Father to love Mother again and ask them to move back into the house.

Oxana cursed quietly. "He's a shit," she hissed. "A no-good piece of shit." She spun around and began to put on her heavy coat.

Mother didn't move. In fact, it didn't even look as if she had noticed.

"Where are you going?" asked Olga.

"I'm meeting Comrade Semienova down at the school."

"But we just got home."

"Yes." Oxana smiled faintly. "But we are so busy, and Comrade Semienova has said that I, Leda and Jegor may sleep in the schoolroom when we've finished writing our article. We're going to have potatoes and salt pork and real tea that Comrade Semienova has had sent from Leningrad."

"But what if Grandfather—"

"Grandfather is an old drunk. He doesn't understand that these are new times."

Olga looked over at Mother and Kolja, who sat still as pillars of salt at the table. It was already getting dark, and when Grandfather came home, he would have emptied the rest of his vodka bottle and be tired and hungry and mean. "Can I come?"

Oxana looked at her in surprise over her shoulder. Then she laughed. "That wouldn't do, Olga. Remember that both Leda and Jegor are fourteen. You're only eight."

"So what?" protested Olga. "You're only ten."

"That's different," said Oxana, holding her head high. "Comrade Semienova says I have a very early understanding of the issues."

Olga felt an odd desperation creep up on her. A night without Oxana. She had never tried that before. Never. And especially now, when Grandfather would be angry and crazy, and Mother just sat there staring into empty space. "But did Mother say you could go?"

Oxana glanced quickly at the two unmoving shadows at the table. "Honestly, Olga," she said, lowering her voice, "Mother can't even take care of herself right now. I need to be the strong one. Do you understand what I mean?"

Olga didn't, but Oxana clearly wasn't planning to explain any further. She just tied her scarf under her chin and looked at Olga with a steady gaze. "Make sure to keep the fire in the oven lit, but don't light the lamp before it's necessary. We're almost out of petroleum, and what we have is rubbish anyway. It's better used on the lice."

Her hand touched Olga's shoulder lightly. "Trust me, Olga."

She opened the door and stepped out into the fall dusk. Olga looked after her as she tramped through the mud in the same direction that Grandfather had disappeared. Then Olga bent down and began picking up the shards.

"YOU NEED TO speak to Heide," Søren was told. "And she's still out at the scene."

Michael Vestergaard had been found some hundred meters from his home in Hørsholm—in this weather at least a forty-minute drive from central Copenhagen. It wasn't that Søren minded the distance. If he was going to get involved in the investigation, he might as well do it properly. He was just a bit reluctant to drag Babko with him as long as he didn't know to whom the GUBOZ man reported. There was still no word of or from the missing Colonel Savchuk. On the other hand, the possible connection with the killing of Pavel Doroshenko was one of the things Søren needed to discuss with Mona Heide, and Babko was the best witness they had in this respect.

"Where are we going?" said the Ukrainian when Søren asked him to come along.

"To talk to one of my colleagues."

Babko looked as if he thought the answer was somewhat lacking, but he didn't say anything else—at least not until they reached the garage in Hambrosgade, and Søren unlocked the car door.

"Is this your car?" asked the Ukrainian.

"Yes," said Søren.

And then Babko's laughter exploded, loud and unreserved.

Søren considered the light blue Hyundai and didn't think it looked especially funny. "Is something wrong?" he asked.

Babko shook his head. "No, my friend. Nice little car. All is well."

Søren sighed. They might in theory speak the same language, or at least something closely related, but the cross-cultural understanding was still far from perfect.

"Get in," he said. "We're going to a place called Hørsholm."

THE COLD BEGAN to eat its way through the soldered seams of Søren's North Face jacket as soon as he got out of the car—so much for being "designed by mountain climbers and athletes." The sun, which had offered a certain illusion of warmth earlier in the day, had disappeared behind a dark grey, snow-heavy cloud cover, and an arctic wind blew across the hedges.

Tundra Lane. The name fit. Even Babko, who presumably was used to these kinds of temperatures, swore and shivered in his suede jacket. He took a small, round, knitted cap out of his pocket and pulled it down so that it covered the tops of his ears.

This wasn't the quiet residential street that Søren had imagined. True, there had been a suitable number of symmetrical housing estates just before the GPS directed them down a narrow side road. But this part of Tundra Lane was little more than a wheel track with snow-covered bogland and forest on one side and soft, hibernating golf course hills on the other. It was surprisingly isolated, considering that they were only about twenty miles from the center of Copenhagen.

Vestergaard's house turned out to be a big box of a McMansion, made of white brick with panorama balconies in the gables and wide, shiny squares of double glazing. Several police cars were parked out front, including the incident van. It looked more like a moving van than a police vehicle, thought Søren, in spite of the orange stripe with the POLICE label. He showed his ID to the frozen uniformed officer who stood by the police tape, then went over to knock on the door of the van.

"I have an appointment with Mona Heide," he said when a young guy in a black down jacket opened the door.

"She's still at the scene," said Down Jacket. "But you can wait in here."

Søren nodded. Even though he was curious, he had known ahead of time that the investigators were unlikely to let people they considered irrelevant stomp around the scene of the crime. He crawled up the ladder-like steps and introduced Babko in English.

"Pleased to meet you," said Down Jacket. "Asger Veng, North Zealand Police."

The inside of the van was somewhat reminiscent of a building site trailer, thought Søren. One end was set up as a kind of miniature cafeteria, with a dining table and minimal kitchen facilities; the other served as office and command center. Between the two sections there was an even more minimal toilet. The facilities were not particularly cutting-edge technology-wise, and the comfort was pretty limited, but at least it was warm, and an industrial-strength coffee machine stood gurgling by the sink.

"Coffee?" asked Veng, who'd noticed the direction of his gaze. "They have just concluded the on-site inquest, so it won't be long now."

"Where did they find him, exactly?" asked Søren.

"A few hundred meters into the bushes behind the golf course. He was sitting in his own Mercedes, wearing a seat belt and everything, but in the passenger seat."

"So he probably wasn't driving."

"No. And the only purpose of that drive must have been to get away from the house. It's not a real road, just a track for working vehicles—tractors, that kind of thing—almost impossible to navigate in this weather. Getting the car out of there again should be really interesting . . ."

"Who found him?"

"The neighbor. She was out walking her dog. Thank goodness for dog walkers. If not for them, any number of bodies would remain unfound." Veng poured coffee into white plastic mugs and waved a hand in the direction of a pair of black folding chairs at the dining table. "Have a seat."

They had barely had time to follow orders before there was the sound of steps in the snow outside.

"There she is," said Veng a bit unnecessarily. The door opened, and something that looked like a slender and athletic Teletubby swung into the van. Police commissioner Mona Heide pulled the protective suit's hood off with an impatient gesture and revealed a becoming short, ash-blonde hairdo and a pair of tasteful gold earrings.

"Heide," she said, offering her hand. No first name, no invitation to collegiality. She projected authority and professionalism that was in no way softened by the gold earrings or the confident, but not exactly subtle, makeup.

"Kirkegard," Søren said, instantly provoked into the same formality.

"It's nice of you to sacrifice your weekend." She didn't ask him why directly, but she was clearly wondering.

"No problem," he said, ignoring the unspoken question.

"We're happy to have the help in any case." She gave a short nod at Babko, who returned the nod politely but with a bit of reserve. He still didn't know why they were there.

"I understand that you can help us with the Ukrainian connection?" Heide continued.

"Probably," answered Søren. "I assume you already know that

Lieutenant Babko and his colleague Colonel Savchuk are here because of a death in Ukraine back in two thousand and seven?" He used their names on purpose so that Babko would know they were talking about him.

"Yes, Natasha Doroshenko's husband. We are, of course, interested in hearing more about the particular circumstances."

"Is she your chief suspect?"

"Let us say that we consider it likely that she is involved."

"More than one perpetrator?" he guessed.

She didn't answer at once. He could feel her reluctance to bring others into the confidence of her small, well-functioning group. She didn't want to discuss her murder theories with him. He waited without pushing.

"We believe he was killed where we found him," she said at last, "and that there were at least two people at the scene of the crime. A woman and a man." And as if this admission had resolved her internal debate, she offered him the rest freely. "Michael Vestergaard was found at a quarter past eight this morning by his neighbor, Anna Olesen, who was out walking her dog. She called us from the crime scene on her cell phone and stayed there until the police arrived. Pretty impressive for a lady of more than eighty, you have to admit. The coroner believes time of death was sometime between eight and eleven, but there's a significant factor of uncertainty because of the cold. It's hard to judge what is rigor mortis and what is just deep freeze."

"But the neighbor was sure that he was dead?"

"Yes. His throat was cut. That doesn't leave much room for doubt."

"Were there any other marks on him besides the cut throat?" asked Søren.

"Several blows to the face, some broken fingers—seven or eight. We won't know for sure until we get some X-rays taken."

Broken fingers . . . it sounded like the sort of coincidence that wasn't one. Still, Søren would like to make the link a certainty rather than a question mark.

"Are there any photos that Lieutenant Babko could have a look at?" he inquired.

"Not yet. Why?"

"Pavel Doroshenko had four broken fingers. It's apparently a common form of torture. It would be nice to know if Vestergaard's killer did it in the same way."

Another reflective pause. Then Heide abruptly got up and opened one of the steel cabinets that stood along one wall of the bus. She tossed two protective suits in crackling plastic onto the table.

"Here," she said. "You can look at him in the hearse. They'll be bringing him out in a little while."

WHEN YOU'RE GOING to see a dead person in a hearse, you expect them to be lying down. Michael Vestergaard wasn't.

"We couldn't get him out of the seat without damaging him too much," the coroner said apologetically to Heide. "It was easiest to cut the bolts and bring the lot."

Michael Vestergaard sat straight up in his car's front seat, which had been cut free and then secured inside the white Ford Transit. It had been sixteen degrees below zero the previous night, and the chill was immediately evident. Vestergaard's once-white Hugo Boss shirt now created a dark armor of ice and frozen reddish-brown blood across his chest. The head lolled backward and to one side, and the lower part of his cheek was stuck to his shoulder, frozen solid. His well-trimmed hair was white with frost.

"Isn't he unusually . . . frozen?" asked Søren. "Of course, blood freezes, but—"

"Blood, waste and other bodily secretions. But it also looks as if water was poured over him," said Heide. "Possibly to wake him from a faint or as a form of torture in itself. They weren't exactly gentle with him."

Søren suddenly had a flashback to a POW exercise in the distant days of his youth. The abrupt cooling, the short sensation of drowning when you inhaled water instead of air. It wasn't quite as cruel and systematic as waterboarding, but in the right—or perhaps the wrong—hands, a simple bucket was a pretty effective instrument of torture. With the current chill factor, it could also be a murder weapon, but Vestergaard had not lived long enough to die of cold.

"His hands?" said Søren. "Is it okay if Lieutenant Babko has a closer look at them?"

"Be my guest," said Heide in English.

Babko apparently understood the ironic English phrase, because he climbed into the hearse with Søren.

The frozen body curved in a way that somehow contradicted the backward-lolling head, as if two opposing forces had been at work at the moment of death. Automatically, Søren's mind began to replay the scene. He sensed the threat that made Vestergaard crouch forward, cradling his ruined hands against his stomach. Then the grabbing of his hair, the head that was wrenched backward, the knife slicing through tendons and arteries and throat cartilage. What Natasha had not managed a year and a half ago was now completed in one abrupt slash without hesitation or failed attempts.

"The hands," he said in Russian to Babko. "Is it the same sort of damage as to Pavel Doroshenko's?"

Both hands were swollen, blue-black and bloody, and on the left, especially, there were several obvious breaks. The cold and the stiffness of death had frozen the damaged fingers into a position that looked more like some marine life-form than a human hand—a meat-colored starfish, maybe, or a shattered coral formation. The outermost joints of the little and ring fingers were bent all the way back. On the middle finger, the tip was simply missing, and you could see the bone sticking out through the tissue.

With a careful, plastic-gloved finger, Babko bent the shirt's frozen cuff back to get a better look at Vestergaard's wrist. "There," he said. "You can see the mark."

There was a deep, dirty groove along the cuff edge. Thinner than a rope, thought Søren, perhaps a cable or a wire of some sort.

"Method is same," said Babko in English so Heide and the technicians could understand him. "Same, Doroshenko."

"Punishment or interrogation?" asked Søren, first in Russian and then in Danish.

Heide tilted her head a bit as she thought about it. "That hurt," she said. "If it was to make him talk, he was either very tough—or he couldn't give them what they wanted because he didn't know."

"Poor devil," said the technician.

Søren didn't say anything. Instead, he studied the shattered hands one last time. He had read the reports from the trial against Natasha, including the doctor's testimony that described in detail what Vestergaard had done to his then-fiancé. Maybe someone, somewhere, considered this fair retribution.

"ARE YOU OKAY?"

Magnus leaned against the doorframe with a coffee cup in one hand and a well-worn copy of *Car Magazine* in the other. The lines in his good-natured, dog-like face had begun to take on a permanent nature lately, thought Nina. Concern lines—was that a word? Like worry wrinkles, only more altruistic.

"Yes," she said, attempting to convince the machine to deliver a cup of instant coffee with powdered milk. "Rina has eaten a banana, and we are working on a cheese sandwich."

"What was that about her father?"

"She hasn't really said anything else, and I don't want to press her. But apparently it's true. I asked one of the guys from the Mondeo gang. He actually blushed and admitted that they had discussed it while Rina was listening. They didn't think she spoke Danish. What did they imagine? She has damn well lived here for more than two years."

"She doesn't say much," said Magnus. "It's easy to read her incorrectly. Those guys are actually pretty nice."

"That's what you think about everyone," Nina said.

"No," he said with a crooked smile. "Only about the ones who deserve it." He swatted at her with the magazine, looking almost frisky—like an overgrown foal with giant, knobby knees and a stubby tail. Where did all this awkward enthusiasm come from?

Sex, of course. What exactly was it that happened to men when they got a bit of not particularly fantastic sex? Now that it appeared Rina's physical crisis was over, Magnus exuded well-being. Why didn't Nina feel that way at all? Why the hell couldn't it be like that for her—as easy as taking a hot bath and feeling recharged afterward?

The phone vibrated in the pocket of her jeans. She answered it with a small, apologetic grimace in Magnus's direction.

It was Søren Kirkegard, the PET-man who wasn't an idiot. She felt a tug in the pit of her stomach. Why on earth had she called him? He was PET, damn it, not a lifeline in a quiz show. And not at all a friend.

"I wanted to update you," he said. "And ask you a couple of questions, if you don't mind?"

She couldn't really say no. After all, she had called him. "Yes. Okay."

"Good. How long have you known Natasha?"

"Since she came to the camp for the first time. It must have been . . . oh, I don't remember exactly. October or November, two thousand and seven."

"And how would you describe your relationship?"

Nina had to think about that. "It mostly centered on Rina," she said, stirring the liquid in her white plastic mug with her white plastic stirrer. For some reason the water in the coffee machine never got as hot as it was supposed to, and the powdered milk had a tendency to just float on top in small, yellowish lumps. "She had asthma even back then and . . . certain psychological problems. Nightmares. Anxiety attacks. It's of course not that unusual among the children here, but . . . well, anyway, we did our best for her."

"I understand that you were the one Natasha called after her attempt to kill Vestergaard?"

"How do you know that?" The words flew out of Nina, hostile, distrustful, before she had time to consider. He didn't answer her directly, but he didn't need to. He probably already had a whole pile of reports lying on his table. Why had she called him?

Because you needed help, she told herself.

She glanced at the clock above the serving hatch. Morten and the children were presumably eating dinner now. It wouldn't be pizza or some other kind of junk food—Morten was good at all that healthy stuff, always making sure they got enough vegetables and slow carbohydrates. She closed her eyes a moment so she couldn't see the clock's digits. She knew that her time-checking was more than a bad habit. "OCD Lite," so to speak. Not quite on par with the poor people who scrubbed their hands bloody for fear of germs, but . . . she had to get it under control.

She saw the minute hand move down to 18:21. Tomorrow it was Fastelavn Sunday. Not content with merely importing American Halloween customs, Denmark still stuck stubbornly to her own homegrown equivalent as well, so now there were twice as many costumes to be produced by long-suffering parents. Except this year, Nina wasn't long-suffering, she reminded herself; Morten would have seen to Anton's outfit for the school carnival. But she would still get to see Anton, and maybe even Ida too, if it wasn't beneath the dignity of a fourteen-year-old to participate.

"I'm just trying to get a clear picture," said Søren the PET-man on the phone. "You called emergency services, but you also went out there yourself?"

"Yes. I wasn't sure . . . sometimes people get flashbacks. Or hallucinations. Natasha was pretty incoherent on the phone; I didn't know how serious the situation was."

"So you were, in fact, present just after the EMS got there?"

"Yes."

It came rushing back: the heat that felt more like August than September, the dark hedges, the house with the front door wide open and all the lights on. The police hadn't come yet—just the ambulance. It was parked in the driveway, its back doors open. The EMS people were already rolling in the gurney, and she could hear the bastard shouting hoarsely.

"She stabbed me! She goddamned stabbed me!"

Natasha just sat in the middle of the lawn with her skinny bare legs pulled up toward her chest, gazing up at the moon as if the activity around her had nothing to do with her. She barely looked at Nina, even when Nina touched her shoulder and asked if she was okay.

"Take care of her," was all she said, and she didn't need to explain who she meant. "You take care of her."

"Where is she?"

"Neighbor. Neighbor Anna. Nice lady. She is safe there."

That was part of what had later been used against her at the trial—that she had carefully arranged for Rina not to be in the house that night. A premeditated, well-planned act, the prosecutor had said.

"Did you get any sense that there might have been other people present at the house? Besides Natasha and Michael Vestergaard?"

Nina had never been asked that question during the entire unbearably long police and court procedure afterward. "No. I'm pretty sure they were alone."

"And Michael Vestergaard hadn't suffered any injuries other than the cut in his throat?"

"No. What kind of injuries do you mean?"

"To his hands, for example."

"No. Why?"

"Sometimes people get defensive cuts," Søren said. "If they have time to try to fight off their assailant."

"I think it came as a complete surprise to him that she could turn on him like that," Nina said, with a sense that he knew very well there were no defensive cuts. That must be in the report, along with everything else. What was he getting at?

"But you knew Natasha well enough that you were the one she called," he said. "Why do you think she did that?"

"Because of Rina. She wanted me to take care of Rina."

"Did Natasha ever say anything about why she had fled from Ukraine?"

"No, we almost never talked about her past. She clammed up if you tried."

"I see."

"That's not very unusual," said Nina defensively. "I think that's true for at least seventy-five percent of the people here."

Her gaze wandered automatically around the half-empty passage in which she stood. Sometime back in the '90s, most of one wall in the barrack's passageways had been replaced with huge windows in a well-intentioned effort to transform the dim, nicotine-stinking smoking zone into lounge areas with green plants, lights, a view and a certain modernity. That just meant that many of the camp's inhabitants stopped using the rooms completely or huddled in the darkest corners where there was most cover. This was especially true of the people who had lived with the constant threat of snipers, in Kosova and elsewhere. The windows were still there, of course. They had been expensive.

"I'm aware of that," said the PET-man. "But did you get any sense of it?"

"Only that she was afraid. That she would do almost anything not to be sent back. I didn't even know that Rina's father was dead."

"No, I can imagine she didn't talk a lot about that."

"Did she really do it?" asked Nina. "And why? Was he a sick bastard like Vestergaard?"

"There's nothing to suggest that," said Søren. "I'll call again when

I know more. Take good care of the girl. There must still be police on the premises?"

"And how," said Nina.

"Good. We'll talk soon."

Nina stood for a few seconds with the silent cell phone in one hand and the coffee stirrer in the other. An update, he had called it. But the only one who had been updated was him. She had answered his questions without learning anything in return. Nonetheless, she felt a peculiar relief again, as she had when he had said he would "see what he could do." She threw the stirrer in the garbage next to the coffee machine, nodded briefly at Magnus and set off down the hall toward Rina's room.

She checked her watch. 18:27.

That must be it. For almost seven minutes, she had had the sensation of not being alone.

"THE NEIGHBOR WHO found him," said Søren. "Do you mind if I have a chat with her? She apparently knows Natasha Doroshenko pretty well."

Heide deliberated. "If you bring Veng with you," she said. "And a tape recorder. We've questioned her once, but of course we need to speak with her again. It's the yellow farmhouse, just on the other side of the hill."

Someone had cleared the road with a tractor, as evidenced by the broad, ribbed tire tracks. When you lived out here, you probably couldn't sit around and wait for the municipal snowplow to stop by. Babko slid into the passenger seat in the front and Veng into the backseat, and the Hyundai bravely struggled up the hill and down to "the yellow farmhouse."

It had probably once been quite a sizable farm, thought Søren. Four wings and various outbuildings washed in a traditional yellow ocher with shiny black wooden trim. The main house and one side wing had newly thatched roofs, golden and unweathered; the two remaining wings still needed a loving hand. Red tarp covered the most serious holes, and one gable looked as if it was mostly supported by chicken wire and rusty iron struts. A dog barked loudly from inside the house, and Søren saw one of the shades move.

Veng rang the doorbell. "It's us, Mrs. Olesen," he said. "DI Veng, remember me? And this is Inspector Kirkegard and a Ukrainian colleague, Police Lieutenant Babko."

The woman in the door considered them with a face devoid of expression. The dog, a classic Danish hunting breed, tried to work its way out of her grip on its collar, but apparently she was holding on tight. Her eyes moved from one to the other, a bit on her guard, thought Søren, but then, they did outnumber her—an invasive force.

"Come in," she said after a few seconds. "Is it okay if we sit in the kitchen? It's warmest there."

"Of course," said Søren.

"I just have to . . . Maxi, go to your basket!" She shooed the dog into the utility room, where it reluctantly lay down in a basket by the boiler. "It's this way."

Given the rural surroundings, Søren had unconsciously expected a kitchen like his parents' in Djursland—vinyl squares on the floor, scratched white-laminated cabinets from the mid-90s, mail-order pine furniture that had never quite been in fashion even when it was brand new. But this was, after all, Hørsholm, home of golf enthusiasts and would-be country squires.

The room was large and well lit—clearly several old rooms combined—with double glass doors leading out into the snow-covered garden, new floors of broad, rustic oak planks, white walls and a high-end, designer kitchen. A comfortable heat radiated from a massive brick wall oven that divided the kitchen area from the dining room.

"Ahhh," sighed DI Veng spontaneously and unbuttoned his down jacket. "Nice to come inside and thaw a bit."

Babko smiled as well. "We have this kind of oven in Ukraine," he said. "Out in the country. That's the only thing that works when it's really cold."

Anna Olesen looked at Babko. Her gaze remained cautious. "What is he saying?" she asked.

"That it's a good oven," Søren translated. "They have them in Ukraine too."

"This one is Finnish," she said. "The old oil-burning boiler is on its last legs, so it's not just for decoration."

Heide had said Anna was over eighty, but she moved like a much younger woman. Her hair had to be dyed, but it was done so skillfully, in a variety of golden-blonde shades, that the result looked completely natural. A pair of red reading glasses sat in her hair as if they were an intentional part of her styling, and the comfortable-looking oatmeal-colored mohair sweater hung loosely over a pair of neat grey wool pants. Søren also noted the high-heeled black shoes, the pink lipstick and the discreetly penciled eyebrows. In no way did she look like a shaken elderly citizen who had just found the body of her neighbor.

"I know you've already spoken with the police," said Søren. "But unfortunately, we'll probably need to inconvenience you several times."

"Yes," she said. "I understand that."

"Do you live here alone?"

"Since my husband died four years ago. The plan is for my daughter Kirsten and her family to move into one of the wings when we finish restoring it."

"But you were alone last night?"

She shook her head. "I wasn't here last night. I was having dinner at the house of some friends of mine and didn't get home until after midnight."

Søren didn't ask about the dinner—Heide's people would definitely check on that if they hadn't already. "Did you go past Michael Vestergaard's house on that occasion?" he asked instead.

"No. I came the other way, from Kokkedal."

"Did you meet anyone on the way?"

"No. As I told you, it was midnight, more or less. And this isn't exactly downtown during rush hour. But someone had been here. I could see car tracks in the new snow."

Søren looked quickly at Veng, but the detective inspector shook his head. "It had been cleared again before we got here," he said.

"Henrik does that," said Anna Olesen. "Henrik Rasmussen. He also takes care of the golf course. Groundskeeper. Or whatever it is they call it in golf-speak." A glint of humor lightened the guarded blue gaze.

"When was the last time you saw Michael Vestergaard?"

"Saw? I've seen his car a few times over the last couple days, but we didn't say hello."

"Was that unusual?"

"No. We used to be a bit more in touch, actually. He could be quite helpful on occasion."

"Did you see Natasha Doroshenko often when she was living in the house?"

Anna picked at a thread on her mohair sweater. "We met now and again. Her little girl liked to help feed the cats. We talked about her getting a kitten, but . . . Well, that never happened."

"What was your impression of her?"

"My impression? She was a nice young girl. Much too young for him, of course, but in her situation, security is probably not an insignificant attraction. I thought they were fine together until . . . well." She interrupted herself in the same way as before. "I had no idea things were that bad."

"I understand that you were out walking the dog when you found Vestergaard?"

The pink lips tightened. "It was more like the dog walking me. I had let her out when I got up, but she didn't come back in. That happens sometimes. She doesn't stray, not really, but she might take a little excursion if I haven't walked her enough. When my husband was alive, she would never have considered setting as much as a paw outside the garden without him. He used to take her hunting and had her trained to perfection, but now . . . Anyway, when she had been gone for an hour, I realized I would have to put on my rubber boots and go search. And then, of course, I heard her."

"She was barking?"

"Yes. She was sitting next to the car—that is, Michael's car—and barking as if he were a fox in a hole. And then I could see . . . Well. I called the police right away."

"And stayed there, I understand?"

"Isn't that what you're supposed to do?"

"Did you notice any traffic during that time?"

"No. It was Saturday morning, so the few commuters we do have weren't going anywhere."

There was a very faint lilt to her voice that somehow wasn't pure Hørsholm. It could be the remains of a regional dialect she had shed, from Fyn or Bornholm, maybe. He couldn't decide.

"Were you born here on the farm?" he asked.

Again the guarded glance. "No," she said. "It was Hans Henrik's childhood home. We didn't move here until nineteen eighty-two, when his mother and father really couldn't manage it anymore. Before that we lived in Lund for years."

"In Sweden."

"Yes. I taught at the university. Classic philology."

Not your typical housewife, in other words—and more than averagely intelligent, thought Søren. Something about her aroused his curiosity, and he felt a sudden urge to rummage through her belongings, though what, exactly, he would be looking for, he didn't know. He had no legal grounds for such a search. If anyone was to do so, it would have to be Heide, he thought, with a grudging pang of envy.

UKRAINE, 1934

"NO, NO."

The protest was so faint, it could barely be called a protest. More like a kind of moan. Nonetheless, the young, beautiful GPU police officer immediately hit Marchenko across the mouth so the blood began to seep from his lips and gums. Marchenko bent forward and let it drip on the newly fallen snow. For some reason that was where Olga's eyes focused.

The red color against the blindingly white virgin snow was so vivid that it seemed almost supernatural in the midst of the grubby chaos. Behind Marchenko, most of his family's former belongings were bundled together in a tall, ungainly load on what had previously been his cart. There were a butter churn and pickling troughs and blankets and clothing and sacks. At the back of the cart sat a few sheaves of straw and the bucket from the farm's well. All of it had been tied to the cart by a couple of men from the kolkhoz. The three horses hitched to it stomped their hooves impatiently in the frozen wheel tracks and whinnied so the steam enveloped their muzzles.

Olga stood so close, she would have been able to stroke one of the horses' flanks if she stuck out her hand. But she didn't. The horse didn't look nice, she thought. The lower lip hung down so you could see the long yellow teeth, and its coat was bristly, mud caking its flank. She was closer than she wanted to be and also close to the scarlet blood spot in the snow in front of the cart.

Olga didn't quite know why she kept standing there instead of going home. Marchenko was the idiot Fedir's father and a kulak, and everyone knew that he had been behind with his grain deliveries for a long time. He had said that he didn't have any, and the village soviet had until now chosen to ignore his negligence. But today Jana had reported at school that the GPU had ransacked the Marchenkos' property and found grain as well as potatoes stowed away in a dugout under the house's foundation. It was the fault of him and the likes of him that everyone was starving, Olga knew that well, but somehow none of them looked quite like the fat kulaks on the poster outside the village soviet's office—especially not Fedir's little sister, who hung on her mother's arm. Her face was narrow and her eyes large. She wasn't much older than Kolja, and every so often she opened her mouth and cried out, a long, thin scream like a hare in the claws of an eagle. The family had been sitting outside in the cold all day, waiting for their judgment, and the child was blue with cold and exhaustion.

The cries made Olga feel sick deep down in her stomach, but still she couldn't tear herself away.

"There are at least one hundred twenty funt," said Oxana, pointing at the six sacks of grain that were just then being carried out and placed on a separate cart. "Just think how many mouths that can feed."

Olga nodded. She couldn't remember ever seeing so much grain at once—and not just any grain, but wheat, supposedly. She had heard that from the talk among the gathered villagers. Most of them had come to say goodbye. Marchenko's brother was there, and several of his neighbors, noted Olga. The men were smoking and talking quietly while the women had pulled their shawls close around their shoulders and were glancing nervously at the four armed GPU officers.

A GPU officer shouted something, and now the driver from the collective climbed, huffing, onto the load. He swung the whip over the sharp backs of the horses. The animals leaned forward heavily in their harnesses, but for a long moment seemed stuck in place until the wheels finally scrunched along in the slippery tracks and the cart began to move.

For a moment Marchenko looked as if he was planning to follow it, but he remained standing next to the four bundles that the family had been allowed to keep. What he had now was an idiotic son, a wife and a small daughter, thought Olga. Because Fedir was definitely an idiot. Even though he was fourteen, he stood sobbing as loudly as his little sister, and it was almost unbearable to keep watching. And yet she couldn't stop.

One of the remaining GPUs apparently felt the same way, because now he poked Fedir in the side with his rifle and told him to start walking.

"Where to?" Fedir stared at him with his wild, cross-eyed gaze, and the GPUs laughed almost kindly.

"To the station in Sorokivka. You're going on a trip, comrade."

Fedir smiled back in confusion, hoisted two of the family's bundles on his back and, neck bent, began to make his way through the crowd of gathered neighbors. One woman tried to sneak him a piece of bread, but he saw it too late and dropped it awkwardly on the road. When he straightened up, he saw Olga and Oxana and froze in his tracks.

"Oxana," he said. A special light slid across his face. "I'll come visit you when I get back."

Oxana lowered her eyes and nodded briefly, and just then Olga noticed the silence around them. As if all sound had been sucked out of the world. For the longest time, people stood mutely, staring at Fedir and Oxana. Then Oxana pulled her scarf closer around her face, turned her back on Fedir and began to walk away. Olga hesitated.

The young, smiling GPU officer poked Fedir again and drove him in the opposite direction down the main street of the village along with the rest of the family. Marchenko was silent now and walked with heavy, stooped shoulders while behind him, his wife struggled to keep the child in her arms. Only Fedir turned back one more time and raised his arm in a farewell that was impatiently swatted down by the boyish GPU officer.

Oxana marched with quick steps toward the stream, and Olga began to run to catch up with her. At the same moment, she felt a sharp stab of pain in her shoulder blade. Something hard and pointy had hit her, but when she looked over her shoulder, she couldn't see anything but the frozen ground and the fine dusting of new snow behind her. She increased her speed but stumbled and fell in the stupid bark shoes on the stupid cloddy ground. "Oxana, wait."

Oxana turned. She backtracked two steps and offered her hand to Olga, who got to her feet, swaying, just as she was hit by an even harder smack. This time it was on her forehead, and she felt a warm trickle of blood run down over her cheekbone. She didn't understand at all, but apparently Oxana did. Oxana raised a fist toward the Marchenkos' house just as another stone whistled toward them.

Oxana's eyes threw off sparks. "Act like it's nothing," she said breathlessly, pulling Olga along toward the stream. 'It's just Sergej, that idiot."

Olga tried to walk as fast as Oxana but stumbled and fell again. She couldn't help looking back.

No more stones came.

THE INCIDENT VAN was still pretty empty, noted Søren. Some of Heide's people were searching the house in Tundra Lane. Others were going door to door in the adjacent housing estates in the hopes that someone had noticed a car or anything else of relevance. Michael Vestergaard had not been considerate enough to get himself murdered in a public place with frequent traffic and CCT cameras. On a pitch-black, ice-cold winter night out here in the no-man's-land between the golf course and the so-called urban development, they would be lucky to find even one pathetic jogger.

Veng poured coffee on automatic pilot, but before Søren had a chance to drink it, his cell phone rang. It was Susse.

"Are you busy?" she asked. Her voice was so stressed that it sounded like a stranger's.

"What's wrong?"

There was silence for a short moment. Then she began to cry. In the background he could hear unfamiliar sounds of steps in long corridors, mumbled voices, metallic clicks and a sort of hydraulic hissing.

"Susse . . . What's wrong?"

"Ben," she managed to say between muffled sobs. "Sorry. There's no reason to cry now. It's just . . . he felt ill. We're at Herlev Hospital. They say it's a little blood clot in the heart."

"Do you want me to come?"

"No, no. It's okay now. But . . . if you have time. The dogs."

"Of course I have time."

"Thea is on a ski trip with some kids from her class. And the neighbors are on Fuerteventura. They'll be home tomorrow, and Barbara is on her way home too, but she's stuck in the snow somewhere outside Fredericia. So . . . so you're the only one here who has a key."

Barbara, Susse's oldest, was at the School of Design in Kolding. A long trip when the snow made train travel irregular.

"Susse. Stop. Of course I have time. Are you okay?"

"I was okay until I heard your voice. Then it all came crashing back again. Sorry. I was so afraid. He was in such pain, and I could see in his eyes that he thought that . . . Damn it, Søren. He's fifty-three. He can't be turning into a heart patient."

Ben had lived the hard life of a touring musician and had smoked twenty cigarettes a day for most of his life, although now he had quit. In Søren's opinion, this placed him dead in the center of the target group for a heart attack, but there was no reason to say that out loud.

"I'll take care of the dogs," he said. "Call if there's anything else I can do. Any time."

"Thank you."

He stood for a moment, thinking. Babko's restless energy had worn off, and he was sitting in a slump.

I could get a patrol car to drive him back to headquarters, thought Søren. But on the other hand . . .

On the other hand, he was convinced that Babko could tell him more if he could just poke a hole in the Ukrainian's jovial but uninformative façade. Perhaps it would help to get away from the uniforms and the coffee-and-adrenaline atmosphere. "Do you feel like helping me feed my ex-wife's dogs?" he asked.

• • •

THERE WAS A string of belated Christmas lights along the white fence. There were birdseed balls on branches of the pear tree and dog tracks in the snow. Susse's two cocker spaniels were barking eagerly, and even through the door you could hear the soft slaps of wagging tails hitting walls and furniture.

Søren unlocked the front door, and the dogs came leaping. They needed to pee so badly that they barely took the time to say hello.

"You meant it," said Babko.

"Yes, of course. What did you think?"

Babko just shook his head. "Your ex-wife?"

"Yes. Her husband ended up in the hospital with a heart attack." Common-law husband, actually, but Babko probably didn't need those kinds of nuances. "Come on in. We might as well have a decent meal. You must be getting tired of cafeteria food."

He could see that Babko was . . . shocked was probably too strong a word, but thrown off-balance, at least. This was unexpected for him. He looked around at the white hallway, the rows of shoes and coats, a couple of Barbara's watercolors, the old school photos of Thea and her that hung on the wall facing the living room. Ben's African-American genes revealed themselves in the form of dark, bright eyes and a warm skin tone. They were attractive children.

"They aren't yours?" said Babko and pointed.

"No," said Søren. "But I'm the godfather of the youngest one."

Søren saw that the information was received and stored in the Babko computer, but what the Ukrainian thought about it, he couldn't tell. Suddenly he himself grew uncertain about whether this was a good idea. Handcuffs and beatings with filled plastic water bottles. Fingers crushed in car doors. If Babko was one of the nasty boys, it wasn't a good idea to show him a vulnerable point. Susse and her family might not be Søren's family in a conventional way, but they were definitely a vulnerable point.

Trust. To earn it, you have to give it.

The dogs came racing in with snow pillows under their paws and snow in their fur. Søren gave them what he thought was a reasonable amount of dry food in the ceramic bowls in the kitchen. Then he opened the refrigerator. There was a pot with some kind of chicken stew, smelling of curry and onions—and a couple of good Belgian beers.

Might that not be enough to build a relationship of mutual trust?

BABKO PUSHED HIS empty plate away, stretched and yawned deeply and sincerely.

"Sorry," he said. "I didn't really get any sleep last night."

"Didn't they offer you a bed?"

"Yes, but . . . I hoped Colonel Savchuk would return."

It was the first time Babko had voluntarily mentioned the SBU colonel—a breakthrough for bicultural understanding? Søren decided to consider it a step forward.

"Why is it that both SBU and GUBOZ are so interested in the Doroshenko family?" he asked and took a modest sip of his beer.

Babko looked around the kitchen. Susse and Ben had combined the old kitchen with the dining room, so they sat at a large flea-market find of a table, surrounded by plants, IKEA shelves with books, records and CDs behind shiny glass doors and with a view of the bird feeder in the garden through a blue terrace door.

"It's nice here, " he said.

Søren didn't answer. He let the question stand.

Babko smiled crookedly. "You're a patient man," he said.

Søren continued to wait. Babko took a swallow of the Belgian beer. He sighed, an unusually deep sigh that would have seemed overly dramatic coming from a Dane. But it wasn't. The sigh came from the same place as the laugh—from the bottom of his chest and possibly also from the bottom of Babko's Ukrainian soul.

"Once," he said, "I must have been eight or nine years old, it was a few years before the Independence . . . once we were going on a school trip, and the bus that came to pick us up was so dirty, you could barely look out the windows. My teacher asked the driver if he could at least wash the windshield so he could see safely. The driver just pointed to a certificate that indicated that the bus had been washed that morning, less than an hour ago. It clearly hadn't been, but it didn't matter; the certificate, with signature and stamp and everything, said it was clean, and so it was clean. My friend, do you understand what I am saying?"

"I'm not sure." Søren was having a lot of trouble seeing the connection to Natasha Doroshenko, but he was willing to listen.

"The truth. The truth is what it says on the certificate. It's completely beside the point if the window is covered in dirt and crap, as long as you have the paper saying it's clean. That's the way it was in Ukraine. That's the way it still is, except that the people writing the certificates are replaced once in a while. And when you meet a man who actually looks at the window and not at the certificate, at the truth and not at the most convenient version of it—a man who wants to change Ukraine if he can—then you don't believe it at first. You look for the hidden motives. You look at the money and wonder where it comes from. You wonder how he has gotten so far if he is really so clean."

Søren sat completely still. He didn't fidget with his utensils; he didn't touch his beer. He didn't want to risk interrupting Babko's monologue. For the first time, he felt he was getting some insight into what went on behind the jovial mask.

"During the Orange Revolution, we thought there would be a new day," Babko continued with a sudden hand gesture as if he were cutting something away. "We thought that corruption and the misuse of power would disappear or at least shrink, but nothing happened.

There was just a new group of people writing the certificates. So you don't believe it. For a long, long time you don't believe it."

Søren waited, but this time it seemed as if Babko had come to a halt again. "But then you become convinced?" Søren attempted to prompt him, not too lightly, not too hard, just the right amount of pressure.

"Little by little," said Babko. "Little by little. When you have kept this man, this very clean man, under observation for more than two years on the orders of his opponents. After two years, you are convinced and deeply depressed."

"Why?"

"Because he doesn't stand a chance. We've been ordered to find something on him. We don't find anything. Suddenly there is nonetheless a file of well-documented accusations, of corruption, witness statements, confessions and an arrest order. Fabricated from beginning to end, but it doesn't matter. There are stamps and signatures and certificates, pages and pages of them."

"Is he arrested?"

"Not right away. The folder . . . is lost. But a new one quickly appears. And then he is arrested. Detained. And in Ukraine, that is . . . no fun."

"No. I know." Plastic bottles and handcuffs. But Babko wasn't one of the torturers. Søren believed that now. He was a person who longed for decency and integrity, the way a man longs for a woman he can't have.

"I thought, he's done for. That was that. They got him. But that's not how it goes. Suddenly he is released again. The prosecutor has to apologize and say that the evidence was flawed."

"It was."

"Yes, but that doesn't usually mean anything. It didn't mean anything this time either. That's not why. Someone made the accusation go away, as it so often happens, even in the cases where you've seen the proof yourself before it disappeared."

"So your clean man isn't so clean, after all?"

"That's the odd thing. I think he is. Why else would he want to investigate who made the accusations disappear?"

"And that's what he did?"

"Yes. Most people would have thanked their lucky stars for the unexpected justice and let it go at that. Not him. He discovered that I was the one who had made the original file disappear."

"Did you get an appropriate thank-you?" Søren couldn't quite keep the irony out of his voice.

Babko laughed—a somewhat quieter version of the volcano laughter that could make people turn around to look at him. "That depends on what you mean by 'appropriate.' He grilled me several times to find out if I knew anything about the prosecutor's sudden change of heart. That's gratitude for you . . ." But the thought seemed to cheer him up. Cheer him up immensely, in fact.

Søren thought about his own boss. A career man, true, fixated on competition, but basically decent. He backed up his people, he followed most of the written and unwritten rules, and it was absurd to imagine that he would consciously hang someone on trumped-up evidence. That was not how he played the game.

Babko came from a country where that pretty much *was* the game. Søren tried to imagine what it would be like never to know if you'd been bought or sold, who was the buyer and who was the seller, and what version of the "evidence" you were using any given week. Of course the Danish system had its flaws. There were omissions, excuses and lies; there were favors and nepotism, of course there were. It happened from time to time that loyalty to the team degenerated into cover-ups—yes, it happened, but it was the exception, not the rule. It was a rare Dane who believed he could avoid a ticket by adding a bill when he handed his driver's license to the officer. Søren didn't feel amazed gratitude for having a boss who had reached his position with his personal integrity more or less intact. He took it as a given.

Babko did not have that luxury.

"Who is he, then—your clean man?"

"Filipenko. Nikolaij Filipenko. Have you heard of him?"

Søren thought. "I don't think so," he had to admit.

"He was an amazing soccer player, had twenty-one games for the national team before he was injured. That's why almost everyone in Ukraine knows him. That's probably also why he was elected to Verkhovna Rada the first time, because people knew and liked him. Otherwise it can be expensive to run an election campaign in Ukraine. And though he has money, he doesn't have *that* much money."

"So he's a member of Parliament?" The way Babko had discussed Filipenko, Søren had gotten the impression that he was a superior within the police.

"Yes. For Ukrainska Justytsiya, a small centrist party. They probably didn't believe their own luck when he wanted to run on their platform; otherwise they would never have gotten a foot in the door. He's on the parliamentary committee for the Eradication of Organized Crime and Corruption. Many hope he'll be our next minister of the interior. And Colonel Savchuk is his brother."

At last. The connection.

"So you're saying that the man we have . . ." Søren was about to say "lost," but the colonel wasn't a missing wallet, after all. ". . . lost contact with . . . that he may be the brother of the future Ukrainian minister of the interior?"

"Half-brother. And not many people know. They didn't grow up together. Savchuk is twenty-six years older. An entirely different generation."

"Same father or same mother?"

"Mother. Tetjana Filipenko. She owns U-card." Babko must have seen that it didn't mean anything to Søren and explained briefly, "It's a Ukrainian credit card. Like Visa or American Express."

"It sounds as if she's fairly wealthy."

"Extremely. U-card let the average Ukrainian acquire all the consumer goods we felt we had to have after the old regime fell. *Who do you call when you need a bit of cash? U-card, U-card, U-card . . .*" The last was offered in a mellifluous falsetto that made both dogs lift their heads.

"So there's nothing odd about her son being able to afford to run a Ukrainian electoral campaign?"

"U-card has supported the campaign with exactly 30,000 hryvnia. No more, no less. They've made a big deal out of that, and it's true. I've spent over two years checking. Nikolaij Filipenko is not a man who built his career on his mother's money."

"He sounds . . . remarkable."

"He is."

"And you still haven't answered my question. Why are you here? You and Savchuk? Why the two of you specifically?"

Babko closed his eyes for a brief moment, as if there were something written on the inside of his eyelids that he needed to read. "My friend," he then said, "be happy that you drive a small car."

"Why?" Søren recalled Babko's volcanic eruption of laughter at the sight of it.

"Because if you drove a big one, I'd never tell you this."

Søren forced himself to be patient. "What?" he asked.

"No one in GUBOZ or the regular criminal police knew that Natasha Doroshenko was in prison in Denmark until Savchuk appeared and requested an extradition order. Maybe SBU knew. Maybe it was something Savchuk had found out on his own."

"Okay."

"I was added on at the last minute."

"Why? Why you?"

"Because someone has asked me to start an investigation of Savchuk's circumstances."

"You're his guard dog."

"Yes."

"And what do you expect to find?"

"My friend, I have no idea. I have a suspicion that it was Colonel Savchuk who made the accusation against Nikolaij Filipenko go away back then. But to disprove false evidence is not a crime—at the worst, it is a declaration of war against those who have fabricated it."

"And you still don't know why he's interested in Natasha and Pavel Doroshenko?"

"No. I've poked around in the case a bit, as much as I had time for. The permission to interview Natasha came through unusually quickly."

Søren couldn't decode the questioning tone in the last statement. "What do you mean?" he asked.

Babko shrugged. "Perhaps the Danes are just efficient at that kind of thing. What do I know? But in Ukraine, if you need to speed up the paperwork . . ." He let the sentence dangle there unfinished.

"Did you think that Savchuk had bribed someone?"

A shrug. "As I said, my friend, it's good that you drive a small car. Honest cop car."

Søren finally understood Babko's appreciation for his practical little Hyundai. Ukrainian police with well-paying clients in the corruption shop apparently didn't drive Korean dwarf cars.

"What kind of car does Savchuk have?" he asked.

Babko laughed. "A huge BMW. But maybe his mother gave it to him." He rolled his shoulders a little. "In fact, he's got it with him."

"I thought you flew."

"*I* flew. He was already here. He was kind enough to pick me up at the airport, but that might have been because I had the extradition order."

"You don't by any chance have the registration number?"

A quieter version of the volcano laughter. "My friend, I just happen to." Babko pulled a small notebook out of his pocket and wrote it down. He knew it by heart, Søren noted. Then Babko tore out the page and handed it across the table. Søren received it with the appropriate gratitude.

Darkness had long since fallen outside among the pear trees. Babko yawned again, and even in the soft light from the Tiffany lamp his face looked worn.

"Do you want me to drive you to a hotel?" asked Søren. "Or do you want to go back to headquarters?"

"Headquarters." Babko yawned again. "There's nothing wrong with the bed there. And if Savchuk checks in, it's best if I'm there."

"You don't like it—that he doesn't check in."

"No. It's not good. For him or for me."

Without a doubt that was why the little piece of paper with the registration number had been handed over.

"Can you give me what you have on the Doroshenko case?" asked Søren to see if the cooperation stretched even further.

"You have the case folder."

"Yes. I mean *everything* you have."

The quieter version of the laughter. "Okay, honest cop. But I need it back." Babko pulled a USB drive out of the inner pocket of his suede jacket and handed it to Søren.

AFTER GIVING THE dogs a final airing in the garden, they drove back to headquarters. Babko disappeared in the direction of the apparently entirely satisfactory bed in the basement, while Søren headed toward the Communication Center under the roof of what had once been the women's prison. The noise was muted but ongoing. Only one of the operators looked up when Søren entered, and her gaze immediately slid back to the screen in front of her.

At the back of the high-ceilinged room sat a nearly bald man with round, well-padded shoulders that filled his light blue uniform shirt to the bursting point. Søren raised a hand. "Hello, Carlo," he said.

Duty officer Peter Carlsen smiled broadly and stuck two fingers in the air, continuing to speak on the telephone without missing a beat. When he was done, he got up and patted Søren on the shoulder with a smack that could be heard even through the stream of reports.

"Sonny boy. What the hell are you doing here?"

"Playing interpreter, for the most part. You've got a Ukrainian in the house."

"Oh, him. Is he of interest to the PET?"

"We're just helping each other out," said Søren vaguely.

Back at the police academy, the girls had given Carlsen the nickname Don Carlo because of a certain relaxed Latin lover charm. The name had stuck long after the pitch-black hair had disappeared and a middle-aged spread had asserted itself.

"What can I do for you?"

"The Ukrainian has a colleague, a Colonel Savchuk, who is . . . well, somewhat Absent Without Leave. He drove off Friday afternoon and hasn't been in contact with anyone since. We'd like to find him, of course." Søren handed Carlo the paper with the registration number. "So if anyone sees this . . . it's a BMW with Ukrainian plates."

"Okay. Is it the PET or headquarters who wants to know?"

"Both. And I'd very much like a personal tip-off right away."

"That'll cost you a beer." Carlo gave him an exaggerated conspiratorial wink.

"You *are* aware that you look like a fawning headwaiter when you do that, right?"

"Deal or no deal?"

"Deal."

"Good. And really . . . don't be such a stranger, huh?"

Søren agreed and headed home to Hvidovre to dig into Babko's files. It wasn't the same as having live witnesses to work with, but right now it was his best chance to get to know Pavel Doroshenko.

IT WAS STRANGE the way a change in your perspective could change a place.

The Coal-House Camp had been Natasha's home for many months, but from the edge of the woods, it looked foreign to her again. She was staring narrow-eyed down at the children's barrack from the little hiding place she had arranged under some low-hanging pine branches. It was dark now and had been for a long time. The evening had drifted into night while she'd sat hunched in her hiding place, but she felt no tiredness—just a background throb in her fingers and toes.

The camp's low barracks seemed stooped against the cold. The snow veiled the walkways, lawns and benches and made Natasha think of the cotton-ball snow landscape Katerina and she had been allowed to construct together in the prison's creative workshop last year. Katerina had arranged a cave for elves under a substantial piece of bark and placed other elves made of pipe cleaners outside the cave and on the little mirror that was supposed to look like a snow-covered pond.

"Should we add a troll too?" she had asked and had hesitantly run a hand through the box filled with wooden beads and pinecones.

"There are no trolls in elf-land," said Natasha.

"And not in real life either?"

Katerina's tone was different, and Natasha's trained ears instantly picked up a change in the rhythm of her breathing.

"Definitely not in real life," Natasha had said, as solidly and calmly as possible.

"But the camp isn't elf land." Natasha could hear Anna as clearly as if she had been standing next to her in the glittering snow. "The camp is a trap. You are the fox, and Katerina is the juicy piece of meat in the trap."

"I know," whispered Natasha. "I'll be careful."

The sense that Anna was with her evaporated as soon as she spoke out loud. No one was looking out for her now. The dark was dark, the cold was cold, and she was alone.

A thin but feminine shape moved behind the third window from the left. She assumed it was Nina. It was good that there was a woman with Katerina, but at the same time, it made things more complicated. Natasha opened and closed her hand around the knife handle in her pocket and attempted to hold back the racing panic that made her heart beat much too hard and fast. She took a deep breath and exhaled slowly, closed her eyes for a moment and concentrated on the weight of her body pressing against the earth, the cold air, the tree trunk's gnarly contours when she leaned back a little.

They had to get away, she and Katerina. Evil had come to Denmark now, and it was no longer safe here. But as long as Nina was awake and sat in Katerina's room with the lights on, Natasha had to wait. Anything else would be too risky. She would be seen. Nina would raise the alarm and call the police.

She tried to think about something else. About the very first days in the camp when Denmark had still looked like a safe haven. In the little leaflet she was given, it said that Denmark was a democracy, and that there were more pigs than people living here, as if the two were somehow connected. On the way here, she had seen the great refrigerated trucks with pictures of grinning porkers on the side, and for some reason it made all the horrors fade a little then. As if nothing wicked could reach her here in this ridiculous little, flat Bacon Land, where even the pigs smiled on their way to the slaughterhouse. Back then the fence had seemed a protection against the dangers she had run from. Even the most ordinary things—for example, the sight of the plastic chairs that were stacked every evening on the tables in the cafeteria with their legs up—brought tears to her eyes because it all seemed so ordered and calm. Even the fact that everything was so worn and nothing was clean for very long, even that was somehow reassuring—they weren't in Kiev anymore, in the apartment's traitorous luxury; it was more like Kurakhovo and the smell of her childhood. Katerina's sheets were patterned with nice little Scandinavian trolls, and Natasha had an odd feeling of being at summer camp with a lot of friendly people who were not out to kill her.

Later the despair set in. The grey fear of rejection cast a pall over the contours of the camp. As inhabitants disappeared, she knew she risked the same thing—knew the only thing she had won with her flight was a delay. She saw the fence for what it really was: a barrier to control the people inside, not a protection against the rest of the world. The greatest danger of all was let in through the main gate in the form of the apparently good-natured policemen who came to collect those who were being sent home. Even the Moomintrolls on Katerina's comforter began to look cruel, with devilish, taunting, superior smiles.

Then she had met Michael. It wasn't the way it had been with Pavel, not a dizzy falling in love, more a form of physical gratitude. Mixed with her desire for him and inseparable from it was the desire for permanent safety. She had loved him because he was a way out. So she had believed back then, and that belief made the camp fade away even while Katerina and she were still living there. It had become insignificant, a temporary refuge, no more. The sheets were weighted with neither hope or despair; they were just sheets.

The light went out in the third window from the left. A kind of electric shock raced through Natasha's body, as if the switch in Katerina's room were directly connected with her own nervous system. Now! Nina had either left the room or gone to sleep. Natasha believed she could overpower the nurse if necessary. Physically she was stronger than ever. It was easy if you had enough time. You stepped onto the edge of your bed and down again—first on your left leg, then on your right—a thousand times in the course of a day, every day. Then you lay down on the cell floor with your arms behind your neck and pulled your head up to your knees just as many times. Then came the push-ups. When she lay in her bed at night, she could feel her stomach muscles under the skin like steely ropes between her pubic bone and her lower ribs. The Barbie doll was no longer soft and smooth and obedient.

How long would it take the nurse to fall fast asleep? Natasha checked her watch. Ten minutes had passed since the light had gone out in Katerina's room, but a faint light still seeped out through the curtains in the room next door. It could be a night-light to calm a child who was afraid of the dark, but Natasha didn't believe it. That's where they were, the policemen.

She closed her hand around the knife in her jacket pocket again. Her fingers felt stiff and strange, as if they were no longer a part of her. But she could move them, and that was enough. Natasha measured the distance with her eyes. First five meters to the fence, and then about seventy meters across the snow-covered lawn. She had found pliers in the car's trunk, and she hoped they would be sufficient to cut a hole in the heavy mesh. Otherwise she'd have to climb across, but that would make it harder when she brought Katerina back with her.

Katerina. Now only minutes separated them, minutes and seventy-five meters. Natasha got up.

Then she heard it. The sound of a motor someplace in the forest behind her where there weren't supposed to be any cars. First a faint growl, then a shift to a lower gear and finally silence. There was no light to be seen through the trees. Only darkness and snow-laden branches. Natasha rubbed her nose with a numb red hand. Waited and listened. Then came the sound of car doors being opened and closed with careful, almost imperceptible clicks. A faint mumbling and the sound of heavy steps in the snow.

Silence again.

The desire to rush across the fence, shatter the window and drag Katerina with her out into the night was about to overpower her again. She was so close. Still, Natasha turned in the direction of the sound, got down on her knees and crept forward among the dark pines. Snow fell in cold showers from the branches onto her head and neck. Her unprotected hands hurt when they sank into the drifts, but she felt it only as a minor distraction. All her attention was focused on the sounds of the night, the whistling of the wind in the trees and the faint growl of trucks on the highway to Hillerød. How could the world make so much noise and at the same time be so still?

She crawled forward and through the next ruler-straight row of pines. The two narrow wheel tracks she herself had followed to the camp were only a few meters away now, and she could glimpse a faint light among the rippling black shadows of the trees.

A car was parked there, obscured by a storm of soft, whirling snowflakes. The headlights were off, but an interior light filled the car and created a faint orange-yellow aura against the black trees.

Natasha stopped in the shelter of a low, prickling pine and stuck her ice-cold hands inside her down jacket, confused. Someone had left the car and plowed a deep track among the trees to her right, but she couldn't see the person who had done it or hear anything but the freezing wind, which blew through the forest. She turned toward the car again.

The driver's seat was empty. But on the passenger seat sat a small, unmoving figure, staring straight ahead. The profile was sharply drawn, the nose aristocratically curved, and around the head was the silhouette of a huge, soft fur hat.

All at once the cold felt as if it came from inside as well as outside. It flowed from her chest through her abdomen and pooled in her arms and legs, making everything stiffen and hurt. Still she managed to move a little farther forward, close enough that she was afraid she would be seen if the woman in the car turned her head. Natasha knew the fear would kill her if it happened, but she had to be certain.

And then the woman did exactly that.

She turned her head slowly on a thin, wiry neck. Later Natasha remembered the movement as in slow motion: The huge gold earrings rocking slightly with the movement of the head, the bright red lips and the carefully powdered pale face. And finally the clear, pale blue eyes that stared into the dark without revealing any kind of emotion.

The Witch had found them again.

Natasha felt everything loosen in her body. She set off in the snow with a start like a hunted hare, stumbling through the trees without sensing the pine branches that whipped her in the face as she raced heedlessly back toward the camp and Katerina.

Seconds later a hollow bang sounded, and she knew she was too late.

DESPITE THE HOUR and the winter darkness, there was a pallid sheen on the walls of Rina's room.

It never got truly dark in the Coal-House Camp. There were lights along the walkways between the barracks, lamps above all the entrances and floodlights along the symbolic wire mesh fence that separated the camp's inhabitants from the rest of the world.

Nina gently stroked Rina's forehead, which was damp and cold with sweat. It was noticeably more quiet than usual in the barrack. Most of the children in the wing had a difficult relationship to men in uniforms and had for that reason been moved to empty rooms in the family wing while the watch over Rina continued. A faint scraping of chair legs and a low mumbling from the room next door was all that Nina could hear.

She found the book she had plucked from a shelf in one of the lounges earlier in the day—a paperback by some American author she had never heard of. She was forty pages into it but couldn't remember what it was about, and it occurred to her that if she was to read it now, she would have to turn on the ceiling light, which was equipped with an aggressive eco-bulb. She abandoned that particular project. Instead, she got up and stretched her legs, feeling the restless energy that always set in when she had nothing to do.

The room was small and claustrophobic, and the curtain-less

windows gave her an uncomfortable feeling of being watched. *Take good care of the girl*, PET-Søren had said, as if some other danger greater than Natasha lurked out there in the dark. It didn't exactly relieve her paranoia to see the personal attack alarm lying on the desk and staring at her with a glowing red eye in the gloom.

Nina took another look at Rina before she picked up her empty coffee mug and walked down to the coffee machine at the end of the hall. The machine hummed and sputtered and reluctantly sprayed the tepid coffee into the mug, and in the middle of a gurgling spray, she suddenly thought she heard something else. A low, flat bang, not a noise she recognized from the camp's usual nighttime soundtrack.

0:06. She stood for a few seconds with the plastic mug in her hand and listened while she gazed down the deserted grey corridor.

Silence. Then a soft bump and a faint scraping against the floor behind one of the doors. Silence again.

She realized that she had been dumb enough to leave the alarm in Rina's room. She swore softly, set the cup down and ran with silent steps toward the door to the room where the two policemen were sitting. She didn't waste time knocking. If anyone was in Rina's room, they needed to react instantly. Still, she was careful enough to let the door swing open without too much noise. A faint, sweet smell hit her.

The window was shattered. That was the first thing she saw. One officer was slumped across the table with his arms hanging heavily along his sides. She couldn't see his face but knew at once that he was either dead or unconscious. The same went for his colleague, who lay in a sprawling heap on the floor behind the table.

The shock propelled her back into the corridor, and she registered almost instantly that she was so dizzy, she had to support herself against the wall with one hand.

Gas. It was gas she could smell.

Without waiting to regain her balance, she tumbled the few meters to Rina's room. She didn't turn on the light but found the attack alarm on the table and pressed the button. Then she half-pulled, half-lifted Rina out of bed.

Rina hung dazedly in her arms but woke quickly enough that she could stumble along on her own two feet after Nina hauled her out into the corridor. They headed toward the coffee machine and the barrack's kitchen and dining hall. The dizziness was dissipating, but the walls were still trying to topple onto Nina, and the corridor stretched out ahead of her, elastic and unending, until she suddenly reached the door.

Behind them there was yet another hollow bang, and glass rained down over the linoleum floor. The big wall of windows in the lounge area had been shattered, and heavy feet stepped across the shards with a crunching sound. Nina jerked Rina along down the rows of tables and chairs and into the kitchen. She had seen the walk-in refrigerator clearly in her mind's eye even as she yanked Rina from her bed. It was the size of a broom closet, but it was airtight.

The heavy steel door was locked. Naturally. There were things that could be stolen in there, and this *was* a refugee center. Even the canned tomatoes were heavily guarded here. Nina fumbled with her passkey in the pallid light. The heavy lock clicked just as the door to the cafeteria was slammed open, and a broad, dark figure stepped into the dining hall behind them.

Nina pulled Rina into the narrow room with such force that the child whimpered as she hit the shelves of milk and cheese and juice. Nina had no time for consolations right now. She slammed the heavy steel door and heard the lock click once more.

She didn't know if he had had time to see them or to hear the slam and click from the lock. Her nausea closed in again; it was as if the gas's sweetish smell had coated her mouth and throat so that it was impossible to spit it out or cough it up. Next to her she could hear Rina's rapid, wheezing breaths in the dark. They stood so close together that they couldn't avoid touching. She put both arms around Rina's head, both to muffle the sound of that awful wheeze and also to remind Rina that she was still there.

Had he seen them? Did he know where they were? She strained her hearing to its utmost but couldn't hear anything but Rina. At least not until something hit the door to the walk-in with such force that the glasses on the shelf behind her clinked against one another.

She spontaneously tightened her grip on the girl's head, much too suddenly and tightly. But Rina didn't react. Said nothing, didn't gasp, didn't even alter the rhythm in her breathing. Not even when the second blow fell.

NATASHA DIDN'T EVEN make it to the fence. A broad, dark figure came running toward her, and the camp behind him was no longer a sleepy and deserted landscape—there were shouts, lights, people standing in the snow in various stages of undress, from overcoats to pajamas to vests and jockey shorts.

None of it mattered if he had killed Katerina.

The thought alone made her black and dead inside. She stood still because it was all she could do. Just breathing seemed a near-impossible task.

He ran past her, maybe forty of fifty meters away. Much, much too slowly she turned around, got her arms and legs to function, moved forward, a stumbling step and then another, until she was finally running, running as fast as she could, after the man who had perhaps murdered her daughter.

It was as if he could see in the dark. He didn't crash into the trees and branches as she did. And when an especially large branch hit her right in the throat, she collapsed and lay on her back gasping for a few seconds.

He stopped. Maybe he had heard her. He turned, and instead of a human face, she saw an insect-like creature with three protruding eyes that glinted faintly in the dark.

He can see me, she thought. Now he'll kill me. And if Katerina is dead, we'll meet in heaven. The thought did not offer any consolation.

From the camp there were more shouts and dogs barking, and just then a light blinked on right behind him. The Witch had opened the car door, and the interior light shone out onto the snow.

"Jurij?" she said. "Where is the child?"

"It didn't work," he said. "Some woman dragged her into a walk-in refrigerator."

"A walk-in . . ."

"Mm-hmm. I couldn't get the door open before the other guards showed up."

There was more barking. Natasha wasn't sure if it was from the handful of pets that lived in the camp or because the police had brought dog patrols. Possibly the man had similar doubts or else he hadn't spotted her, after all. At any rate, he quickly slid into the driver's seat and started the motor. The heavy car slid forward, headlights off, and within minutes the winter forest had swallowed car, man and evil Witch.

Natasha sat up. Katerina was alive. With those words everything existed again. An entire universe could be turned on or destroyed that quickly; that was how frail the world was.

THEY HAD BEEN living in Kiev for a few years when Natasha first discovered how easily everything could come apart. It began with a knocking on the door—loud, impatient raps, as if whoever was out there was irritated that the door hadn't opened at the first knock. Katerina was in her high chair eating pierogi, which Natasha had cut into bite-sized pieces for her. She dropped one of them on the floor in fright. "Whooo?" she asked.

"I don't know, sweetie. But now Mama will go look."

On the landing stood an older man in a suit, a brown case under his arm. He smelled of licorice and had a yellow-black licorice stain at one corner of his mouth.

"What is this?" he asked, waving a piece of paper in her face aggressively.

"I don't know," said Natasha, confused.

"The rent," he said. "You haven't paid the new rent."

"I don't know anything about that," she said. "My husband takes care of all that."

"Then you can tell your husband that he has to pay the same rent as everyone else in this house. It's been in effect since March. But he hasn't paid!"

"That must . . . be a mistake," she answered uncertainly. "I'll tell him when he gets home. He'll take care of it."

"I certainly hope so, little lady. If I have to come back, I won't be coming alone."

As soon as he had left, she called Pavel, but even though she tried for several hours, she didn't get hold of him. She felt as if the house had turned to glass. If anyone knocked on the door, it would all shatter and break. Natasha's magical castle, her beautiful rooms and all the beautiful things in them, the view of the National Museum, the trees outside, everything could disappear because of an old man who smelled of licorice.

Katerina sensed her anxiety and whimpered and fretted. Natasha attempted to calm them both.

Pavel will take care of it. Pavel will fix it, she told herself.

Finally Pavel did come home, exuberant and happy as usual. He kissed her on the mouth, deeply and hungrily, and lifted her up off the floor. This was when Natasha usually put her arms and legs around him, as if she were a child who needed to be carried. But not today.

"I tried to call," she said, and then the tears came rushing along with the rest of the story, even though she knew he hated crying. "A man came . . ."

"Stop. Dry your eyes, my love. You're scaring Katerina."

She sensed he was angry. She didn't know if it was at her, and she definitely didn't feel like making it worse, but she asked anyway.

"Pavel, is it true? Are we behind on the rent?"

"No," he said. "We pay exactly what we are supposed to."

"But why isn't it the same as what the others pay?"

"You don't need to worry about that, my love. I just need to make a call, then everything will be fine again."

And it was. Less than an hour later, there was another man at the door. He didn't smell of licorice but of expensive aftershave, and his cuff links were shiny and black, with a leaping golden jaguar.

Pavel did not invite him in even though it was terribly rude to leave him standing there in the doorway. "Natasha, this is Vasilij Ivanovitsj, who owns this beautiful house. Vasilij, this is my even more beautiful wife."

"It's a pleasure to meet you, Mrs. Doroshenko. And I regret that you were subjected to that unfortunate incident this morning. It was, of course, a mistake, and it will not happen again."

Natasha nodded silently. The man bowed gracefully, turned and left.

"You see," said Pavel and kissed her. "There's nothing to be worried about. Worrywart."

"I'm sorry," she said. "But I don't understand why we pay less than the others."

"Because Vasilij is a good friend," said Pavel. "That's all."

Natasha wanted so badly to believe it, and she almost succeeded. But if they were such good friends, then why hadn't Pavel invited him in? And why had Vasilij Ivanovitsj turned when he was halfway down the stairs and stared up at Pavel with eyes that were narrow and dark with hate?

THE DOGS BARKED. Natasha got up as quickly as she could. If she stayed here, she would be found. Katerina was once again out of reach, but at least she was alive.

SHE FELT AS if she had been beaten up. Nina's ears were buzzing, her entire body ached and there was a point at the back of her neck, at the meeting of spine and skull, where it felt as if a burning needle had been inserted.

She held Rina close despite her uneasy awareness that she was the one deriving comfort from the gesture, like a child holding a teddy bear. There was no reciprocity; Rina might as well *be* a stuffed animal. If it hadn't been for the loud, gasping wheezes that constituted the girl's breathing, Nina might have been tempted to check for signs of life.

Magnus and Pernille arrived with the oxygen. Magnus maneuvered Rina out of Nina's embrace with his usual calm authority. "Okay, Rina. Now we're going to make it easier for you to breathe."

Nina had to fight a spasmodic tension in her arms, forcing herself to let go. "She also needs salbutamol," she said before she could stop herself.

Magnus just nodded as if there were nothing odd in a nurse attempting to dictate a treatment he had undertaken hundreds of times.

It was 2:03. Forty-six minutes had passed since she had heard a key click unsuccessfully in the walk-in door.

"Nina, are you in there?"

It wasn't a voice she had immediately recognized. She was paranoid enough to hesitate for a second.

"Nina Borg? Police."

"Yes," she shouted. "We are here."

It had taken another fifteen minutes to get the door open. The lock had been damaged by the attacker's attempt to break it open, and in the end, they had to cut the hinges instead.

Outside there were people everywhere—or at least that was how it felt. There were probably only seven or eight, but the only one she knew was the camp's technical director, Henning Grønborg, who had apparently taken charge of the blowtorch himself. The rest was a whirl of yellow police vests, black SWAT uniforms and young policemen's faces wearing oddly nerdy protective glasses. Like well-behaved children at a New Year's party, thought Nina.

They tried to take Rina from her at that point, but she resisted. "Get Magnus," she had repeated, over and over again. "It has to be someone she knows."

Now she had finally let go. Her arms hurt just as much as the rest of her, in spite of the fact that she had only suffered a handful of bruises from furniture and doorways and whatever else she had bumped into on her confused, unsteady flight from Rina's room.

Pull yourself together. You are not exactly dying, she told herself.

A shiver went through her that had nothing to do with cold, though it felt that way. Right now she was deeply grateful for Magnus's insistence on heating the clinic to a temperature that would do credit to a steam bath.

2:11.

The children were sleeping now, she thought, Anton under his Spider-Man comforter and Ida presumably in sheets that were as pitch black as most of her wardrobe. For a while she had had Legolas from *The Lord of the Rings* on her pillow, but lately she had been talking about "the cynical abuse of Tolkien's work in merchandising," and Nina had had to quietly exchange a few Christmas presents before they reached the tree. The first post-divorce Christmas. Only Nina's first childhood Christmas without her father had been worse.

2:13.

Stop. She turned her watch so the face was on the inside of her wrist. It made it a little more difficult to check the time and normally helped her control her own personal mini-version of OCD. The improvement was relative—the compulsive checking of the time was replaced by involuntary movements in her lower arm every time she caught herself turning her wrist.

After her divorce, an exciting new development had occurred in the neurosis, she observed dryly. Now the checking of the time was often accompanied by an automatic picturing of what Anton and Ida were doing; she wasn't quite sure if that was better or worse.

"Nina Borg?"

She looked up. Yet another unfamiliar face, this time a younger man in civilian clothes.

"Detective Inspector Asger Veng, North Zealand Police," he introduced himself.

"Yes," she said tiredly. She couldn't even manage a politely encouraging question mark in her tone.

"May we take a few moments of your time? We have a couple of questions."

Yes, of course they did. If he had asked her to crawl naked through icy mud, her enthusiasm might have been at much the same level, but it was probably best to get it over with.

"WHAT HAPPENED?"

The shout sounded across the parade ground from a small group of freezing people who were huddled in the doorway of one of the family barracks. Nina recognized one of the camp's long-term inhabitants, a man from Eritrea, but she had to cast about for his name. Rezene, that's what he was called. He suffered from violent reflux attacks, so they saw him relatively often at the clinic.

Nina didn't know what to answer. When it came to the spreading of rumors among the camps' inhabitants, "wildfire" was an understatement, especially when the police were involved, and rumors were never harmless. They all lived with the threat of deportation as a constant stress factor. Even though Magnus did what he could to minimize it, there were a lot of sleeping pills and sedatives in circulation, and not so long ago, an Iraqi mother had shown up with three packs of nitrazepam that she had recovered from her sixteen-year-old son. When asked what he had been intending to use them for, he said that it was in case the police came to get them, because he would rather die in Denmark than in Iraq.

"It's okay," Nina shouted back in careful, simple English. "Someone tried to take a child. The police stopped them."

It was important to keep statements clear and uncomplicated.

"What child?" shouted Rezene.

"Rina. The little Ukrainian girl."

"Why ambulance?"

"Some policemen were hurt."

Detective Inspector Veng put a gentle hand on her elbow. It was presumably meant as a polite reminder of their real errand, but the touch irritated her.

"Yes, all right," she hissed. "It's hardly surprising if some of them want to know what the hell is going on."

"Your director *has* informed them," said Veng.

Nina had no doubt. Birgit Mariager had been the camp's director for almost five years now, and clear communication had quickly become one of her main concerns. But Nina also knew that even the clearest communication in the world couldn't prevent speculation, questions, rumors and doubt.

"Are they okay? Your two colleagues?"

"We don't know yet," he said. "They used a pretty nasty form of gas."

"There was only one person," Nina corrected him. "A man."

"Yes. I heard you said that."

They had asked even before they managed to open the walk-in. Nina understood that they needed to know who and how many people they were searching for and what kind of resistance they could expect to encounter if they found them, but it had seemed almost brutal to have to bellow her answers through the thick steel door when every shout made Rina's body start.

The ambulances were gone now, but the children's barrack was still closed off. Powerful projection lights made the snow glitter, and technicians were busy picking up glass shards and photographing footprints.

"We've got permission to use the director's office," said Veng. "Let's get you inside where it's nice and warm, all right?"

He was trying to be friendly, Nina told herself. It wasn't reasonable to hate him just because he was young, rested and professionally kind.

The two women who waited in the director's office were remarkably similar as far as height, weight, dress and hair color were concerned. Slender, blonde, well-dressed and well-groomed. In spite of what must have been a very rushed departure, Birgit had had time to put on both makeup and a freshly ironed white shirt. A fine gold chain ringed her still almost unwrinkled neck.

"Nina. Are you okay?"

Nina nodded. Birgit was actually okay. Most of the time.

"Please let me know if there's anything I can do."

The other woman, the Birgit clone, presented herself as Deputy Chief Inspector Mona Heide. At least *her* white shirt didn't look as if it had just come out of its cellophane wrapper. Her face didn't either. In spite of the careful makeup, the exhaustion was evident.

"I'll try to be brief," she said. "But it's important for us to find out as much as possible as quickly as possible."

"Okay."

"When did you first become aware that something was wrong?"

"I heard a crash. It must have been the gas grenade, or whatever it is they used, shattering the window."

"And when was that?"

"Six minutes past twelve."

Heide raised a well-plucked eyebrow. "You're very precise."

"I looked at my watch immediately after." Nina didn't think there was any reason to mention the OCD.

"Where were you?"

"By the coffee machine."

"Not in the girl's room?"

"No. But I had only been away for a few minutes."

"What happened then?"

Nina explained her quick look in on the policemen, hurrying to Rina's room, pressing the attack alarm, the clumsy flight to the walk-in.

"Why the walk-in?"

"It's airtight. I was pretty sure there was gas."

"And then?"

"And then he came in through the window in the lounge area."

"You're sure it was a man?"

"Yes." She recalled her brief but definitive glimpse. "He was big—both tall and broad. Completely black, including his face—he must have been wearing some kind of mask or hood."

"And it was just him?"

"Yes."

"You're sure?"

"Very sure. Listen, it wasn't Natasha. I know what you're thinking, but it wasn't her. She's a slight, slender girl. Smaller than I am—one meter sixty at the most, I would guess. And he was alone."

Heide eyed her calmly. "People often perceive events in a distorted way in situations like this. Everything happens fast, it's violent, you're afraid . . . few people ever describe an attacker as small."

"He *was* big."

"Precisely where and for how long did you see him?"

"It was only a glimpse; I was busy trying to open the door to the walk-in. He was entering the cafeteria."

The crunching of glass, Rina's breathing, the sweet-and-sour taste in the mouth that was a mixture of adrenaline and gas. The figure behind them, a faceless monster with three shiny eyes . . .

Three eyes?

"I think . . . it looked to me as if he had three eyes."

Veng and Heide exchanged a glance.

"Maybe he was using IR equipment," said Veng. "Combined with a gas mask?"

Heide nodded. Nina noted that they had finally begun to say "he" and not "they" or "her."

"Professionally done," said Heide dryly. "If you can say that about a failed mission."

"It wasn't Natasha," repeated Nina, just to make sure.

"I understand you've worked with the family for a few years?" said Veng.

Nina's mind tripped over the "family" part. In her world, an isolated and traumatized girl with a dead father and a mother who was in prison wasn't much of a family.

"Since they came here," she said.

"What has Natasha told you about her life in Ukraine?"

"Nothing. She never talked about her background."

"So you didn't know that she was wanted in a criminal investigation there?"

"Of course not. I didn't even know that she had a husband or that he was dead."

"Did she have any confidantes here? Among the other inhabitants of the camp or in Denmark in general?"

"Not that I know of. She did get engaged and moved in with . . . Vestergaard." At the last moment, she avoided calling him "that bastard" as she usually did. "The only other person I think she really spoke with was a neighbor. I don't remember her name."

"Anna Olesen?"

"Yes. That's right. Neighbor Anna. That's what Rina called her. I think she was kind to Rina while they lived there. At least I know that Rina liked her, and it usually takes her a long time to attach herself to a new person. I also got the impression that Anna was one of the few people Natasha trusted."

"And you don't know anyone else? Anyone from Ukraine, for example?"

"No." She thought about it. "We have had other Ukrainians here, but I think . . . I think Natasha avoided them on purpose. It's a little unusual; often they are very happy to have each other. Have the chance to speak their own language with someone who understands them."

"Letters? Emails? Telephone contact?"

"I don't know." Nina considered. "If she was in contact with anyone while she was serving her sentence, then Vestre Prison must know. While she was here . . . Of course, Natasha spoke on the phone now and then, but I think it was mostly with Michael Vestergaard or perhaps with Anna. In English, at least, and in the bit of broken Danish she knew."

"You haven't heard her speaking Ukrainian with anyone?"

"I don't think so. All I know is that she was terrified of being sent back. Most people here are, but with Natasha it was . . . unusually evident. And she was right to be afraid."

"What do you mean?"

"I think it's pretty obvious now. Someone is after Rina and her."

Heide gave a little, irritated shake of her head, causing her gold earrings to dance. "Not much is obvious about this," she said.

"We can at least agree that Rina is in danger," said Nina. "What are you planning to do to protect her?"

Heide looked at her coolly. "It wasn't the girl who was gassed," she said. "It was the people trying to protect her. It appears as if it is pretty risky to stand between Natasha and her daughter."

"Damn it. How many times do I need to say it? *It wasn't Natasha*."

Easy, easy, Nina told herself. She knew that swearing and yelling would not make this calmly collected woman listen any better to her—on the contrary.

"I think we're done," said the deputy chief inspector. "At least for now. If you remember other contacts Natasha may have had, we'd very much like to know, and we will naturally need to ask for a formal statement at some point."

"So you're not planning to do anything?"

"We have two colleagues in the hospital right now," said Heide. "One of them is in critical condition. You may be sure that we are planning to 'do something.'"

Nina's stomach hurt. It was perfectly clear that Heide's priority was the hunt for the gas man and Natasha—not Rina's safety.

Veng had gotten up, a clear sign that Nina was supposed to do the same. He handed her a single sheet of paper. Nina glanced down at it automatically.

Victim support, she read. *If you have been the victim of violence, rape, a break-in, robbery, an accident, etc., it is natural and completely normal if you experience reactions such as feelings of unreality or loss of control, the inability to act, hyperactivity, emptiness, memory loss, fear of being alone, fear of recurrence, stomach pain, an elevated heart rate, difficulty sleeping, nightmares, guilt, despair.*

"They are very good," he said. "And you are welcome to contact them."

Nina snapped.

"What the hell makes you think," she said in her most glacial voice, "that I am anybody's *victim*?"

NATASHA HAD PARKED the car in the forest on the other side of the camp this time. The view of the children's barrack wasn't quite as good—the depot shacks were in the way—but there were still searching figures with lights and dogs in the woods around her former hideout. The snow had finally stopped falling. It covered the roadblocks and the cars and created an almost unbroken surface between the fence and the barracks, more orange than white because of the sodium vapor in the camp's streetlights. She couldn't see Katerina or Nina anywhere. Of course not. It had to be at least at least ten degrees below zero, and it was only 4:30 in the morning. She rubbed her tired eyes. It was useless. Even if she did see Katerina, what was she going to do? Freezing to death was about the only thing she could accomplish by remaining here, if someone didn't spot her and catch her first. It was unwise, but she couldn't help herself.

When she realized that the nurse had saved Katerina from the Witch, Natasha had felt a relief and a gratitude so powerful that the darkness around her spun dizzyingly as if she had drunk too many of Robbie's whiskey shots. The relief was still there, but the gratitude was receding. On the other side of the fence and the sodium lights and the police barricades, that skinny Danish woman was lying with her arms around Natasha's child, and although she knew that it was neither reasonable nor sensible, Natasha had never for a second been as jealous of the women in Pavel's life as she was of Nina right now.

YOU'RE TOO CLINGY *with that child*, Pavel had said. He had imagined that they would go on vacation together, just the two of them, maybe to Krim, or why not abroad? Why not Berlin? He spoke the language; there was so much he could show her. Or Paris or London if she preferred.

Seventeen-year-old Natasha would have been beyond thrilled. This was precisely the world she had hoped would be waiting out there once she had escaped from Kurakhovo. Nineteen-year-old Natasha, however, would rather sit on the grass in the park and stop Katerina when she tried to put ants or ladybugs in her soft little mouth. Kiev was enough. The apartment, Pavel, Katerina—why would she need anything else? Occasionally she had agreed to hire a babysitter so they could go to a restaurant, but she would be restless the whole time, constantly remembering something she had to call and tell the young sitter. It was someone Pavel knew. He said she was studying medicine and wanted to earn a little cash. Natasha would have worried less, she thought, if there had been a more grandparent-like person available, but Pavel's mother had died several years ago, and it was too far from Kurakhovo for her mother to come for a single evening.

Gradually he stopped asking. If that was how it was going to be, he said, then he wanted to hear no complaints if he went out on his own. That was when her jealousy had crept up on her. She sniffed him like a dog when he came home and tried to smell where he had been. She looked at his cell phone when he was in the bath and found a lot of unknown numbers and messages from people she had never heard of. Some of them were women, and she noted every female name. She turned out his pockets meticulously before she did the wash. And she couldn't help asking, "Who is the Anna you call so often?"

He looked astonished. "Anna? How do you know that?"

"Who is she?" she repeated.

"My God," he said and laughed. "Now you're being silly. It's my mother's old nanny. She's almost eighty, and she lives in Denmark. See for yourself." He showed her the number and then had to explain, and she was embarrassed and really did feel silly and stupid because she hadn't known that there was a difference between the numbers abroad and the ones in Ukraine. But how was she to know? She had never known anyone who lived abroad.

"Why did your mother have a nanny from Denmark?" she asked.

"It's a bit complicated," he said. "*Everything* was complicated then—Poles, Germans, Russians, Ukrainians, Galicia was one big mess, and nobody knew what would happen from one day to the next. Anna ended up in Copenhagen and got married there. But Mother never forgot Anna, and they kept on writing to each other for many years, even back when half their letters were snatched up by the censors. I've visited her several times, and, yes, I call her now and then to hear how she is doing. I care a great deal about her, in fact."

Nina put her arms around his neck. "That's okay," she said. "You are allowed to care for almost eighty-year-old ladies. Just as long as you love me the most."

"Silly thing," he said. He pulled her close, exactly hard enough that she knew he wanted to make love to her, and a powerful surge of heat exploded somewhere under her belly button, shot downward and then spread up to her breasts and neck. She gasped, and he laughed and let his hands slide down to cup her buttocks. They never made it to the bed.

IT WAS BECAUSE of Anna that she had chosen Denmark later, when all the bad things happened. When Pavel was dead, and Katerina and she could no longer be in Ukraine. Denmark was the only other country that Natasha had been to—Natasha, Pavel and Katerina had visited together twice—and Anna the only person she knew abroad. And when her caseworker began to look worried, and Natasha was terrified that it was her turn to be deported . . . then it was Anna who had made sure she got to meet Michael.

She felt a stinging pain in the pit of her stomach at the thought. She took out a piece of chocolate and let it melt on her tongue. Then, slowly and with difficulty, she chewed a slice of the dark Danish rye bread that looked just like the Ukrainian bread she was used to on the outside but that tasted completely different. To think that she had been so stupid. To think that she had been so happy. So happy that she would be allowed stay in Bacon Land forever, where everyone lived high off the hog, and no one needed to be afraid of anything.

ABOUT HALF AN hour later, Nina emerged from the children's barrack with Katerina. Natasha was out of the car before she knew it and had taken nine or ten steps toward the fence. Dangerous steps. A few more meters and she would have been completely visible from the camp.

She saw Nina speak with one of the officers who stood at the barricade around the barrack. The nurse pointed toward the clinic on the other side of the big, open grounds where the kids played soccer in the summer. The policeman lifted the striped plastic tape and let them through.

But Nina didn't go in through the clinic's front door. She and Katerina disappeared around the corner, then appeared again a bit later by the main entrance and the parking lot. The nurse took Katerina's backpack and made her get into an ugly little yellow car.

Natasha began to run. Just then she didn't care if all the policemen in the world saw her. She plowed a way through the high snow along the fence, but she was too far away. The little yellow car had started and was rolling out of the parking lot, slowly and carefully on the icy road, but still much too fast for Natasha to reach it.

Still she kept running, until her foot caught on a hidden tree root and she fell headfirst into the snow. And then she had to run all the way back again to the stolen Audi, which in her rush she couldn't figure out how to start.

When she finally got the cold motor going and made her way back to the road, the yellow car was gone.

Natasha pulled over to the side and bent forward over the steering wheel. Acid burned in her stomach; she could barely breathe. In all the time that she had been parted from Katerina, she had always known where her daughter was. The little man on the Google map could find her. Natasha could plan the route and calculate the distance; she knew what direction she needed to go.

The Google man couldn't find Nina.

Or wait. Could he?

"I know where you live," she whispered. She could feel the knowledge loosening her chest so she could breathe again. She had been there once, long ago, when she and Michael had just gotten engaged and it looked as if everything would be safe and all right again. When both she and Nina believed that Natasha's life could go on quietly in a house in Hørsholm, behind a hedge of flowering lilacs. In Bacon Land.

They had sat drinking coffee on Nina's sofa in her messy apartment full of books, children's clothing and rubber boots. Natasha wasn't sure what the street was called, but she remembered the house—an old red-brick building on a narrow side street off the same wide boulevard where, months later, Natasha had bought the knife she meant to stab Michael with. Jagtvejen. That's what it was called. The boulevard. Surely she would be able to find it. It wasn't a route she had practiced, the way she had practiced the way to the Coal-House Camp, over and over again. But the Audi had a very high-end GPS.

It might even be better this way. After all, there were no fences and no guards around Nina's house.

UKRAINE, 1934

OLGA KICKED HER way through the snow to the stable, where the cow lay waiting patiently in the dark. That was something cows were good at. Olga sometimes tried to imagine what it was like to be a cow and lie there on the cold earthen floor and wait for someone to appear with water and hay and potato peels and let light into the stable and shovel shit from the gutter and whatever else a cow needed to stay alive. Did Zorya even know that summer would return? And was she ever afraid of being forgotten?

If she was, she hid it well. Her large, glassy eyes rested calmly on Olga in the gloom. She lay on her side with the clumsy yellowish hooves pulled up against her stomach, which appeared unnaturally large and swollen in comparison to her flabby, shrunken udders.

Olga grabbed an armful of hay and loosened it carefully, trying not to get pricked by the many thistles. Then she threw it in front of the cow, who stuck her long blue tongue all the way out and pulled the hay toward her without getting up.

Frost covered the walls and straw like a fragile white spiderweb, and the water in the trough was frozen, but not so hard Olga couldn't make a hole in the ice with Grandfather's sickle for Zorya to drink from. Then she scraped the cow shit to the side and cautiously poked the cow to see if she wanted to get up. She didn't. Milk for Kolja would have to wait. If the cow stood up, Olga would also find some fresh pine boughs for her to lie on, because even though she had her usual thick winter coat, you could see her bones like thick branches under the skin. If the cow wasn't lying on something soft, those bones would gnaw through flesh and skin, and she would get sores and die.

Mother didn't take care of the cow.

She took care of the pigs in the kolkhoz and had the responsibility for all the squealing, hunchbacked beasts in Stable Number Two. Every morning she fought her way down there through the drifts to fatten up the swine. And that was fine with her. Or so she said. She might not be as strong as she used to be, but she was still a damn sight better than those two sluts from the Caucasus who were supposedly in charge of Stable Number One, but who, according to Mother, drank vodka and whored worse than the swine. Back when Father was still living with them, Mother wouldn't have said such things, but her speech had become coarse and rude now, especially when she talked about younger women.

"They can fuck, but I can work," she said, her laugh brief and hard, not at all like the way she used to laugh when they still lived in Kharkiv.

Olga stroked the broad, greasy bridge of the cow's nose and thought that it would have been nice to sit here with someone. Jana. But the mere thought of Jana gave her a clenching sensation in her stomach.

After Oxana's pioneer meeting, a number of children in the school fawned over her in a dog-like manner. Nadia and Vladimir and little Veronica, who was really a *niemcy*, an ethnic German, and had been forcibly relocated here from Galicia, but who still loved Comrade Semienova and the Party and all that meant in terms of khaki-colored uniform shirts and red banners. Her eyes were glued to Oxana in the schoolroom, and when Olga talked about the counterrevolutionary cells in the village that had to be crushed, little Veronica opened her tiny bright red mouth and sighed with devotion.

But not everyone looked at Oxana and Olga with such adoration. Some eyes were lowered when they turned around in the schoolroom. Whispering would suddenly cease when they walked by and later start up again behind their backs. Olga knew what they were whispering, even though no one had said it to her face. She had listened and picked it up piece by piece. They were whispering about Oxana and Fedir. They said that Fedir had been in love with Oxana, and that Oxana had gone for long walks with him down by the frozen stream. She had lured him into telling her about the wheat under the stable floor, and afterward she had reported it to the chief of the GPU in Sorokivka.

Everything had gotten worse after the letter arrived from the Marchenko family. Fedir's sister, the little girl with the hare-like scream, had never made it to their destination, which was so far north that you had to travel by train for a full fourteen days. She had stopped screaming on their third day in the cattle car. They had left her someplace along the tracks between Kharkiv and Novokuznetsk. No one knew exactly where.

Jana was one of the whisperers now. Fedir was her cousin, and even though Jana had made fun of him when he still sat in the back of the class, his disappearance had broken something between Jana and Olga, something that couldn't be put back together again.

That was the way things were, and there was nothing Olga could do about it.

She was not responsible for Fedir's banishment, but she was tied to Oxana by blood, just as Jana was tied to Fedir. Therefore they had to be enemies now, and it was a war that Jana threw herself into with a bloody rage.

Jana said that Olga was ugly and had body lice, and that she didn't want to sit next to her in school. Jana also said that she was just as dirty as her swine of a mother. Jana told the others in school how their old house sparkled now that Svetlova had taken over the housekeeping and that Svetlova was expecting a child who would soon replace Olga, Oxana and Kolja.

Outside the cow barn, Grandfather was making his way to the woodshed, coughing. Olga stood with her hand on the cow's neck and listened to the sound of the axe splitting wet birch wood until it hit the chopping block with a faint echo in the ice-cold air.

Then came the roar.

He was calling Mother, Olga could hear, and afterward he also called Grandmother, even though she had been dead for several years now. Olga felt a gust of terror blow through her. She wrenched open the door and raced across the yard to the woodshed.

Grandfather lay with the axe in his shin, cursing and shouting for vodka. Olga and Oxana had to hold down both him and his leg while Mother pulled the axe free from the bone. There was blood everywhere. Even the bone bled, it seemed to Olga, and she knew bones couldn't bleed.

Mother sent Oxana off to get the barber, telling her to run as fast as she could. Olga got rags and blankets, and Mother tore a wide strip of linen from a sack and made a tourniquet right above the cut. She used the axe handle to tighten it and turned it around and around even though Grandfather screamed like an animal going to slaughter and cursed her to hell and back again.

"Would you rather die?" Mother just said when he stopped screaming for a moment out of sheer exhaustion.

Finally Oxana returned with the barber. He tied a piece of bluish-white sheep gut around the biggest of the pumping arteries and sewed the tear together with needle and thread. Only then could they help each carry Grandfather into the house.

Even after the barber was done, Grandfather didn't stop bleeding. Mother sat next to him and pressed one rag after another against the cut, her grip hard and frantic. Grandfather had drunk so much vodka that he could no longer speak, and spit and drool trickled from the corner of his mouth into his beard. There was a wet rattle in his chest. Olga wasn't sure if she was more afraid of him dying or of him waking up again. She was feeling sick and couldn't stop shaking, but Oxana was pale and calm and looked as if she were thinking of something else completely.

"If he dies, he is no good to us," she said gravely to Olga. "And even if he lives, he is no good to us. It is winter, and we have no man in the house."

Olga looked over at Grandfather. The darkness in the room was oppressive, and the glow from the oven illuminated it only enough that she could see the growing pile of soaked black rags on the floor next to him.

Olga knew that she shouldn't be thinking of herself, but still. Grandfather did more than just administer hard, unexpected slaps to the face and neck. Grandfather chopped wood and laid traps in the woods. The skins he sold were their only source of cash and goods like meat and sugar and tea and salt and petroleum; how would they do without?

The barber had cost rubles, Olga knew. Rubles and bread. And today there were no rations from the kolkhoz's communal kitchen because Mother had stayed home and left the pigs to the Caucasian whores.

LATER, WHEN GRANDFATHER was fast asleep, and dusk had fallen outside, Father suddenly appeared in the doorway.

Olga's heart gave a little jump for joy in the middle of all the sadness and nastiness. Father must have heard about the accident and had come to . . . to take Mother back. Now that he knew she was completely helpless in the world, he had realized what a big mistake he had made. The widow and the baby had to go, of course, but that would be okay. The baby would be small and could live in a smaller house. And in any case, that was Svetlova's problem, not theirs.

Father carefully stomped the snow off his boots before he stepped inside. His broad shoulders filled the whole room, thought Olga.

"*Tatko!*"

Without thinking she rushed over and threw her arms around him. She took in the familiar smell of sawdust and pine sap and noticed that it was now spiced with a very faint new scent of chamomile, which probably came from Svetlova's body. She didn't care. She burrowed her face into his open coat and pressed her nose and cheek against his woolen shirtfront.

He pushed her away.

His eyes were swimming a little, and Olga realized that nothing was exactly as it should be. He had been drinking, she could see, and behind him Oxana now stomped into the room and shot Olga a cranky look.

"You wanted to speak with me?" Father said to Mother, his expression foreign and hostile.

Mother got up on uncertain legs, nodding to Father as she smoothed her hair. Olga could see that she was attempting to hide the gaping holes in her rows of teeth when she spoke. "We need money, Andreij. Or at least some of your rations from the kolkhoz."

"Sell something," said Father. "The old man still has a cow, and that's more than most people. That it was allowed to survive last winter was a miracle in itself. Fat and pregnant as it was. If I were you, I'd eat it now before it is collected for the kolkhoz. That's the best advice I can give you."

Mother lowered her head but went on. "But your children," she said. "Will you let them starve because of this new bastard of yours? What kind of man are you?"

Grandfather stirred uneasily in the gloom behind her. He made a drawn-out, whimpering noise that sounded more like an animal than a human. He lay with his eyes closed, his breathing labored.

Father had narrowed his eyes to slits, and the rage and vodka made his face ruddy in the light from the oven. Olga was afraid now. It seemed like an eternity since he had sat on the veranda outside the house in Kharkiv and called Olga his "most highborn princess" and Mother "the most beautiful flower in the field."

Now he was a person she didn't know at all, and she realized that there was also more than one truth about her father. The man who loves and smiles one day can hate the next. Turn your back for a moment, and feelings will change and flow in new directions.

"*Tatko*," she whispered and grabbed hold of his hand. But he didn't notice her.

"I have been man enough for you," he hissed. "Now I am man for another woman, and I cannot support two families. It's hard enough with one."

Mother's face distorted in a terrible grimace. "You're lying," she said. "I know how much you have put aside over time. Jewelry from your mother. My silk shawls from town and my sewing machine. At least give me those things, Andreij, so I can take care of your children."

Father stepped forward and raised his hand. Even though he lowered it without striking, Olga knew that Jana had been right. He had chosen the widow and the new child, and she and Kolja and Oxana were nothing to him.

WHEN HE HAD left, they sat for a long time in the silent gloom. Then Oxana finally got up and began to get ready to go out again.

"Where are you going?" Mother's voice was flat and low, as if she were speaking from the bottom of a grave.

"To school," said Oxana. "There's something I have to discuss with Comrade Semienova."

THE DOORBELL'S SYNTHETIC ding-ding hammered at Søren's eardrum. He had a confused sense that it wasn't the first ring but perhaps even the fifth or sixth. He had been going through Babko's case files, both the official ones and the unofficial USB-key, until almost one o'clock, when he had had to admit that he couldn't think straight any longer.

He tumbled out of bed, still with a heavy sensation of sleep and unreality weighing down his body, and lifted the shade a bit so he could see who it was ringing his bell at whatever hour it was in the night.

An adult and a child. They were both bundled up in down jackets and scarves, and it was probably more a sense of inevitability than actual recognition that made him conclude that it had to be Nina Borg and the girl. What was her name? Katerina?

He looked down at himself. Bare, middle-aged legs and boxer shorts. Where was that robe Susse had given him for Christmas? He grabbed a pair of sweatpants instead and pulled them on over his hairy legs.

He turned on the light in the hall and the entranceway. Through the flecked glass of his front door the figures were just vague silhouettes, but he had been right. It was Nina holding the hand of a skinny blonde girl. The girl was clutching a pink backpack.

"You were in the phone book," said Nina. "Your address and everything. I didn't think that was allowed when you were in the PET."

"It doesn't say than I *am* in the PET," he said, feeling stupid with sleep and thoroughly unprepared. But despite the untimely invasion, he was glad to see her. "Come in."

"They don't know I'm here," she said.

"Who?"

"The police." She looked at him and corrected herself. "That is, the other police."

"What happened?"

"He tried to kidnap Rina."

"He?"

She gestured impatiently with her hand. "Someone. Not Natasha. Someone who uses gas grenades and infrared goggles."

He took a deep breath. "What happened to the guards?" he asked.

"They . . . one was taken away in an ambulance. Because of the gas. A very young man. They say it's critical, that he might die. He stopped breathing. He is under observation for brain damage. I took Rina and locked us into the walk-in refrigerator. Otherwise they would have taken her. Or rather, he would have. I didn't see more than one person."

Her eyes were huge. She was speaking calmly even though her sentences weren't quite coherent. She looked peculiarly happy, like someone who has said all along that it would end badly and finally has been proven right.

"They still think it's just Natasha," she said; this time she apparently meant the police. "They don't understand that Rina is in danger. But . . . you do. Am I right?"

"Maybe," he said. He wouldn't give her too much.

"You have to help me protect her," she said. "Will you?"

The words came out all edgy and awkward. He sensed that she didn't often ask for help.

"At least come in and have some breakfast," he said. "I have to call my boss. You understand that, right?"

A cop killing. If the young policeman died, it would be a cop killing. No one would condone Nina's disappearing act then. But when he looked at the little Ukrainian girl, about to collapse and breathing like a leaky balloon, he couldn't quite blame her.

"Is he . . . not an idiot either?" she asked.

He wasn't quite sure if Torben, with his adherence to rules and career focus, would be able to live up to her definition of non-idiocy. "He usually knows what's what," he said. "And he's super smart."

"Okay," she said, as if he needed her permission.

TO BE WOKEN up in the middle of the night—or in this case, at a quarter to five on Sunday morning—was of course a part of the job for a man like Torben, but that didn't necessarily mean he liked it.

"What is it now?" he said shortly.

"Everything has gone pear-shaped," said Søren quickly. "Someone tried to kidnap the daughter from the Coal-House Camp, and one of the men from the guard detail is in intensive care. They say his life is in danger."

There was silence for a few seconds.

"Could it be the girl's mother?" asked Torben.

"It was a man. Of course you can't exclude the possibility that it was at the mother's request. But I'm calling because the girl is sitting in my kitchen right now with Nina Borg. And no one else knows."

"For fuck's sake, Søren. Why?"

"Because Nina is convinced that the girl would be in imminent danger if she stayed in the camp."

"That woman is hostile to authority and borderline paranoid," said

Torben. "How on earth did she manage to walk off with the kid without anyone noticing?"

"I haven't asked yet. But I would like you to contact our colleagues and explain to them that we are planning to provide Katerina Doroshenko with the necessary personal protection."

"Søren, I can't do that. Especially not if they have a dead colleague on their hands!"

"Maybe precisely for that reason. The girl's safety is not their priority. They just want to get hold of the perpetrator and Natasha Doroshenko—and that's not necessarily the same thing."

"Do you know something? Or are you just guessing?"

"The original Ukrainian case against Natasha Doroshenko, that is, the killing of her husband, is based primarily on two circumstantials: the fact that she fled the country, and a confession from a violent criminal who claims that she paid him to attack Doroshenko."

"That latter is perhaps more than circumstantial."

"Torben. It's Ukraine. You can extract confessions like that in so many ways."

"Okay. I hear what you are saying. But who is 'you' in this case, and why would 'you' do so?"

Søren tried to structure his argument before answering. "The Ukrainian policemen who originally came up here to interrogate Natasha are from two different services—as you know, Lieutenant Babko is from GUBOZ. His colleague, a Colonel Savchuk, is from SBU."

"Hold on," said Torben. There was a creaking, followed by footsteps and the sound of a door being closed carefully. Torben had left the bedroom, Søren guessed, in order not to wake Annelise and to be able to speak freely.

"GUBOZ *and* SBU," said his boss thoughtfully. "You have to ask yourself why they are interested in Natasha Doroshenko."

"Precisely. Especially when one of them disappears without a word to anyone, apparently blindsiding his GUBOZ colleague completely. A colleague who was sent up here specifically to keep an eye on him."

"What do you mean?"

As briefly as possible, Søren told Torben about Babko's admissions and about the connection between Savchuk and Nikolaij Filipenko, Babko's "clean man." "Unfortunately, I think Nina Borg's concern for the girl's safety is well justified."

"Because of Savchuk?"

"I have no grounds for claiming that. Not at the moment. One might equally well argue that Savchuk is missing because during his search for Natasha Doroshenko, he got in the way of the person or persons who attacked the Coal-House Camp."

"But you don't believe that?"

"Right now I don't believe anything. The closest I can come to a theory is that everything is connected to the killing of Pavel Doroshenko."

"Mmm." Torben had the habit of humming inarticulately when he was thinking something he wasn't saying. "Go on."

"It's speculation."

"Go on anyway."

"Doroshenko was a journalist."

"Yes."

"I've looked through his articles. He published a good deal of controversial material with sensitive personal content."

"Okay."

"Presumably you remember the Gongadze case?"

"The journalist. The headless corpse, which they at first tried to avoid identifying. When they couldn't get away with that any longer, it came out that the murder was committed on the orders of the interior minister, what was his name . . ."

"Kravchenko."

"Yes. Him. He got the journalist eliminated because he wrote critically about the administration's abuse of freedom of speech and civil rights, wasn't that the way it was?"

"More or less. Four officers from the SBU were sentenced for the murder, and the investigation of who gave the order stopped with the death of Kravchenko. He was found with two bullet holes in the head a few hours before he was to due to be interrogated by the public prosecutor, and Oleksandr Turchinov, Savchuk's boss in the SBU, closed the case with a declaration that Kravchenko had committed suicide."

"Very convenient."

"Yes. Of course, it *is* theoretically possible the first wound wasn't fatal and the suicide candidate was very determined, but . . ."

"It's pretty rare for people to shoot themselves in the head twice," said Torben dryly.

"Precisely. I'm not saying that Pavel Doroshenko is another Gongadze; I don't have any proof of that. But what if . . . what if he was killed by someone in the system either because they were hired to do so or because they were protecting one of their own? Then you can't really find fault with Natasha's decision to leave the country in a hurry."

"And where in this speculative scenario do you place Colonel Savchuk and his brother the politician?"

"Half brother. I don't know. I have no idea whether Savchuk is a hero or a villain in this." Among Doroshenko's articles there had been nothing about Nikolaij Filipenko, his half brother or their mother. Nothing that tied Savchuk to the case. "It's hard to get a sense of the relationship between the two brothers. There's such a great distance between them age-wise and . . . historically. Savchuk was born in the postwar years with a supposedly 'unknown' father, an army brat who himself made a career of the military. From what little I've been able to dig up on him, it seems he was with the Russians in nineteen seventy-nine when they moved into Afghanistan. Later he joined the KGB and just continued on to the SBU after the Independence. A bit of a Cold War dinosaur, it looks like, but there are a surprising number of those in that part of the world, and a wise man doesn't turn his back on them. Filipenko, on the other hand, was born in nineteen seventy-two. A completely different life—glasnost, perestrojka, independence. And it looks like a completely different personal life as well—the mother had at that point married a man who was somewhat younger than her, an engineer who later became a diplomat under Gorbachev. There are a number of foreign postings, two years of boarding school in England, engineering studies because he apparently wanted to follow in his father's footsteps, then soccer hero status, which he begins to turn into a political career in the late nineties. Apparently Filipenko is a humane, well-intentioned, decent man who wishes to get to the bottom of corruption in his country. What Savchuk is . . . That's more of an open question. And until now there was no other connection to Pavel Doroshenko than his energetic efforts to get the widow extradited to Ukraine."

"What does your friend Babko say?"

"He doesn't know either. He has given me a lot of material that I am trying to understand. Among other things I have a sense there is a pattern to the articles Doroshenko published, but I can't quite make the pieces fit together. I would like to speak with Babko again. But first I want to solve the problem I have sitting in my kitchen."

A pause. He could hear the refrigerator door open and the sound of something being poured into a glass. Tomato juice, if he knew Torben. Once in a while the juice was accompanied by Tabasco, ice and vodka, but not now, not when there was work to be done.

"Are you really convinced that the girl is in danger, and it's not just her mother who has tried to get hold of her?" his boss asked.

"If that was your daughter, would you have used gas? A grown man almost died from it. Would you risk it with your daughter—when that daughter suffers from severe asthma attacks?"

There was a swallowing sound as Torben took a sip of his juice. "No," he said. "I wouldn't. I would go as far as to say that it certainly doesn't sound like the mother has had complete control over the person or persons responsible for the attack."

"Then you agree that the girl is in danger."

A sigh. "Yes. That would follow. But listen. You know exactly how Heide and her people will react if we just waltz in there and take things over."

Søren was well aware of the tensions between the PET and the other divisions of the police. It was not the PET's primary job to make sure that those who committed criminal acts were taken to court and sentenced, and there were times when a prosecution would directly interfere with the security concerns of the PET. Once, in 1988, that schism had even cost the life of a young policeman, and the wounds still ached.

He could understand Heide's resistance and her fear that the PET's involvement might make it more difficult to construct a case.

"I'll call Heide," said Torben. "But only to make your collaboration easier. You're going to have to work it out between you. We have to make her feel safe. Make her understand that we want to help, not obstruct."

"And can personal protection of Katerina Doroshenko be a part of that help?"

"What level were you thinking of?"

"First, that the girl doesn't have to go back to the Coal-House Camp or any other place where she is easy to find."

"Okay. I think I can sell that—on the condition that they have access to both Borg and the girl when they are needed for questioning. But are you imagining an actual safe house?"

"If that's possible. Wouldn't that also make Heide feel safer, knowing Natasha Doroshenko would have a very hard time getting hold of the girl? She's unlikely to try to leave the country as long as the girl is here."

Torben snorted. "I can try. Okay. You stay where you are for the time being. I'll call when I have something for you. And keep a close eye on that paranoid nurse of yours, okay? We don't want her to give us the slip."

THE PARANOID NURSE sat at the little table in the kitchen with her head against the wall. Her eyes were closed, and Søren guessed she was close to nodding off if she wasn't asleep already, despite the hardness of the chair. She was still wearing her coat, and a little pool of water was spreading around her boots as the snow stuck in the treads melted.

The girl, on the other hand, was wide awake. She didn't look at him directly, but there was a guarded glitter from behind her lowered eyelashes.

He squatted down in front of her. "Are you hungry?" he asked her in Russian.

He saw Nina jolt and open her eyes. The child just shook her head.

"Sleepy?"

A single nod.

"Proshoo," she whispered then. *"De tut tualet?"*

"It's right out here in the hall," he said, still in Russian. "Do you want me to show you?"

She got up, still holding the backpack tightly. He didn't try to get her to put it down. Nina sat completely still and observed them with a carefully neutral expression. She didn't interfere with his attempts to make contact.

He showed the slight girl to the bathroom and turned on the light for her. Built-in halogen spots threw shiny reflections back from shiny black granite tiles and lacquered white cabinets. There were no calming bath toys and happy frogs on the shower curtain or anything else that might make a child feel at home, but at least it had just been cleaned, so hopefully it smelled more of Vim than of urine.

"Thank you," Rina said politely. She was clearly waiting for him to leave.

He closed the door but remained outside for a moment, listening. She didn't lock it, he was happy to note. He had no desire to deal with a child who had barricaded herself in his bathroom, either on purpose or accidentally—his six-year-old nephew had once gone into a panic when he couldn't unlock the door.

She stayed in there for a while. He let her be and went back to the kitchen to offer Nina a cup of coffee.

"That's unusual," she said.

"That I offer coffee?"

"No, that Rina speaks to someone she doesn't know."

"Maybe it was because I spoke Russian."

"Yes. Maybe. What did your boss say?"

"He's going to call me back. But we're trying to get you a safe house. Do you know what that entails?"

"Kind of . . . well, not really."

"Milk?"

"No, thank you."

"It can be more or less institutional, with more or less in the way of surveillance and guards, depending on how we evaluate the level of threat. The most important thing for Rina's safety right now, in my opinion, is that we make her hard to find. That's the best protection we can give her."

Nina put both her hands around the mug of instant coffee that he handed her. She sniffed the scent as if it were perfume. "So she's not going back to the camp?"

"No. Not if we can help it."

"I knew you weren't an idiot," she said and flashed him something that was more of a relieved grimace than a real smile.

"A few ground rules," he said. "If you haven't done so already, you need to turn off your cell phone. You can't use it. In fact, I'd prefer if you gave it to me." Søren didn't know what resources his adversary could draw on—if the adversary was Colonel Savchuk, with his rank and standing in the GPU, it was probably a considerable amount. Tracking a cell phone was not, these days, a PET monopoly, more was the pity.

"Okay." She must have figured out why, because she didn't ask any questions. She just fished her phone out of her pocket and handed it to him, meek as a lamb. Would wonders never cease?

"Does Rina have a telephone?"

"No."

"Good. Where is your car?"

"I parked it a few streets away. It's pretty recognizable."

"Good thinking. Do you have any sense of whether you were seen when you left the camp?"

"It's hard to say. Everything was still pretty chaotic. But if the deputy chief and her troops had seen me, I guess they would have stopped me."

She cleared perceived the police as the enemy. Again, Søren experienced that odd, don't-let-her-fly-away sensation mixed with a dose of wonder that she was sitting here. That she trusted him at least that far.

"Until we have the opportunity to move you to a more secure location, this is your safe house," he said. "That means that neither you nor Rina may leave the house—not even to go outside to smoke or anything like that."

"I don't smoke."

He considered the situation. The house was neither more nor less secure against break-ins than any other suburban house—or secure against escape, for that matter. It was easy for Torben to tell him not to let Nina wander off, but in reality there wasn't a whole lot he could do if she really wanted to leave. Not without restraining her physically—and wouldn't that be a fine thing for the fragile trust he hoped they were establishing?

"Would Rina understand if we tell her she has to stay here? That it's dangerous to go out?"

Nina hesitated. "Rina has lived in the Coal-House Camp for a long time now," she said. "She understands about rules. But . . ."

"But?"

"She really just wants to be with her mother. So if Natasha finds us, Rina is gone. You can bet on that."

"Do you think that Natasha would recognize your car?"

"It's not the same one that I had when she was in the camp. No, I don't think so."

At least Nina had been smart enough not to park it in the driveway, but his own professional paranoia would have preferred it to be even farther away.

He got up and went into the hall. Listened at the bathroom door.

The girl was talking to someone.

He stopped breathing for a moment to listen better.

"Are you coming soon, *Tatko*?" Søren could just barely make out the soft, quiet child's voice through the door. "We miss you. And Mom is . . . Mom is in the kitchen making poppy seed cakes. Guests are coming. Anna is coming. And Great-Grandmother. Oh, it would be *so* nice if you could come too. You *are* coming? Oh, that's good. Three o'clock. Kiss, kiss. I love you!"

Tatko. He was fairly sure it meant "father," even though it wasn't something a Russian child would say.

He quietly opened the door. Rina was sitting on the toilet, but on the lid, holding a cell phone up to her ear.

"Who are you talking to?" he asked.

She stiffened. "No one," she whispered almost inaudibly.

"May I see your phone?"

She held it tightly against her chest for a few seconds. "It's mine."

"Yes. I just need to have a look at it."

Rina handed it over reluctantly. Her breathing abruptly became even worse, wheeze in, wheeze out, a labored and uneven rhythm.

The cell phone was turned off. Dead. It was an old model, at least five or six years old. The display had a thin black crack across the upper left-hand corner; the back cover was cracked too, and absolutely nothing happened when he tried to turn it on. Presumably it hadn't worked for a long time.

He handed it to the girl. "Thank you for letting me see it."

She quickly put it away in her backpack.

Dear God, he thought.

"Who gave it to you?" he asked.

She didn't answer. Just stared at him, blankly and fearfully, gnawing at her lower lip as if she were trying to eat it.

"Your Tatko?"

She nodded. An almost invisible nod.

"I can see why you treasure it," he said.

NINA SCRUTINIZED THE young man who sat in Søren's kitchen. He was tapping away with concentration on some kind of cell phone/computer hybrid. Not an iPad—she knew what they looked like, at least, because Ida wanted one. This was something more exotic. The man's powerful jaw worked ceaselessly, giving a little irritating click with every chew, and a pack of nicotine gum peeked out of his breast pocket. Nina didn't really think he looked like a PET-man. He certainly didn't look like Søren. And he *wasn't* Søren, a fact that irritated her even more than his constant cud chewing.

She had slept for a few hours in Søren's guest room with Rina nestled against her. The sleep had been amazingly dream free. Even though she had been so tired her whole body buzzed with exhaustion, Nina hadn't expected to fall asleep so quickly and so deeply. Søren had had to shake her shoulder lightly to wake her up.

"I didn't want to just leave you," he'd said. "This is Mikael Nielsen. He'll be on watch for the next six or seven hours."

Nina was taken aback. She hadn't expected Søren would personally hold her hand twenty-four/seven; of course he would have other things to do too, and it was pretty generous of him just to provide his house. But the cud-chewing young man didn't seem an especially committed or confidence-inspiring replacement, and all her defenses rose up anew. The few questions she had tried to ask him were answered monosyllabically without him raising his gaze from his electronic thing even once. It was hard to determine if he suffered from what the Coal-House psychologist called "communicative issues" or whether it was just professional distance. One thing was certain—Rina would not begin to chat cozily with *him*. Especially not after he had insisted on taking away her security blanket cell phone to be *completely* sure it didn't work.

Nina was still amazed that Rina had spoken to Søren. Yes, he had an advantage because he could speak Russian with her. But that wasn't all. There was something solid about him. Quiet but immovable. Apparently his Paul Newman–like aura also worked wonders on traumatized eight-year-old girls.

She went back to the living room, where Rina was now lying on the couch with a comforter around her, her face turned toward the television screen. Little Japanese figures, looking to Nina primitively drawn or at least very stylized, raced by in a melee of explosions. Rina's eyes were almost shut. Nina debated whether she could get away with turning off the television but decided not to. It would be good if Rina fell asleep again—she needed it.

9:26.

Still an hour and thirty-four minutes to go until she would get to see Anton. The school carnival began at 11:00.

Rina was still clutching her backpack. The by now somewhat grubby mini Diddl mouse attached to the zipper appeared to be staring at Nina with supersized eyes. Nina wanted to hug the girl, silly stuffed mouse backpack and all, but she knew it was her own need and not the child's.

9:28. Morten might already be helping Anton with his costume. This year Nina hadn't been the one left with the choice between spending a fortune at the toy store or spending a weekend creating a costume. Anton usually had firm opinions about what he wanted to be. She remembered the year he insisted on being a traffic light—in terms of costume construction one of the easier options—it could basically be produced from a cardboard box, a couple of mini flashlights and some silk paper. But he had had a ball running around and yelling, "Stop! Red light!" to innocent passersby.

This year she had been left completely out of the loop. Morten hadn't even told her when the carnival was; she had had to track down that information herself on the school's intranet page.

She went back into the kitchen, where she had a better view of the street outside. Magnus would be here soon. He had promised to stand in for her so that there would still be someone familiar there for Rina. When she entered the room, the cud-chewing ceased for a moment or two before the PET guy lowered his gaze and continued tapping on his not-quite-an-iPad.

There was a faint noise from the living room. It was barely audible through the sound effects from the cartoon, but still reached Nina's Rina radar. She listened to Rina's whispering voice. For more than two years, she had seen and heard Rina use the broken cell phone. Not until yesterday had she seriously begun to worry whether it was something other than a game—perhaps a somewhat obsessive game, but still a game. Never in all that time had she guessed that what Rina was really doing was talking to her dead father.

Blind. Deaf. Dumb. How could Nina *not* have seen it? It made her wonder how well she actually understood the traumatized people who surrounded her. Maybe she wasn't really any better at solving their problems than at handling her own.

The thought gave her a hollow feeling inside. Her entire adult life, she had seen herself as someone you could count on when the going got tough. Someone who "made a difference"—that worn phrase used about everything from people who sorted their garbage and once in a while took the bus to those who went on dangerous, potentially deadly peacekeeping missions. She knew that she *had* been party to saving lives, to improving them. The cost had been her own family.

Or not quite.

It wasn't quite that black and white, she did realize that. Morten would probably have been able to live with the fact that she had a job that consumed her, that sometimes demanded so much of her that there was too little left for him—and sometimes too little even for Ida and Anton. That wasn't why he had ended it.

It was because she always had to go right up to the edge—and then take one more step. Because she, in his words, had transformed her life into a war zone. It wasn't enough to take an extra shift at the Coal-House Camp and attempt to help the people shipwrecked there. She had promised not to go on missions abroad anymore, and she had kept that promise. Instead, she had committed herself to aiding people Danish society considered "illegals." The ones who couldn't go to the emergency room or see a doctor, the ones who couldn't go to the police when they were the victims of crimes. People like Natasha who had to accept squalor or abuse, either because they had no choice or because almost anything was better than being sent back where they came from.

She was *good* at it. In a crisis situation she was calmly efficient, perfectly able to act, to think, to do something. She missed that capable version of herself when things became too humdrum. For Christmas this year Ida had given her a T-shirt she had managed to get hold of from some ad campaign extolling the virtues of public transportation; it was bright green and had the words WORLD SAVIOR printed in big letters across the chest.

Nina wasn't stupid. She had done therapy, and she knew perfectly well where it came from, this compulsion to save the ones no one else wanted to bother with. She could say precisely, to the minute, when it had begun: the day she had run home from school during the lunch break and had found her father in the bathroom in the basement.

She forced herself to remember. Consciously, dispassionately. *Don't avoid it. Confront it.* Water on the floor. Blood on the floor. Blood in the water. Her father lying in the water with all his clothes on, turning his head slightly to look at her with eyes that resembled those of a fish. That far she could go.

It was the hour following that she couldn't account for. No matter how hard she tried, all she could remember was going next door to get help. Right away. *I went over there right away.* She had repeated it again and again to the police, to the therapists, to the doctors and all the other grown-ups, even though they all kept on telling her that it couldn't be true. She remembered how frustrated she was that they wouldn't believe her, that they tried to make her accept their correct, adult, superior understanding of time and place. And the ugly, world-swallowing vortex she found herself floundering in when she began to realize that they were right. Almost an hour *had* passed between the moment when she went down into the basement and the moment when she came up again. And during that hour, her father had died.

Morten knew, of course. For many years he had understood, condoned, shielded and protected when she would allow him to do so. He knew the gap was there and what it cost her not to fall into it. What he couldn't accept was that their children also had to live on the edge of that abyss.

She listened to Rina's whispering voice and did not interrupt. Let the girl speak with her father, she thought. Who am I to tell her that she's wrong, that the phone doesn't work, that her father can no longer hear her and is never coming back?

When Nina had the sense that Rina was saying goodbye, she stepped into the living room. And it was only then that she saw that the phone Rina was speaking into wasn't the broken cell phone but the landline on Søren's desk.

"Who were you speaking to?" she asked.

Rina started. "No one."

Who did Rina even know that she would think of calling? Someone at the Coal-House Camp? Natasha? Rina had been speaking Ukrainian, but how on earth could she have gotten a number that would connect her with her mother?

"Was it . . . your father?"

Rina shrugged and bowed her head. "It doesn't work anymore," she said.

"Why not?"

"It's broken. He said so. The policeman."

Nina went over to the phone and pressed REDIAL. The telephone rang five, six, seven times. Then a friendly man's voice said, "You've reached Anna and Hans Henrik Olesen. We can't come to the phone right now, but leave a message, and we'll call you back."

Hans Henrik Olesen? She had never heard of the man and she couldn't figure out how Rina knew him.

But maybe Rina didn't know him. Maybe she had pressed the numbers randomly or called one of the numbers in the phone's memory.

"Rina. It's important. Were you trying to call your father?"

Rina stood there for a moment, gasping with her mouth open, and Nina was sorry to have pushed her. The girl's narrow face puckered and distorted as if she was going to cry, but no tears came.

"I just want to talk to him," she said at last, and the air wheezed in and out of her lungs, worse and worse, it seemed to Nina. "I miss him so."

So do I, thought Nina. How could he do that to us?

She put her arms around the girl, this time not caring whose need she was responding to. Rina felt light as a bird in her arms, a small, damp burden weighing less than it ought.

The time was now 9:42.

THEY CAME FOR Father in the beginning of December, and he didn't have time to say goodbye to anyone besides Vladimir Petrenko and the widow.

It was Jana who was able to report it in school, and maybe she did feel a little sorry for Olga, after all, because she let Olga sit next to her on the steps while the children gathered around her during the break.

"He was yelling and screaming all the way down to the crossroads," said Jana. "And Svetlova, big as a house, came waddling after on bare feet and tried to hit one of the GPUs with a log. Like this."

Jana got up and ran with heavy, spread legs over the lumpy, frost-covered ground, screaming, "Oh, oh," holding her stomach with one hand and swinging an imaginary piece of firewood in the other. The others laughed, and Jana happily repeated the performance a few times before she tired of the applause and stopped, cheeks glowing and feet apart. Her breath emerged in a white cloud from her mouth.

"Did they hit him?"

Olga thought Jegor looked almost eager. Her stomach had tied itself into a hard knot, and the air she breathed into her lungs was so cold, it seemed to make her chest freeze solid.

Jana didn't answer right away but remained standing, scratching her hair thoughtfully. She had lice, Olga observed. Jana's mother had

had a fever and a cough for the last two weeks and had not had the strength to comb Jana and her little sister with the lice comb the way she usually did. Even at this distance Olga could see the big, fat creatures crawling around in Jana's pale hair and was secretly pleased. Maybe that would teach her to lie about Olga's body lice. But it still hurt all the way down into the pit of her stomach. In the old days, she would have offered to crack the lice for Jana during recess, but now Jana would just have to crack them herself, if she could catch them.

"I think they did hit him once with the rifle," said Jana then. "Across the back of the neck. Afterward, he did what they told him to, even though he kept screaming."

"Too bad."

The boys had hoped for more, Olga could see. They had played Capitalists and Communists all recess long, and the capitalists had been beaten as usual. It was clear, they said, that Andreij should have been beaten much more severely for his crimes. As head of the kolkhoz, he had not only protected the kulaks, who should have been deported long ago, he had also ignored several thefts from the state's grain stores, even though the thieves had been caught. Those kinds of thefts could be punished with deportation or even death, but Andreij had openly flouted the law and neglected to report the episode to the GPU. He had even accepted a young mother who had been classified as a Former Human Being into the collective farm and had fed her kulak children through all of last winter.

In his house he had hidden several things that made him a class enemy. The GPUs had dragged both Mother's sewing machine and a silver candelabra from the house, and the widow Svetlova had brazenly worn a zobel fur and had owned two big copper pots. Even one would have been a conspicuous luxury; two copper pots was a clear crime against the people, who had toiled in the mines to bring up precious metal for the industry.

The boys then tried to guess where Andreij would spend his time in deportation. Obdorsk, or Beresovo, or maybe Samarovo. The farther north it was, the worse it would be. People got gangrene and lost arms and legs in the Siberian cold, and that was true both for those who ended up in a prison camp and for the more fortunate ones who were deported but allowed to live as free men. Letters from Siberia were full of horrors.

For the widow, it was a different matter, or so Jegor claimed. True, she had been forced to depart in woolen socks and without either zobel fur or overcoat, thrown out on her ass and ordered to find a place to live outside the village. She had a bad record now, but she probably had an old mother someplace with whom she could seek shelter from the winter cold for her unborn child.

Olga sat stock-still, picking at her felt boots and trying not to think the incomprehensible. Her father wasn't a class enemy, and she didn't understand how it had come to be that he was one anyway. It wasn't easy either, to figure out why some of those who had been deported were to be pitied while others apparently were getting what they deserved. Every day offered new truths that grated against one another inside her head, as painfully as sharp stones under one's feet. The others seemed to have no problem understanding. Self-confident Jana, Jegor and Leda and Oxana, yes, even Sergej, that little shit, knew when you were supposed to smile proudly and when you had to duck your head in shame. Knew which truths you should grab on to and which ones you should let go.

Old truth: Olga's father is Andreij Trofimenko, a trusted man in the village, a loving father and a loyal husband.

New truth: Olga's father is Andreij Trofimenko, class enemy and traitor, deportee and Former Human Being, a lousy father and deceitful husband.

Unwelcome pictures began to swim past her inner eye, even

though she bit herself hard in the cheek and tried to think about the soy candy from Petrograd that Comrade Semienova had offered Oxana and her last week.

Her father living in a hole in the ground like the ones the Former Human Beings dug among the birch trees up in the hills. His hands that had split the year's first melon two summers ago in the garden of their little townhouse . . . in her imagination, those same hands were now black and stinking with gangrene, even as he held the sparkling red fruit between his fingers.

"Eat, my lovely," said Father and handed the melon to her while he smiled with a toothless mouth. His nose was as black as his fingers, and he smelled of rotting flesh and vodka.

"I feel sorry for the baby," Veronica said and shook her head sadly. In the battle against the kulaks and the capitalists, she had had a passionate skirmish with Sergej and had her kerchief pulled down over her shoulders. "That a mother would do that to her child."

"Save your pity," drawled Jegor. "The brat isn't even born yet, and maybe Svetlova still has time to go to a doctor in Kharkiv, and that's the end of that, and nothing will ever hurt it again."

"Shut up."

Olga knew she should keep her mouth shut, but the words shot out. Her voice broke, sounding stupid and babyish. She wished Oxana was here, but Oxana was in the kolkhoz, arranging yet another political meeting, and now Jana looked at her with a mixture of pity and glee.

"What's wrong? I thought you didn't like Svetlova."

Olga shrugged, got up and quickly brushed off her dress. Her fingers were red and numb because she had left her mittens in the schoolroom, and she had forgotten to hide her hands in her coat sleeves. Right now she couldn't feel them, but when she went inside, her fingers would hurt, and the skin would split and itch. To her amazement, Jana brought her face so close to Olga's that their foreheads almost touched, and Olga had time to think that now she would definitely get lice.

"You better watch out for yourself," whispered Jana. "Your father may be a class enemy, Olga, but your traitor sister has blood on her hands now. Her own family's blood. If I were you, I would watch my back around her."

NATASHA PULLED HER coat closer to her body and glanced at her watch. It was almost eleven, and she had been sitting on the steps here for an hour and a half already, but she didn't dare leave now. Not even to find a place to pee, though it was starting to feel pretty urgent. If she left . . . if she as much as looked away for a moment . . .

She had found the street; she was sure this was it. The little corner store, the miserable-looking birch trees along Jagtvejen's median strip. It was here. But the houses looked more alike than she had remembered. The same worn red-brick fronts, the same anonymous brown doors. There was no ugly yellow car parked on the street, and she had looked at all the intercoms without finding Nina's name. But sooner or later they had to come out, Nina or the husband or the children, and then she could ask. Then she would make them tell her where Katerina was.

She had pulled the hood of Robbie's grey sweatshirt over her head in order not to be recognized. It would have been better to sit in the Audi, but cars lined the street bumper to bumper, and she had had to park elsewhere. What would they think, the Danes inside their apartments, if they looked out their windows and saw her now? Would they think that she was homeless, like one of those people who periodically froze to death during Kiev's cold winters in a stairwell like the one she was huddling in now?

She had been surprised that there were also homeless people in Denmark. More, it seemed, than in Kiev. But maybe that was because there were fewer police. In Copenhagen there weren't two policemen on every other corner. Here people could camp out in peace and quiet with their bags and packs and cardboard to sit on. Was that what she looked like? She was beginning to smell that way, that was for sure.

BEAUTIFUL, BEAUTIFUL NATASHA.

That was her, and of course that was what Pavel had fallen for, even though he said back then that it was her eyes and her smile, quite simply *her* that he had fallen in love with.

He spoiled her and treated her like a lady. He brought her to the expensive stores in the mall under Independence Square and discussed what suited her best with the salespeople while Natasha stood there without saying anything, because if she opened her mouth, they would be able to tell that she wasn't from Kiev. The clothes were different from the ones she would have bought herself. Narrow skirts that reached her knees. Soft silk blouses and white shirts and glittering bracelets, wide belts and high-heeled shoes. Classic, he said, because Natasha was a "classic beauty." He said the same thing to the hairdresser, who apparently felt duty bound to tell her how much eyeliner and mascara it was appropriate to use in Kiev. What she was wearing was too much and too cheap, and had a tendency to clump on the lashes. And the lipstick should not be pink and glossy.

"You're not in Donetsk any longer, honey," the lady had said and told her about Dior and Elizabeth Arden and other companies she had never heard of. Then she had cut Natasha's hair shorter than she'd ever had it before, to her shoulders, and with new sharp angles and waves. The color was fine as it was—like a Ukrainian wheat field, with touches of brown and gold.

"From now on, you need to come see me every third week, honey. Or there'll be trouble. Hair like yours can look like a million dollars if you take care of it."

Pavel kissed the new hair and new color on her lips and said that she was completely perfect.

Only much later did she realize that he also loved her for her ignorance—all the things she didn't know about him, about the world. He loved her because she was beautiful and dumb, *because* she was seventeen and came from Kurakhovo. A woman from Kiev, a woman his own age, would have asked more questions. Natasha didn't question. She only loved. She loved him, she loved the apartment, she loved that he went to work every day and wrote in the newspapers about important topics and spoke with important people.

She kept the apartment so clean that everything shone. She changed the sheets every day, like in a hotel. And she cooked the way he wanted her to. Traditional, he called it. Beautiful braided paska bread for the holidays, borscht, cabbage rolls and little pancakes with fried farmers' cheese, honey and sour cream, jam or apple sauce. In return he took care of her. She didn't need to work in a dirty factory or stand in the unemployment line. Katerina was born in a private hospital with brilliant white towels in the bathroom; a drip of clear anesthesia was inserted into Natasha's spine and took away all pain and worries. To Natasha, that had been the final proof back then that her life really was a fairy tale, so far removed from those girls from Kurakhovo, who, in the coming years, would be lying on rusty hospital beds with dirty covers, bellowing like cows as they brought their children into the world in a flood of shit and blood and torn placenta.

Pavel held her hand through every single contraction, because that was what men did in Kiev, at least the educated ones. And when Katerina finally lay in her arms, Pavel looked at her with so much tenderness that it was almost more than she could bear.

Beautiful, beautiful, stupid Natasha.

She didn't know it then, but she had learned it now.

In this world, you were punished for your stupidity, and you were punished hard. That was just as true in Copenhagen as it was in Kiev.

IT WAS COLD sitting on the steps, but it still felt more natural than standing. She would have liked to have a smoke, a refugee habit she had picked up in the camp and which had intensified in prison. Cigarettes were fantastic props during life in captivity because they gave you the feeling that you were doing something other than just waiting. You pulled smoke into your lungs and blew it out again, and you turned the cigarette in your hand and looked at it while it got smaller and smaller.

A door opened, and for a brief moment, Natasha thought she saw Nina's slender figure step out onto the sidewalk. It was the same impatient toss of the head, the same quivering energy in the body, but it was still wrong. This was not a woman but a girl in skinny jeans, basketball sneakers and a heavy leather jacket. A boy followed in a baggy ski jacket and an eye-catching black mustache taped to his upper lip. And then finally a man that Natasha recognized with certainty as Nina's husband, even though he somehow had become thinner and older looking—dark eyes and a broad jaw under a black cap. He was dressed like a teenager in worn pale jeans and a yellow down jacket. He must be forty, thought Natasha, but Danish men dressed like boys, not men.

Michael had been an exception, of course. He preferred classic shirts and dark pants and expensive jackets that had to be dry-cleaned and pressed and steamed, and somehow she always managed to get it wrong so that he got angry or irritated. Maybe her life would have looked completely different if she had met a boy-man like Nina's husband instead. If someone like him had lived in the house next to

Anna's farm. Natasha doubted that Nina's husband had ever touched the nurse in a way she didn't like. If he had, Nina would probably have exited both the bedroom and the apartment and slammed the door behind her. That was a luxury Natasha had not been able to afford.

Nina's husband, son and daughter walked toward her without noticing her. The boy wore lurid electric-blue pants and a pair of ludicrously oversized shoes that would barely stay on. Still, he had that energy in his feet which she recognized from the boys at home. He kicked stones, balanced on the curb and made small, energetic jumps to smack a flat hand against the traffic signs.

She got up, went over to them. Attempted to smile.

"Is Nina home?" she asked in her best Danish. After more than two years, she understood most things, but Danish words still felt like slippery stones in her mouth—foreign objects that didn't belong.

"Why?" The man gave her a cool, measuring look.

Maybe Nina had asked him to be on guard. Maybe she had said he should keep his mouth shut and not reveal where Katerina was.

"Katerina," she said anyway and stood her ground, blocking their way on the sidewalk. "Tell me where my daughter is, please," she said in English.

The boy with the big black mustache stopped abruptly and looked questioningly at his father.

"What is she saying?" he said. "Dad, come on. We're going to be late."

Nina's husband definitely looked unfriendly now. He stepped into the road to get by her, with the boy and the scowling teenage girl right behind him.

"I don't know what you're talking about. Nina doesn't live here anymore, and I don't know where your daughter is."

They couldn't leave. She had waited for hours; they couldn't leave.

Natasha grabbed the boy's sleeve and held on. "Have you seen Katerina? My girl? Is she at your house?"

The boy attempted to pull away, but she had a good grip on the soft down jacket and held him back. Grabbed hold with her other hand as well, on the collar under the boy's chin. His skin felt burning hot against her stiff, cold fingers. His eyes were wide open in surprise.

Then Nina's husband shoved her hard, forcing her to take a step back. Natasha's eyes slid from the boy and back to the man. She could see he was surprised, but he was also angry now. His eyes were dark, narrow slits in his winter-pale face.

For a moment she was sure he would hit her. Punish her, like Michael would have done. Pavel had never touched her, of course he hadn't—he had been too busy constructing pink castles in the air where violence would have clashed with the stage sets. Michael had had different ideas, and maybe Nina's husband wasn't as unlike him as she had first thought.

Natasha let go of the boy's jacket and took a step backward. "Please, tell me. I need to see Nina. She know where is my daughter. I have to talk to her," she said in her best English.

Nina's husband was walking away, shielding the children from her with his body. "Welcome to the club," he said over his shoulder. "The rest of this family has tried to make contact with her for the last fifteen years. So good luck with that. I have no idea where she is, and I don't care."

Natasha touched the knife in her pocket. But he was already on his way with both children ahead of him as if they were chickens he was shooing into a henhouse. Only the girl looked back.

THE GYM SMELLED of apple fritters and coffee and faintly of sour gym sneakers. Nina's gaze moved like a radar shadow across everything that was shorter than a four and a half feet: Spider-Men, musketeers, carrots with legs, Tiggers, pirates, a slightly dated Ninja Turtle, a pumpkin—recycled from Halloween?—and a couple of witches, a Darth Vader and a knight in a silver helmet and a homemade coat of chain mail. My God, Nina thought, how many hours had it taken to sew all those key rings onto the leather vest—and what did it weigh?

She had to check the knight and Vader twice, but then she was certain.

It was 11:02, and Anton wasn't there.

The noise was earsplitting. Excited children's voices climbed to a register that would make any soprano envious, and the parents' attempts at chatting had begun building in a slow but relentless crescendo in order to be heard above the children and themselves.

"Coffee?" yelled a mother from Anton's class and handed her a mug without waiting for an answer. "Where is Anton?"

"He's coming with Morten," Nina yelled back and saw the mother's expression change because she suddenly remembered the divorce.

"Oh, right," the mother said. "But how nice that you can do this together."

"Yes." Nina smiled mechanically. 11:06, and still no Anton. Morten was usually early for these kinds of things.

"There's Minna," said the mother and pointed. "She wanted to be a shower stall this year. Isn't it amazing how creative children can be?"

Minna. Yes, that was her name. A highly energetic and slightly trying little red-haired girl whose freckled face right now was sticking out of a box affixed with a flapping plastic curtain, real faucets, a soap dish and a little steel basket with shampoo and a sponge. The red hair was, of course, crammed into a flowered bathing cap.

"We got most of it for next to nothing at IKEA," said Minna's mother happily. "She even has a spray bottle, so she can squirt people if they want a real bath experience."

"Fantastic," said Nina. 11:14. The teachers had already begun to herd the children toward one end of the room, where they were lining up. Two barrels hung from the rafters on blue nylon ropes, waiting to be beaten to a pulp in time-honored Danish carnival tradition. At least there were no longer live cats inside them, thought Nina with an involuntary shudder, looking at the grinning black paper cats that adorned the outside of the barrels.

"Little ones to the right and bigger ones to the left," shouted one of the phys ed teachers, a tall man from southern Jutland called Niels, who was currently dressed in a Robin Hood cape and a green crepe paper hat with a pheasant feather.

"Am I little or big?" peeped a Tigger who was definitely no more than four.

"You are little."

"What about meee?" hollered a brawny nine-year-old, a Frankenstein's monster rubber mask his only nod to dressing up.

"What do you think, Marcus? Back in line you go. You were behind Selma."

There he was. There they were, all three of them, Morten and Ida and Anton. Ida had not stooped to fancy dress, but the fact that she was here at all was a major concession. Anton was wearing a pair of blue overalls with extra big yellow buttons sewed on, a red shirt, white gloves and a red cap with a white M on the front. His eyebrows had been drawn on with a thick makeup pencil so they looked like black slugs, and a bushy black mustache decorated his eight-year-old upper lip.

Nina's heart flickered in her chest.

"Mom," he yelled and came racing through the crowd. "Look! I'm Super Mario!"

"Yes, you definitely are," she said. She couldn't stop her hands, which, entirely following their own agenda, tugged at the blue suspenders, touched his warm cheek, rested against his soft neck under the pretext of straightening his cap. He didn't want a hug, she knew that, not here, not now, while all his friends were watching. But her hungry hands couldn't quite let him be.

She could tell by Morten's tight shoulders that something was wrong, but she didn't know if it was simply because she was here. Should she have asked? No, damn it. She had a right to come see her son hit the carnival barrel without asking him first.

"Hi, Mom," said Ida.

A year ago it had been "Nina." Now she was Mom again. Ida also looked a little less like a caricature than usual—not so much doomsday mascara and a T-shirt that wasn't actually black.

"Hi, sweetie. It was nice of you to come."

Ida shrugged. "I've promised to cheer for the little maggot if he gets to be the Cat King," she said, referring to the honor bestowed on the child whose blow finally cracked the barrel. "Plus I made the cap."

"He looks totally cool," said Nina and, to her horror, felt a burning flood of tears well up. She had to control herself! Ida would never forgive her if she suddenly started blubbering in front of most of the school.

Anton had already moved on, in a peculiar gait that was supposed to look like the way Super Mario moved in his favorite Nintendo game. Ida gave her a quick fist bump on the shoulder—the height of teenage affection—and waved at another big sister who stood at a careful distance from the noise and the barrels, contriving to look bored.

"Millie! Hi, Millie!"

As soon as Ida was out of hearing, the question jumped out of Nina's mouth without permission. "What's wrong?"

Morten didn't answer right away. "I didn't know you were coming," he said.

"Of course I was coming. I usually do."

"When you have time . . ."

"Morten, can't we . . ."

"I may need to move," he said.

Her chest felt wooden. "Where?" she croaked. "Why?"

"I don't know," he said. "Far enough to rescue the children from your war zone."

"*What?*"

"You promised to stop."

"I have stopped. The network doesn't exist anymore. Besides, a clinic is being established, a clinic where people can be treated anonymously . . ."

He didn't even look at her. She could see that his entire body was on high alert. He was repressing an anger so great that there was barely room for it inside him.

"What?" she asked. "What is it you think I've done?"

"She touched Anton. She grabbed him. Do you know how frightened he was?"

"Who?"

"I don't know. Some disturbed woman who said she was your friend. She was looking for her daughter."

Natasha. It couldn't be anyone else.

"Where did you see her?"

Now Morten gaped at her. "Oh, I knew it," he said. "You know what? It would almost be easier if you were an alcoholic. Then at least there'd be Antabus."

Bang. The first blow connected with the decorated barrels to general cheering and applause. Bang, bang.

Nina stared at Super Mario Anton, almost wishing that Morten *would* move away with the children, at least for a while. Until . . . until this was over. Natasha had grabbed Anton. What would have happened if Anton had been alone? Natasha was desperate. Exactly how desperate Nina could tell from her own irregular heartbeats. And she no longer had any idea where Natasha's limits lay. "A child for a child—give me my daughter, and you can have your son." Would she do that?

Nina had no idea.

NATASHA EASED THE knife blade between the door and the doorframe and forced it. The frame shattered, and with a few extra wriggles, the pawl broke loose from the lock.

There had been no answer when she had tried the buzzer downstairs or later when, after making it into the stairwell on the heels of someone's pizza delivery, she rang the bell at the nurse's front door. But she had to check. She had to know. She walked rapidly down the hall, throwing all the doors wide open.

No one was there.

In the kitchen there were still dirty dishes by the sink, and someone had left the milk out on the counter. The girl's room was surprisingly neat, almost neater than the rest of the apartment. The walls were dark purple; all the furniture was black. Small, powerfully scented candles stood in red and orange glasses. The boy's room was one big chaos of sheets, LEGO blocks, stuffed animals and small plastic figurines that it seemed he collected; most of them looked to be some kind of monster.

Nowhere did she see anything that could be Katerina's. And the double bed in the bedroom only had one pillow on it.

Nina's husband had told the truth. Nina didn't live here anymore. And this wasn't where she had gone with Katerina.

Natasha knew that she shouldn't stay here, that every second increased her risk of being discovered. But her bladder was about to burst. She found the little bathroom at the end of the hall, closed the door and peed so hard, it splashed in the bowl.

Her thoughts were leaping in all directions, like the grasshoppers in the long grass next to the railroad in Kurakhovo. Katerina wasn't here. Nina wasn't here. She had broken into someone's apartment for nothing.

Alarms. Were there alarms? She hadn't heard anything, but perhaps not all alarms rang as earsplittingly as the one Pavel had installed in the apartment in Kiev.

IT HAD BEEN of no use. During the last eighteen months they had lived there, they were burgled four times. The first time she had been at the doctor's with Katerina and came home to an open door and an apartment that had been searched.

"In the middle of the day," she had said to Pavel when she called him, with a childish sense that break-ins were supposed to happen after dark. "Should I call the police?"

"No," said Pavel. "I'll take care of it. Where are you now?"

"In the apartment," she sniffed. "Where else?"

"Take Katerina to the park," he said. "Or wherever it is you usually go. Do it now."

"But the door won't shut. And everything is a mess."

"Just do as I say. I'll come get you when everything has been taken care of."

And he did. Everything had been cleaned up, the door was repaired and there was a new lock. If it weren't for the smell of fresh wood and paint, you would think it had never happened. He had even bought shashlik, rice and salad from the Tatar restaurant in the square so she didn't need to think about dinner. And when she wanted to talk about it, to tell him how afraid she had been, to tell him about the open door that she at first thought she had forgotten to lock, about the sensation in her throat when she realized that someone had been there, someone had gone through their things and taken her new iPod and earrings and necklace . . . then he had hushed her.

"We'll forget this," he said. "You can't worry about things like that. Life is too short."

The second time, he had bought extra locks and a safety chain. The third time she had been home alone. She had fallen asleep on the couch and woke up to the sound of a screwdriver splintering the doorframe. She had stood in the hallway screaming hysterically—"I'll call the police, I'll call the police"—so loudly that Katerina had woken up and begun to cry.

"There's a lot of crime in Kiev," said Pavel. "There's no avoiding it."

The fourth time . . . she didn't want to think about the fourth time.

SHE WASHED HER hands and her stiff, cold face and dried them on one of Nina's towels. Nina's husband hadn't wanted to say where Nina lived now. But sooner or later she'd have to go to work. Sooner or later she would have to drive down the narrow, winding road to the camp in her ugly yellow car that was only half the size of Natasha's stolen Audi.

More waiting. But Natasha had become very good at waiting.

UKRAINE, 1934

THERE IS NOTHING greater, nothing worse than death.

Or maybe there was. Maybe hunger was worse. It hurt when fat and muscle shrank away from your bones. In hunger there was, beyond the pain, also the fear of death, and maybe it was really fear that trumped both hunger and death, Olga thought. Maybe fear was worst.

Olga turned over one more time—carefully, so as not to wake up Oxana and Kolja. She was in her old sleeping place in the house in the village, on the bed shelf above the huge brick oven. The wood shavings in the mattress were fresh, and for once the lice kept their distance. In a way everything was as it had been before, and yet nothing was the same. The house still smelled of Father and Svetlova and the life they had lived together, and Father's absence filled the whole house—on this night worse than ever. Butka, who worked down at the lumber mill, had come to see Mother today and had told her that Father had not been sent to Siberia, after all, as Olga had imagined. In her thoughts she had followed him in the cattle car to the endless snow-covered steppes. She had felt his thirst and hunger and had hoped . . . had even prayed to the nonexistent God to protect him and bring him home whole, with all his arms and legs and toes and fingers still there.

In reality, he had made it no farther than to the GPU's headquarters in Sorokivka, where he had been held in the cellars for a while before finally being tied to a pole and shot. That had happened yesterday. Butka was sure, he said, because he had seen it with his own eyes, even though it had been hard for him to recognize Father. He had been terribly thin after just three weeks in prison. But they had shouted his name, Andreij Trofimenko, counterrevolutionary and Former Human Being, and he had confessed to all the charges, they said.

Mother cried, and Butka stood awkwardly in the living room with his fur hat in his hands, but Olga refused to believe it.

"Prove it," she said softly. "Prove that it is Father who is dead."

It sounded so terrible when she said it. Real.

At first Butka looked a bit uncertain, but then he seemed to remember something, dug into his goatskin coat and pulled out Father's little red party book. He handed it to Mother with a solemn expression.

"They let me bring this to you," said Butka softly. He neglected to mention the widow. She was gone now, and it was as if she had never existed. "It was the only thing he thought to take with him when they came to get him."

Mother opened the book with shaking hands, then let it drop to the floor. It remained there until late in the evening when Olga had surreptitiously picked it up. Small, dark flecks of blood covered the book's cover like freckles. Inside was a picture of Father with his hair combed back and a steady gaze that looked as if it was focused on a finer, better future—the one he had once said he would build with his own hands.

Olga had hidden the party book under her pillow. She could feel it as she lay here now thinking about hunger, fear and death, and what had been the worst for Father as he hung there on the pole and waited for the bullets to drill through his body. She was too tired to cry anymore.

She turned over again in the dark and bumped into Oxana's knee under the blankets. Oxana moved a bit in her sleep, but her breathing was heavy and calm. The familiar sweet scent of her breath, skin and hair surrounded her, and suddenly made it difficult for Olga to breathe.

Oxana had cried today too; big, shiny tears had run from her cornflower-blue eyes. She was the one who had opened the door and received condolences from the few neighbors who had dared to come by in the course of the day. Jana's mother had arrived with vegetable soup and freshly baked bread, and Oxana had answered virtuously, had carried the soup to the table and offered tea from the samovar and had drip-drip-dripped her tears into the tea and across the floor.

Olga breathed carefully through her mouth and turned away from the spicy scent of thyme and garlic and warm girl-body. She tried not to touch Oxana, not to think about her. Not to think about Father and not to think about Grandfather, who had been lying there for three weeks after the accident with his leg, unable to either live or die. He had become feverish and had drunk a lot of vodka, and in his fever had staggered over to the barn to brain the cow so the Reds wouldn't get her. Poor Zorya had been hit with the sledgehammer first across one knee, which had collapsed, and then twice on her broad, quivering neck, until he had finally managed to aim at her forehead and finish her off. The farm and the tools had gone to the state, but they had eaten meat at Grandfather's funeral.

Don't think, she told herself.

She tried to just lie there, completely still, and listen to the wind that grabbed hold of the house and made the woodwork sing and creak under the sky, which Olga knew was black and cloudless and filled with stars.

"Don't be angry at Uncle Stalin," Oxana had said. "The Revolution demands sacrifices from us all."

"IS SHE DIFFICULT?" Mikael Nielsen had asked when Søren turned over the watch to him back at the house on Kløvermosevej.

"She has actually been pretty cooperative," Søren had assured him. Now he wondered whether he should have warned Nielsen about Nina's oddities anyway. Small talk and bedside manners were not Nielsen's forte, nor did his restless nature adapt particularly well to the long, dull hours of surveillance during which nothing happened. But he was Søren's man, and he was available and willing to sacrifice his Sunday, and thanks to all his gadgetry, he saw pretty much everything that moved, even though he might not look particularly alert. He had immediately distributed a number of small webcams both indoors and outside, and if Søren knew him at all, he was currently engaged in tracking them all simultaneously on his self-designed tablet computer, colloquially known as The Gizmo—possibly playing Battleship or indulging in a game of chess at the same time.

Søren would have preferred to be there himself. But he needed to talk with Babko, and in spite of the new era of bicultural trust and peace, he had no intention of letting the Ukrainian anywhere near Rina. Apart from Søren's own people, at this moment only Heide and Heide's boss knew where the girl was. He had promised to bring both Nina and Rina in for a more thorough interview Monday morning if the girl's health allowed.

Babko had shaved and generally looked fresher and sharper today—Søren was in no way sure that the same thing could be said about him.

"I managed to get through most of it," he said, poking the substantial pile of papers. The printer had been going for almost two hours; it wasn't among the fastest, but it had been easier than going to Søborg to use the one at the office. He was still better at reading things on paper, and when he was also faced with a linguistic challenge, he needed all the help he could get. His reading speed had definitely not been optimal.

"Did you find it interesting?" asked Babko.

"Much of it, yes."

Pavel Doroshenko had been born and had grown up in a little village south of Kiev. His father was a dairy worker, and his mother had been employed at the same dairy for most of her adult life. The most unusual thing about the family was the mother's background. She was originally from Galicia in eastern Ukraine, one of the local minority of ethnic Germans who had been blown hither and thither by various national and military storms around the time of the Second World War. First the area had been under Polish rule, then the Soviets came, then the Germans, with a short-lived attempt to create an independent Ukrainian state, and finally the area had again been absorbed by the Soviet Union. Galicia's history was more turbulent than most, and Søren wondered how it had shaped Pavel's mother.

"You wrote 'Mama's boy' in your notes," said Søren. "Why?"

"She died in nineteen ninety-seven, so it's an entirely secondhand impression. I spoke with the father; he is still alive but hadn't been in contact with Pavel for several years. The marriage wasn't exactly harmonious. It's a small town, everybody knows everybody's business, and if Pavel was a ladies' man, he didn't get it from strangers."

"But they didn't get divorced?"

"No. You're familiar with the *propiska* system?"

"Yes." During the Soviet era, one needed an internal passport, a propiska, to live in a certain place. The propiska simultaneously served as right of residence to a specific address. "Is that still in use in Ukraine?"

"It was officially judged to be unconstitutional in two thousnd and one, but not a lot changed. So with certain modifications, yes. The short answer is that even if Pavel's parents *had* divorced, they couldn't just split up. At least not without exchanging the propiska on their little house for two propiskas to much less desirable apartments. Pavel's mother defended her right to the house with tooth and claw, understandably so. The result was that they lived like a dog and a cat. Funnily enough, most of the villagers sided with the husband, perhaps because her Ukrainian was pretty poor. She'd grown up with German and Polish, of course. Pavel was called Niemcy, 'the German,' in school, or 'the Nazi brat' if they were being particularly cruel. And apparently they spoke German together, his mother and he. She called him Paul. So you could say he grew up strongly motivated to succeed. He was going to show them all."

"And he did, didn't he?" said Søren, thinking of a few pieces he had found on the Web. German television in particular had apparently used Pavel as a local expert a few times. "A career as a journalist, a good income, an apartment in Kiev and a young, beautiful wife . . . to them, he must have looked every inch the successful media star."

"At least to his mother he did, though she didn't get to see the final chapters."

"I've looked at everything you found on him," said Søren. "His stories are generally pretty black and white, aren't they?"

Pavel Doroshenko never seemed to just write about people. He wrote about villains or heroes. The heroes acted "without thought of personal gain" and "with great personal courage" and were "tireless," "selfless" and "determined," whether he was describing a fireman in Chernobyl, a local businessman, the director of an orphanage, a mayor who fought crime in his city or just a retiree who had defended himself against a pickpocket. The villains were similarly described as "calculating" and "greedy"; they were "caught in their own snares" and could often look forward to "many years behind bars"; people foolish enough to defend them were described as "collaborators" or "coconspirators" without it being clear what the conspiracy consisted of. Pavel fairly often cited family background or ethnicity, creating the impression that evil was genetic rather than personal. To Søren, the rhetoric seemed oddly old-fashioned and pretty tiresome.

"You think so?" said Babko. "A lot of people write like that. At least in Ukraine."

"I haven't been able to find anything that explains Savchuk's interest in his widow."

"No, me neither."

"Is he another Gongadze?" Søren said, although broken fingers and a heart attack did not quite seem to match the gruesomeness of the decapitation of that particular heroic journalist.

Babko shook his head. "I don't think so. The people he would attack were mostly nationalists. At the beginning of his career, he was more politically focused—accusing the early nationalists of being a collection of Kosak-romantics, bumpkins and anti-Semites. Later his attacks became more personal, though funnily enough, most of the people he attacked still belonged to the Orange faction. The Blues—that is, the more ethnic Russian- and Moscow-friendly wing—he never wrote much about them, although there would be no shortage of material if he had wanted to have a go at them."

"Are his personal beliefs a factor here?" asked Søren.

"Possibly. Or it might just have been to please his audience. For a time, he lived and worked in Donetsk, which is a predominantly

Russian-speaking area. His motives could also have been more narrowly financial. There was and still is a lot of money flowing out of Moscow to willing mouthpieces in the media world. How else did you think Yanukovytsj managed to get himself reelected a mere six years after the Orange Revolution threw him out?"

Was that the pattern Søren's tired brain had tried to decipher last night? No. He didn't have Babko's local knowledge and couldn't automatically recognize the party colors of the people Doroshenko had written about.

"I wonder about two things," he said. "First of all, I think his style changes. It becomes even more purple yet at the same time less precise, wallowing in phrases like 'could it be that . . .' or 'might not stand up to closer examination.' In his earlier articles, he is sharper and produces names and facts. Secondly, as his income grows, the apartment in Kiev and so on . . . he writes less and less, and for more local and smaller media. The year before he died, he published almost exclusively on some Web news site, what was it called . . ."

"*Velyka Tayemnitsya*. The Big Secret, in the English version."

"Yes. It seems paradoxical."

"That's because he is no longer a journalist in the true sense of the word. He was producing *kompromat*."

Søren's inner dictionary managed to provide a definition a second before he had to ask. *Kompromat*—by now a fairly old Russian abbreviation for "compromising material." A tactic in the information war that had roots all the way back to Stalin and which, in all its simplicity, consisted of digging up, fabricating and throwing as much dirt as possible at the person or persons with whom you were at war. American election campaigns were like Sunday school sessions by comparison.

"It's still used a lot?" he asked.

"Oh, yes. Big Bizniz. Now also as a more private enterprise. And the richest *kompromat* producers are usually the ones who don't print what they write."

"Blackmail?"

"Yep. As a *kompromat* producer, you always have two potential customers—the person who has paid for the dirt and the person you're planning to throw it at. The latter usually pays more."

"And the vague articles that just make suggestions but don't name names . . ."

"Those are warning shots. They let the victim know what he can expect if he doesn't pay up."

Søren looked at the pile of articles with renewed interest. That meant that the "warning shots" offered up a number of people who had good reason for murdering Pavel Doroshenko and possibly also for pursuing his widow. That is, if Søren and Babko could figure out whom the warnings were directed at.

14:11. EXACTLY A minute had passed since she last checked. Not good.

The sky was so thunderously grey that it might as well have been evening. Nina knew that she checked her watch more frequently on days when the sun didn't give her a natural sense of the time, but this was more than that. She pulled over to the side of the road, and only then did she realize that she had subconsciously been headed for Fejøgade.

Fuck.

"You don't live there anymore," she told herself. She said it out loud because she wanted her subconscious to *listen* this time. Damn it. If Morten saw her, he would probably think she was stalking them. Like one of those rejected ex-husbands who went home and polished their army reserve rifle and put on their best clothes before blasting off the backs of their skulls. That is, if they didn't take out their whole family first. Contemptible shitheads.

She carefully placed her hands on the steering wheel again. 14:11. Fuck.

"I just want to take care of them."

And they said that too, the men with the army reserve rifles. I just wanted to take care of them. When they shot the children, it wasn't to *harm* them. Shitheads.

14:12.

But the thought that Natasha had been there. At her home. Well, okay, at Morten's and the children's home.

14:12. Fuck. Fuck. Fuck.

I just want to take care of them.

"Are you having a nervous breakdown?" she asked out loud in English.

Why she was speaking English to herself she didn't know. And then she actually did know. English was the language of crisis. In Dadaab and elsewhere. And flying conditions were lousy.

"Nina, damn it."

She breathed very consciously now. Long, deep breaths. "Allll the way down to the pit of your stomach," as an instructor had once said. Panic-reducing big breaths.

The black anxiety inside her paid no attention. Nina didn't get it. Natasha wasn't more dangerous than the Finnish psychopath who had kidnapped Ida last year. And in that situation she had been able to think and act; she had done what was necessary for Ida to be rescued. Natasha was no more dangerous. Definitely not. Natasha was just a poor Ukrainian girl who had landed in some bad shit.

A poor Ukrainian *mother*, Nina reminded herself. And you have taken her child.

14:13.

She knew that it wasn't always the obvious crises that made people crack. An Iranian man who had survived multiple arrests, torture and threats without breaking down had completely lost it and had tried to smash a radiator one evening in the Coal-House Camp's recreation room. Afterward he explained, crying and incoherent, that it was because the noise from a defective valve reminded him of machine-gun fire.

But you haven't been tortured, she reminded herself. So how about turning down the drama a notch or two?

Outside on Jagtvejen traffic glided by in its lazy Sunday rhythm. A mother passed her with two carnival-costumed children, one in a stroller, the other lagging a few feet behind on tired cat paws.

For the rest of the school carnival, Nina had barely been able to keep it together. She had smiled and clapped for Anton's sake. He had been so caught up in the barrel-smashing and apple-bobbing and all the other hullaballoo that he hadn't noticed anything. But Ida had immediately spotted that something was wrong.

"What have you done now?" she asked, lashing out at Nina with all the old hostility that had seemed to be receding.

"Ida!" said Morten. "Speak nicely to your mother."

Nina felt a surge of wobbly and yet more destabilizing gratitude to him for defending her, even if the defense did sound a bit tired and hollow because he basically agreed with Ida. As soon as the bottom had fallen out of Anton's barrel, releasing oranges in all directions, she had kissed Super Mario on his cap and raced out the door.

Would you take my child, Natasha?

And Natasha answered her, a whispering voice somewhere inside: Why not? You took mine.

"No," Nina protested. "You *asked* me to take care of her. That's what I've done. Just that." But it was a lie, a big, fat lie. When the gates to Fejøgade had been shut in her face, banishing her from what right now seemed a perfect Eden, though it hadn't been so at the time . . . in that moment of despair and rejection, it had been Rina she had clung to. There had been so many nights when she had slept next to Rina ostensibly "to keep an eye on that asthma," but really because her own bed in the new-divorcée apartment had been unbearably lonely and impossible to sleep in.

So no, she couldn't go to Fejøgade. But the thought of returning to Søren's tidy suburban home made her panic accelerate. Magnus was there, she thought. Magnus would have to manage a little longer. He had a caring but more professional relationship to Rina.

She could go get the asthma medicine. Yes, that's what she would do. They had already used more than they should have, and they couldn't afford to run out. The drive back and forth would consume over an hour of unruly, fundamentally un-checkable time, and by then she might have calmed down a bit.

She started the engine again and headed for the Coal-House Camp. The time was 14:19.

UKRAINE, 1935

STOMP, STOMP, STOMP.

Olga stared down at the frozen wheel tracks as she walked. It wasn't all that far from the school to their old house on the outskirts of the village, certainly not anywhere near as far as it had been to Grandfather's farm up in the hills. And yet it felt farther.

Her heart beat hard and fast under her coat, and she increased her tempo, forced herself to breathe slowly and deeply, forced herself not to run. The heavy white blanket of snow that had fallen in the night hushed all sound, but she still caught most of it. Oxana's steady, confident steps to her right. A door that opened and closed in the house next to the cooperative shop. A quiet conversation between two men over by the sawmill. She could hear the way they stomped their feet and clapped their hands hard together to stave off the cold. Their cigarette smoke hung in the ice-cold air like a faint bluish veil.

They walked quickly. Olga because she was afraid. Oxana more likely because she was angry.

COMRADE SEMIENOVA LOVED Oxana. Leda and Jegor loved Oxana, and Mother and Kolja loved her too. But that winter it was as if everyone else had begun to hate her.

It had begun with Sergej's stone, the day the GPU had come for Fedir and the rest of his family. And after that the hatred had grown.

Although Olga caught only a sort of echo of it, as if the hostility bounced off Oxana and hit her instead, she felt it as a resistance in her body that made it difficult to move and breathe. It showed in all the little gestures, she had discovered. Men stuck their hands in their pockets and turned away. Conversations ceased. Smiles faltered and eyes were averted when Oxana and she walked by. People didn't yell or call names anymore; the hatred was in the silence and in the air she breathed into her lungs. So it wasn't until she was inside, at home with Oxana and Kolja and Mother, that she could breathe freely.

Uncle Grachev's house had become a dangerous place to pass, because even though Father and he had often argued about who would provide bread and vodka for the old folk, they had had a lot in common and enjoyed drinking and playing cards in the evening. Uncle Grachev was Father's brother. He had a huge beard and an odd, hiccupping laughter, and he used to pinch Olga and Oxana much too hard on the cheek. Olga had also seen him pinch Mother's behind when he was really drunk and had lost both kopeks and rubles, but Mother had never paid much attention, and luckily Grachev had his own wife, who was named Vira and was big and strong as an ox and ruled over both Grachev and the three large cousins with a firm hand. Their house was also big enough that Grandfather and Grandmother Trofimenko could live there, and when Mother and Father and Olga and Oxana and Kolja had first come to Mykolayevka in the fall, Vira and Grachev had invited the whole family to celebrate the first harvest after the great hunger. They had had honey cakes and tea and had listened to Cousin Fyodor's stories about his time in the army in Afghanistan. To think that the Afghan women were dressed in tents and were only allowed to see the world through a mesh of horsehair, while the men sat around smoking water pipes! Unimaginable wonders like that were blissful when served with tea and cake.

Olga missed Vira and Fyodor and even Grachev, in spite of the cheek-pinching, but since Father's death their house had been closed to Olga as well as Oxana. Vira pursed her lips together when they met her in the street, and the two youngest cousins, Vitja and Pjotr, ran between the houses with Sergej and threw hard, little icy snowballs at Olga and Oxana and even at little Kolja when he came along. Once Vitja had pushed Oxana into the open gutter, so she had fallen on the layers of frozen shit from the Lihomanovs' house.

Olga and Oxana always walked by as quickly as they could, making sure not to expose themselves unnecessarily; they were especially careful with their throats, eyes and cheeks, which they covered as best they could by bending their heads, hunching their shoulders and pulling their kerchiefs close around their faces. It was no longer a good idea to stop and warm their hands or chat with the other girls. Even Leda and Elizaveta, who, like Oxana, were eager young pioneers, steered clear of them in the open street.

The worst thing was that Olga liked Vitja and Pjotr and Fyodor and Grachev and Jana. Even now, even when they were being so awful to her. Last summer, before all the trouble with Father and the widow, she and Pjotr had gone down to the river together to fish several times. Once in a while they caught one of the fat barbel, a fish that could get so big, it required all the strength and concentration an eleven-year-old boy could muster to drag it to shore. Other times they had to make do with small fry that Mother made into fish soup with the head, tail, eyes, guts and the lot.

But that was over now too.

STOMP, STOMP.

Olga knew that she would be able to see their house now if she raised her head. Once home, she and Oxana would be responsible for building a fire in the oven, collecting water at the well if it wasn't frozen over, or melting snow on the stove if it was. Mother wouldn't be home until the pigs were fed for the last time that day.

She placed one felt boot in front of the other and tried to calculate how many steps were left. Probably about a hundred steps to the Petrenkos' house and from there another twenty to their garden fence. She fought the desire to look up. And then it came anyway, the sound she had feared since Comrade Semienova had closed the school door behind them.

Running feet in the snow.

Coming from behind, from the shortcut by the shoemaker's house.

The next second Olga felt the first hard blow against her shoulder. Little Sergej had caught up to them and now ran right behind them, buzzing like a wasp around rotten plums. Olga tried to slap him, which made Sergej laugh hilariously.

"Oxana," he said, "you're so good in school, you must also know that Noah had three sons. What was it they were called, Oxana?"

Now Pjotr and Vitja had arrived and were blocking their path. Olga also saw Jana's big brother Vanja and felt a new prick of terror. Vanja was seventeen and as broad-shouldered as a grown man.

"Come on, Oxana. What were they called? Sing for us."

Sergej yanked Oxana's kerchief down around her shoulders so she stood with her head bared. A lock of blonde hair had been torn from the tight braid at her neck and flapped across her face. Her eyes flashed angrily at Sergej and the other boys. Her mouth was a narrow black line in her pale face.

"Leave us alone," she said and tried to push her way past Pjotr. "Or I'll report you to the GPU. You have no right to bother me and Olga."

Vitja hit Oxana so hard across the mouth that her lip split and blood dripped down into the snow. Olga halted as if paralyzed.

"What were Noah's sons called, Oxana? Answer!"

Oxana pressed her felt glove to her lip and glared furiously at Vitja.

"Every idiot knows that Noah's sons were called Sem, Kam and Jafet," she said finally.

Sergej's little pockmarked face contorted in a sneaky grimace that revolted Olga. If only he had died of pox or hunger typhus or something even worse. It seemed to her that cruelty almost radiated out from his small, skinny body.

"Then I must be an idiot," yelled Sergej triumphantly. "I thought Noah's sons were called Sem, Kam and *Judas*." He hit himself across the forehead. "But you know that better than I do, Oxana. Thank you."

Sergej's words seemed to hit harder than Vitja's fist, because now Oxana blushed, and for the first time, she lowered her eyes. The loose strands of wheaten hair blew in the wind. Vitja gave her a vicious shove, so that Oxana lost her balance and had to fight to remain standing.

"Leave us alone," screamed Olga. She was afraid now. This wasn't like the other times, when ice chunks and rocks had hit them from secret hiding places. This time they were standing in the middle of the street. Two workers from the kolkhoz walked by, and Olga knew who they were and wanted to turn to them for help, but it was as if they looked right through her. They were talking and smoking and continued on without stopping. Now she noticed cousin Fyodor and Uncle Grachev a bit farther up the road, standing with parted legs and folded arms.

"Shut up," screamed Petjr. "Just shut your mouth."

He brought his fist down on Olga, but she managed to turn away from him so he hit her shoulder instead of her face. Then he grabbed hold of both kerchief and hair and yanked her head back hard. She fell. Pjotr dragged her across the trampled, hard-packed snow of the road and didn't let her go until she lay in the frozen sewage gutter with her face pressed against the ice. She could hear the sound of blows against Oxana's body, some hushed by overcoat and mittens, others clearer as they hit her face and other exposed bits of skin, but Olga didn't dare look up. She just stayed where she was like a coward hunched in the snow until she heard Vitja swear faintly; he was out of breath.

"Damn. We better get out of here," he said.

Olga lifted her head in time to see little Sergej kick Oxana in the stomach one last time before he set off running down Shoemaker Alley with the others. Farther down the road she could see the reason for their sudden departure: two riders down by the sawmill wearing the easily recognizable uniforms of the GPU, rifles over their shoulders.

Olga got up. The snow had crept in under her jacket and kerchief and now ran in small, cold rivulets down her neck and chest. Oxana lay a little distance off. In her overcoat and thick felt boots, she looked like a lifeless pile of clothes in the middle of the road, but she finally moved, stuck a leg out to one side, steadied herself with her hands and raised herself into a sitting position. They hadn't killed her.

Oxana brushed the snow off her pummeled face. One of her eyebrows was bleeding, as was her nose, and her cheeks were as red as poppies from the cold and the many blows.

"What are you staring at?" she said. "Help me up."

THE AREA AROUND the children's barrack was still closed off, and plywood covered the place where the glass wall had been. That was just last night, thought Nina. Less than twelve hours ago.

She walked over to the policeman who stood at the barrier. "Excuse me," she said, "I just wanted to know . . . How is your colleague doing?"

He looked at her with a measured gaze. He was older than the plainclothes men from the Mondeo brigade, which she at first perceived as odd, perhaps from a vague impression that seniority was supposed to get you out of uniform at some point.

"I can't say," he said formally.

She'd have to ask Søren, then. Or even the cud-chewer with the iPad that wasn't an iPad.

She walked across the old parade ground to the clinic. Oddly, the door was locked. Officially, the clinic was closed on Sundays, it was true, but it was rarely possible to adhere to the scheduled hours. When 400 traumatized people were crowded together in sixteen barracks, there was almost always someone with a medical need. But apparently not right now.

She went in and unlocked the medicine cabinet, found the little blue plastic box labeled *Rina Dmytrenko* and put the Bricanyl and Spirocort in her pocket.

On the shelf below stood another little blue box with another name on the label. Nina knew it contained a ten-pill foil pack of Valium. And she knew the pack would not be used because the Somali woman for whom it was intended was no longer in the camp.

She closed her eyes for a moment. One small pale blue pill. Ten milligrams. That was all she needed to make her anxiety go away. And no one would notice that there was one pill missing from the packet next time the cabinet was put in order.

But she had to go back to Søren's house. She had to be able to drive. To function. After a traumatic night, and less than three hours of sleep . . . no. No pill.

She *was* a bit calmer now. She had only checked her watch three times in twenty minutes, which was close to normal. It had helped to move, as if driving eased certain ancient fight-or-flight instincts.

She locked up the clinic again. When she passed the guard in the gatehouse, little more than a shed, she waved casually. He nodded briefly and raised the barrier. He knew her and wasn't surprised to see her on a Sunday.

It had started to snow again. All that snow, all that ice. It would probably be late March before they saw the end of it. She drove slowly to give the Micra a chance to handle the curves. The wipers squeaked across the windshield, struggling to push the heavy flakes aside. She should probably have cleared the car of snow again before she started, but it hadn't had time to cool down completely while she collected the medicine, and the problem would be solved within a few minutes.

Suddenly there was a light among the trees in a place where it shouldn't have been. With a muted roar of acceleration, a car shot out in front of her into the middle of the road.

Where did he come from? Where the hell did he come from?

She took her foot off the gas, shifted gears and stomped the brake to the floor, knowing perfectly well that none of it would help. Desperately, she wrenched the steering wheel to the left and managed to turn the Micra part way around, but it still sailed forward into the collision. She hit the snowbank and the other car at the same time with a muffled bang, and was jerked forward against her seat belt and then thrown back as the airbag exploded in her face. There was the sound of shattering glass.

She couldn't move. The airbag's material stuck to her face, as if someone were trying to choke her with a pillow. Something had happened to her hand. The Micra's motor was still on, but the sound was a forced insect-like whine, and after a few seconds, it ceased. At that moment the front door was yanked open, and someone attempted to pull her out of the car. It didn't work; she was still wearing her seat belt. Nina herself groped for the release button. The belt sprang loose, and she slid sideways, upper body first, out of the damaged car.

Cold air, snow, grey sky over dark trees.

Was she missing time? Seconds, minutes? She tried to lift her left arm to check her watch but couldn't.

"Where is she? Katerina. Where?"

Nina was lifted up and thrown into the snow again. She still couldn't catch her breath.

It was Natasha. Natasha had driven into her car. Her brain couldn't quite comprehend it, but that must have been what had happened. The Ukrainian girl sat on top of her, a knee on either side of Nina's chest. Her hair hung in iced clumps, and the Barbie-beautiful face was merciless and set in stone. She let go of Nina with one hand, but only to bring up something made of bright, glittering steel. Nina felt a sharp jab under her chin, the coldness of metal against her neck.

"Tell me. Where?"

"The police," gasped Nina. "The police have her. I don't know where. In a safe place."

"*Brekhnya*. You're lying."

"No. Natasha, you're only making it worse for yourself. Go to the police, give yourself up. Otherwise, you will never get to see her again."

Natasha's eyes became totally black. Her hand jerked, and Nina felt the metal point pierce through her skin to her windpipe. She's going to kill you, Nina thought, coolly and clearly. It'll end now. You'll be found lying in the bloody snow, and Ida and Anton will cry at your grave. She suddenly saw it with excruciating clarity in her mind's eye, like an over-the-top sentimental scene in an American B movie. It was filmed from above. The camera zoomed down on the coffin and the open grave, people with black umbrellas, the freezing minister. Then a close-up of the two black-clad children, Ida holding Anton's hand and shouting, "You're a lousy mother! How could you do this?"

She didn't know what time it was.

Then the pressure disappeared from her neck. Natasha remained sitting on top of her a little while longer, and Nina could see that the murder weapon—the potential murder weapon—was an ordinary kitchen knife, the semi-Japanese kind with a triangular blade, especially efficient when cutting meat.

And windpipe cartilage, Nina said to herself. If Natasha had pushed it any farther in, you'd be dead now, or at least in a few minutes from now, choking on your own blood. Murdered with a kitchen tool by one of the so-called poor wretches you thought you could help.

"You must know," said Natasha in English. "I saw you. Katerina was in your car. I saw it! You know where she is, you must know, you must . . ."

"No," said Nina. "They keep that kind of thing secret. It has to be secret, or it's not safe."

"Safe," repeated Natasha.

"Yes. They'll keep her safe. I promise."

Natasha rose to her feet and disappeared from Nina's rather blurred field of vision. Nina heard seven or eight stumbling, uneven steps in the snow. She stayed completely still except for reflexive blinks when sharp snowflakes grazed her eyelashes. Listening.

The sound of a car door. A creaking, scratching sound of metal against metal, an uneven acceleration. She turned her head and felt a delayed snap in her neck, like a gear falling into place. From her unfamiliar frog's-eye perspective, she saw the back of the other car come closer, felt the spray of the snow thrown up by the rotating rear wheels. Then Natasha drove forward again, the back end of the car making a few slalom-like sweeps from side to side before the tail-lights disappeared behind the snowbanks at the next turn.

Nina lay unmoving. She didn't know if she was hurt. Right now all she could think was, She's gone, and I am still alive.

THERE WAS BLOOD on the knife. The nurse's blood. Natasha had cut her neck. Not as badly as she had done with Michael, nowhere near, but worse than she had meant to. Natasha felt a deep shiver spread from her core.

Blood.

Nina hadn't screamed, hadn't flailed her arms as Michael had done. She lay still in the snow, looking up at Natasha. Her voice was calm, as if it were a normal conversation and Natasha had just asked her a completely ordinary question.

"It has to be secret, or it's not safe."

Danes didn't lie as much as Ukrainians did. It was as if they believed the truth made them better human beings. A Dane would feel the need to tell a terminally ill patient the entire truth about the cancer that would choke him in the end. For his own good, of course. "I have to be honest," a Dane would say, and afterward he would be relieved, and the one who had received the truth would be crushed. Natasha preferred a considerate lie any day, but she hadn't encountered many of those either in or outside the Coal-House Camp.

Was the nurse lying now? Natasha narrowed her eyes, looking down at the sprawling figure she was straddling.

It has to be secret, or it's not safe.

"Safe," she said thoughtfully, trying to understand the word. Safe was to be in a place of safety, a place where no one could harm you. Where the Witch couldn't reach you. But the price was that it was secret, and no one could know where you were.

That was a calculation she understood completely. It was in her bones. It had been in the pounding, chilly pain in her crotch and abdomen, the smell of sweat and semen, the near-throttling pressure against her throat and in the silence that could not be broken, no matter what form his anger took. With Michael, *that* had been the price of safety. She had paid it for Katerina's sake.

You can endure anything, she had told herself, as long as Katerina is safe.

Could she also endure the thought that Katerina would be safe in a place where Natasha couldn't reach her? Could she stand it if safety meant she could never touch her daughter or see her again, not even on wrenchingly brief prison visits?

Some women gave their children up for adoption so they would have a better life. Natasha would rather die.

Nina was saying something. Natasha didn't catch it all, she just heard the repetition of the word "safe."

The crushing, unacceptable truth was penetrating her, jerk by jerk, even though she didn't want it inside her. The nurse didn't know anything—even bleeding, even with the knife against her throat, she couldn't tell Natasha anything.

With a sharp wrench of translucent pain, the last connection to Katerina was severed. The trail of bread crumbs through the forest was gone; the birds had eaten it. There was no longer a way home.

A HOLE IN time, a sudden shift.

She was in the car. She was driving the car. Headlights approached her in pairs. The snow was drifting across the windshield. She had no idea where she was, didn't remember how she had gotten there. The knife lay on the seat next to her, still with blood on the tip. Inside her there was no longer a goal, no longer any direction or any meaning at all. The temptation to head for a pair of the lights moving toward her was overwhelming.

Suicides did not go to Heaven.

"Don't fill the child's head with that superstitious foolishness," Pavel had said. "There is no Heaven."

It was the day that Natasha's grandmother was being buried. September, but still so warm that the air shimmered above the asphalt outside the airport in Donetsk.

"Why not?" asked Natasha. "You don't know what happens when we die either."

"I know that there won't be any angel choirs and harp music for me," he said.

Katerina had been five. She listened when the grown-ups talked. Not always obviously, but with a silent awareness that made it seem as if she was eavesdropping even when she sat right next to you, as now, in the back of the taxi.

"So Daddy won't go to Heaven?" she whispered to Natasha.

Pavel heard it even though he was helping the taxi driver put the bags in the trunk. He also saw the silent pleading in Natasha's eyes.

"Sweetie pie," he said and slid into the seat from the other side. "That's a long time from now. We don't need to think about it."

"But Great-Grandmother is dead," said Katerina. "Where is she going if there is no Heaven?"

It wasn't as if Katerina had seen her great-grandmother all that often. Still, the question was serious, as was Katerina's worried gaze.

"Are you sad that she is dead?" asked Pavel.

Katerina considered. "She made good poppy seed cakes," she said.

Pavel smiled. "Good," he said. "Then we agree that there is a Heaven and that Great-Grandmother is there now. She has just baked a poppy seed cake and made us tea, and we can visit her when we sleep so she doesn't get too lonely. I'll just have to try and see if I can stand the harping."

Katerina accepted this and looked relieved. Death without lifelines was hard for a five-year-old to take on board, and Natasha was happy that Pavel had been as accommodating as he had and that Katerina couldn't see the irony in his eyes.

Twelve months later Pavel was dead. And for some reason Natasha had a hard time imagining that he sat next to God looking down at them. He no longer took care of them; in fact, he never had. It had just seemed that way until the day the Witch arrived.

SUDDENLY NATASHA KNEW what she needed to do. The world fell into place around her, and there was meaning and order again. She could protect Katerina, even though she no longer knew where Katerina was. She could make sure that safe really meant safe.

Once she had wondered at the fact that murderers could get into Heaven when people who committed suicide couldn't. Wasn't it worse to kill someone else? Now she was glad that was the way it was. She listened, but Anna-in-her-head apparently had no opinion of her new plan. Still Natasha felt calm, cold and determined. If Katerina really was to be safe, there was only one thing to do.

The Witch had to die.

"THIS ONE," SØREN said, pointing at one of Pavel Dorshenko's many articles. "Why do I have a special feeling about this one?"

Babko stretched and stuck out his hand for the now fairly grimy paper. "May I see?"

> *"Solovi, solovi, ne trevozhte soldat . . ."*
>
> *Nightingale, nightingale, do not wake the soldier, for he has such a short time to sleep. Which of us has not heard this sentimental but beautiful song, whether it was Evgeny Belyaev, who thrilled us with his fantastic tenor, or the Red Army's talented male choir or more modern soloists? But who was this nightingale really, and whom did she sing for?*

Babko took a sip of his lukewarm coffee.

"It doesn't seem quite like the stuff he usually writes," he said. "But I can't see any great potential for scandal. Most of this is generally known. Kalugin's Nightingale. The story was even turned into a *Carmen*-like musical a few years ago."

They had had to return the borrowed office to its owner and were now once again sitting in the headquarters's dove-blue coffee room.

A Sunday lull had descended; only a single uniformed policeman was reading the sports section from one of the tabloids as he consumed his breakfast roll. Søren scanned the text once more. He could grasp the general sense—that it had to do with the world war and the dogfight over Galicia—but his knowledge of contemporary Ukrainian history wasn't sufficient for him to catch all the nuances.

"What does it mean?" he asked Babko. "The stuff about the Nightingale?"

"She was a kind of Ukrainian Marlene Dietrich," Babko said and tapped a specific paragraph with a broad index finger. "Oletchka Marasova, she was called. She sang for Bandera's nationalist troops. She kept up morale and that kind of thing. But it turned out that she sang in more ways than one. She informed on several of them to the KGB, to a Colonel Kalugin—hence the name."

"Dramatic," Søren observed. "I can see why someone thought it would make a great musical."

"It was terrible," said Babko dryly. "Plot holes you could drive a cart through and so overacted and tear-jerkingly sentimental that some of the audience began to giggle. Very unhistorical and slightly embarrassing."

Søren sensed that Babko had been one of the gigglers.

"Doroshenko's version is not much better," said the Ukrainian. "Some of it is taken directly from the musical, as far as I can see. Other parts are tall tales and myth; he doesn't distinguish. All that stuff about Kalugin discovering her at an orphanage concert, for example, is nonsense. She did come from an orphanage, true, but she didn't meet Kalugin until she was grown. And she probably doesn't have quite as many lives on her conscience as Kalugin claims. She was given credit for a good part of general informer activity. The national army was, to some extent, an underground army and therefore very vulnerable to that kind of traitor. Many were accused, arrested and executed. Bandera was murdered by the KGB as late as nineteen fifty-nine, in Munich, I believe. And he is still a divisive figure. Some see him as a Ukrainian freedom fighter, a hero; others accuse him of war crimes and point out that he allied himself with the Germans for a while. A Ukrainian battalion was created under the banner of the Wehrmacht, and do you know what they called it?"

"No," said Søren, a bit irritated. This wasn't a quiz show.

"The Nachtigall Battalion. Funny, don't you think?"

"Does it have anything to do with her? Kalugin's Nightingale?"

"Probably not. Or if it does, the connection may run in the other direction—it made the nickname even more appropriate."

Søren skimmed the article one more time. If you ignored the tragic background of the war, it was basically a banal honey-trap story. It had even been illustrated with photographs of scenes from the musical, he saw, and an apparently random picture of two little girls in some kind of national costume. There were no captions to explain why that was relevant.

"It doesn't include an accusation," he said. "None of those badly veiled suggestions that there is a 'basis for a closer investigation' and so on. And it all happened a long time ago. So why do I still keep coming back to it?"

"Perhaps because it was published on September eighteenth, two thousand and seven," said Babko suddenly.

It took a few seconds. Then Søren felt an abrupt desire to smack himself on the forehead. "The day before Pavel Doroshenko was killed," he concluded.

UKRAINE, 1935

"YOU'RE LIKE A dog. A little, stupid one."

Olga looked at Oxana across the narrow table but didn't have the energy to answer, just waited for the next attack. Oxana wasn't really angry, she knew that. There was something teasing in the blue gaze. An invitation to a game of the kind they had played when they were a little younger in Kharkiv and even in Mykolayevka before everything went wrong. But Olga didn't accept.

"A dog sticks its tail between its legs and hides because it doesn't know any better. What's your excuse?"

There was a smile but also a flicker of irritation in Oxana's voice now. Olga still chose to ignore it. They were having oatmeal today. Water softened the oats so they somehow filled you up more than millet porridge and bread, and if you ate very slowly, it worked even better.

Olga emptied her bowl at a steady rate. She inhaled its smell and felt warmth spread through her whole body.

Mother also sat silent with her own portion, which wasn't much bigger than those she had served the children. She gave them a little hunk of bread each. Olga broke hers in half, carefully cleaning the bowl with the soft side of the bread before stuffing it in her mouth. Afterward, they cleaned the pot together in the same way. Oxana poked at Olga's hand, ruffled her hair and nipped playfully at her ear, but Olga pulled away instinctively. That was just the way it had become. She could no longer stand to be touched by Oxana.

She got up abruptly and began to comb Kolja's hair for nits. Mother had had to cut it very short, because when Kolja was being looked after at the kolkhoz, he often played in the collective house, where whole families slept, cooked and ate on the floor. Lice and other bugs jumped on him even though Mother made sure to wash him every day and had somehow even acquired some bars of real soap. They managed, as Mother said. There were oats and cabbage and winter carrots, and the fist-sized bread ration that Mother brought home with her every day from the kolkhoz, a chunk for each. But hunger stayed with Olga like a toothache. When she got up, when she went to bed and now while she was rinsing the pots and checking Kolja's soft short hair for lice.

Olga kissed him carefully at the nape of his neck and spun him around once. Mother had made a new coat for him from the red wool dress she had brought from Kharkiv. "Here I'll never need such finery anyway," she had said. "The hogs don't care what I wear."

"How nice you look," said Olga and smiled. "A real little man."

Kolja nodded. "I'm going to show it to Viktor and Elena and Marusja," he said but then got a worried wrinkle in his forehead. "Should I be the father or the big brother when we play family?"

Olga considered for a moment. "You should be the father," she said. "You're a father who has just come back from Moscow after an important meeting with Uncle Stalin, and he has given you this fine coat as a thank-you for all that you have done for the Soviet Union."

Kolja stood up straight and gave Oxana a serious look. "Like you, Oxana. I am going to build a better future with my own hands."

Oxana was putting on her coat. She looked at Kolja and smiled crookedly, but she didn't say anything. Oxana had become quieter lately. She was thinking of the cause, she claimed, but her spontaneous speeches about the better times that awaited them had become less frequent, and they warmed neither soul nor stomach the way they had done in the past.

Olga felt sore and tired to the bone, which really wasn't very far if you thought about it. Her ribs were visible just beneath the skin, and her hipbones jutted out so far that it really hurt when she knocked into a table or a doorframe. And she did that often. Hunger made them all clumsy, and Kolja fretful and whiny, but they were still alive while others were dead—Father and Grandfather and Jana's mother too, who had succumbed to tuberculosis just a month ago. Olga had watched from the window when she was sung out of the Petrenko house. Jana walked behind the funeral procession with her shoulders pulled all the way up to her ears, scratching her hair once in a while. She and Olga no longer spoke.

Mother had tied on both shawl and kerchief and reached for Kolja with an impatient gesture. "We have to go now, Kolja," she said in a thin voice. "Otherwise Mama Hog will get impatient."

Mama Hog, the largest of the breeding sows, was Kolja's favorite, and for her sake he was usually willing to hurry, but today he pulled himself free of Mother's hand and stuck out his lower lip. "I have to bring my rifle."

Olga looked around and caught sight of the stick that he had whittled smooth and nice and free of bark, and which had now been designated a weapon in the Red Army. She handed it to Kolja, who stashed it under his coat with a satisfied expression.

"Now we'll go," he said.

"Yes, now we'll go."

Mother and Kolja opened the door, walked out to the road and turned in the direction of the kolkhoz. Oxana remained in the doorway, looking at Olga.

"Come with me," she then said. "It will be all right. They won't dare to do anything."

Olga shrugged, not meeting Oxana's eyes. They had had this conversation before, and she knew what Oxana was going to say. Olga ought to go to school both for her own sake and for Uncle Stalin. She and all other children were the future of the nation. Oxana had reported the beating to the village soviet, and no one would dare to attack them again. That's what Oxana would say, but it would be lies, most of it, and even Oxana knew it.

Why else would Oxana go to so much trouble to get to the school without being seen? Olga knew which way she went. Instead of taking the long main street through the village, she snuck out through the orchard and followed the narrow path to the river. From there you could walk among the closely spaced birch trees to the back of the cooperative store without anyone seeing you unless they were really close. If you went through the gap between the wagon maker's shop and one of the village's deserted houses, you could reach the school without meeting a living soul.

But Olga wasn't having any of it.

After what happened with Vitja and Pjotr, she left the house only reluctantly, and when she did, it was mostly to collect water or logs or to stop by the Arsenovs. They subscribed to the local newspaper for Kharkiva Oblast and let Mother read it in return for helping them with their washing.

Oxana thought Olga was scared, but it wasn't just that. It was an unclear sensation of shame, even though Olga didn't think she had done anything wrong. It was the thought that she had been lying there in that frozen sewage ditch in the middle of the main street, her cheek pressed against the grubby ice and the sound of the boys' excited and breathless laughter in her ears. And as for Uncle Stalin—Olga had begun to grimace in her head every time he came up—as for good old Uncle Stalin, Oxana could take him and stick him up the ass of a cow, if she could find one that was big enough.

She didn't want to go to school, where Jana would be staring at her and Sergej would stick his oily face close to hers to whisper ugly words. And she didn't want to walk beside Oxana. Ever again.

OXANA FINALLY LEFT. Olga closed the door behind her and was alone.

That was okay. Better than going to school, at least, but she had to keep herself constantly occupied in order not to think too much. Today she was going to put their blankets out on the veranda. It was still cold, and with a bit of luck, the frost would kill some of the lice.

Olga took the birch broom and swept the floor as best she could, but the work quickly made her dizzy and short of breath, and in spite of the heat from the brick oven, she felt the raw cold through her underwear, dress and shawl.

She lay down on the oven shelf and covered herself with the heavy blankets and goat hides. The warmth from the heated bricks immediately made her doze off and dream uneasy dreams. Father was tied to a pole with his hands behind his back, and next to him stood the widow Svetlova dressed in a zobel fur and with her great, round stomach exposed and vulnerable to the gun barrels that pointed at them both.

Olga tried to wrest herself free from the dream, but the pictures kept coming in a swiftly flowing stream no matter how hard she squeezed her eyes shut. And then the pole was suddenly gone, and she was back in their own house and Father was outside hammering on the door with huge, heavy fists and screaming that she was to let him in.

She was still dreaming. It had to be a dream. But the insane hammering continued.

"Where is she? Where is your devil of a sister?"

I'm not going to open up, she thought. Why can't they all just leave us alone? The living and the dead.

A POLICE CAR FOUND her. Nina had made it into sitting position but no farther, her back propped against one of the Micra's front wheels. She wondered if the patrol car would be able to stop in time or would just continue into the Micra.

Luckily, the police had begun to equip their vehicles with winter tires. The patrol car came to a controlled stop ten or twelve meters from her. One of the cops got out; the other remained seated behind the wheel.

"Do you need any help?" asked the one who had gotten out.

Help. Yes, she did. All kinds of help.

"What time is it?" she asked instead.

The police woman squatted next to Nina. "Could you look at me for a moment?" she said. "Can you tell me what happened?"

"She drove into me," said Nina. "She must have been parked between the trees. She was waiting for me to come, and then she drove right into me."

The policewoman smiled in a calming way, but there was a bit of skepticism in her very young, very pretty face. "I think we need an ambulance for you," she said.

Nina decided she had been sitting there long enough. "No," she said. "I'm okay. Pretty much."

She thought she could feel a fracture in her lower left arm, but that wasn't exactly life threatening. She got to her feet on the first attempt but then had to lean discreetly on the Micra to remain upright until the dizziness wore off.

The hood was cold, she noticed. Fuck. That meant time had passed, and she had no idea how much. Her usual loss-of-time panic set in, but it was a familiar panic; she could control it. As long as someone told her the time *soon*.

"My name is Nina Borg," she said. "I'm a nurse at the Coal-House Camp. I was on my way home when another car suddenly appeared. I don't have a concussion; I'm completely oriented in time and place"—well, place at least—"and my own data. All I need right now is a taxi. And maybe a mechanic for the car."

The other officer, also a woman but somewhat older, had left the car and approached. "As long as you're not actually bleeding to death, we'd better set up a few warning reflectors. We prefer to deal with one accident at a time. What about the other driver? Did she just take off?"

"Yes."

The accident had been no accident. Natasha had been parked and waiting for her on one of the tracks the forestry workers used when they were transporting lumber. That much Nina had pieced together in her head while she was sitting in the snow, trying to muster the energy to get up. Belatedly she realized how they were likely to react when—or if—she told them who the woman was. It felt wrong, even now, to give Natasha up like that, to make it easier for them to find her.

"The other . . ." she said.

"Yes?"

"It was Natasha Dmytrenko."

"The one who . . ."

"Yes."

The treachery was complete.

One of the policewomen was already speaking very quickly into her radio. "Which way did she go?" the other asked. "And what kind of car was she driving?"

"I didn't see it very well," Nina said. "I think it was black or dark blue. Big. A heavy car. Maybe a Mercedes or an Audi? She drove that way, back toward Værløse."

The other officer cursed into her radio. "No, damn it. We can't even give pursuit while that stupid little car is blocking the way. Can we get some help out here in a hurry?" She shot a quick question at Nina. "When did she take off?"

"I don't know exactly," said Nina. "Five or six minutes after three, I think."

The policewoman lifted her well-functioning arm and looked at her well-functioning watch. Nina was jealous.

"So you've been sitting there in the snow for almost forty minutes?"

Forty minutes. Fuck.

"I guess I must have been," Nina said.

THE TAXI LET her off on Kløverprisvej at what she considered a suitable distance from Søren's house. She was gradually managing to bend and stretch her arm better. She still couldn't rotate it, so something was wrong, presumably a minor fracture. It might have been the airbag explosion itself that caused the damage, but it was still a lot better than banging her head into the steering wheel.

It was the cud-chewing Mr. Nielsen who let her in.

"It's after four," he said. "The boss has called twice to ask where you were. Fifteen minutes more, and we'd have had to upgrade our coverage."

"I'm sorry," said Nina. "Something unforeseen happened."

He looked at her as if nothing unforeseen ever happened in his world. And maybe it didn't. He looked like a man who not only had a Plan B but also Plans C, D, E, F and all the way to the end of the alphabet.

Magnus stood in the kitchen door. "*I* was starting to worry too. How did it go? Did Anton get to be Cat King?"

"No, but he was Super Mario and super stylish. How is Rina doing?"

"She's sleeping."

She knew she should tell them about Natasha and the accident, but she didn't have the energy right now. She had already been grilled twice by two different sets of police. The Coal-House Camp and Michael Vestergaard's house in Hørsholm were under the jurisdiction of North Zealand Police, while it was Copenhagen's Prison and Probation Service that was officially responsible for following up on Natasha's escape and her physical assault on an officer on duty. Nina felt as if she had repeated her story endlessly. All she had received in return was the information that the young policeman from the gas attack was conscious and out of danger. It was a huge relief—at least the officers hunting Natasha no longer thought they might be tracking down a cop killer.

Nina no longer knew how she felt about Natasha; she no longer fitted into any of the usual boxes. Some of the time Nina still saw her as Rina's mother and therefore a persecuted victim to be helped and protected; then Natasha would suddenly shape-shift into something wild and unpredictable to be kept at bay, a threat to Anton, a car waiting among the trees, a knife against the throat. Nina collected a little spit in her dry mouth and swallowed. She tried to concentrate on the present.

"What did Søren want?"

Nielsen Cud-Chewer paused for a second, possibly to indicate that he didn't completely approve her casual use of Inspector Kirkegard's first name.

"He had some questions. You can call him from my phone."

"In a little while," she said. "I just want to check on Rina. Here . . ." She awkwardly reached across her body to take the Bricanyl from her left pocket. "I went to get the last of her medicine."

The Cud-Chewer—who had stopped chewing cud, she noticed—looked like he was considering forcing her to call right this minute, but instead just activated the phone himself.

"She's back," she heard him say as she headed for the living room.

"What's wrong with your arm?" asked Magnus.

"Nothing," she said. "Nothing important."

In the living room, the television was still on, playing an eternal loop of noisy cartoons. Rina's socks stuck out from under the comforter at one end, but her head had completely disappeared. Perhaps the noise from the television was disturbing her sleep. Nina turned it off and switched on one of the two lamps on the windowsill. Rina didn't like waking up in the dark.

Then she noticed two things simultaneously.

The terrace door was slightly ajar. And in the silence that set in when she turned off the cartoon inferno, she couldn't hear Rina's breathing.

NATASHA FELT COOL and clear-headed. It was as if she was better able to think and act now that half her brain was no longer occupied with keeping track of where Katerina was. She dumped the damaged Audi in a snowdrift by a small forest and hoped that the snow would soon cover it so it would be just as hard to recognize as the other snow-covered roadside wrecks. There were plenty of those on a day like today.

She had to walk for a few kilometers along the road before the solution to her acute transportation problem revealed itself in the form of a long, sprawling inn with wide-open doors and men in shirtsleeves who stood in the doorway smoking. From inside the inn she could hear the loud, homemade songs that were a part of most Danish family celebrations, with the addition of jovial bass line, electric piano and a slightly tinny drum machine.

She edged her way past the smokers into the outer hall and proceeded down into the cloakroom in the basement without anyone taking any particular notice of her. In one of the many heavy overcoats hanging from the rack, she found a key ring with a Suzuki logo. The parking lot was behind the inn, next to the main entrance, and when she pressed the key's remote control, a helpful blinking light guided her to the right car. It was a small, ugly blue one, but it started without protest, and she drove unchallenged down the road and farther into the anonymous drifting snow.

She had no idea how to go about killing someone like the Witch, but it couldn't be that hard. Not when you were bigger and stronger than the person who was to die. And Natasha certainly was, because the Witch was tiny and more fragile than an egg. She pictured the old woman as she seen her in the backseat of the car in the winter forest, and in spite of her determination, Natasha felt a jolt of fear that she immediately tried to suppress. Stop thinking like a mouse, she said to herself. Now you're the hunter, and *she* is the one who has reason to fear. The days of shivering in the dark are over.

IN COMPARISON WITH the fourth break-in, the three first had been amateurish and almost peaceable. Natasha was wrenched from sleep straight into terror. She couldn't breathe, couldn't see. An unidentified pain raced up through her stomach, and it was only in the seconds that followed that she realized someone had hit her, and that the reason she couldn't scream was because something moist and acidic had been pushed into her mouth. An apple. They had stuffed an apple into her mouth as if she were a cartoon pig about to be roasted. The juice ran into her throat, and she tried to cough it out but couldn't. A hand in her face forced her head back against the bed's headboard.

"Not a sound. Get it, bitch?"

She did not get it. She didn't understand anything. There were two men in their apartment, and Pavel was nowhere to be seen.

"If you scream, we'll kill the kid. Do you understand that?"

She nodded, her fear choking her.

"Where is he?"

She assumed they meant Pavel, but she just shook her head. She tried again to spit out the apple, and this time they let her.

"Don't know," she gasped. "He isn't . . . don't know . . . where . . ."

"Listen, you whore. If you don't do exactly as I say, we'll fuck you till you can't walk. And afterward we'll do the same to the kid."

The words hit her harder than the heavy, brutal hands. She felt them inside her head, blows you couldn't block or duck.

"I don't know," she moaned. "He isn't here. I don't know."

"You can tell him that if he writes another word, we'll be back."

"Yes," she said. "I'll tell him. I will."

Not until they had left did she remember that Pavel was in Denmark. With Anna. He wouldn't be home for several days. She crept along the wall of the bedroom, down the hall and into Katerina's little room. The light was on, but Katerina was asleep. She lay with warm red cheeks and the blanket half kicked off, but she was all right; nothing had happened to her. Natasha let herself sink to the floor and sat with her knees folded up against her chest for almost an hour before she felt strong enough to get up again, find the telephone and call Pavel.

It was as if he didn't understand what had happened. Even though she told him, *told* him what they had said, told him that they had been *there*, in the apartment, he still didn't understand.

"But didn't the alarm work?" he asked, as if that meant anything.

"They said they would . . . Pavel, you have to come home. Now. Do you hear me?"

"I'll come as quickly as I can," he said. "Can't you go stay with your mother and father? My love, I understand that you are frightened, but that's what they want. That's why they do it."

"You're not going to write anymore, are you?" she said. "You'll do as they ask, won't you?"

There was a pause on the other end.

"Did they say what it was I couldn't write?" he asked.

"No. Just that you should stop."

"But it's my work," he said. "What we live on. I can't just stop."

She cried so hard, the snot was about to choke her. "You can just write good things," she said. "Things everyone will like."

"You can't live on that," he said.

She couldn't go home to Kurakhovo until the morning, when the trains would be running again. Instead, she got a knife from the kitchen and began breaking open his desk drawers, the ones he kept locked and didn't want her to look in. There wasn't much there. She knew there used to be more—old photographs, newspaper clippings. He had bought a scanner after the first break-in and used it frequently, so maybe it wasn't necessary to keep so many paper pictures around. There were some bank payment statements, some empty envelopes, a Dictaphone. The new digital camera he had just bought. A pack of condoms, which under normal circumstances would have made her insanely jealous. Now she barely cared.

It took her a few minutes to figure out how to make the camera show pictures on the little display, and it was hard to see them properly. There were pictures of various people and places, nothing she recognized. She turned on the Dictaphone, but there were no recordings on it. It was no longer the one he used when he talked with people, she remembered. His cell phone recorded the conversations for him now and stored them on a little flat memory stick.

Finally she looked at the payments. They were from U-card, the credit card that Pavel used most frequently. She was surprised to see how much he owed. And why was it that nothing was ever paid in? She looked down the long row of numbers. Nothing but outgoing payments, no deposits. Even though she let Pavel manage their budget, she knew this wasn't normal. You couldn't have a credit card like that, with everything going out, thousands and thousands of it, and nothing ever being paid back in.

Maybe it was like the rent—Pavel didn't have to play by the same rules as everyone else.

All at once she realized there *was* a link to some of the pictures in the little camera. She wasn't sure what it meant, but there was a connection. Two pictures showed a little old lady. In one a large man in an overcoat was helping her out of an even larger car. In the other she stood smiling broadly up at another man, a man Natasha knew mostly because he had once been on the national soccer team. Nikolaij Filipenko. And the woman holding his face between her hands was his mother, Tetjana Filipenko. Who owned U-card.

"WHO DO YOU call when you need a bit of cash? U-card, U-card, U-card! You call: zero, eight hundred, four hundred and two hundred twentyyyy."

She sang the little jingle aloud to herself, as Pavel had done when he flashed his gold card in expensive clothing boutiques and good restaurants. Happy, greedy Pavel who had treated that U-card like a goose who shat golden eggs, golden eggs he never had to pay for.

Natasha turned off the country road she was on and pulled over to the side. She drew the numbers with a finger on the fogged-over car window so she wouldn't stumble: 0-800-400-220. Then she found Robbie's cell phone in her pocket and called.

"U-card customer service. How may we help you?" The voice was young and mild and could almost have belonged to one of the scantily clad girls from the commercial. In the background Natasha heard the faint clatter of hundreds of fingers on computer keyboards.

"I would like to speak with Tetjana Filipenko."

"I'm sorry?"

Natasha waited a moment. "Tell her that Natasha Doroshenko wants to speak with her. Tell her to call me at this number."

"I think you have the wrong number." The voice at the other end had developed a sharp edge. "You have called U-card's customer service. We can block your card if it has been stolen. We can make a transfer for you. We can assist you with your . . ."

"Do you want to die?"

Natasha's question stopped the girl's memorized service patter, and the phone became silent. She could still hear the faint clicking from all the other keyboards and the soft buzz of other young women's voices in the background. Natasha pictured the young woman, far away in Ukraine, looking around for help. Considering her options. But she was surrounded by young women like herself, and they were all busy blocking U-cards and sending money through cyberspace.

"Tell Tetjana Filipenko that I called, and she should call me at this number. Natasha Doroshenko. Tell her."

She hung up and remained sitting with the phone in her hand. Closed her eyes and waited. The Witch would call.

UKRAINE, 1935

NO ONE WAS allowed to see the dead.

Not even Mother, although she screamed and cried herself hoarse in front of the village soviet's office. Comrade Semienova put her arm around Mother's shoulders and cried too, but she was still the one who held Mother back and prevented her from storming into the building where the GPUs were busy still. She had to wait until they were done examining the bodies, said Semienova. Nothing was more important right now than finding out what exactly had happened.

Olga stood behind her mother and could not cry, even though a hard, sharp pain had lodged itself just below her breastbone, like it sometimes did when something heavy hit you in the stomach. She couldn't cry, and she could barely breathe.

They had killed Oxana. That was what Comrade Semienova had told them. Down by the stream, with knives. The attack had been so violent that the blood had sprayed out over the snow and the naked birch branches in an arc several meters wide. That last detail Olga knew from Leda and Jegor, who had gone out with Comrade Semienova to look for Oxana. The first thing they had seen was little Kolja lying on the ground, staring emptily at the sky. His toy rifle was nowhere to be seen. Olga didn't know why she asked about it at all, but for some reason it felt important. As if the rifle could have made a difference. But he didn't have anything in his hand, said Leda, and he was dead, she could see that at once because his throat gaped like a broad red extra mouth under his chin.

Oxana had been lying a little farther off.

I want to die too, thought Olga. I want to die and lie together with little Kolja and even with Oxana, because now they no longer feel anything, while I hurt everywhere.

But she didn't die, and she couldn't think of anything she might do right now to make death happen. She could only stand there behind Mother and listen to her hoarse screams and look at Comrade Semienova, who had red, swollen eyes. Today she wasn't showing her dimples or smoking cigarettes.

During the night Mother finally stopped screaming, which was both a relief and a source of new fear, because what if she died of sorrow? Olga knew it was possible, because her own soul felt like it was twisting inside her and attempting to escape her body. Olga had heard that there was no greater sorrow than the one a mother feels when her child dies. And Mother had lost two children at once, and maybe that was more than heart and lungs and intestines and all the other things inside the body could endure.

Olga curled up, listening for Mother's breath in the darkness. She finally caught the sound, the kind of small, hiccupping gasps that small children sometimes made when they had cried deeply and for a long time. It was impossible to tell if Mother was sleeping or if she was awake. But at least she wasn't dead. Not yet.

Oxana would never sing again, and Kolja was done playing family and fighting great battles for the Red Army. Now he lay dead in the headquarters of the GPU. Olga suddenly wondered if all the lice on his head would follow him into the ground. The thought nauseated her, but she couldn't stop herself. Pictures kept popping into her mind, pictures of Kolja with his throat cut and lice that crawled slowly across his cold, pale scalp; of Oxana's sparklingly happy blue eyes that day when she had learned that she would sing at the Pioneer meeting in Kharkiv.

"You shouldn't have gone, Oxana," Olga whispered into the mattress. "I told you not to go."

IN A FEW quick frames of the footage, Rina slid down from the couch and under the coffee table. It took less than six seconds. Another camera had caught her at the garage and a ways down the sidewalk, a sequence of twenty-one seconds. Both recordings were almost two hours old.

"She's alone," said the Cud-Chewer and searched on among the not-an-iPad's stored pictures. "It's not a kidnapping."

"I thought you were watching her," said Nina. "I thought you were fucking professionals. What good is all that equipment if you can't even keep track of one little girl? She's eight, damn it!"

"The camera is set so that it registers ordinary movement in the room. I wasn't expecting her to worm her way across the floor!"

"Did she see you place the camera?"

The Cud-Chewer was practically chewing his jaw off its hinges. "Maybe," he admitted. "I thought she was asleep."

"Why exactly is it that people think she is deaf, blind and dumb just because she doesn't say very much?" Nina snarled.

Mikael Nielsen didn't answer. He was making a call, presumably to his boss.

The trick of placing a couch pillow under the comforter so that it looked as if there were still a sleeping girl there—Rina might have picked that up from countless television films. The ruse with the stuffed socks was all her own—it had probably been easier for her than to make than something that looked like a head.

Nina stared blindly out the window at the snowflakes that glittered whitely in the light from the streetlamp. It was freezing out there. Pitch dark. And Rina was alone.

Mikael handed her the telephone. "He wants to speak with you."

She took the phone silently.

"You know Rina," said Søren. His voice sounded calm, almost as if the world hadn't exploded around them. "Where would she go? Where would she think of going?"

Nina thought desperately. "The Coal-House Camp, maybe. One of the policemen out there was kind enough to point out that it was where her mother would look for her first."

"Okay. How would she get out there? Does she know how to take the bus?"

"Maybe. She doesn't know her way around the city as such, but she knows the right bus number."

"Would she talk to strangers? Ask for help?"

"I don't think so. You've met her. She barely speaks to people she's known for years."

"Other places?"

Nina tried to imagine Rina's mental map of Denmark. Where had she actually been? Not a whole lot of places other than the camp.

"Vestre Prison. We visited her mother there. But she knows Natasha isn't there anymore. Michael Vestergaard's house, of course. Hørsholm. It's close to Hørsholm."

"I know. Other places?"

"Not a lot. Tivoli, that kind of place. The National Aquarium. I think they once did a project about fish with the Coal-House children. I don't know!"

"That's fine. That's a good start." She could hear the professional, calming tone she herself had often used. Praise made people relax—and it worked on her too, even though she knew perfectly well why she was being praised.

"What will you do?" she asked.

"We'll check the places you have given us, and the routes there, focusing primarily on the camp and Hørsholm. We'll send people out to look in nearby areas too—garden sheds, tree houses, that kind of thing. Does she have any money?"

"I think so. They get an allowance. Natasha has sent her a little as well, and she doesn't really use it."

"And she doesn't have a cell phone other than the old broken one?"

"No."

"Too bad."

"Søren."

"Yes?"

"She used your telephone."

"Mine?"

"Yes, the one in the living room. I thought she was just dialing randomly; she said the old one didn't work anymore. The policeman had said it was broken. I don't know if it was you or . . . or your colleague she meant."

"Okay."

"I thought she just wanted to speak with her father, but what if that wasn't what it was? What if she called someone? In real life, I mean."

"Let me talk to Nielsen," he said, and she handed the telephone back to the Cud-Chewer.

Nina zipped up her jacket. Luckily, she could open and close it with her left hand.

"Hello—where are you going?" asked the Cud-Chewer.

"I'm going to look for her in the neighborhood," she said through clenched teeth. "She may not have been able to get very far."

"Wait." Magnus had followed her. "Wait a second, Nina. We can't just run around randomly."

"It's urgent," she said.

"Yes, but we need to be a bit systematic. You go this way"—he pointed toward Kløverprisvej—"and I'll go this way. We'll meet again at the corner in half an hour."

Nina nodded, desperate to get started. Rina had run away before; they had done this before. And we found her then, she told herself. We will this time too!

She had spoken to two neighbors and looked in three garages when the realization hit her. *You have reached Anna and Hans Henrik Olesen. We can't come to the phone now . . .* Because of the male voice she hadn't put two and two together. But the wife's name was Anna. Like Neighbor Anna. The Anna she had met, the Anna who had taken such loving care of Rina the night Natasha had decided to try to kill her fiancé.

"Olesen, that's what she was called," she said aloud to herself.

On the other side of the street, going in the direction of Hvidovrevej and Damhusdalen, was a taxi. The green FREE sign shone like a signal in the dusky gloom, and before she had time to think, she had leaped into the road with one arm in the air.

SOMETIMES WHEN YOU have to do a really hard thing, you can't let yourself think. No looking down and discovering how deep the drop is beneath your feet, and no looking ahead either. You balance on a wire, and it can be ten or a hundred meters long. It doesn't matter, because you can't run anyway, and you can't jump the last bit to make it across the abyss. You can't cheat. All you can do is place one foot in front of the other. One step at a time.

Natasha was kneeling in the snow between the dense bushes, gazing out at the parking lot. The afternoon darkness had turned the snow grey. The sky above her was dark blue with faint, glowing streaks of light in the west, and she could feel the temperature dropping in the air around her, burning her fingers and toes.

She hadn't made a real plan. She knew it, but the simplicity of her idea still gave her a kind of solace, because she only needed two minutes. Maybe less.

One hand rested lightly on the tire iron from the car's trunk. It was heavy enough. More than heavy enough, she thought. And the wait would soon be over.

A group of half-grown boys crossed the farthest end of the parking lot. They ducked in turns, shoveling little piles of frosty snow together with clumsy mittens and throwing loose handfuls of it at one another in fun. The snow was probably too powdery for real snowballs. The sound of their shouting and laughter cut through the clear air, but besides that there was no sound except the faint rush of cars on the distant main road. Kastrup Fort, with its old fortifications and dungeons, lay deserted and empty in the winter dusk.

She knew the place from her time with Michael. He liked to bring them here when the weather was good, her and Katerina. There was a playground at the bottom of the grounds and a few beat-up, green-painted toilets with lots of graffiti. A bit higher up lay the restaurant with the large green clover lawn and the view over the ramparts, where weeds grew dense and wide-leaved in the summer and smelled sharp and sweet at the same time.

Michael and Katerina had played hide-and-seek on the steep stairs and labyrinthine paths that wound through the thicket of whitethorn and bramble on their way to the top of the fort. Once there had been lookouts here, soldiers and cannons. Now only bare cement circles were left. Natasha knew that it would be a good place to meet your enemies, exactly as it had been in the past. There were only two real bridges over the moat, but today that didn't matter, because the moat was frozen and covered with snow, so she could theoretically disappear in any direction. Theoretically. Whether she got away or not was of little importance. One step at a time. One foot in front of the other.

THE CAR ROLLED into the parking lot ten minutes before the agreed-upon time. Natasha recognized it from the woods behind the Coal-House Camp, long and black and shiny, like a hearse. The license plates were no longer Ukrainian but Danish, she noticed. The Witch might be a queen in Kiev, but here in Bacon Land, her power was reduced, and she had to hide like the freak that she really was. Natasha felt a fleeting sense of cold triumph as she crouched even lower behind the cover of the bushes. She hoped that her tracks in the snow wouldn't be too visible in the dusk and that the man and woman in the car would not be too on their guard.

A broad, slightly hunched figure got out and remained standing for a long moment with his hands on the car roof, looking around. She knew exactly what he could see because she had paced the parking lot herself several times: On one side, naked trees and dense shrubbery sloping down to a snow-covered moat. On the other, the old dungeon which Michael had said once held ammunition for the fort's four cannons. The stairs up to the meeting place she had suggested were narrow and icy, and as the man took the first step, he slipped and had to grip the steel railing in order not to fall.

He returned to the car and opened the door for the woman in the backseat. It was too far for Natasha to see anything but a shadow moving behind the man's back and a glimpse of a pale, upturned face. He said something, and Natasha knew what it was. Or at least she thought she did.

"You can't come up there with me. The stairs are slippery, and you're old. I will go up to the top and meet her alone."

That was about what he said, because that was how she had planned it. The old woman would probably resist. She wanted to come, thought Natasha, because what she wanted from Natasha meant so much to her that she had dragged her old, rotting body all the way up here through half of Europe.

Natasha held her breath while the man bent down to the old woman. Gestured. Eventually, it seemed, the old lady accepted. She moved farther into the backseat with her hands pulled up to her fur collar to shield herself from the cold. The interior light hit the sharp features of her powdered face for a second. Then the man slammed the door, and the old woman became nothing more than a dark profile behind the car window.

The man looked at his watch. It was hard to determine his age at this distance, but he wasn't young, thought Natasha. It was the heft that she noticed, the width in his body that didn't belong to a young man. Nonetheless, he moved up the stairs with surprising speed. She would not have long to enact her plan, most likely not more than a few minutes. That would have to be enough.

When Natasha could no longer see him because of the thicket of thorn bushes, she carefully counted to thirty. He should be approaching the meeting place. He wouldn't turn around at once, he would think that she was on her way, that she would appear from the sheltering bushes up there any moment.

It was quiet around her now, and she closed her hand more tightly on the tire iron. It felt heavy and cold and right.

One foot in front of the other.

Springing to her feet, she sprinted across the parking lot. The distance to the car seemed to stretch elastically, and twice she almost stumbled on the packed ice under the new snow, but she stayed on her feet and tried to increase her speed. She ran with the tire iron hanging like a dead weight in her right hand. Not until she reached the car did she raise it and hit the car window with full force. A hard, flat thump resounded in the silence, and her fingers lost sensation from the blow. Still, there wasn't much to see other than a long, thin crack that ran across the side window. The Witch's face had turned toward her. The eyes were narrow black slits, the lips pulled back in a grimace that revealed long, crumbling teeth. Natasha imagined how thin the skull would feel under the soft fur hat and the thin, downy hair. What it would sound like on impact. Like a nut being cracked inside a fur bag.

She raised the tire iron again, and this time she used both hands to follow through. There was another odd, dead thump, and the pain in her hands raced all the way up to her wrists. The face behind the window was now partially obscured by a white cloud in the glass. But the window remained intact, and the woman in there stared directly at her, as if Natasha were an interesting natural phenomenon of the kind you can go to see in a safari park.

She sensed the abyss beneath her.

Then she grabbed the car door and pulled the handle, without luck. Of course.

She had been so unbelievably stupid. Of course the Witch was still untouchable. Of course she couldn't kill her.

Natasha hit the window again, hammering away, and with every blow, the face became harder to make out.

"Die." Natasha was winded now, and her words sounded just as dead and flat as the impact of the tire iron. "Please—just—die."

She closed her eyes and struck again, and this time there was a little hollow sound like when a hard-boiled egg hits a table, but it wasn't just the sound that made her look carefully at the window's cobweb pattern. She could feel in her fingers that something was finally yielding. And true enough, a little black hole gaped in all the whiteness, and she hit the window again with full force in precisely that place and felt the euphoric sensation of almost reaching the goal when the glass yielded even further. One foot in front of the other.

As she raised the tire iron once more, someone grabbed hold of it and jerked it back with such suddenness that she swayed and tumbled backward into the snow. Blows fell on her face, hard and precise and in a steady rhythm. She felt two of her molars shatter and cut into her tongue, already warm with blood.

"Natasha Doroshenko?"

She was too confused to answer. Just shook her head stupidly and tried to get up.

New blows. Fast and hard.

"Natasha Doroshenko?"

This time she managed to answer yes, but in the instant that followed, everything rushed away from her in whirls of grey and black and red. The wire under her feet broke, and she dropped and fell straight into the abyss below.

UKRAINE, 1935

THE PARTY BURIED Oxana. And Kolja too, even though he was neither a hero nor a pioneer. For Mother's sake, as Semienova said. So Mother wouldn't have to think of anything but the heroic deed her daughter had done, and for which she had bravely paid with her life.

"Your daughter is an example to Soviet youth," said Semienova. She didn't have red eyes any longer and now seemed more angry than sad, and with the anger, some of her shining energy had returned. She had become beautiful again. "A visionary little girl who valued solidarity above all else, even her own family. A true pioneer."

Olga couldn't help wondering whether she would also have been buried by the Party if she had been murdered along with Kolja and Oxana. Would Semienova have made a beautiful speech about her?

Mother sat with her head hanging limply on its thin neck and didn't look as if she was really listening to anything Comrade Semienova was saying. She hadn't lit the oven, and she hadn't swept the floor or cooked the porridge or done the washing. The whole house smelled like a dung heap, thought Olga, and she was constantly freezing.

"But there should be a panachydy," Mother mumbled then. "There should be a singing. My children must be sung out with 'Vichnaya Pam'yat.' Forever remembered, forever loved. I have to call a priest."

Comrade Semienova shook her head. "Oxana was not religious, and she had a strong will. A priest at her funeral would be an insult to everything she stood for. The funeral should be in her spirit, and the Party Committee has already—"

"And Kolja?" Now Mother lifted her head and stared at Semienova with a look that frightened Olga. "Must little Kolja be shut out of Heaven too?"

Comrade Semienova just smiled a sad little smile and stroked Olga's hair before she left. Olga had hoped she would stay a little longer because it was not nice to be alone with Mother, who just sat staring into the blue. But it was as it had always been. Comrade Semienova was busy with Oxana, even now when her body lay cold and hard in a coffin somewhere, and she could neither sing nor engage in interesting political discussions in the classroom. Even now, Oxana was more interesting than Olga.

Olga knew that it was wrong to think this way. In fact, she should feel nothing but sorrow now that Oxana was dead and had been murdered by the kulaks, as it said in the newspaper, but it was as if she couldn't stop the forbidden thoughts no matter how hard she tried. In fact, it was as if they grew and swelled the more she tried to drive them off. Like the time when Jana and she had begun laughing in old Volodymyr Pavlenko's class and had just laughed louder and louder the more he scolded them. It was as if they had been hit by a kind of madness that wasn't cured until he slapped them both quite hard.

Please don't let Semienova see what I'm thinking, prayed Olga quietly. She must not see what I'm thinking about Oxana . . . but now Semienova was on her way out and only turned in the doorway to say goodbye to Mother.

Mother didn't look up, but suddenly some force inside her seemed to come alive again. "Damn you, Semienova. Damn you to hell—you and all your fine friends in the Party." She wasn't speaking very loudly. "They were my children, and now you won't even let me see them. Not even in death can I get them back."

Olga held her breath, and Semienova, who had been about to close the door behind her, hesitated. She opened it again, and an ice-cold blast of winter raced through the living room, even though Olga had thought it couldn't possibly get any colder.

"Watch what you say," said Semienova. She looked shaken and upset, and Olga understood her. Mother should not be scolding her like this, and Olga felt sorry for Semienova. "I like you and your daughter, but I can't protect you from everything. Your ex-husband's family has already been arrested and is on their way to Sorokivka. There will be a harsh reckoning with the kulaks and their anti-Soviet propaganda."

It was no use. Mother couldn't be stopped. Her eyes were black pieces of coal in her pale face. "None of this would have happened if it wasn't for you," she hissed. "You have blood on your hands, and it will never come off."

MOTHER MADE AN effort to stay upright for the funeral. She did not brush her own hair or change her clothes, but she washed Olga's face and braided her hair, her touch gentle. Olga found her good dress, the one she had worn in the picture Semienova took; it was still pretty, although the sleeves were now too short. Oxana's dress would have fit her better, but Mother had given it to Semienova so Oxana could wear it in the coffin. A waste. Wouldn't it have been better for Olga to be dressed nicely for the funeral and for Oxana to be in the too-small dress rather than the other way around? The coffin was closed anyway.

Olga pictured Oxana lying there beneath the heavy lid with her hair spread out on the pillow. Kolja was to be buried in his new coat, although without his rifle. Even though Olga had searched and searched for it down by the stream, she hadn't been able to find it.

Then they were off. Down the main street, where the snow had started to melt and turn to mud. Spring would come without Father and Kolja and Oxana, even though Olga had not thought it would be possible.

IN THE GRAVEYARD, a brass band was playing, and the pioneer division from Sorokivka had come. Some of the older children must have met Oxana, because they stood with tears in their eyes when Comrade Semienova stepped forward to speak. She looked wonderful in pants and a man's jacket, her mouth painted red. She spoke of how Oxana had wished for freedom for the workers and the peasants, and how she had often talked about how unfair it was that the kulaks still had so much when others had so little. Too good for this world, Comrade Semienova concluded. The people's nightingale had fallen from the sky, but her song would still sound in everyone's hearts.

No one said anything about Kolja.

NATASHA WAS PRETTY sure that she was going to die.

Not because the man next to her had said anything particular to her or had been deliberately threatening. It was more the way that the woman in the backseat and he spoke to each other—so quiet and relaxed, as if Natasha had already been taken care of and never would be a threat again.

"Did you speak to Nikolaij?" asked the man.

"No. No, I'll wait to call until we get home again. He thinks I'm in Odessa. I couldn't say . . ."

"No, I guess you couldn't." The man's tone had become dry and distant.

"Jurij, you know it's different with him. He doesn't understand these things."

"I know. Forget it, Mamo. It'll work out. We can leave tonight if you want. Then we'll be home by Tuesday morning at the latest. I need some proper food; I'm about to throw up from all the hot dog buns." He laughed a brief, explosive laugh and slammed one hand flat against the steering wheel.

Even though he was probably the one who would be in charge of the actual execution, it was the old woman who made the hairs at the back of Natasha's neck stand up. She made Natasha intensely uncomfortable, and Natasha couldn't help turning her head every other second so she could at least see her out of the corner of her eye. The Witch noticed and sent her a brief, unreadable look before turning her head toward the side window.

"What are we looking for, Jurij?" she asked. Passing headlights and the white overhead flicker of the streetlamps illuminated her narrow face and made deep black shadows of the furrows around her mouth and eyes.

He shrugged. "A good place," he said.

Natasha sank a little deeper into the seat. The blood kept collecting in her mouth, and she was tired of swallowing it. She considered how he might react if she spat it out, either on the bottom of the car or in a dramatic red splatter on the side window. She caught sight of herself in the side-view mirror, her ghostlike reflection flashing back at her each time they passed another streetlight. Her face looked battered and distorted. One of her eyes had almost disappeared in a swelling that seemed to grow with every glimpse. Strands of hair had come loose from her ponytail and were matted against her forehead, nose and swollen eyelid, but she was unable to push them aside or scrub away the bloody tracks under her nose. The man, Jurij, had bound her hands behind her back with thin plastic strips of the kind normally used to organize cables or attach plastic toys to brightly colored cardboard backgrounds.

Like a Barbie in a cardboard box, she thought. The face in the mirror, which was no longer really hers, crumpled and emitted an odd, sobbing snort, neither laughing nor crying. Little flecks of blood hit the man's hand on the gearshift. He shot her an irritated look, reached across her and searched for something in the glove compartment. Finally he found a pack of wet wipes and wiped his hands, cursing softly, before once more turning his full attention to the road.

The traffic abruptly slowed down and then almost stopped. Up ahead Natasha could see blinking blue lights and men in yellow reflective vests. Some of them read POLICE.

She considered whether there was anything she could do. The nice Danish policemen probably wouldn't be quite as nice now that she had attacked one of their own, but they wouldn't kill her and bury her in "a good place." But it was hopeless. She could neither wave nor knock on the window, at least not unless she began pounding her head against it. Jurij glanced at her and pulled aside his overcoat in a relaxed way so she could see the butt of a black pistol.

"First I'll shoot you," he said. "Then I'll shoot them if necessary. But first you."

She sat passive, her head bowed, while they passed the police car and the tow truck that was in the process of pulling two cars apart.

WHEN THE POLICE came to say that Pavel was dead, she hadn't been surprised. That is what happens when you don't believe in the reality of wolves, she thought. Meanwhile, her body registered an inner breakdown, as if her spine had finally succumbed to some long-term pressure and collapsed. Her legs became numb, and she could no longer feel her face. Her hearing came and went, and she had to ask the policeman to repeat the message several times to catch it all. In a car. At Lake Didorovka. What had he been doing there?

"Did he come off the road?" she asked, because maybe there was still a chance to normalize his death into the comprehensible everyday universe. But no. Of course not. It was homicide. A "suspicious death," they called it. That didn't surprise her either.

What took her by surprise was that they wanted her to say she had done it.

They brought both her and Katerina to the station and placed Natasha in a little room with green walls and both bars and netting in front of the window. Katerina was not allowed to stay with her. Natasha could hear her crying in the next room. It was a terrible sound; it filled her so she couldn't think, it made her chest and stomach ache, and she tried to make the officers understand that she would listen if she could just comfort Katerina first.

They asked her why she had done it.

Done what? she asked.

And then they explained that it was usually wives who killed their husbands, and she had probably grown tired of him and wanted his money. He has no money, she said, while Katerina cried; he owes several hundred thousand. To whom? To U-Card.

That made them hesitate. They went out into the hall and spoke quietly. Then one of them disappeared. The other asked if she wanted tea. No, no tea. Just Katerina. Yes, of course. Something had changed, as if "U-Card" was a magic formula that opened locked doors. Suddenly she was allowed to see her daughter. After a little while, the second policeman left too. Only a secretary remained, sitting at a desk.

Natasha lifted Katerina up onto her hip and asked if she was charged with anything. "No," said the secretary. "They just want a statement from you."

"Then it'll have to be after I go to the doctor with my daughter," said Natasha, with a new authority. "Can't you hear how labored her breathing is?"

She left the station. All they had with them was Katerina's little backpack and what Natasha had in the pockets of her coat; she didn't even have her wallet. She had to go back to the apartment even though her instinct screamed that she had to get away while she could.

Instead of going up directly, she rang the downstairs neighbors' buzzer. They had an au pair, Baia, a young girl from Georgia who for some reason was always in a good mood. She and Natasha had taken the children to the playground together on a few occasions—the neighbors had twins, a boy and a girl—but Natasha had the feeling that Baia had been told not to associate with her. There was a certain glint in Baia's eyes, a secretiveness in her giggling, that made it seem as if they were two teenagers playing hooky from school to smoke cigarettes behind the bicycle shed.

Today Baia wasn't quite as upbeat as usual.

"I've heard," she said. "Terrible. And the police have been here, also SBU, and they asked a lot of questions and stomped around upstairs for several hours."

"Have they left?" Natasha asked.

"Yes, I think so. It's quiet now."

Katerina stayed with Baia and the twins while Natasha snuck up the stairs. The door was wide open, just like with the first break-in. It was quiet in there, but as Natasha ventured into the front hall, she heard a faint noise from the living room. She glided silently toward the door and looked in cautiously.

Everything had been worked over. Drawers pulled out and overturned, books cleared from the shelves, pillows and cushions cut open so the filling lay like snow across the wreckage. And in the middle of everything, there she was. The Witch. A tiny, bent old woman with white hair and a coat that reached almost down to her ankles and her shiny, high-heeled red shoes. She stood half turned toward the window, and the light shone right through her thin white hair so you could see her scalp and the outline of her skull.

Baba Yaha, thought Natasha, the old witch who lives in a cottage in the woods, a cottage that has legs like a hen and can run around like a living creature.

She stood with a picture of Katerina. The newest one, which they had had enlarged and framed so it could stand on Pavel's desk. Katerina wore braids and smiled shyly, but there was a sparkle in her big, beautiful eyes. "She looks like someone who is up to mischief," Pavel had said and had kissed the picture, and then the live model, six or seven times right under the hair at the nape of the neck, until Katerina screeched and said it tickled.

Baba Yaha ate children who came and knocked on her door. The fence around the chicken-legged house was made from human bones.

The old woman suddenly slammed the picture against the side of the table so the glass shattered and shards spilled across the desk and floor with a shrill tinkling. With her thin fingers, she peeled the photograph out of the frame and stuck it in her coat pocket. Natasha only managed to pull back her head just in time as the old woman began to turn around.

There was no time to think. Natasha grabbed her bag from the coatrack in the front hallway and raced down the stairs to Baia. An hour later, she was on her way to the Polish border in a rented car with only the clothes she had on, but with Katerina in the seat next to her, so close that she could touch her once in a while, as if it was necessary to make sure she was still there.

THE BIG MAN, Jurij, had taken them off the main road and into a semi-deserted summerhouse area. The road was only partially cleared, and the small wooden cabins on both sides were dark and cold. Natasha thought she could glimpse the sea among the trees at the end of the dead-end road. Her every instinct told her that this was it, they were going no farther. This was the place where Jurij would do what he planned to do. When he finally slowed the car, there were no longer any houses around them, and the road had narrowed even further. The car's tires spun a few times in the snow, caught hold and then finally stopped completely when Jurij turned the key and shut off the motor.

For a moment they sat silently in the faint interior light, all three.

"We've been looking for you for a long time," said the big man. "But you know that. Of course you know that."

He turned in his seat and gazed attentively at her, as if he was searching for an answer in her exposed and battered face. He was old too, thought Natasha, sixty years or more, and he didn't look anything like the tiny woman he had called mother several times. His face was meaty, his lips broad and spotted by age and tobacco. Only in his brilliant blue eyes could you clearly see that mother and son were related. Even now, in the gloom, and with the eyes partially shaded under a pair of heavy, baggy eyelids. The Witch had given birth to a monster and had suckled it at her own breast. This was not the son the little woman appeared with in the papers. He wasn't the suit-wearing, beautiful, clean politician. This son was a man who used his hands and got things done. Not the kind who built things but the kind who demolished them.

She avoided his gaze, feeling the blood pooling around the teeth in her lower jaw once more. She didn't dare spit but instead bent forward and let the blood dribble over her down jacket.

"Your husband, Pavel, was a coward," Jurij continued, unaffected. "Many believed he was a hero, a journalist who wrote the truth because he was a man with honor and integrity. In reality he only wrote what he was paid to write. And it was almost always lies. The truth, on the other hand, he was well paid to keep hidden."

Natasha didn't answer. Her tongue kept getting cut by the jagged edges of her broken molars, and what he said was not news to her. She had known it for a long time. Pavel was no hero.

"The question is," said the man, and again she felt his searching gaze. "How well did he hide his secrets, and where did he get them? How much does his pretty wife know? And what about his daughter? Even little pitchers have big ears."

Natasha tried to control herself, but the mention of Katerina made her twitch. And she knew he saw it and would store her weakness somewhere in his memory.

"I know nothing," she said. The blood sloshed under her tongue and made it hard to speak clearly. "Pavel never told me anything."

He sighed. An old man's exhaustion. The big hands rested on the steering wheel.

"Nonetheless," he said, "I will give you a chance to try and remember something. Where did he hide his papers and pictures?"

Natasha shook her head. "There were only the things in the apartment," she said, slurring her words. "There wasn't anything else."

She sensed at once she'd made a mistake by acknowledging that she knew something. She could see it by the tiniest of twitches in the heavy eyelids. "The things in the apartment . . ." he repeated. "You know we were there. You know we searched it."

It was quiet between them for a long moment, during which Natasha heard nothing but the faint hiss of small, hard snowflakes against the car's windows. Then the man opened the car door with a quick, angry jerk and stomped through the snow to the trunk. The old woman behind her emitted a long sigh and leaned back in her seat. Natasha caught the scent of her perfume and the musky smell of her mummified old body.

"I know nothing." Natasha turned as far as she could and tried to catch the old woman's gaze. "I don't know what you are looking for. Please don't touch Katerina."

She would have said more, but it was as if her words hit an invisible glass wall. The old Witch just looked at her. Her narrow face looked almost childish under the dome of the fur hat.

Then the car door on Natasha's side was thrown open, and Jurij grabbed hold of what was left of her ponytail and pulled her forward until she sat with her face between her legs. He worked fast, cutting the plastic strips off her wrists and attaching her right hand to the seat belt's buckle with a new one. Then he made a loop around her left hand—a thin rope—no, not a rope, a wire, a plastic-covered wire of the kind used for pulling boats up on the shore.

At the police station, they had shown her pictures of Pavel. Of his shattered hands that looked as if someone had hit them with a hammer. They had asked her why she had done it. Not *if* she had done it, just why.

She looked up at the man with the heavy eyes and the heavy body and understood for one burning second what he was planning. She opened her mouth without wanting to and felt her ruined lip tighten over her broken teeth, but there was still nothing she could tell him. If she had known, if she had been able to give him what he wanted, she would have.

He tightened the wire and pulled her left arm across the empty driver's seat, then disappeared out of her field of vision. She could feel by the pull in the wire that he was fastening it to something, but she didn't know what. He looked over his handiwork, growled, made some adjustments. There was nothing she could do. The seat belt and the plastic strip immobilized her in the seat; she had just a few centimeters' leeway. The strain in the arm stretching across the seat was uncomfortable, but that wasn't the problem. The problem was that her hand was positioned precisely where it would get caught when he slammed the door a few moments from now.

"I know nothing," she repeated, without any hope that it would stop him.

Surprisingly, he nodded and bent down so that she could see his face better. "I believe you," he said. "But sometimes one remembers the most incredible things." He looked like a kindly teacher awaiting an answer from a fumbling student. "I have asked you a question now. And your brain, the computer you have that remembers and thinks, is already hard at work. A little man has been sent down to rummage through the files in the archives, and I'm sure he will come back to us with something. Don't you think?"

Natasha shook her head silently. The details in his heavy face were imprinting themselves indelibly in her—the drooping cheeks, the burst blood vessels at the point of the cheekbones, the chin covered with bristly stubble, the five or six long hairs from each eyebrow that hung down over his Santa Claus–like blue eyes. She would remember that face till she died.

Which wouldn't be long—less than half an hour, most likely. That knowledge hit her once again, like a fist under her ribs.

"Look," he said. He took a folded piece of paper from his coat pocket, smoothed it out and held it so the interior car light illuminated it clearly. It was a printed copy of a black-and-white photograph of two girls. It was old, and the girls were wearing traditional Ukrainian dresses, like the ones folk dancers still used. "Where did this come from?" asked Jurij. "Where did your husband get this picture?"

"I don't know," she whimpered. "I know nothing."

She could feel the icy edge and the mechanism of the lock with the back of her fingers. She tried instinctively to pull her hand back, but the wire didn't permit it. Jurij straightened up and reached for the car door.

If all my fingers break, I can't drive, thought Natasha. If my fingers break, I can't turn the key and shift gears, and I can't . . . It felt as if her heart stopped in her chest for a moment. I can't kill the Witch.

Then he slammed the door. Natasha screamed, but she no longer attempted to pull back. Instead, she pushed her hand as far out of the car as it would go, so the door hit the her wrist and the heel of her hand rather than the fingers. The pain was excruciating, but she could feel that the bone was intact. She wasn't incapacitated. Not yet.

Suddenly she thought of aspirins.

Why? Why aspirins?

Jurij had opened the door again and was looking at her.

"Yes, it hurts," he said, as if he were a doctor who was sorry that a necessary vaccination involved a needle prick. "What about the little man? Has he found anything in the archives?"

Little man? There were no small men in her brain. Her brain was a mouse at the bottom of a tin pail, a mouse that raced around, jumped for its life and scrabbled at the smooth surface to find a way out.

He stepped back behind the door, ready to slam it again.

"No," she said. "No . . ."

And then it came. An image of Anna's home. She and Pavel and Katerina are at the dining room table eating cake. It is summer. The first visit to Denmark, and Katerina's second year in the world. Pavel would have preferred to go alone, he said, because he had many meetings to take care of, and he thought Katerina was still too little to fly. But Natasha pleaded and begged, and at last he'd given in. So now she is here in Denmark with Pavel's mother's old nanny. Anna is stern and distant, thinks Natasha, except when it comes to Katerina. With her she chatters cozily in a steady stream of Danish and a few Ukrainian words Pavel must have taught her. "Dog." "Cake." "Thirsty." "Sleepy." Short children's words that Katerina understands. Anna stuffs her with chocolate cake and brightly colored chocolate drops. Natasha is tired and has a headache.

"You can take a couple of my pills from the drawer in the bedroom," says Anna, now in English, which is the language they speak when Natasha is there. Otherwise, Anna and Pavel mostly speak German. It is all a big mess, and it's so hard to talk to anybody, and maybe that is why Natasha's head hurts so much. She has the sense that Pavel and Anna share something, that they are keeping her in the dark by speaking a language she doesn't understand.

"Panodil, aspirin or codeine," says Anna. "I think I have all three."

Natasha gets up and goes up into the bedroom and pulls out the top drawer of the dresser. She finds a plastic bottle marked aspirin, unscrews the lid and tips two pills into her hand. A few other pill containers rattle around in there, and at the back, some yellowed photographs lie loosely piled on the flowered paper lining the drawer. One of them shows two girls. It is very old and faded. The girls are dressed in the finest and most festive of traditional styles, and they are both looking seriously into the camera. It isn't Danish, she can see that, both because of the clothes and because of the lettering that reads, "Mykolayevka. Two nightingales." It's a little odd that it's here, she thinks, but maybe Pavel gave it to Anna. He has his own drawers at home, always kept locked, and in them are many old photographs that he doesn't want her to tidy or "mess up," as he calls it. This was before the first break-in. Before he got the scanner.

Natasha leaves this picture alone too. What does she need the past for? The present is bright and happy, at least most of the time—Natasha has discovered that it is entirely possible to be jealous of old ladies, even ones who decidedly do not want to sleep with her husband. Why do they have to chat so intimately in German all the time? Then she scolds herself as he would have, stupid Natasha, silly Natasha, takes the aspirin and joins the others again. They revert to English when they hear her on the steps, and Anna asks if she is feeling better now.

"ANNA!"

Jurij had opened the car door wide, ready to slam it again when Natasha suddenly said the name. Now he hesitated.

"I know where it is," said Natasha. "The picture. I know who has it!"

Jurij let go of the door. She felt the relief flood her like soft, warm water. Could it really be that simple? Was that really all they wanted? A picture from Anna? Her wrist pounded, sore and painful, but she could still move her fingers and hands, and in a miraculous way she now had a new chance to save Katerina.

"Where?" asked Jurij, and Natasha felt the wire loosen around her aching wrist.

"It's here," she said. "In Denmark. I'll show you where it is."

"WE SENT A man over there," explained Heide with somewhat exaggerated patience. "They are packing up out there so they can get home before the roads close, but Veng fought his way through the snowdrifts, and there was no one home. No sign of the girl, and Anna Olesen only showed up while he was actually knocking on the door. She had apparently been out searching for that dog again. He went through everything, including the stables, and the girl wasn't there."

"That's the number Katerina phoned."

"Yes, I understand that. But she isn't there."

"Okay. Thank you for trying."

"We'd like to find her as well," said Heide, refraining—pretty generously, Søren thought—from commenting on the fact that he—and the PET—was the one who had managed to lose the child in the first place. "Has her description been circulated?"

"Yes." Søren stared out across Polititorvet without really seeing his surroundings. "Will you keep me posted if something happens at your end?"

Heide promised. He knew she had her hands full, not just with the investigation of the Vestergaard killing, but also with the coordination of the hunt for Rina's mother. Natasha had been observed close to the Coal-House Camp earlier in the day when, according to the first brief report he had received, she had hit another car and fled from the scene of the accident. In spite of the apparently fairly definite identification, they were having trouble locating the fugitive. The weather was so bad that there was no point in using helicopters. On the smaller roads, especially north of Copenhagen, the snow had started to make its own roadblocks—and snow made no exception for patrol cars.

He had so far declined to put out an appeal in the media for information regarding Rina's disappearance. There was no reason to let the bad guys know she was out there, vulnerable and alone, if they didn't know already.

His stomach rumbled sourly. Too much coffee and not enough proper food. He hadn't eaten anything except two dry breakfast rolls and a cheese sandwich from the cafeteria since Susse's chicken stew the previous evening.

Susse. Ben. He had totally lost track: Herlev, the heart attack, even Susse's tears on the phone. Damn it. He quickly dialed. She was still in the hospital, he could tell from the background noise, but she sounded less distraught.

"It's better now," she said. "He slept well last night, and we're out of intensive care now. He says to say hello. And thanks for taking care of the dogs . . ."

"Anytime. You know that."

Babko, who was by now starting to find his way around the police headquarters's labyrinthine corridors like a native, came in and placed a cup of coffee in front of him, this time accompanied by a pastry.

"You look like you need this."

"Thanks," Søren said, though his stomach didn't quite agree.

"And one of the Danes gave me this."

It was a yellow Post-it note with a scrawled message from Don Carlo in the Radio service.

Call me. Car spotted.

Søren looked at his cell again and noted that Carlo had tried to reach him several times. Before he'd called Susse and Heide, there had been a number of conversations about mobilizing the search for Rina as well as a lengthy telephone report to Torben. He dialed.

"Hi, Carlo."

"Sonny boy. You asked us to let you know if anyone saw a Beemer with Ukrainian plates."

"Yes."

"We haven't. But a colleague who was on duty at a road accident on Englandsvej saw a black BMW 5 with Danish plates. He noticed it because one side window was smashed. He didn't get the whole number, but the Register can't find any BMWs with the partial he noted."

"Stolen plates."

"Yes. Almost certainly."

"Put out an APB. And alert the airport just in case that's where he's going." It was, after all, right around the corner from the Englandsvej sighting.

"Done, my friend."

"Thanks."

"No prob."

There could, of course, be several reasons for a BMW to drive around with false plates, but it was the first possible trace of Savchuk they had had at all.

Søren quickly put Babko in the loop. "There wasn't anything wrong with the window in the BMW when you saw it, was there?" he asked.

"No. But that could have happened later."

Søren checked his other missed calls. Don Carlo wasn't the only one who had called in vain. Mikael Nielsen was on the list too. Søren called him back.

"Yes?"

"Mrs. Borg walked out."

"What?"

"She and the Swede went out to search in the immediate vicinity. The Swede has just returned. He hasn't found the girl, and now he can't find the nurse either."

What was the matter with this case and these people? Couldn't Søren turn his back for one second without someone else disappearing?

"Hang on a sec."

He put Nielsen on hold and called Nina's cell. A second later it rang cheerfully in his inner pocket. Damn. He had taken it from her himself. For safety reasons . . .

"How long ago?" he asked Nielsen.

"They went out to search forty-five minutes ago. They went in opposite directions and had apparently arranged to meet again after thirty minutes. The nurse didn't show up. The Swede is worried."

So am I, thought Søren.

THE WIND WAS picking up. A corner of the red tarp on the stable roof flapped wildly, and the snow blew like smoke from the ridge of the thatch, so that for one distorted second, Nina's eyes insisted on telling her that the roof was on fire.

The light was on in the main house and in the courtyard, but otherwise the sky was dark, the pitch black that was a winter night in the country.

She gave the driver her credit card and blindly signed the receipt he handed her. He hadn't been eager to come all the way out here, had cursed the weather and the driving conditions and the long trip back to town. But she had said something, she didn't even remember what, that had made him to shut up and drive pretty abruptly. Now he was so eager to get out of the yard again that his wheels started to spin by the gable, and he had to let the car roll back a length before he could clear the little rise that led to the road.

The light came on in the hall, and the front door opened.

"Can I help you?" A small, slender silhouette stood in the lit square of the doorway.

"Anna?" said Nina. "It's Nina Borg. I don't know if you remember me."

A moment passed. Then Anna Olesen took a step back so the light fell on her hair and face.

"The nurse," she said. "You were here the night when Natasha . . ."

"Yes."

"Come in."

THE FIRE GLOWED behind the glass doors of the big white brick oven between the kitchen and the living room. Anna placed a Bodum glass mug in front of Nina.

"It's tea," she said. "I can make coffee too. But that'll take a few minutes."

"Tea is fine."

Tea, coffee . . . Nina didn't care. Her gaze wandered across the neat dining room table, the stove with two bubbling pots, preparations for dinner. For one or for two?

No Rina, anyway. Not here.

"I came to ask if you had seen Rina."

Anna wrinkled her eyebrows. "Little Katerina? A man came to ask the same thing a little while ago. But why on earth would I have?"

"She has disappeared from . . . the camp." At the last minute Nina chose to simplify the explanation. "And our only clue to where she might have gone is that she called here."

"Here? When?"

"This morning. Between nine and ten." Between 9:40 and 9:42, to be exact, but Nina had learned that people usually looked at her oddly when she gave the time down to the minute.

"I was probably still out with the dog then."

"Who was the man? The one who asked for her?"

"One of the policemen searching Michael's house. A DI somebody or other, I don't recall his name. But why would Katerina call me? I haven't seen her in . . . well, since then."

"She's had a couple of hard days. Maybe she needed to talk with someone who would understand her." But that person couldn't have been Anna, Nina thought suddenly, because Rina had spoken in Ukrainian. "You haven't seen Natasha, have you?" she asked casually.

Anna pushed her reading glasses into her hair and smiled sarcastically. "My dear, I know that Natasha is wanted by every police authority in the entire country. If I was really hiding her in my leaky hayloft, do you think I would tell you? But you're welcome to look."

"No, no, it doesn't matter." If Natasha was here, it certainly wouldn't be in the hayloft. But Nina couldn't really believe that she would dare to come here. Michael Vestergaard's house lay just on the other side of the hill; it must have been swarming with police for the past twenty-four hours. No doubt Anna had been questioned as well, by people who were somewhat more professional at that kind of thing than Nina was.

"How long has Katerina been missing?"

"For almost four hours."

"If she was really on her way here, she should have been here long ago. Unless . . ."

"Unless what?"

"The bus doesn't go down Tundra Lane; its nearest stop is at Isterødvej. That's quite a walk. And in this weather . . ."

"Are you saying you think she might have gotten lost?"

"Henrik cleared the road with the tractor again just before you came. You and your taxi were lucky you didn't try an hour earlier."

"We have to look for her. Or . . ." She glanced at Anna and noticed, really for the first time, that she was, in fact, talking to a fairly senior citizen. "I have to, anyway."

"Wait," said Anna. "I'll come. I just need to put some proper clothes on."

Five minutes later they were on their way out into the blizzard, armed with two powerful flashlights and, in Anna's case, a handful of dog biscuits and a leash.

"If that stupid dog would only come when I call her, she could help us. She's actually a trained scent hound."

Nina had only the vaguest notion of what that meant. Something to do with finding animals hurt or killed in traffic. Or something.

Killed in traffic. She stared out into the darkness and wished those words hadn't popped into her head.

UKRAINE, 1935

THE COURTROOM WAS small and crammed with people Olga didn't know, and she felt as if just breathing was a difficult undertaking. She couldn't help thinking that it would have been better if she had been allowed to stay at home with the lice and the cockroaches, but there was no way around it, Semienova had said. Olga was a witness, and it was important that she repeated everything she had already told the GPU. Several times. About Uncle Grachev and Fyodor and Pjotr and Vitja. That they were kulaks, that they had attacked Oxana because she was pure of heart and fought for the Soviet state and had reported Father, who had always been a kulak and an enemy of the people. Kulaks could not tolerate that there were people like Oxana. Kulaks spread hunger and destruction so that they themselves could eat until they became fat, and Oxana had been a threat to them. She was pure of heart.

"Pure of heart, pure of heart."

Olga formed the words silently. She knew what she was supposed to say because she had said it many times already. The truth. Everything she now knew about her Uncle Grachev and Aunt Vira and Pjotr and Vitja and Fyodor and even Grandfather and Grandmother Trofimenko, who had been jailed three months ago along with the rest of the family. They had all been a part of planning the murder of Oxana and little Kolja. It was revenge for Father, and Oxana's punishment because she was pure of heart and the people's nightingale. That was what Grachev had not been able to stand, coward that he was, and the GPU police had nodded and smiled kindly at her every single time she repeated it, and now—today—she carried the truth with her like a small, well-polished pearl, waiting to be presented to the judge, who had come all the way from Leningrad. There was even a great author who insisted on attending the trial, and Olga thought she had seen him among the spectators, a little man in a dark suit with sharp, pale eyes.

Olga straightened her back and glanced at Mother, who sat unmoving next to her. If she was pleased that Oxana's murderers would soon be held accountable for their misdeeds, she didn't show it. Her face expressed neither happiness nor sorrow, and her eyes had begun to look odd, as if they had been painted on her face in black. Her flat and lifeless gaze moved slowly around the room and seemed to focus too long on things that no one else took serious notice of. One of the judge's boots, the heavy ceiling beams and the whitewashed wall behind the desks and judges, which was greyish and had cracks in it. Someone should have whitewashed it again, thought Olga, just as Mother whitewashed the walls at home with the straw whisk that she dipped in lime. Her hands would become red and cracked and sometimes started to bleed as she worked.

Here the picture of Uncle Stalin was allowed to hang on a shit-colored wall, and that was wrong, just like everything else. The angry mumbling from the listeners, the stiff GPU people and the author and the pioneers, who had pushed their way into one of the front rows of spectators and stared at Olga warmly and eagerly.

The truth.

It shouldn't be so hard, but Olga's stomach hurt, and she felt as if she was going to throw up when Uncle Grachev was led into the room, accompanied by a wave of excited talk and hushed comments.

He was wearing a clean shirt, and his dark beard was washed and trimmed, but he looked older than she remembered him, and it was as if he was squinting against a light that wasn't there. Grachev hid his hands in his shirtsleeves, which hung loose and flapping on his thin arms. He admitted that he had killed Oxana. And he admitted that he was a kulak. And he admitted that he had hated the girl deep in his cowardly kulak soul because she was clean, and because she sang so beautifully. He said that he had murdered Oxana, but that he had done it alone. His sons were innocent and so were his parents.

"You've always been full of lies, Grachev!" a man behind Olga shouted spitefully, and several others availed themselves of the opportunity to spit angrily on the floor. Olga recognized the first one as Uncle Grachev's neighbor and card-playing friend. Olga had often seen them sitting together by the samovar, smoking and drinking tea and vodka. The neighbor also used to borrow her uncle's cart when he had to bring in the hay or needed to go to Sorokivka.

The truth.

Grandmother and Grandfather Trofimenko were dragged in and placed together before the judge. Grandfather had trouble staying upright and had to lean on the GPU officer who had led them in. Grandmother, who was tiny, smaller than Olga and stooped, stood without help but couldn't seem to understand what the judge was asking her. She just cried.

Kulaks, like their sons. People spat again, and Olga stole a look over at Comrade Semienova, who stood against the wall almost next to the judge's desk. She looked at once strict and sorrowful, exactly as she did in school when someone answered an important question incorrectly or maybe even said something stupid about Uncle Stalin. When that happened, she frowned exactly as she was doing now and tilted her head as if she was trying to figure out how she could best show them all the beautiful pictures of the future that were in her head. She had never looked at Oxana in that way, but sometimes at Jana and Olga when they giggled in class, and it was such a sad expression that Olga always wanted to apologize because she had upset Semienova.

Today she wanted to show Semienova that she had understood everything. That she knew what was needed to fix everything that was wrong in the world. Both Grandmother and Grandfather Trofimenko were beyond redemption, that much she could see already, but she could still make Semienova proud.

"Uncle Grachev is a kulak," said Olga. Her eyes met Semienova's, and Semienova smiled encouragingly at her. "The day Oxana and Kolja were murdered, my cousin Fyodor and he came to look for Oxana. She was to die because she was a communist."

"And what did you do?"

Olga sat so close to the judge that she could smell the strange, spicy scent of his grey coat, but she didn't dare look up at him. He seemed so stern, and he had large, springy grey hairs that sprouted like brushes from his ears and even from his nostrils.

"I cried," said Olga. "I begged for her life, but they wouldn't listen to me. They wanted to kill the people's nightingale, they said."

Someone patted her on the shoulder when she sat down on the bench next to Mother. She pulled herself together to smile faintly, but she couldn't really feel anything anymore. She didn't know if she was a hero or a sinner, and she caught herself envying Oxana her fate.

Oxana was a hero. Of that there was no doubt.

The newspaper had written about her, and Semienova asked the party leadership in Moscow for money to erect a statue of Oxana in pioneer uniform in the square in Sorokivka. The people's nightingale.

Olga clenched her teeth and stared down at her hands, which lay like dead birds in her lap.

The truth had left a sharp, metallic taste on her tongue. Nothing else.

THE BUS STOP sign cleared the snowdrift by only about a meter and a half, and the wind still whipped more snow across the open fields. They had called and shouted all the way down here, without result. Nina searched her pocket for her cell phone but then remembered that she had given it to Søren. Her left arm ached steadily, a deep but not especially insistent note of pain, like a soft bass line somewhere beneath the main theme: the fear of what had happened to Rina.

"Do you have a cell phone I can borrow?" she asked. "This isn't going to work; we need dogs."

Anna shook her head. Here was a woman who understood how to dress for the weather, thought Nina. A bright red ski suit covered her from head to toe and made her look like an overgrown kindergarten child on an excursion.

"I have one somewhere, but I rarely use it. I don't even think it's charged. We'd better go back to the house. Then you can call from there."

Why aren't they already here? thought Nina. Chains of men with Alsatians, lights, search teams? Sending one policeman to look around couldn't exactly be called a search.

And she felt almost certain that this *was* the place they needed to search for Rina. There were probably just two places in Denmark that could have activated Rina's homing pigeon instinct. One was the Coal-House Camp, the other was here. And it wasn't the Coal-House Camp that Rina had tried to call.

They turned around and walked back toward the house. Anna moved at a steady clip, and in spite of legs that were somewhat longer and younger, Nina had to quicken her pace to keep up. At first it was nice to have the wind hit her other cheek for a change, but it wasn't long before that cheek was just as numb as the one that had been frozen on the way out. When they were almost all the way back to the farm, a large, brindled dog came running toward them.

"There you are!" said Anna sharply.

The dog didn't pay any attention to the cool greeting. It jumped around, shaking its head so its ears flopped, and wagging its entire rear. When Anna didn't pay it much attention, it thrust its pinkish-brown nose into Nina's hand, so that her glove was soon covered by a fine glaze of dog drool.

That was when she discovered that it had something in its mouth. At first she thought it was a mouse, and in a way it was—a stuffed toy mouse with oversized ears, eyes and feet.

It was the Diddl mouse that had been attached to the zipper on Rina's backpack.

"MY HUSBAND TRAINED her," said Anna. "She never really bothered to listen to me."

"We have to try," Nina insisted. "What is her name?"

"Maxi."

Maxi had exchanged the Diddl mouse for a dog biscuit, but Anna still didn't show any sign of encouraging the dog to search, and Nina's experience with that kind of thing was limited to having seen cadaver dogs work. She attached the leash to its collar and then held the drool-covered toy mouse in front of the dog's nose.

"Search," she said as authoritatively as she could. "Maxi, search!"

The dog looked up at her, and she thought it looked as if it was grinning foolishly.

Something occurred to her then. "We should be able to see where it came from. It must have found the toy somewhere."

"The snow is already covering the tracks," said Anna.

"Yes, we have to hurry." She remembered that she was, in fact, dealing with an elderly woman. "You don't need to come," she said. "If I can just borrow Maxi."

"You don't know your way around here," said Anna. "We can't have you getting lost too."

THEY HAD WALKED perhaps four to five hundred meters in the deep snow—about as exhausting as wading in seawater at mid-thigh height—when Maxi finally seemed to understand what the exercise was all about and set off with a tug that almost dislocated Nina's one functioning arm.

"She's got a scent!"

"Yes," said Anna. "Let her get on with it. Hold the leash tightly, but go with her as quickly as you can. Run if you can."

The flashlight's cone of light danced across the snow. Shrubbery and saplings were bent low under the heavy snow, and once in a while Nina's foot caught on a branch or a stone she couldn't see. A fence blocked the way on the left—that must be the edge of the golf course. This was neither woodlands nor a real field, but a scruffy sort of in-between-ness, like the meager plantings the municipality tried to establish on highway embankments and the like. Nina had to halt the dog for a moment while she climbed over a partially fallen barbed-wire fence, then on they went through the drifts. Her jeans were ridiculously unsuitable for this, and the snow worked its way up her pant legs and melted down into her socks and boots.

Suddenly Maxi gave a high-pitched, sharp bark and threw itself forward with so much power that the leash slid between Nina's gloved and frozen fingers. She managed to keep her flashlight on the dog long enough to see it disappear into one end of something that looked like a scrapped railroad car.

She ran as quickly as she could.

The first thing the light illuminated inside the car was a tea table. A cardboard box covered in a flowered tablecloth, four unmatched cups and a teapot without a lid. Napkins had been set out, and three cookies were neatly arranged on each of the napkins. The cups had been filled with a red liquid that didn't quite look like tea. Juice, maybe. Only one cup appeared to have been drunk from.

"Rina?"

Nina listened anxiously. No one answered, but she could hear the familiar sound of Rina's asthmatic breathing. She moved the flashlight around and saw in dancing glimpses that the freight car's raw wooden walls were covered by cutouts from magazines, photographs, plastic flowers, pale green glow-in-the-dark stars and planets of the same kind that Ida had once been briefly infatuated with, posters of large-eyed animals and long-legged pop starlets, but most of all photographs and ads and newspaper cutouts with one thing in common: they all showed fathers with their children, fathers who pushed strollers, father who held the reins of ponies in amusement parks, fathers who pushed swings, played, built, swam or just smiled and laughed with happy daughters. A secret den, thought Nina. A Father Temple.

"Rina!"

She was lying curled up under a pile of old blankets and towels in the corner farthest from the heavy sliding door she probably had not had the strength to shut completely. Her eyes were closed, her lips pale and wax-like, and beneath her eyebrows was the reddish-brown pinpoint bruising her asthma attack had given her, dark freckles against the almost blue-white skin.

Maxi barked once more and then began to eat the cookies.

Nina pulled her gloves off and placed her fingers against Rina's neck. The difference between her own cold fingers and Rina's skin didn't feel as significant as she had feared it might.

"Rina! Rina, wake up. Look at me."

She pinched Rina's earlobe. No reaction whatsoever.

"Oh, the poor little thing." Anna had appeared in the door. "What's wrong with her? Is she very weak?"

"She is unconscious," Nina said but couldn't see why.

"It must be the cold."

"Possibly." There was no doubt that Rina was colder than was good for her, but there was no stiffness in the muscles, no sign of the confusion that sometimes made hypothermia victims act paradoxically by, for example, beginning to take off their clothes.

Then there was a sudden exclamation from Anna. "Oh, no. What has she done?"

"What?"

Anna held up a pill bottle in a red ski mitt that matched her suit. Nina shone her flashlight in her direction but couldn't see what it was.

"These are mine," said Anna. "How did she get a hold of them?"

"Give them to me!"

Anna handed them over. Nina grabbed them and finally was able to decipher the writing on the damp, half-dissolved label.

"Diazepam," she said. "How many were in the bottle?"

Anna's wide eyes glittered in the glow of the flashlight. "It was almost full," she said.

"HERE?"

Jurij stopped the car at the turnoff and squinted down the narrow track that ran between the snow-covered fields.

Perhaps he hesitated because the road was so small. There were only four houses in all: Michael's, Anna's farm and then two smaller houses almost all the way down by Isterødvej. Not many cars came this way. In the summer the grass grew so tall in the middle that it brushed against the bottom of the car. In an odd way that was precisely what had made Natasha feel at home. Not in Michael's house, but on the road that led there. When she lived with Michael, she sometimes did stupid things when he wasn't home. Walked out of the house and across the pebble-covered front drive, crossed the gravel road on bare feet and continued into the wilderness of knee-high grass and wild oats and clover and elder trees. And then she sat down in the middle of it all, so that she couldn't see the brick house or the garage or the pebbles, and turned her face to the sun, breathing in the spicy scent of grass and feeling the tiny legs of insects as they crawled across her feet. Strangely enough, it was neither Pavel nor her luxurious life in Kiev that she missed when Michael and she moved in together, but the flowering verges of her childhood. The kind that lined the road when Father and she rode their bikes to Grandfather's and Grandmother's farmhouse, the kind she had sworn never to return to. Natasha moved a little in the seat to wake up her hands, which were now bound behind her back again. She let her tongue slide across her broken molars and split gums, which had finally, finally stopped bleeding.

Tonight there was no green anywhere. The snow blew into the wheel tracks, but the road had been cleared not long ago.

"It's not a one-way street. You can drive through to the big road," she said.

He didn't answer. Just turned off the lights and got out of the car. She saw his dark shape pace down to the first turn in the gravel road and disappear. The car quickly became cold now that the motor was turned off. The hole in the side window was already providing plenty of fresh air. Natasha pulled halfheartedly at the narrow plastic strips but quickly gave up. Her right arm and wrist ached, throbbing violently, and the jerky movements only made it worse.

The woman in the backseat shifted uneasily. Now that there was no longer a fresh supply of warm air circulating through the car, Natasha could sense the Witch's rotten breath. Baba Yaha who ate children.

Jurij returned and got behind the wheel, cursing. He maneuvered the car decisively in between the snowbanks, headlights still off. The snow was falling more heavily. The snowflakes were hard and grainy and rattled against the window like claws.

Jurij wanted to turn in at Michael's house, but Natasha stopped him.

"It's farther on," she said. "The next house." She saw with a certain relief that there was no sign of life in there. Michael wasn't home.

The she saw the yellow-and-black tape. POLICE, it said. Her chest constricted, and she couldn't tell if it was from fear or hope. Right now she'd like one of the nice Danish policemen to come save her from the Witch and her son. But there were no policemen at the barrier, which was disappearing into the snow.

What had happened at Michael's house? She guessed a part of the answer before she asked, and she had little doubt that Jurij, with his large and capably destructive hands, would be the right person to answer her, if he wanted to.

"What happened?" she said.

"We had to have a chat with your fiancé to find out where you and the girl were," said Jurij. "He didn't even know that you had run off, but at least he told us where we could find the little girl. We didn't think you'd run far if we had her."

"Did you kill him?"

Jurij didn't react. "Where are we going?"

Michael was dead. She recognized that in Jurij's indifference. For him Michael was just as irrelevant as Natasha, who would also be dead in a very short time and therefore had already been removed from his calculations.

"Farther along," she said flatly. "On the other side of the hill."

Jurij engaged the gears again and let the car eat its way up the rise and down the other side. Behind them, Michael's house disappeared from sight. He was gone. Everything he had been, everything he had done to her, was gone now. She felt nothing at the thought.

Jurij let the car roll into the drive that led to Anna's farm.

"I'm going to park it behind the stable over there." Jurij pointed at one of the farm's yellow outbuildings. "It's best if the car can't be seen from the road, so there'll be a little bit of walking, Mamo. Are you sure you want to come?"

Natasha sensed the old woman's movements in the backseat. A determined nod, she assumed, because Jurij sighed, resigned.

He parked behind the low half wall that had once encircled the farm's midden. They got out and walked along the sheltered side of the stable where the snow wasn't piled as high, Natasha in front, with her hands still bound behind her back. Then Jurij and the old woman, side by side, like an aging couple. The old woman kept up surprisingly well, noted Natasha, in spite of the fact that the snow was ankle deep here and in several places slippery and uneven in the deep tracks left by a tractor.

The light in the hall was on, but Jurij didn't waste any time knocking. He pushed at the door, and when it opened—as usual, Anna hadn't locked up—he shoved Natasha ahead of him onto the pale golden floor tiles. Anna's rubber boots and clogs were arranged along the wall on clean and dry newspapers. The heat from the large kitchen hit her, and the snow brought in by their shoes melted almost instantly, making small, dirty pools on the floor. Poor Anna would have to get out the mop, thought Natasha, and marveled at how ordinary the thought was.

The old woman had followed her son and now approached the huge oven in the middle of the room with outstretched hands. Heat emanated from it and made the air billow in waves around the birdlike figure.

I could kill her when he turns his back, thought Natasha. Maybe she wouldn't even need her hands. She pictured herself rushing toward the old woman, cracking her own head against that frail old skull. Would it be enough? Or a kick. Maybe she could knock her down and kick her in the head. That was probably better.

Jurij had promised that he would leave Katerina and her alone as soon as they had found the picture. Beautiful, stupid Natasha would have believed him. In fact, she wanted to believe it, just as she also wanted to believe his promise not to touch Anna. But she was no longer beautiful, stupid Natasha, and she had seen her future in his indifferent gaze.

"Call her," said Jurij quietly. He had already checked both the boiler room and the kitchen and had taken the safety off his gun, which he now directed at the door to the living room.

Natasha felt her fear return. "Is that really necessary?" She nodded at the gun.

Jurij shrugged but apparently saw no reason to put it away. "Call her."

Natasha called Anna, halfheartedly but still loud enough that Anna should have been able to hear her. Anna's hearing was fine, she knew. There was no answer, and she realized that she hadn't heard the usual clicking of dog paws across the floor. No barking and no wagging mutt, whacking its tail into cabinets and chair legs.

"The dog," said Natasha and nodded at the water bowl that sat on the floor near the door to the hallway. "She must be out with the dog."

"In this weather?"

Jurij looked skeptically out the window above the kitchen sink. Snow whirled among the rosebushes in the yellow glow from the patio lights. He slammed open the double doors leading to the living room, walked with long strides into the room and started to systematically open cabinets and drawers.

As the work progressed, he spread papers and folders in a thin layer across the floor. He picked up a few and threw them on the floor again. Lingered briefly over a small tape recorder, but let it go and continued with a row of cans decorated with flowers that stood on the shelf above the couch. He pulled off the lids and upended them so that the contents—buttons and sewing material—flew out in all directions and hit the floor with small, distinctive whacks.

"Where was it you found the picture?" he asked then. "Show us."

"Upstairs," she said. "In the bedroom."

He made her go up the stairs first. She could feel the light pressure of the gun barrel under her right shoulder blade and tried to calculate what the bullet would hit if the gun went off right now. Probably a lung. And her heart, depending on the angle. She had never been particularly interested in biology, but she had, after all, seen pigs slit open, with intestines and kidneys and liver hanging out of the body cavity. She knew where the organs were, and none of them were expendable.

"But he won't shoot you, right? Not yet." Natasha formed the words silently with her lips. Here in Anna's house, the voice that usually lived in her head had gone conspicuously silent. She forced herself to look at the staircase in front of her. One step at a time. The Witch was also on the stairs now, but Natasha was already up. Too late to let herself stumble backward and crush the bird skeleton in the fall.

Jurij turned on the light in the bedroom and ordered Natasha to lie on the floor, which was surprisingly difficult with her hands bound behind her back. She managed to get on her knees, and Jurij pushed her the rest of the way so that she fell forward and hit her shoulder and chin on the wooden floor.

Then he opened the dresser drawer and emptied its pill containers and papers out onto the bed. The picture of Anna and her husband on vacation with palm trees and a light blue pool in the background fluttered to the floor in front of Natasha's face. Then the tips of Jurij's shoes approached her forehead.

"You didn't lie, did you? Sometimes people lie because that's all they can remember how to do. Maybe you are like your husband."

He touched her very lightly with the tip of his shoe. The sole scratched the bridge of her nose. The shoes were still wet. She turned her face away and waited while he looked under the bed and behind the wardrobe's enormous mirrored doors. She could see that the Witch had entered the room now, her feet making their way around the bed. Then she stood still and looked at the wall Anna had covered with pictures of her daughter. Natasha knew the pictures well. The daughter was called Kirsten and in the first pictures had been photographed at age three while she held an old-fashioned red phone in her hand and smiled in a friendly way at the photographer.

Farther down was a row of more or less anonymous school photos in which the girl's hairdo varied between short and slightly longer. In two of the pictures, her teeth were covered by braces. Then came the graduation photo, pictures of Kirsten with Anna's grandchildren, pictures of Hans Henrik and Kirsten at an amusement park with the kids. Katerina loved the photos, and for some reason the Witch also remained standing in front of the portraits. Natasha could see that she was leaning forward. Her head moved in small, uneven, hen-like jerks. Then she turned to the nightstand and picked up Anna's and Hans Henrik's wedding picture.

The Witch's hands shook so much that the picture rattled between her fingers. How old was she? Eighty-five? Eighty-six? Too old to lay a fair claim to more years in this life, and yet she was winning and Natasha was in the process of losing.

"Who is that?"

The Witch held the framed photo out to Natasha. Natasha couldn't see it properly from her position on the floor, but she remembered it from the many times she had been lying in this room, on Anna's bed, while everything hurt and she had fled from Michael, and Anna was patting her hair and murmuring, "There, there, there," as she tried to console her. Anna had said that Michael was better than Ukraine, and that was true, at least most of the time.

Natasha had looked at it so often. The picture of a woman who had married a good man and had lived a long life with him in peace and safety in Bacon Land. Wedding Anna smiled a bit crookedly and had her eyes partially closed against the sun. Her hair was in thick, roller-induced '50s curls under the veil, and she was made up almost like a movie star. Hans Henrik was young and strong and kind, had shiny, brushed-back black hair and didn't look like the thin and aging man she had come to know on her first visits to Denmark those last years before he died.

"That's Anna," said Natasha tiredly.

The old woman in front of her looked as if someone had physically shoved her. She tottered in her impractical half-heeled boots. Even now, with death so close that the old biddy must be able to feel the cold gust of annihilation through all the layers of shiny sable fur, she insisted on dressing like a woman.

"That's a lie. You're lying."

Jurij, who had stopped in the middle of dresser drawer number three, turned around and stared silently at them, and Natasha shook her head. She couldn't do anything more than that because of her awkward position on the floor. She tested her strips again, but nothing yielded even slightly.

The old Witch leaned against the wall for a moment. Her breathing had become heavier, and she picked up the picture from the floor again, narrowing her eyes as she studied it.

"You don't need to search any further," she said to Jurij. "Finish here and come downstairs. We'll wait for her by the oven."

Jurij grabbed Natasha's armpit and hauled her to her feet, but the faint sound of a motor from outside stopped him mid-gesture.

"Shit!"

He released her and let her tumble to the floor so he could reach out for the light switch and turn off the light in the bedroom.

"Stay where you are," he said to his mother. "I'll take care of this."

He grabbed hold of Natasha and dragged her across the bedroom floor to the little bathroom Anna had had put in so she didn't need to go downstairs at night. He swore the whole way but didn't let go until he had thrown Natasha on the tiles by the bathroom door. This time, she fell flat on her face and chipped her front tooth. He kicked her the rest of the way in, took the key and locked the door behind him.

Natasha lay on the floor and felt her tears burn in the cuts on her cheek. She was dizzy and wanted to let herself fall into unconsciousness, the way she had sometimes done when Michael was at his worst. Anna wasn't there to help, neither in reality not in Natasha's head. And maybe she would never help again after what Natasha had done.

SØREN POSITIONED HIMSELF behind a snowplow on Isterødvej and stayed there. The driving had been bad even on the main highway to Elsinore, and after the exit, it had gotten much worse. It did no good to push it, especially not in a flimsy little car like the Hyundai.

"We run the risk of not being able to get back to the city tonight," he said to Babko. Not so good when Torben had made it very clear that he wanted Søren back at his usual post on Monday morning.

"I think I've had about enough of your headquarters," said the Ukrainian. "Fancy though it is."

The message that the BMW with the shattered window had been spotted at the exit to Isterødvej had come in almost three-quarters of an hour ago and had set off a whole chorus of alarm bells in Søren's head. It was simply way too close to two of the central locations of the case: the scene of Michael Vestergaard's murder and Anna Olesen's house, which was the address Rina had telephoned a few hours before she disappeared. He had practically dragged Babko with him out to the car and on the few stretches where conditions had allowed it, the little Hyundai had had its not particularly impressive acceleration pushed to the utmost.

Tundra Lane. He almost missed it even though he had been there the day before. Snow and more snow. The visibility was terrible. But it looked as if the tractor had been by relatively recently, and it wasn't as impassable as he had feared. He stopped and got out of the car to look at the tire tracks, but the snow was blowing so strongly, he could only determine that one or more cars had driven this way not too long ago. Whether one of them was a BMW with a defective side window, he could not say.

They stopped at the barricade by Michael Vestergaard's house.

"You go one way around; I'll go the other?" he suggested to Babko. He wished he had taken the time to get the Ukrainian a radio. Søren had a "colleague in trouble" button, but Babko didn't. The only channel of communication between them was their cell phones.

Babko nodded. Out of old habit, he patted himself where at the moment there was neither radio nor service weapon nor bulletproof vest, and grimaced. "Sorry," he said. "I feel a little underdressed."

Søren just nodded. They ducked under the tape, which in any case was being quietly buried in a snowbank. Søren turned on the flashlight he did have and then turned it off again. He had no idea what to expect if they came upon Savchuk. It would depend on the situation, and he would like to have the option of observing before he was observed.

The wind moaned around the corner of the house, but otherwise he couldn't hear anything except his own footsteps. It didn't look as if a car had come through here. Behind the bungalow he met Babko, who had just as little to report.

"Let's go see the lady with the good oven," suggested the Ukrainian.

When they were still about a hundred meters from the yellow farmhouse, Søren stopped the Hyundai in the middle of the road.

"Same procedure?" asked Babko.

"Yep."

There was a light on in the yard, but the only car parked there was Anna Olesen's red Mazda. Babko headed down along one stable wing; Søren turned his attention to the farmhouse. There was no dog barking, but there was a light on in the hallway. He went along the gable and into the garden to get a discreet look through the kitchen windows.

Just then his cell phone vibrated in his pocket, a single buzz. A signal from Babko.

The car is here, the text message said.

"LIEUTENANT BABKO, I see you've been busy."

Søren stopped mid-step, on his way around the stable corner. He carefully set his foot down into the snow again. In front of him, a few steps away and with his back to Søren, stood a large, broad-shouldered man in a long, classic overcoat. Babko was facing Søren but carefully avoided looking in his direction.

"Colonel. You've been missed."

"Really. By whom, Mr. Lieutenant? Who has such a burning interest in what I do?"

Søren had absolutely no intention of interrupting this fascinating conversation. He took a slow, silent step backward in the direction of the half wall around the old midden.

"The Danish police do," said Babko. "It's an unfortunate situation. If you have news of Natasha Doroshenko, you should report it to the Danes."

"And why would you think I have such news?"

"Among other reasons . . . because you are here. So close to where her Danish fiancé was murdered."

"The Danes won't know I'm here—unless you tell them."

Søren slid behind the half wall and began to crouch down to be less visible. In the middle of the move, his bum knee, the one that he'd had surgery on, cracked loudly.

Savchuk spun around. His hand disappeared into his coat, but at the moment the gun came out, Babko hammered the edge of one of his large, bony hands against the Colonel's neck.

The blow didn't hit with true precision, partly because of the thick, woolly overcoat, but mostly because Savchuk was moving. The gun was free of its holster, but by this point, Søren had left his half-covered position to come to Babko's aid. He threw his flashlight as hard as he could in Savchuk's direction just as the first shot rang out.

Savchuk fell over in the snow with Babko partly under him. There was yet another shot, a second before Søren kicked Savchuk under his jaw with all the strength he could muster. He grabbed the bigger man by the arm and rolled him on his stomach. Søren didn't have handcuffs, but right now there wasn't any resistance in the arm he was holding. Savchuk was unconscious.

"Are you okay?" Søren asked. His sense was that both shots had been fired in his direction without hitting him.

It took awhile for Babko to answer. "Not quite," he said.

Søren whirled around. Babko sat in the snow with both hands pressed against one thigh. Blood was seeping through his fingers.

Søren let go of Savchuk. He pressed the ASSISTANCE NEEDED button on the radio with one hand. Where the hell was the gun? It must be lying somewhere in the snow.

"Where are you hit?"

"On the outside of the thigh."

Better than the inside, where a huge artery supplied blood to the entire leg.

"We have an alarm from you," came the dispassionate voice over the radio. "What is the emergency?"

Something hit Søren in the side with a whistling kick, and suddenly he didn't have the air to answer. The radio slipped from his hand. He stretched his hands out in front of him without quite knowing why, maybe to support himself so he wouldn't fall. He still ended up in the snow, with a growing worry about where his next breath was going to come from. The kick had completely knocked the air out of him.

By the stable wall stood the tiniest, most ancient woman he had ever seen. Her mouth shone red in a powdered beige face, and in front of her she held a pistol that looked grotesquely huge in her wrinkled hands. She took aim again.

It was only then that Søren realized that he hadn't been kicked.

Fuck, he thought. I've been shot by a little old lady. And in another second, she'll do it again.

IT TOOK FOREVER to get the plastic ties off.

Natasha found the light switch after some fumbling and pressed it with her elbow. Anna had a first-aid kit in her linen closet, she knew—Natasha had needed it several times when she lived with Michael. And in that kit were scissors.

She managed to open the closet and, with her chin and shoulder, maneuvered piles of towels, cleaning rags and toilet paper onto the tile floor until she found the red plastic pouch with the white cross. It landed on the floor too. With difficulty she got down on her knees and slid sideways onto her bottom like a clumsy mermaid. The flap on the case was closed with a button that took several more minutes of fumbling to open. She shook the contents onto the floor, found the scissors with her stiff hands and guided the two short, slender blades to the black plastic bands.

Snip.

Her arms fell forward and suddenly felt twice as heavy and sore, which made no sense. But there was still a locked door between the Witch and her. She pressed her shoulder against it, testing. Her weight didn't seem to make any impression on either the jamb or the door.

She pushed the small angled overhead window open instead. A whirlwind of snow hit her, pricking her skin like the metal spikes on a hairbrush. She could hear voices somewhere in the howling of the storm—voices speaking Ukrainian. She thought one was Jurij's but couldn't be sure.

Suddenly she saw dancing lights along the road. Someone on foot was coming around the bend where the fat electrician and his wife lived, and when they passed under the lamppost in his driveway, even at that distance she recognized the dog, Anna's red snow suit and . . .

And Nina Borg. With a child in her arms, a child wrapped in a blanket, but it could only be . . . It made no sense, but it had to be Katerina.

A lie. The Danish nurse had failed her own gospel of truth and had lied to her. Katerina was not with the police, and she was not, *not* at all "safe." Hatred and panic rose in Natasha with equal force. The Witch was here, downstairs in Anna's house, and the nurse was on her way to the Witch with Katerina. For a moment she thought the Witch had paid Nina Borg to lie and now was sitting in her chicken-legged house, waiting for Nina to bring her the child she was going to devour.

But the Witch didn't know everything. She could not have known that Natasha would lead them to Anna's house. There must be another explanation.

Then the next wave of emotion arrived, and this time it was pure, unarticulated panic.

Katerina. The Witch. Katerina.

Natasha planted her foot on one of the closet shelves and was now halfway through the narrow window without having thought about how she would get down from the roof. But it turned out to be easy. The snow lay in drifts around the rosebushes beneath her, and she just jumped, hung in the empty space, then hit a snow pillow and thick, bristling rose stems and finally the cold ground. Seconds. She only had seconds to get to them and stop them before they were within reach of the Witch.

She had turned one knee in the fall but still ran, slipping and limping, through the deep snow. Behind her came the sudden sound of two dry bangs in short succession. Shots. But who had shot whom?

The dog barked briefly and started to run as if it were expecting a couple of ducks to come drifting down from the sky for it to collect. The flashlight figures hesitated. Then Nina put her burden down in the snow and ran after the dog, toward the farmhouse and the yard, in the direction from which the shots had come.

How stupid was that?

Natasha ran in the opposite direction, toward Anna and Katerina.

Anna, squatting in the snow next to the child, looked up in surprise when Natasha came running. She said something or other, but Natasha wasn't listening. She pulled the blanket aside, and Katerina's face appeared, closed and pale like the faces of the dead saints Mother had hanging above the kitchen table.

But Katerina wasn't dead. She couldn't be. Natasha desperately attempted to quiet her own hectic breathing so she could hear Katerina's, pulling her onto her lap and hugging her tightly.

"What's wrong with her?" she asked. "What happened?"

Yet another shot, followed by a piercing howl from the dog.

Anna jumped. Instead of turning around, she walked past Natasha on stiff legs and toward the yard, stupid as a pig that wanders into the slaughter stall without noticing the blood on the floor, just because someone jangles the feed bucket. She had lived too long in Bacon Land.

When she got to the corner of the main house, she stopped. She only stood there for a moment before she took three quick steps backward and turned around, but the light from the lamps in the yard had hit her, and yet another flat slap sounded.

The pig is dead, thought Natasha, and in a moment it will fall over on the bloody floor. But Anna was still standing. Natasha felt

Katerina move, a slight scraping of one knee against her thigh, and she got up quickly with her daughter in her arms and stumbled away from the road, into the deep winter darkness. She sank down into the drifts behind the rose hedge, better hidden by the darkness than by the leafless stalks, but she knew it wasn't enough. If the Witch had a light, if she looked this way . . .

The car. Could she make it to the car? No, it was no good; the keys were in big Jurij's pocket. Natasha wished that she had listened more closely back when acne-covered Vasyl had tried to impress her by hot-wiring his father's ancient Lada. But she remembered something about hot-wiring not working on new cars anyway, so perhaps it made no difference.

She saw Anna back away from the corner of the house and down the road, her hands held out in front of her.

"Stop," the Witch commanded. "One more step, and I'll shoot."

THE DOG HOWLED as if possessed. Long, piercing screams, as only an animal in pain can scream. Nina ran in the direction of the sound. It was where the two first shots had come from too. She fumbled in her pocket for her cell phone and only a second later remembered yet again that she had given it to Søren that morning.

She found the dog first. It had been shot in the back and was attempting to crawl through the snow to the house, leaving a wide and scarlet track behind it. She forced herself not to meet its gaze.

Behind the stable a big black car was parked, half hidden by the old midden wall. There was an unreasonable amount of blood in the snow, and it wasn't all the dog's. A man lay on the ground with his face downward, unconscious but alive to judge by his labored breathing, and a few meters from him another man sat on the ground, half bent over a third man, who was Søren. Had they shot each other? She couldn't see a gun.

She had recognized Søren immediately even though she couldn't see his face, just his back and neck. She fell to her knees next to him.

"Help," said the man who was still sitting. It was not a plea for himself but more of a calm instruction. "Shot. Chest. Get help. Him."

The telegram style was clearly caused by linguistic difficulties, not panic, though she could see that he himself was bleeding pretty heavily from a wound in the thigh.

I can't see anything, she thought. How can I help him when I can't see anything?

Søren was breathing, but not well. There was a bubbling sound.

"Let me," she said. In Danish. Of course it didn't help. "I'm a nurse," she attempted in English. "Let me take a look."

She was able to turn him over partially so she could see his face. His eyes reacted when he saw her, but he was gasping too hard for air to be able to speak. Blue lips. Hypoxia. She suddenly realized that what looked like red and white snowflakes on his chest was down—from where the shot had torn a hole in his jacket. Entry wound and no exit wound. His back had not been bloody. Pneumothorax. The lung had been punctured and was in the process of collapsing. With every breath he took, he was dragging air through the hole, air that was caught between the lung membrane, compressing the lung further.

A syringe, she thought, where the hell am I going to find a syringe? The only place there was even the tiniest chance of finding something she could use was in the house.

"I'll be right back," she said to Søren's conscious gaze. She ran, trying to calculate how many minutes he had left.

THE GUN WAS so large that the Witch had to use both her ancient hands to hold it. Natasha shrank down with Katerina in her arms, much too close, and with only the snow, the darkness and the rose hedge for cover. She was terrified that the Witch would hear Katerina's breathing, but it seemed as if the old woman only had eyes for Anna. The light from the gable illuminated Anna's hair and face and made the red ski suit glow like a torch in the middle of the whirling whiteness of the blizzard. Natasha couldn't see the Witch's face. Only the fur and the boots with the too-high heels that sank into the packed snow with every step the old woman took, making deep, precise holes, like punctures.

An odd silence had fallen. It was as if even the snowflakes stopped in midair.

"Are you a ghost?" asked the old woman.

"No," said Anna. She took half a step toward the old woman and held her arms out like you do when you want to embrace someone. She wasn't planning to embrace the Witch, was she?

"Stand still."

Anna stopped. She understands Ukrainian, thought Natasha. She doesn't usually. But when Anna began to speak again, it was in Ukrainian.

"They thought I would die," she said. "But I survived. And that wasn't so good, because by then the trial was already over, and the murderers condemned."

"I think you *are* a ghost," said the Witch. "How otherwise could I have stood by your grave?"

"It wasn't my fault. Semienova . . . They couldn't admit that a mistake had been made. Semienova had me placed with a family in Galicia, with the brother of an aunt of hers. Pötsch, they were called. They were ethnic Germans. And later . . . later it was easier to pretend that I was German too, otherwise I would have been sent back to Stalin."

"And so what? You were a hero, right? The people's nightingale?" The Witch spat out the last two words as if they hurt her mouth.

Anna stood still. Her face had transformed as her language had changed. There was an expression now that Natasha had never seen on a Dane. The unmoving mouth, the eyes that slid to the side . . . No, you couldn't break it into parts. It was just Ukrainian. If Anna had ever looked at Natasha with that expression, Natasha would have known right away that she wasn't born in Bacon Land.

"A dead nightingale," she said. "A dead hero. Who was still alive. How long do you think it would have been before they corrected that mistake? They had shot Grachev and Grandfather and Grandmother Trofimenko and . . . all of them. For my murder. If you have a murder trial, you also need a corpse."

"Kolja was dead. But maybe he doesn't count? *He* didn't get a statue, you know."

"Olga . . ."

The Witch laughed. A laughter without much sound, just a series of short hisses. "Olga? It has certainly been a long time. Several names ago. They are used up so quickly, it seems to me."

She began to cock the gun with shaking but competent hands.

"Are you going to shoot me?" asked Anna.

"Why not?"

"Haven't we lost enough? Olga, we are the only ones, the only ones who are left."

"So perhaps that was why you thought you had the right to bleed me for money? You milked me like one milks a cow."

"That wasn't me. It was Pavel. I shouldn't have told him as much as I did."

"No, you probably shouldn't have. Sister."

The Witch completed her gesture. Natasha could hear the small click as yet another projectile shot forward in the gun's chamber. Katerina stirred in her arms and made a tiny, sleepy sound.

Natasha knew that she wouldn't have more than this one chance. She was barely able to make herself let go of Katerina. But she did it. She placed her little girl softly in the snow and silently promised that she would return very soon. As soon as she was done.

She actually didn't much care right now if the Witch shot Anna. Because now she knew that it was Anna who had brought the Witch into their lives. All that time when she thought it was just Pavel's stupidity, Pavel's greed . . . It was Anna's too. That much she had understood. Because she had also watched Anna become wealthier. Had seen how there was money for a new kitchen, for the newly thatched roof, not just on the main house but also in the wing where Kirsten was going to live. She crept closer to the spot where Anna had dropped her flashlight.

"Olga, don't do it!" said Anna. It was clear she hadn't spoken Ukrainian for a long, long time. She sounded like someone in an old film.

"It's not a crime to shoot someone who is already dead," said the Witch. And at that moment, Natasha struck and felt the blow hit home, in spite of the fur hat, all the way to the frail, old eggshell skull.

The Witch fell forward, almost disappearing into the snowdrift by the gable. Natasha kneeled beside her and raised the flashlight again just to make sure.

This time no Jurij came to stop her.

ANNA STOOD IN the middle of the yard with a peculiar look on her face. At her feet crouched the dog, which had finally stopped howling. Nina didn't know if it was because it was feeling better or worse, but it wasn't dead yet.

"A syringe," she said to Anna. "Do you have one?"

Anna stared at her as if she had fallen from another planet. "Why would I have that?" she asked.

"Because I need one!"

"I don't."

"Something else. Some kind of tube. A pen."

Anna Olesen just shook her head, and Nina gave up on getting anything useful out of her. She ran up the stairs and into the house. The boiler room. A toolbox? Not a lot of slender tubes in there. The kitchen . . . She needed a knife in any case. Maybe there was a pen too.

She opened cabinets and tore out drawers and barely registered that there was already a mess that hadn't been there when they had gone out to look for Rina. Knives. Yes. Sharp enough to pierce the wall of the chest, though that in itself would not create a passage. She chose a slender, very sharp fillet knife with a patterned hilt. The blade was twelve to thirteen centimeters long—that had to be enough. The next drawer was full of spice glasses and completely useless. The next drawer . . . baking paper, tinfoil, plastic containers . . . Wasn't there a damned pen anywhere?

She looked around wildly. The seconds were passing. Her well-trained sense of time could feel them like an extra pulse, tick, tick, tick.

On the refrigerator hung a pad with a magnet and a pen on a string. Nina tore it down and took it apart with quick, sure hands. Out with the tip and the cartridge—it was only the hollow plastic part that she needed. She had her tube and her knife.

HE WAS STILL breathing—much, much too fast, and his gaze was hazier than it had been.

"Hurry," said the man who had been shot in the thigh. As if that wasn't what Nina was already doing.

She tore open the jacket and the shirt beneath it, drew a mental line from the nipple to the armpit and jabbed the knife in between the fourth and the fifth rib. It required more strength than she had anticipated. The muscles lay like tough, flat cables across the chest, and she needed to get past them and to the lung membrane—six, maybe seven centimeters. Thank God it was on the right so she didn't need to worry about the heart.

The thigh-shot man exclaimed, most likely something to the tune of, "What the hell are you doing?" She ignored him. When she pulled out the knife, there was a groaning sound of air being let loose, but only momentarily. She forced the sharp end of the pen through the cut she had made and sent a prayer to gods she didn't believe in. *Let it work.*

If her hopelessly improvised procedure worked, the air that was now trapped between the lung membranes would be released. The lung would have room to expand again, and Søren would be able to breathe.

She hadn't looked at his face at all while she did it. She had sensed his reaction to the pain, but only distantly. It had been necessary to think of his body as something mechanical, a question of tissue, anatomy and function. That perspective collapsed more quickly than his lung had when she met his gaze. It was darker than usual but already less hazy. He still needed proper drainage, oxygen and so on, and somewhere inside him was a projectile that would need to be removed. Lying on the cold ground wasn't helping him either, but right now it was too risky to move him. She had bought time; that was what was most important. Enough time, she thought.

She felt a jab in her left lower arm, and only then did she realize that she had been using it without even feeling the fracture.

She turned to the guy with the thigh wound, but he quickly held up a hand in front of himself. "Okay," he said. "I'm okay." He obviously had no wish for a taste of the Borg version of first aid.

The snow crunched. When Nina turned, she saw Natasha standing by the black BMW. Her face was so damaged that Nina only recognized her because she had Rina in her arms.

Rina. The pills. Rina.

She started to get up.

"Don't try," said Natasha. "Don't try to stop me." She opened the back door and carefully set Rina down on the seat.

"Natasha, Rina needs to go to the hospital." Nina got up, took the first step. "She has had an overdose of diazepam. Valium. She needs to be under observation; you can't . . ."

Natasha turned around and hit her straight across the mouth, a blow that hammered Nina's lips against her teeth and made her neck snap back with a whiplash jerk.

"You said, 'I'll take care.' You said, 'like my own child.' But you don't even know her right name. KA-TE-RI-NA. And you didn't take care."

"She needs treatment," Nina said. She felt the blood run down her chin on the outside and pool behind her teeth on the inside of her mouth. "Natasha, you're risking her life. She needs to be in a hospital."

Natasha shook her head stubbornly. She shoved Nina aside and went over to the third man, the one who lay on his stomach in the snow and hadn't moved at any point, even though she could hear him breathing fairly normally. Natasha rolled him onto his back. Then she kicked him in the face hard. She stuck her hands into the pockets of his overcoat and fished out a set of car keys and a wallet. A pair of black cable strips followed, but those she threw aside in the snow. She sent Nina a furious black look.

"All the time, you think, poor little Natasha, she can do nothing, she is so stupid. Poor, stupid Natasha. Beautiful and stupid, and people do what they like with her. But I'm not stupid. Katerina is *my* child. *I'll* take care now. You lose your children, but you can't take mine."

She got behind the wheel of the big BMW and drove away.

NINA SANK TO the ground next to Søren. The blood from her split lip dripped into the snow, dot, dot, dot, like the first third of a Morse code emergency signal. She observed it without emotion.

So much for Nina Borg, World Savior, she said to herself. That was that. Soon there'd be nothing left but the T-shirt. If there was one thing Natasha had managed to knock into her head with that blow, it was that she hadn't saved anyone from anything, and that there was, in fact, no one right now who wished to be saved by her. Rina was gone. Katerina, she corrected herself. You are a shitty mother even to children who don't belong to you. And flying conditions are still lousy. No help from above would be forthcoming.

She felt a hand on her ankle. It was Søren.

"Are you . . . okay?" he asked. The pause was the result of not being able to finish a whole sentence in one breath.

She looked down at him. His color was better, the lips a little less blue. He still had a hole in his lung. It was at once laughable and unbelievably touching that he was asking if *she* was okay.

She placed her hand on top of his. A little too cold, she noted, still in mild shock.

"I'm a hell of a lot healthier than you are," she said.

UKRAINE, 1935

"EAT!"

The lady at the end of the barrack stood with her arms folded behind her back, her eyes raking down the bench rows, and even though Olga hadn't been in the dining hall before, she immediately knew what was expected of her, and what the consequences would be if she refused. She could see it in the other children's faces; they had odd, rigid eyes and didn't look up or to the side, and she knew it from the two other orphanages she had stayed in over the course of the late summer.

What was expected of her was obedience. Nothing else. The consequences if she refused would target her body first. There would be locked doors, darkness, heat, beatings, hunger or thirst. But they might also be accompanied by humiliation. The recitation of Father's crimes against the Soviet state, or even worse, the story of Father's death on the pole where he had "howled like a dog." All the children around her were orphans like her. Children of class enemies, of the deported or just of parents who had fallen victim to hunger in the great hunger year. Still, the shame burned in her cheeks when the orphanage lady talked about her father. As if the very way that he had died was more undignified than everything else. Up against a pole. Howling like a dog. Thin and bony and beaten and toothless.

Olga shrank down over her plate and stared into the whitish-yellow mass of overcooked potatoes. The soup was covered in flies, which moved only lazily and unwillingly when she pushed at the spoon. Some remained lying there belly-up on the sticky surface, legs kicking. Olga was hungry after the trip from the station to what was called Lenin's Orphanage Nr. 4. She was someplace near a town called Odessa, she knew, but the orphanage was a lonely and windswept building stuck in the middle of the steppe, and even though there was now a touch of fall in the air, the midday heat was indescribable.

"Eat."

A sharp elbow poked her in the side, and she glanced at the girl who sat on her right, shoveling down her soup, quickly but at the same time carefully so not a drop was lost between plate and mouth. A pair of buzzing flies that were trapped in the sticky mass went right down the hatch too without the girl taking any notice.

"Eat it or let me have it," she whispered, looking impatiently at Olga. "The food will be cleared away in five minutes."

Olga's stomach growled a warning, unwilling to accept her indecisiveness, and she breathed deeply. She scraped some of the wriggling flies off the soup and brushed them off the spoon with her index finger. The first spoonful was the worst, but afterward it went pretty well. She took a mouthful and let it glide down her throat in one rapid movement, so that she didn't have time to either taste or feel it in her throat. Her benchmate followed her spoon with hungry eyes, but when Olga had scraped her plate completely clean, the girl took the time to examine Olga.

"What's your name?" she whispered.

"Oletchka," said Olga. That's what it said in her papers now.

"Did you just arrive?"

Olga nodded but wasn't sure she felt like doing this. She had already met and said goodbye to lots of girls since they had come to take her away from home.

It was the day after they had driven off with Mother. Olga had slept alone in the summer darkness the last night and had lain listening to the grasshoppers and the crickets that chirped in the grass outside in the overgrown garden. Mother hadn't touched the vegetable plot since Oxana and Kolja died, and through all of July she had just sat on the crumbling clay bench under the porch roof in front of the house, staring into space. Sometimes, not very often, she cried. Other times she asked Olga to sing, and Olga sang quietly and softly, almost as if it were a lullaby, and if she sang long enough, Mother might make a faint grimace which looked like a smile and say that she sang almost as beautifully as Oxana. Her daughter and the people's nightingale.

Uncle Grachev and Grandmother and Grandfather Trofimenko had been shot in the square where the statue of Oxana was to be erected, but neither Mother nor Olga talked about that during the dark summer nights. In fact, they didn't speak at all. The neighbors took turns bringing them a little food. Mother didn't eat anything much, but Olga took what she could get. And waited for something to change. For Mother to either die or get up again so that life could go on. But neither one happened. They just came to get her one day and said she had to be in a hospital because she was ill, and the day after, they also picked up Olga and drove her to the first of the orphanages. She was there for ten days. She lived in the next home for almost a month, and now she was here. With a new lot of strange children. Olga lowered her head, but the girl next to her wasn't put off that easily.

"Were your parents enemies of the people, or are they just dead?"

"Both, I think. I don't really know. My sister was a hero."

The girl stared at her with renewed interest. "What do you mean?"

"My sister is the People's Nightingale. They've erected a statue of her in the square in Sorokivka."

The girls sitting around them turned toward her, and Olga felt small and miserable and much too visible at the long table.

"I've heard of her," said one of the girls, her eyes narrowed. "There's a song about her. She reported her father for stealing grain."

It got completely silent, and Olga followed the skinny little flies wandering across her underarm. Didn't know what more she should say.

"But if she was your sister . . ." said a girl, hesitating. She sat right across from Olga. She was a little older, maybe thirteen, with a broad face and black eyes. Probably a Tartar from the Crimea. Olga had seen them at the market back when they were still living in Kharkiv. "You're full of lies," the Tartar girl continued. "Because if your sister is the People's Nightingale, then why are you here?"

"I don't know," mumbled Olga and wished she was just as dead as the rest of the world from which she came. "But I can sing too. I can sing 'Zelene Zhyto'—about the green, green wheat."

"By heart?"

The girl's tone seemed to Olga a bit more friendly, and almost against her own will, Olga felt herself grasp at that kindness, cling to it.

"Yes," she said. "I know a lot of songs by heart."

THE WORLD WAS so damned small when you thought about it. Where could you live in peace? Was there a place anywhere where you could hide forever? Not in Denmark, at least, thought Natasha, and especially not now.

She let a finger run across Katerina's soft white forehead. She had fallen asleep again, on the worn sofa in front of the stove. The warmth in the living room had loosened her shoulders, so that she now lay like an infant with her arms stretched above her head, hands open and unclenched. Her hair was still damp from the bath, and her cheeks and lips blushed in the heat, ruddy and full of life. Right now Natasha was the only one on guard.

She had stolen a new car before she crossed the bridge to Malmö in Sweden, and with Jurij's money she had bought two frozen bags of corned beef hash in the tiny supermarket they had passed on their way north. Katerina had thrown up twice but had otherwise slept most of the way. The Danish blizzard had not come this way, and after a few hours on fairly clear roads, Natasha had found a dark farm that sat abandoned and neglected under the black pines. It was not a vacation home of the kind the Danes bought and upgraded with heated floors and running water. Here, the old furniture was covered in dust sheets, and it smelled of pine and soot from the oven and of the old people who had lived here once but were now gone. On a gas burner in the tiny, claustrophobic kitchen, Natasha had heated water so she could wash both Katerina and herself, and when she let the water trickle down Katerina's forehead, she felt almost like she had that morning many years ago when she had stood next to Pavel watching the priest do the same.

They were together, and everything could begin again.

Tomorrow they needed to move on. Through Finland and across the enormous expanses of Russia until they found a corner that was remote enough. Heat billowed from the cast-iron stove in the small, overly furnished living room and made Natasha sleepy, but there were things she needed to do before she could lie down next to Katerina and close her eyes.

She stuck her hand into Katerina's pocket and fished out Pavel's old cell phone. With a broken fingernail, she carefully removed the plastic cover on one side and plucked out the memory stick from the derelict phone. She transferred it to Robbie's little Sony Ericsson and promised herself that this was the last time she was going to use it. Tomorrow she had to get a new one.

The display lit up, and she tapped her way through the menus to the pictures, texts and recordings that were saved on the stick.

With one hand on Katerina's arm, she listened carefully to the scratched recordings, the voices that rose and fell.

If you were going to be invisible and untouchable in the world, you needed money, she knew that now. But you couldn't allow yourself to get greedy or careless, like Pavel. He was the stupid one. Not beautiful Natasha.

The voices on the recording sang in her ears, telling stories people would prefer to forget, and as Natasha felt sleep moving in on her, she hung on to the little phone and reassurance it gave her: once again, she had a future.

They would make it, Katerina and she. They would want for nothing.

IT HAD TAKEN a long time for winter to loosen its grip, and it had also taken awhile before the hospital let him go. But now most of the snow had melted, and Søren was gradually beginning his rehabilitation.

There was a FOR SALE sign from one of North Zealand's fancy real estate agents at the entrance to Tundra Lane, but it wasn't Michael Vestergaard's house, it turned out. It was Anna Olesen's thatched yellow farm.

Søren parked the Hyundai next to Anna's red Mazda. There were pools of melted snow between the cobbles, and crocuses blooming along the house.

It's been two whole months, he said to himself. It's a completely different place now.

Still, he could feel his body's discomfort at being here. This is where you get hurt, it shouted. This is where the pain is!

The old woman who had shot him had been found in a snowdrift by the house's gable with extensive injuries after a series of hard blows to the temple and the back of the head. She had later been transferred to a hospital in Kiev with astounding haste. It was clear that her condition was so serious that it made no sense to prosecute her, but still the case had gone unusually smoothly, Søren observed dryly. You could not say the same for Jurij Savchuk's case. He was still stuck in Vestre Prison, awaiting his Danish trial, and no one in Ukraine had expressed any desire to get him back. Apparently not even his squeaky-clean half brother, Babko had reported. Søren and he had called each other a few times to exchange reports and health bulletins.

There was barking from the front hallway. The dog appeared to have survived.

Anna opened the door. She didn't look quite like herself. It took him a few minutes to realize that she wasn't wearing any makeup. The eyes were older and more tired, the hair less carefully arranged.

"Is it you?" she said without curiosity. "What do you want? More questions?"

"Not really," he said. "I came to tell you something."

She didn't move, clearly preferring for him not to come inside.

"We haven't been able to find either Natasha or Katerina," he said. "And so we haven't been able to ask Katerina what happened that Sunday. We don't know where they are. We don't know how they are doing. We have no idea whether they are still alive."

"That's sad."

"Yes, we are not happy about it. But we have found a witness that saw Katerina get into a red car not far from Damhus Lake." This was a bit of an exaggeration. The witness had seen "a child who could be Katerina" and the description of the car was equally vague—it was red.

Anna didn't move a muscle. She didn't even glance at the Mazda, which Søren had kind of hoped she would. It would have been a lovely, unconscious confirmation.

"Why are you telling me that?" she asked.

"Because I do believe that children can grieve. I do think an eight-year-old girl can miss her dead father terribly. She would probably also be able to buy the juice and cookies herself, in spite of the fact that we haven't been able to find a store with anyone who remembers seeing her. But there's one thing I don't believe. And that is that she would steal a bottle of Valium and try to kill herself."

Anna Olesen observed him for a long time. Then she closed the door. After a little while, she opened it again.

"I would appreciate it if you would get off my property," she said. "If there is anything else you feel you have to tell me, you can contact my lawyer."

Søren remained standing there for a little while, just to irritate her.

ON THE WAY home, he called Nina.

"Did she say anything?" Nina asked.

"Not a word. Not a useful word, at any rate."

"Do you still believe she did it?"

"Yes."

"Why? Why would she hurt the child? As far as we know, they had a good relationship."

"I don't know. I'm just sure that she did it. Maybe Katerina posed a threat to her—a connection between her and Pavel Doroshenko's dangerous blackmail. I've spoken to her daughter, Kirsten. She had no plans whatsoever to move into that wing Anna was restoring and had, in fact, asked her not to do it. She was afraid her mother's finances wouldn't be able to cover the expenses, but that doesn't appear to have been a problem. On the other hand, there aren't a lot of bills for the work that was done."

"Off the books?"

"A good way to place money if you can't really explain where it comes from."

"I still don't understand it. There's a long way from a bit of blackmail to . . . to an attempted child murder."

"Katerina called her. Anna came and picked her up in her red car.

Together they went out to Katerina's nest and had that peculiar tea party, with juice in the cups. Katerina's cup contained pulverized Valium. In Katerina's head, they were having a party with her father. Who knows? Maybe Anna was even able to make herself believe that it was for the best. That the child would be spared any more pain, and all that."

"They spoke Ukrainian together," said Nina suddenly. "On the telephone when Rina called Anna. Can that have been enough? Enough to make Rina dangerous for her, I mean?"

Søren considered Anna Olesen's almost perfect Hørsholm façade. She hadn't been able to help herself, he thought. She wanted so very badly to speak to the child, and in the beginning that would only have been possible in Ukrainian. In Anna's eyes, this exposure must have seemed terrifying when she realized that her past was catching up with her.

"I can see how it might look that way to her," he said.

Nina was quiet for a while. "It did seem to me . . ." she said, then broke off.

"What?"

"When we were searching for Rina. Katerina, I mean. In hindsight, I think Anna was trying to make sure I wouldn't find Katerina too soon. She made no effort to tell the dog to search, for instance."

Søren sighed. "Could you swear to that?"

"Not really. It was more of a vague impression."

"Not conclusive."

"No."

Another silence.

"Will you go out there again?" asked Nina.

"Yes," he admitted. "In a little while."

"Do you think she'll say something sooner or later?"

"Not really."

"Why do it, then?"

"Because she needs to know that someone is watching her."

He could almost see her shake her head. "You're not God."

He laughed. "No, unfortunately not."

There was another short pause. Ask her, he told himself.

She said goodbye. He cursed. She had saved his life—wasn't he allowed to ask the woman out to dinner in return? But he didn't do it. Maybe it was because he still remembered with crystal clarity the moment where his crappy middle-aged knee had cracked so loudly that both Babko and he had been shot as a result.

Maybe he needed to find someone his own age.

And maybe he needed a bigger car.

MAGNUS HAD MET someone else. Nina listened distractedly to his careful and considerate explanations, the great respect he had for her as a person and a colleague, how happy he had been that they had been able to help each other through a difficult time, and so on. The concern lines on his friendly dog's face were incredibly deep.

The window was open, and a scent of loam and rain and spring in the air drifted into the apartment's tiny kitchen. In the evening darkness, you could hear the protracted metallic noise from a freight train passing down on the tracks. Nina poked at the rice from the Thai food he had brought—chicken cashew—while she considered how long she needed to let him talk before she could decently interrupt him.

"I'm handing in my notice," she finally said, when the considerate explanations showed no sign of ceasing.

He was jolted, and in his confusion he pushed his glasses into his hair. They were crooked, she noticed, and made the blond Swedish locks stand straight up.

"You don't need to do that," he said. "I mean . . . I'm sure we can figure it out, and if we can't, then I'm the one who'll look for another job."

It took her a moment to realize he thought she was giving notice because of him.

She couldn't help laughing. That didn't make him any less confused, she could see.

"Magnus, damn it," she said. "We're not exactly Romeo and Juliet, are we? I'm not planning to keel over dead on your grave."

"*Jag förstår inte,*" he said, suddenly slipping into Swedish in his total perplexity. "I don't get it."

She spelled it out for him. "I've thought about it for more than a month," she said. "And I've made my decision, so all you need to do is say 'okay' and 'too bad' and then wish me luck in my new future."

"But why?"

She shook her head. "I'm not sure I can explain it. Partly it's because I've come to realize that I'm no longer the same person I was when I took the job. I can't keep defining myself as the one who has to save everyone else."

He took off his glasses and started to polish them with a corner of his shirt. He observed her for a long time, but it wasn't uncomfortable. Then he smiled.

"And here I sat explaining and explaining," he said. "Were you listening at all?"

"Some of the time."

"Okay. I'm . . . I'm going to miss you. In several ways. What do you want to do next?"

"I don't know yet."

"You're not applying for another of those hellhole missions you used to do, are you?"

She shook her head. "That would be a step in the wrong direction, don't you think?"

"Yes."

"Who is she, your new love?"

"Do you really want to know, or are you just being polite?"

She snorted and took a sip of her wine instead of answering.

He got up. "Do you have a date in mind?" he asked.

"May first. But I've done a lot of overtime, so it'll actually be in a couple of weeks."

He gave her a long hug on the way out the door. "Take care of yourself," he said.

"You too."

WHEN HE HAD left, she felt a relief so intense, it was almost as if she were weightless. As if her feet's contact with the kitchen floor was a completely voluntary condition. She went over to close the small window overlooking the railroad tracks, then remained standing, looking down at the lamps along the park path, where a lone jogger came running, slap, slap, slap, along the asphalt ribbon under the blooming trees. She took her cell phone out of her pocket and called Morten's number.

"I quit my job," she said without preamble.

It took awhile for him to answer. "What does that mean?"

"How hard is it to understand? I've given notice at the Coal-House Camp."

"Where are you going now?"

"Nowhere! I just thought . . . I could find something where there would be more time for the kids. Something less hectic."

There was a faint click. He had hung up.

She stared at the telephone. Didn't understand. She had thought he would be . . . maybe not exactly happy, but less cranky. Less annoyed with her.

The telephone rang. Now he was the one who didn't say hello.

"Why now?" he asked, and his voice was so angry, it shook. "Why not one of the approximately six hundred times when I asked you to? One of the times when it would have meant something?"

"I thought you would be . . ."

"Yes. Sorry." He sighed. The anger left his voice as quickly as it had arrived. "Nina, I know it's not your fault, or not just your fault. When I think about what happened with your dad, when I think about the fact that you were younger than Ida is now . . . I can't begin to imagine how someone could make it through something like that in one piece. You are as you are, and . . . and there are many good things about that. But I don't want to renegotiate our agreement and offer the kids the possibility of something more, just because you've suddenly had the idea that you want to be more of a mother to them. And besides . . ."

"Besides what?"

"No. We'd better talk about that another day, when I know more."

"Morten. You can't just say something like that and then leave it there."

The relief had abruptly disappeared. There was nothing weightless about her whatsoever. What was he going to say? Something about the kids? He had spoken of moving, she suddenly remembered. That terrible Sunday. *Far enough away to save the kids from your war zone*. Was that it?

"Are you moving?" she asked.

"I don't know. Nina, there's no reason to talk about it now. I shouldn't have brought it up."

"They are my kids too," she said and hated the meekness that had entered her voice. As if she wasn't sure it was true.

"Yes," he said. "I've been thinking a lot about that lately."

"Morten . . ."

"Good night, Nina. I didn't mean to worry you. Forget it."

SHE LAY IN her bed with the window open just a crack. The alarm clock's large numbers shone in the dark: 2:12.

Okay, she said to herself. So it isn't going to be as easy as you thought. So what? Aren't you supposed to be the great crisis queen?

The clock's digits changed with a barely audible click—2:13.

She rolled out of bed, slowly and deliberately, and padded barefoot into the hall, to the closet where the toolbox was. She chose the bigger and heavier of the two hammers and placed it on the kitchen table. The next step was to carry one of the kitchen chairs into the bedroom so she could take the clock down from the hook on the wall.

There was no reason to get glass all over the place, so she wrapped a kitchen towel around the clock before she placed it in the sink and calmly and methodically proceeded to smash it.

She didn't know how long it took. Nor did she know what time it was when she went back to bed awhile later and eventually fell asleep.

"SHE IS SO small," he says, and there's a frustrated tenderness in his voice. "So small that you think you can pick her up in one hand. But you can't."

The lights are low; the machines are humming quietly. This is not one of Kiev's overpopulated public hospitals. Here, nothing is lacking.

The doctor clears his throat. "She's not young," he says. "And the risk of operating yet again . . . I hope you understand how great it is. It's a minor miracle that she is still alive. But that's the way some people are—the heart just goes on and on."

"Do you think she can hear us?"

"You're welcome to try speaking to her. She is unconscious. We've recovered more than twenty skull fragments from her brain by now, and there is no doubt that certain areas have suffered permanent damage. I honestly don't know how much more we can do."

"You have to try." It's not a request; it is an order, and that is how the doctor hears it.

"Yes, sir," he says.

"You don't know my mother, you don't know how strong her will is. If anyone can survive this, she can. She's not afraid of battle or of pain."

"I can assure you, there is no pain, not now."

"But . . . she's still there, right? There are still thoughts and dreams and memories in there?"

The doctor places a gentle hand on his elbow. "Even if we manage to wake her up, you can't expect her to be the same. The damage is too extensive."

SHE SEES ALL of this from above. Looks down at Nikolaij, her beloved Kolja, as if she was standing in a tower. It is that tenderness. That admiration she cannot do without. She might have been willing to let the rest of the world think what it likes about both the past and the present, if not for him. He has to love her. For his sake, for the sake of that love, she will not let anybody drag her name through the mud. The lies, the secrets, those many, many songs of betrayal, Kalugin's bloody nightingale . . . all that must stay where it belongs, in the tangled, filthy darkness of the past. She will not let it touch him. Whatever the cost, he must not learn the truth.

Then she falls down. Not into her body, but in the darkness of memories, where old ghosts rise from the grave and will not let you be. She can't eat, speak, move; she has a tube in her mouth and another up her ass. Most of the time she can neither see nor hear. But in the darkness she remembers.

UKRAINE, 1934

"WHERE IS YOUR devil of a sister?"

Olga opened her eyes just as a huge hand hit her roughly on the side of the head. She attempted to roll away from the next blow and to sit up at the same time. Attempted to get free of sleep's clutches. It took a long moment before she realized that the man standing in front of her wasn't Father but a man that she had said hello to only a few times down by the cooperative shop. Sergej's father. Fedir's uncle. He wasn't a big man. A bit bent and scarred, like his son.

He looked angry but for some reason Olga was sure that he had just been crying. It was something about his eyes and voice, which was thick and soft as if he had coated his throat with oil.

She didn't dare say anything because the man clearly wasn't normal. Men didn't usually cry. Not in that way, in any case. Olga crept even closer to the wall and pulled the blanket all the way up to her chin, staring at him all the while.

"Fedir is dead," said the man. He seemed to be mostly telling himself. One tear had made it all the way to his frost-cracked lips and hung there for a moment like a small, clear pearl. Then he sniffed. "Tell me. Tell me where she is, that little bitch of an informer."

Fedir. She remembered the infatuated puppy eyes he had made at Oxana the day the GPU officers evicted them from the house and sent them off to Siberia in a freight car. Now he had died somewhere out there, like the little girl with the hare-like cry, and that's why Sergej's father was standing here, shaking her with red, wet hands.

Olga felt a watery fear in her stomach. A nauseating lurch that went both up and down at the same time, so that something loosened in her bowels. And yet there was, somewhere behind the fear, a sense of unholy scarlet glee. At last, Oxana would be punished. Punished for everything she had done.

"Oxana usually walks along the stream on her way home from school," she said quickly. "She's probably on her way home already."

Sergej's father let her go, without a word, without a look. He left the door open on its hinges when he walked out, and Olga lay motionless for a long time, watching as his tracks slowly filled with snow.

ACKNOWLEDGMENTS

IN THE COURSE of the creation of *Death of a Nightingale*, we have come across questions that we couldn't answer ourselves—just as we did with our other books. How do you handle a frozen corpse, what is the PET's department for the Prevention of Organized Crime in common parlance, and how do you say "Where is the toilet?" in Ukrainian? Luckily, we have once again had many, many kind, helpful and wise people to advise us along the way, and with their aid, we hope we've been saved from the worst mistakes. A special thank-you also to family and friends, who again have taken the time to read, encourage and take care of dogs and children when things got hectic.

Thank you:
Nina Gladkowa Johansen
Lone-emilie Rasmussen
Hans Jørgen Bonnichsen
Vladimir Stolba
Henrik Laier
Gustav Friis
Kirstine Friis
Else Rognan
Inger Møller
Marie Friis
Lars Ringhof
Anders and Louise Trolle
Esthi Kunz
Lisbeth Møller-Madsen
Eva Kaaberbøl
Anita Frank
Inga og Henrik Friis
Lotte Krarup

Bibs Carlsen
Inger Johanne and Jakob Ravn
Knud-Erik Kjær Madsen
Erling Kaaberbøl
Lasse Bork Schmidt and Martin Kjær Madsen of SustainAgri

—and thank you also to our Ukrainian friends who have wished to remain anonymous. You know who you are.

Other Titles in the Soho Crime Series

James R. Benn
(World War II Europe)
Billy Boyle
The First Wave
Blood Alone
Evil for Evil
Rag & Bone
A Mortal Terror
Death's Door
A Blind Goddess
The Rest Is Silence

Cara Black
(Paris, France)
Murder in the Marais
Murder in Belleville
Murder in the Sentier
Murder in the Bastille
Murder in Clichy
Murder in Montmartre
Murder on the Ile Saint-Louis
Murder in the Rue de Paradis
Murder in the Latin Quarter
Murder in the Palais Royal
Murder in Passy
Murder at the Lanterne Rouge
Murder Below Montparnasse
Murder in Pigalle
Murder on the Champ de Mars

Henry Chang
(Chinatown)
Chinatown Beat
Year of the Dog
Red Jade
Death Money

Barbara Cleverly
(England)
The Last Kashmiri Rose
Strange Images of Death
The Blood Royal
Not My Blood
A Spider in the Cup
Enter Pale Death

Colin Cotterill
(Laos)
The Coroner's Lunch
Thirty-Three Teeth
Disco for the Departed
Anarchy and Old Dogs
Curse of the Pogo Stick
The Merry Misogynist
Love Songs from a Shallow Grave
Slash and Burn
The Woman Who Wouldn't Die

Garry Disher
(Australia)
The Dragon Man
Kittyhawk Down
Snapshot
Chain of Evidence
Blood Moon
Wyatt
Whispering Death
Port Vila Blues
Fallout
Hell to Pay

David Downing
(World War II Germany)
Zoo Station
Silesian Station
Stettin Station
Potsdam Station
Lehrter Station
Masaryk Station

(World War I)
Jack of Spies

Leighton Gage
(Brazil)
Blood of the Wicked
Buried Strangers
Dying Gasp
Every Bitter Thing
A Vine in the Blood
Perfect Hatred
The Ways of Evil Men

Timothy Hallinan
(Thailand)
The Fear Artist
For the Dead

(Los Angeles)
Crashed
Little Elvises
The Fame Thief
Herbie's Game

Mick Herron
(England)
Down Cemetery Road
The Last Voice You Hear
Reconstruction
Smoke and Whispers
Why We Die
Slow Horses
Dead Lions
Nobody Walks

Lene Kaaberbøl & Agnete Friis
(Denmark)
The Boy in the Suitcase
Invisible Murder
Death of a Nightingale

Martin Limón
(South Korea)
Jade Lady Burning
Slicky Boys
Buddha's Money
The Door to Bitterness
The Wandering Ghost
G.I. Bones
Mr. Kill
The Joy Brigade
Nightmare Range
The Iron Sickle

Peter Lovesey
(England)
The Circle
The Headhunters
False Inspector Dew
Rough Cider
On the Edge
The Reaper

Peter Lovesey cont.
(Bath, England)
The Last Detective
Diamond Solitaire
The Summons
Bloodhounds
Upon a Dark Night
The Vault
Diamond Dust
The House Sitter
The Secret Hangman
Skeleton Hill
Stagestruck
Cop to Corpse
The Tooth Tattoo
The Stone Wife

Magdalen Nabb
(Italy)
Death of an Englishman
Death of a Dutchman
Death in Springtime
Death in Autumn
The Marshal and the Madwoman
The Marshal and the Murderer
The Marshal's Own Case
The Marshal Makes His Report
The Marshal at the Villa Torrini
Property of Blood
Some Bitter Taste
The Innocent
Vita Nuova
The Monster of Florence

Stuart Neville
(Northern Ireland)
The Ghosts of Belfast
Collusion
Stolen Souls
Ratlines
The Final Silence

Helene Tursten
(Sweden)
Detective Inspector Huss
The Torso
The Glass Devil
Night Rounds
The Golden Calf
The Fire Dance

Janwillem van de Wetering
(Holland)
Outsider in Amsterdam
Tumbleweed
The Corpse on the Dike
Death of a Hawker
The Japanese Corpse
The Blond Baboon
The Maine Massacre
The Mind-Murders
The Streetbird
The Rattle-Rat
Hard Rain
Just a Corpse at Twilight
The Hollow-Eyed Angel
The Perfidious Parrot
Amsterdam Cops: Collected Stories